BEAUTIFUL TYRANT

by

C. P. MANDARA

Published by **Chimera Books**
ISBN 9781780806815

Harper

Brandt and Gabriel have me tied down on the bed. While Mal points a gun at them they're going to mess with me a little. Gabriel looks almost gleeful at the prospect, Brandt not so much. It's too bad. He might as well get his kicks in where he can.

After Mal's finished with them, hopefully he'll find something unpleasant for them to do. He always needs a patsy to murder someone or other. My fingers are crossed that the pair can find an opportunity to run and get the hell out of this mess. That's what I'd do if I had the chance.

Unfortunately for me, my last few days are to be spent at Mal's warehouse. The Airfix King is about to take his superglue addiction out on me, before he chops me up into little pieces and leaves me for dead. This is probably not the time to wish I'd killed myself earlier, right?

Everything you've ever wanted is on the other side of fear. George Addair

Chapter One - Harper

I want to cry.

'Get back on the bed, darling.'

Fear crawls up my spine. It feels like a million termites have decided to use my body as their last meal. Something is eating me alive from the inside out, and all that's left for me to do is scream. This can't be happening. *This is happening.* My world is spinning out of control, like a supercell tornado lashing at me with lightning and hail. This is going to be a pivotal moment in my life, and I need to figure out my next move quickly. The trouble is, I am paralysed. I know everything is going down the pan and no matter which way I turn the outcome will be the same.

Mal's eyes are eating my naked body up, while his goons point their guns at me. I am helpless. What should I do?

'Get back on the bed, darling,' Mal repeats, with a vicious edge to his voice. Shit. *Move, Harper, move.* On feet that are about as stable as a new-born lamb's, I stumble over to the bed and almost fall onto it headfirst. Please don't kill Brandt. The words are stumbling over and over in my head, but there is no way I'll ever voice them out loud. If Mal knew what Brandt meant to me he'd be dead in an instant. While he thinks of me as nothing more than a possession, he doesn't want any competition for my attention. He made that very clear with Alex, which is why my late husband is now residing under six feet of particularly wet and squelchy mud. It says something that I consider him the lucky one.

2

The trouble is, Mal is one of those people who likes to play with his food before he eats it. The tube of glue is still spinning around in his hand, and he's looking at me expectantly, with one eyebrow raised. That eyebrow says something along the lines of 'Do you want to do this the easy way, or the hard way?' I already know he'd prefer it if I took the latter option, but I'm not that brave. There'll be plenty of time for the Airfix King to have his fun with me later. Brandt doesn't need to see that. I'm kind of hoping that when death comes, it will be just me and Mal, but that's not very likely. He likes it when people watch. I know this from experience. I think it turns him on in some other-worldly, freakish way. Whoever gets to watch my death is going to need a strong stomach. He's going to pull out all the stops when he begins work on me. He's already told me so.

'Well, what are you waiting for, gentlemen? Go fuck her up a little.' Mal ushers Brandt and Gabriel towards me, and the pair give each other a look, as if to say, what the hell? Some of what I've told them about Mal must have stuck, though, because they don't push their luck. They begin moving towards me.

Gabriel is stumbling slightly, due to the gunshot wound, but by the looks of it the thing is superficial. That's not to say Mal hasn't taken a decent chunk out of his leg, but I can tell, just from looking, that it hasn't severed cartilage or bone. The bullet was a warning. I begin to wonder whether Mal's planned this little scenario from the start. It wouldn't surprise me.

When Gabriel gets to the bed his eyes shoot daggers. He thinks I've sold them down the river, when the exact opposite is true. I'm trying to save them both, but he doesn't know me well enough to realise it.

Moving towards me menacingly, he says, 'I can't wait to get started on you, princess.' That should put the fear of God into me, but I have bigger things to worry about. I need to get these two out of here. Nothing that Gabriel dishes out will compare with what Mal's going to do to me later.

'Shut up,' growls Brandt through clenched teeth, and gives him a look that could kill lesser mortals. Gabriel pauses on his journey towards me and his head tilts sideways. He's wondering what's going on. At least he thinks on his feet. At the moment he'll just assume Brandt is protecting me, when he gets close enough I'll help fill in the blanks. For now, he can hate me all he likes. It will play right into Mal's hands.

'What do you want us to do to her?' Gabriel's voice is vicious as he directs the sentence back towards Mal. It appears he's a bit ticked off about either his near miss with a bullet, or my apparent disregard for his safety.

Mal shrugs his shoulders. 'Whatever you like, just make sure it's entertaining or I'll shoot you both, and I won't miss this time.'

Great. No pressure then, I think wryly. The next hour or two of my life is sure to be hell on wheels.

'Can we tie her up?' Gabriel asks, running a hand through his hair as his abs ripple in the dawn light filtering through the window. His macabre tattoo's look utterly spectacular in every way that counts, and the effect is enhanced by the cruel frown that goes from one side of his face to the other.

'You can do whatever the fuck you like to her, now stop pissing around and get

3

on with it.' Mal was never known for his patience. The guys had better get on with it or he will kill them. Thankfully, Gabriel gets the message.

Grabbing the handcuffs from the bedside table he spins me over and shoves his knee into my back, so he can keep me still while fastening the cuffs around my wrists. I have a serious case of déjà vu right now. It only seems like seconds ago since he got the cable ties out.

Turning to Brandt, Gabriel goes straight for the jugular. 'Do you have a whip around here? Something that'll do a fair amount of damage?' Twisting my head around to watch Brandt's response, I see his eyes flare in horror.

'Hey, the man said to fuck her up; I'm just following orders,' Gabriel says, with a smile upon that beautiful, twisted face of his.

Brandt's fingers clench into fists. 'Gabriel, the woman is mine to torment, not...'

'Children, children; I didn't ask for a discussion,' Mal barks. 'Get the fuck on with it before I whip you both.' He's losing patience.

Brandt pays no attention, however. He grabs Gabriel's arm with a death grip to make sure he can't go anywhere. It's the wrong move.

'Just do it,' I hiss. 'Get the whip. I've had worse. Now go get it quickly before he makes an example of you. The man isn't kidding around.' These two idiots are going to get themselves killed.

Brandt still doesn't let go of Gabriel's arm, and Mal's had enough waiting around. Advancing towards us he lets loose his fist, and it flies straight into Brandt's nose, which is still bleeding from the last encounter. Brandt lets out a whoosh of air and staggers back, reeling from the force of the impact.

'Up against the wall, pretty boy,' Mal sneers. 'It's time someone taught you a lesson.' Mal doesn't give Brandt the chance to obey because he's already gripped the hair on top of his head and is dragging him forward. Oh fuck, no. I can't watch this.

Slamming Brandt into the wall face-first, Mal barks, 'Arms up, over your head!' Brandt obeys him woodenly, which is just as well because I really can't deal with anyone else getting shot.

Mal spins around and looks at Gabriel. 'You,' he growls, 'go get me a whip and make it snappy.' He clicks his fingers, which is Mal speak for it had better be done in three seconds flat or you're dead.

Gabriel, unfortunately, has no idea where Brandt keeps his toys and looks at me helplessly.

'Top drawer,' I whisper. 'Get it now.'

The man jumps off the bed as if fifty hell hounds are on his tail. To be fair, he's not wrong. Yanking the drawer open, he rifles through the contents and finally pulls out a short-tailed whip. It's made of braided red and black leather. I can tell, just by looking, that it will hurt like a bastard. Gabriel then turns his head to glare at me. He is not pleased. While he'd have been more than happy to whip the shit out of me, he doesn't want to hurt Brandt; it won't do much for his reconciliation plans, that's for sure.

'Give him twenty lashes and don't hold back. If you haven't drawn blood by that point, you're next.' Mal motions for Gabriel to get busy. I don't think I can watch.

4

Mal wants to see if I'm affected by this, and I can't be. I have to be indifferent. If he knows how much Brandt means to me, Brandt's life expectancy will evaporate quicker than a teardrop on a hot summer's day. I need to make it clear I could not care less about his fate - even though I'd rather pull out my fingernails one by one than watch this horror story unfold.

"Arper, you watchin' this, babe?' Mal comes to stand behind me, and runs his fingers all over my bruised and battered backside. I know what's coming next, and sure enough his fingernails dig into the raw flesh, pressing so hard it's all I can do not to yell out loud.

When I get my voice back, I say, 'Wouldn't miss it for the world, darling. Do I get a go, or is this game just for boys?' It's the only way I can think of to make sure Mal knows I don't give a crap about him. All other roads lead to bullets.

'Why you fucking bitch,' hisses Gabriel, but Mal's hand waving a gun about silences him.

Angling his head, as if surprised, Mal says, 'You hate him that much, huh?' He's thinking. He's wondering whether he wants to watch me whip the crap out of Brandt. This is the deal I made with the devil, so I have to accept the consequences if I'm called out on it. If I am, I'm in trouble. Hurting Brandt will be more than my already battered conscience can cope with.

'He's kept me locked in a freezing cold cell, naked and leashed to the wall for the last couple of days. He would have kept me down here for five years, if you hadn't come for me, so yeah, he's not my favourite person right now. I'd happily lay into him, given half a chance.' I give Mal what I pray is a hopeful look. My acting skills aren't bad, and they improved no end after marrying Alex, but I'm under a considerable amount of pressure. I just have to hope Mal believes me.

His fingers keep tapping as he searches my eyes, looking for lies, but I don't move a muscle or bat an eyelash. He knows every single tell, and I'm not going to give him anything bar a sly little smile. He can make what he wants of that.

Eventually he reaches a decision. This is going to go one of two ways, and I'm about to find out which.

'And here I thought you liked the guy. Don't tell me you've fallen out with pretty boy? It would be a shame, as you're going to fuck him in a few minutes' time.' Mal is once again amused, and this is almost a relief. If he's being kept entertained, he's having fun, and he won't be shooting anyone.

'Don't make me do this,' I whine petulantly. 'Uncuff me and let me have that whip. I want to get my own back.' I hope I'm not laying it on too thick. If I am he'll get suspicious.

He seems to believe me. In fact, he almost seems pleased. 'My precious little darling is an evil monster at heart, huh? We're a match made in heaven, darlin'.' I almost roll my eyes but stop myself just in time. There's no heaven on earth that's going to accept Mal into its pearly gates, and I don't think I'm up for any saint of the year award, either.

When the silence stretches between us I raise my eyebrows in question. Gabriel then blurts out an expletive and rushes towards me, but Mal grabs him and shoves the butt of his gun under his chin. All the guards rush forward and there's the awful clicking noise of several safety's being removed. The room is now as quiet as a thief in a bubble wrap factory.

'You want me to pop another one into you?' Mal drawls. 'Do you need a bit of longer-lasting, more permanent damage this time?' Gabriel shakes his head, but there's a tick in his jaw that says he's mightily pissed at the moment. I know he's itching to let loose the power of his body, but he's not stupid. He knows that means certain death. For the moment he'll have to play nicely. He can plan his revenge later - if he's not dead.

When Mal presses the gun further into his throat, Gabriel finally shakes his head.

'Then get the fuck over there and start ripping into your buddy. Make sure you put some effort into it, too. If you don't do the job properly, I'll demonstrate how it's done.' Shoving Gabriel away Mal keeps his gun trained on him as he waits to see if he'll obey. It's do or die. The poor fucker has no choice.

Gabriel's jaw tightens as he lifts the whip. I can't even imagine being in his position. My stomach is curdling at the thought. Brandt is looking back at him, and gives him the nod. Brandt always was the intelligent one. He's saying get on with it, so we stand a chance at getting out alive. It's the sensible play.

Gabriel gives him a slow nod of his own and raises his whip hand. Giving me one last look, which should have me shaking in my boots, he flicks the tails back and lets them fly. He's not gentle. By the way Brandt's shoulders jerk back in shock, he's just imparted one hell of a wallop and I clench my teeth to stop myself from sucking in a pained breath. I can't let Mal see I'm affected by it. I know he's eating up the expression on my face because he's looking right at me, and I have to let him know I don't give a fuck.

'Let me have a go,' I wheedle. 'Please? What's a girl need to do to get her own back?' Another smile. There, that should do it. Someone give me an Oscar already.

Gabriel brings his hand back to let loose another vicious crack. Jesus Christ. He's taking Mal seriously. He's not holding his punches, that's for sure.

Mal grabs my chin and brings my eyes up to his. He's looking for emotion, but he won't find any. Not a single flicker of concern flutters across my face. I'm used to this game and I've learnt to play it well.

'Huh, you really do hate him, don't you?' He seems surprised. It's not that much of a stretch, is it? Especially when you consider how the bastard has treated me these past few days. The fact that I still adore him just goes to show what state my mental health is in.

'Let me show you just how much I loathe that fucker,' I growl. I then have to school my features as Gabriel paints another stripe upon Brandt's back. Can I whip him? I'm not sure I have it in me, but on the other side of the coin, I wouldn't be able to do as much damage as the dark angel in front of me. My eyes are mesmerised by the grace of his body as he bends the whip back to let it fly once again. There's a certain erotic beauty in watching his muscles contract, tense and then relax as the whip moves in an arc. I daresay I won't see it in quite the same light when it's my turn to go under it, but it doesn't stop my eyes from staring at the exquisite perfection of his body.

'No, darlin', you can't hit hard enough. You need strong arms to do this kind of shit,' Mal says, equally as entranced at the unfolding performance. It's a relief that his eyes are somewhere else, but I don't let him know it.

'I bet I could do some damage,' I grunt, with a fair degree of menace. It's directed at Gabriel, but he doesn't need to know that.

Mal laughs. 'I don't doubt it, but you won't do nearly as much as he will.' It's no word of a lie. Brandt has his hands flat against the wall and his knuckles are white as he curls them into claws. He doesn't make a sound as the whip crashes into him, and that worries me. That tells me he's familiar with pain - too familiar. I know some of what he's had to endure in prison, and I know I'm directly responsible for that. I have so many sins to atone for, and they weigh heavy upon me.

Mal is content to sit in silence, soaking up the delightful atmosphere, as Brandt takes a beating. I think he'd have enjoyed it more if I'd have appeared bothered by the ordeal, though. Now he thinks I'm not he's likely to move things along more quickly. This is a blessing for Brandt, although I'm sure he wouldn't thank me for it.

Just as I've suspected, after a couple of minutes Mal barks, 'Blood!' He's not interested in watching Brandt get fucked up; he wants to move on to the next course - the one where I'm the main dish.

It takes every ounce of my willpower to pretend to be unaffected as Gabriel goes at Brandt as if he's something out of a Freddy Kruger movie. He knows exactly what he's doing, which doesn't surprise me, and he does it with alarming efficiency. Within minutes Brandt is hissing all kinds of expletives through his teeth, while little red rivers of blood dribble down his back. I want to cry. Instead I smile and try to look at Mal as if he's not a reincarnation of Adolf Hitler. In order to give myself a little extra credibility I also begin humming and bob my head from side to side as the shitshow continues. In the end Mal gets bored, as I knew he would.

'Enough. It's her turn.' Both men turn towards me, as Mal sits calmly beside me with a dark gleam in his eye. He expects me to fight, or at least beg him for mercy. I'm tempted not to bother, as I know it won't get me anywhere, but this is the part that turns him on. Hopefully, if we get it out of the way, he'll want to finish what he's started and this can all be over. I'm not in a rush to fall headlong into my own gruesome death, but neither do I want to drag this awful mess out. I just want it to be over. With any luck the boys can then somehow scrape together an escape plan and get themselves away. There is no chance of that happening for me.

My clock is ticking down to ground zero, but that doesn't mean I have to take everyone else with me.

Chapter Two - Brandt

'Please don't do this, Mal,' Harper whispers miserably. 'Take me home. We can have some fun together there. Don't leave me alone with these monsters.' Her face is pale and her eyes are lifeless. I want to believe that all her earlier words were an act, but my head is all over the place. Which side is the woman on? It takes me a moment to get the facts straight, but when I do I'm sure of my answer.

Mine; if she wasn't I'd already be dead. As it is, we're going to be lucky to pull ourselves out of here alive. I can't say she didn't warn me. Why didn't I listen?

'Baby, you know I love it when you bleed for me, and I haven't seen you in ages, 'ave I? Do this for me, sweetheart. You know how this shit turns me on.' Mal grabs one of her bruised ass cheeks and squeezes cruelly. I want to lump him.

In response Harper nods slowly. This is not acquiescence. She knows she has no choice. She's played this game before. You sick fucker, I think, but wisely keep my mouth shut. The less said the better.

Mal turns to feast his dark eyes on me. 'Brandt, why don't you 'ave a turn with the whip? It's time to get your own back, buddy.' He looks pointedly at Gabriel, who has a firm death grip on the thing and looks very unhappy at the thought of relinquishing it. He's not convinced by Harper's innocence, and he wouldn't mind ripping into her given half a chance. He doesn't know her like I do. Gabriel thinks everyone is a liar until proven otherwise.

Reluctantly he offers the whip to me. I take it and wince; my back is a mess. Now I have to do the same to Harper, and the thought turns my stomach. She has been through enough. This has to stop.

Placing the whip carefully down on the bed, I climb up and straddle her. I think I do it to antagonise the bastard sitting beside her, which is pretty stupid, all things considered, but then again, he's the one sitting there waiting to watch other men fuck 'his girl'. If Harper was mine I wouldn't let anyone near her.

As it happens Mal doesn't say a thing, but he watches me carefully. He's worried I'm about to pull something stupid, but he can rest easy. I'm being a good boy. I'm not going to get a chance to take the bastard out today, but when I do, I'm going to do the job properly. The man is going down like a hooker in an orgy. He's going to hit the floor hard, too.

Lightly brushing my fingertips up Harper's back, I make my presence known. I need to unfasten the cuffs she's wearing, otherwise her arms will be in the way. Grabbing the key from the table, I slip it into the lock and remove them, but when I set them down on the bed Mal is not happy.

'Keep her cuffed. If she can move she'll be running around the room wailing. I want to see her properly punished.'

My jaw stiffens. This means he wants us to mess her up bad, and that's exactly what I'm afraid of. If he takes her away almost crippled with pain, she won't stand a chance at being able to defend herself. Who am I kidding? She stands no chance against the fucker anyway. None of us do.

'I can't whip her back if her arms are in the way,' I say. The cuffs are redundant, anyway. I know Harper won't move once I start laying into her. It's not her style. She'll take everything that's coming, like the meek little lamb Mal has trained her to be. No wonder the poor girl is so screwed up. Getting him out of her head will probably take years of therapy. There's also another reason. If she isn't cuffed we stand a chance at escape. If the guards take it in shifts to babysit us during the night, there might be an opportunity for Gabriel and me to take them on. If Harper is tied up it will make an escape attempt far more difficult.

'Then cuff her 'ands to the headboard, idiot. It's not rocket science. Wait, my mistake, it probably is for you.' That little barb isn't even worth my time. Mal is hardly the smartest man on the planet if he's dealing crack cocaine and heroin, is he?

'Grip the headboard,' I order. My voice is sharp. If Harper's acting I need to follow suit. There's a reason she's doing what she's doing, and I'm sure she'll explain it to me when she gets a chance, but I can probably already join up the dots. Mal is jealous, and if he suspects Harper and I are anything but enemies my life will expire faster than the average celebrity marriage.

Harper obeys instantly. Now I know why she barely batted an eyelid at all the crazy shit I pulled on her when I first brought her to the house. What I did was child's play compared to the stuff she's had to suffer under Mal. I feel like a jerk. If I'd talked to her at the beginning, instead of going gung ho on her, I could have figured this all out and been halfway to Bali by now.

The handcuffs close around her wrists, pinning them in place. Thankfully I can't see her face as it's pressed into the pillow because if I did, my resolve would probably evaporate in an instant. Gabriel is better at this sort of shit. The man doesn't have a conscience. Unfortunately, I do, and if Harper is telling me the truth, the last few days are going to sting when I think about them too carefully. Shit, shit, shit. Is there any way out of this mess?

'I'm waiting, tough guy. Let's move it along now, shall we?' Mal brings me back into the here and now, standing up from his perch so he can watch me from a distance. It's always nice to make sure you have a great view just before some random bloke is about the beat the shit out of your girlfriend.

Hovering over Harper, I feel a moment of indecision. Blinking, I try and clear my head and think about what I'm going to do next.

'Don't hold back,' Harper murmurs, so quietly I can barely hear her. 'If he thinks you're holding back he'll get suspicious. I can take it.'

I sit back and pick up the whip. I can feel both Gabriel and Mal's eyes on me, wondering what I'm about to do. A lot is riding on this. If we want to get out of here alive I need to play my part. So squaring my shoulders I get myself exactly where I need to be. For anyone wondering where that is, it's in a twelve by eight-foot prison cell with Micas standing opposite me.

'Well, well, well,' I purr, donning some familiar armour, 'it appears I have you right where I want you, Miss Wilkinson.' Running the fronds of the whip gently down her back, I watch her shiver. I need to pad this out with as many actions and words as I can. The sooner Mal tires of this little production, the better.

'Get away from me,' Harper grits, and she puts some real venom into the words. I wonder how much of her life has been an act in the last few years. If I had to bet, I'd say almost all of it. We have more in common than I thought.

Bringing my hand down sharply I slap her ass.

'Ah, I don't think so, precious. I think you and I are going to have a lot of fun in the next couple of hours. Isn't that right, Wilkinson?' I don't want to use her first name. It's easier to keep this impersonal if I use her surname. Later I'll just use something derogatory, but I can't call her Harper. If I do, every time I think of her after this episode will be marred with violence, and the thought is horribly sobering.

'Mal, stop this madness,' Harper yells, and begins to rattle the bedframe. I'm sure the bastard is lapping it all up behind us, but we both know he isn't going to call a halt to the proceedings.

Giving her another sharp slap I grab her ass, exactly as Mal had, and knead it with cruel pressure. After the spankings and Gabriel's belt she's going to go into meltdown when I tear into her, but we have no choice. We're out of options.

'In a minute, I'm going to do just what we promised earlier. Both of us are going to fuck you in every hole you possess, and we aren't going to be gentle about it. We're going to eat you alive, Wilkinson, and we're going to make you scream.' There. That should keep the big dog happy.

'Shut the fuck up and whip her.' Or not. Mal utters those words dryly, as if he's seen this all before, and if that's the case, why is he even bothering? Hell if I know. Maybe he's just a really impatient man. Still, the time for stalling is over. I've got to get on with it. Bringing my arm up, I flick the fronds of the whip forward with no warning. They connect on her lower back with a sharp crack, and she sucks in a breath. She can cope with that, but if I start on her ass she's going to freak out. It's already a mess. I'm going to avoid that area at all costs. As it is, she'll be barely able to walk when I've finished. The only reason I'm moving is because I'm running on adrenaline. When that stops I'm going to be a cripple for the next few days.

'What the fuck was that? Put some effort into it. If your best buddy could rip you to shreds, you should be able to make mincemeat of the most hated woman in your life, surely? Or is there something you're not telling me here?' Mal begins pacing up and down, which is never a good sign. This whole thing is a test. He wants to know if I still care about her. That's why she's being such a bitch. She wants to send the message out loud and clear that we can't stand each other. That way there may be a chance he'll let Gabriel and me go. It's not a good plan, though. I can't leave her in his hands. You only need to take one look at Mal to know what he's capable of, and I don't want to be within three miles of him. I need to get her out of here. If I can't do it now, I at least need to be alive to get the job done later, when I can gut the man like a fish. Actually, forget fish. I'm going to slice the bastard in two, and I'm going to start between his legs.

Taking a big, theatrical sigh, I sit up and regard him carefully. I'm buggered if I'm going to kowtow to him. If he wants to shoot me, he can. Otherwise, I'm running this show.

'Oh, she's going to get hers,' I say, 'but I like to start slow. If I rip into her right from the start she'll be in tears within seconds, and unconscious in minutes. No one is going to enjoy themselves very much if that happens, are they?' Mal inclines his head to the side as he takes that in. It's not what he was expecting. Good.

'You really do hate her, huh? I always wondered if you harboured some idea of getting back together with her. She's a pretty little thing, isn't she?' If he's trying to keep me off guard it isn't working. I'm used to reading people and having eyes in the back of my head. It's one of the only reasons I'm still alive.

'Oh no, I worship the ground she walks on,' I say sarcastically. 'Fucking slut had me put away for five years to cover up her shit. We're this close, we are.' I hold my hand in the air and cross my index and middle finger over one another. It's about the only way I can stick my middle finger up at him and get away with it.

Mal's lips twist wryly. 'I told her you'd hate her guts. I'm rarely wrong.' Yeah, well, you royally screwed up this time, mastermind. We were tangled up in the bedsheets not moments ago.

'What are you planning on doing to her, when I've finished with her? Is she going back to your castle, or have you had enough of her?' Turning away from Mal, I bring the whip down sharply on Harper's back, three times in quick succession. She screams out loud and her body goes rigid in shock. I feel like a complete bastard, but what choice do I have? There are guns everywhere. To do anything else would be suicide. If Harper can put me away for five years to save her hide, she can take a beating for mine - although it might kill me to deliver it.

'You like inflicting pain, Browning?' Mal's behind me. The fucker is looking over my shoulder as I work. I want to spin round and smash my fist through his face, but that is not a good idea.

'Is it that obvious?' I say instead, releasing another series of horrible volleys against Harper's back. I hope he stops this soon, but I have a terrible feeling he won't.

'You were a weedy little thing when you were put inside,' he comments. 'I didn't think you'd last a month.'

This confirms that everything Harper has told me is the truth. Mal wanted me put inside, and he wanted me dead. Interesting. I didn't realise I posed such a threat. I now know better. I need to watch myself around her; if we appear anything more than enemies I'm in trouble. It's all beginning to make sense.

'Sorry to disappoint.' My voice is clipped.

'My, you're a cold one. You're not what I was expecting.'

I'd love to know what he was expecting. Fluffy bunnies, coupled with hearts and flowers?

'So would you be after five years in jail,' I point out calmly. I then unleash my temper on Harper's back with a series of slices that would have the devil himself screaming in agony. Sure enough, Harper loses the plot.

'Sure you want me to carry on?' I ask Mal. 'She's going to be virtually catatonic if I continue, but I'm game if you are.' I'm not. She will never forgive me for this, and I can't say I blame her. When I receive no response from Mal I take his silence as permission to continue. Drawing my hand back, I decide I'm going to keep at it, as hard as I can until she passes out. At least she won't have to be fucked over by two men at the end of it. There's some shit you can never wipe clean.

'Stop.' Mal's voice rings out in the air, and his throaty tone makes my stomach lurch. Now what? 'Maybe you're right,' he continues. 'We want her wide awake for when you guys show her a good time, right?'

Wrong. 'You want us to fuck her now?' My voice is devoid of all emotion. I don't want to give the bastard a thing.

'Yes, but I want to make sure you two don't enjoy yourselves too much.' He smiles cruelly, which leaves me to believe I'm not going to like what comes next.

'I think I want a little appetiser first. You and Gabriel; go fuck each other up. Let's see who's the last one standing.' He looks at me and waits. Mal would like nothing better than for me to come roaring at him with both fists blazing, but I do no such thing. I'm not going to give him the satisfaction.

'Is the broken nose and massacred back not fucked up enough for you?' I enquire sweetly.

Mal shrugs and puts his hands in his pockets. For some reason I notice he's wearing suit pants. He's trying his best to be an upmarket thug, though the material and cut of the suit is cheap. These are things I'm trained to spot. Oh, the joys of being raised a snob. If Mal notices me checking him out, he doesn't react. I suspect he's got more important things on his mind.

'Actually, no. Besides, there's method behind my madness. First, I want to see how you operate under pressure, and secondly I want to see if you can 'andle yourself. You're of no use to me if you can't hold your own in a fight.'

I snort. 'No one can hold themselves against Gabriel, but you'll figure that out in a minute. Get the body bag ready.' Standing up, I throw the whip back down on the bed, and try to ignore the sound of Harper's sobs. Less than a day ago the sound of her cries turned me on, but right now they make me sick to my stomach, especially as I'm the one who's caused them.

Facing Gabriel, I get ready to take a pounding. He's faster, stronger, and far more agile than I am. Add to that a decent background in martial arts, and the battle was already won, even before someone took a chunk out of my back and smacked me in the nose. I know why Mal is doing this, and it's not for the reasons he's just stated. He wants to check that Harper really is as impervious as she appears to be. If I'm lying on the floor bleeding out, there's a chance she might crack. It's possible I'm wrong, but I doubt it.

Gabriel is now standing in front of me, hesitating. He knows I'm likely to go down quick, and he also knows if he lays me out cold, he's on his own. That's his problem. I'm kind of looking forward to taking a nap.

When he stands there motionless for a few more seconds, I decide to give him some helpful words of encouragement. 'Come on, big guy. Hit me. I know you can.' Those fucking abs are staring at me, framed by his black pyjama bottoms. My gaze is drawn to them helplessly. I've worshipped his body more times than I care to count, and I have to confess I miss it a little. The man is a god in bed, there are no two ways about it.

Gabriel rolls his eyes at me, but he puts his fists up in front of his chest and adopts his fighting stance. While it's clear he doesn't want to do this, he's going to. Whether it's to save my hide or his own is anybody's guess. At the moment I don't care. I just need him to get on with it.

The first punch that swings my way misses, and for that I can be grateful. Gabriel's hand almost flies into the wall due to the power behind it, but he recovers just in time. He's good like that. I've yet to see anyone get the better of him in a fistfight. But when the second punch comes my way I'm not so lucky. This one connects with a shattering crunch into my jaw. My teeth snap together and my eyes water. Pain splinters up the bone and congregates in my head, giving me a motherfucker of a headache, and we've barely even started. I have a feeling that when this is finished it's going to take someone days to scrape what's left of me up off the floor.

'Come on 'Arper, sit up and enjoy the show.' My head swings round at Mal's voice. He's unlocking her cuffs so he can prop her up and make her watch. Just as I suspected, his motivation isn't quite what it seems to be. As my head turns back to check for the fist that is almost certain to be heading my way, I find it's already hurtling towards my left eye. Gabriel is on a mission to show Mal who's boss around these parts. Jerking my head backwards to try and avoid some of the blow, his knuckles connect just below my eye socket and have me stumbling backwards. Before I have a chance to recover I feel the heel of his foot crunch into my upper right thigh, and I stagger backwards, nearly dropping to my knees. I don't think he realises how powerful his feet are. The man is a killing machine and he has the cold-blooded temperament to match. Will he kill me? Is this what we've come to?

Gabriel delivers another series of kicks and punches, all with his uninjured right leg, which are carefully timed to make sure they do the maximum amount of damage. My body is exploding in pain and I can barely think, let alone move, but I somehow manage to push my head forward and use all the anger bubbling up inside me to hit Gabriel square in the chest. If he is going to kill me, I want to get one in before I send a cheery wave to the man upstairs, or downstairs, because these days I'm not entirely sure where I'm headed.

I manage to hit the bastard, but only because he's not expecting me to retaliate. He probably figured he'd done enough damage to keep me down for a while, and to be fair, there is nowhere I'd rather be right now than gasping for breath on the floor, but I need to stay conscious for Harper. I cannot leave her alone with this pair. They'll annihilate her.

'Stop, I've seen enough,' Mal rasps. 'Brandt, you fight like a fucking girl. Your mate, on the other hand, might be of some use to me. Let's hope you're better at other things.' His derisive comment rips through me because I know what's coming next. He wants us to tag team Harper - and mess her up bad. I almost wish Gabriel had knocked me out.

He claps his hands. 'Right, time for you two to get naked. Let's get the main course over with. This time show me what you're made of Brandt because if you can't fuck worth a damn, after we've finished I'll cut it off and stick it on Harper's forehead as a memento. You feel me?'

Chapter Three - Brandt

'Let's see what you've got, pretty boys.' Mal is very careful to make sure his gaze stays on us from the waist upwards, but I don't think he'll be so careful in a few minutes' time. By the looks of the guy he's strictly heterosexual, but looks can be deceiving. I learnt that the hard way.

'Are we allowed to do anything we want?' Gabriel has to get that out there, and I want to strangle him. It's about time he learnt to control that temper of his.

'Yes; that's kind of the object of the exercise,' Mal says, talking back to him as if he's three years old. Gabriel's back stiffens. Serves him right.

We then both stand there like lemons, wondering what to do next. There's four guns trained on us, so it's not a particularly romantic setting, and the last thing I feel like doing is getting my shit on, but beggars can't be choosers. When Mal raises his eyebrows, we know our time is up.

'Which end do you want?' Gabriel asks me. It's like we're discussing a side of beef. How the hell am I supposed to get my head around this?

'I'll take the top end,' I say dryly. In fact, I'd take any end I could get my hands on, but I need to be able to speak to Harper. Besides, if Gabriel marked that pretty face I'd never forgive him.

'Suits me. Are we tying her up?' Harper is sat on the bed where Mal left her. Her face is vampire-style white, and it looks like all the blood in her body has gone on holiday. That was probably the result of our little fight a moment ago. I'm hoping she managed to look bored and smile through it, but she looks pretty rough now.

'Do we need to? There's two of us, and one ninety-pound weakling of a girl. I think we can probably handle this.' I don't want Harper tied up. If there is any chance of escape, no matter how small, I need her to be ready to take it.

'It's more fun when they're tied up. They scream more.' I think Gabriel is trying his best to impress Mal, and sure enough, the bastard smiles.

'When she starts wriggling we'll tie her up. For now, let's just get on with it.' I hope I sound suitably indifferent to the whole ordeal. I'm trying my best.

'Suit yourself.' Gabriel pats Harper's thigh and gives her a look that suggests she's soon about to be fish food. 'Why don't you get up on your hands and knees for us, sweetheart?' Her sable eyes expand to the point where they nearly blot out her entire irises, and I can feel her fear. She's already had a taste of Gabriel before, and she knows exactly what he's capable of.

'What are you going to do to me?' she whispers, not moving an inch. I want to take her in my arms, right there and then, and promise everything will be okay. I want to tell her that there's no way I'll let anyone hurt her, now or ever again. Of course, I do no such thing. In a few moment's time I'm going back to being the aggressor in our partnership, and I've lost the taste for it. I want to scream out in frustration.

'We're going to fuck you up, you heard the man.' I flick a finger backwards to indicate Mal and then pat the centre of the bed. 'Come on, Wilkinson, let's not keep everyone waiting.' My voice is laden with venom. I am playing my part to the best of my ability, and Harper's acting skills aren't bad, either.

'Get away from me,' she whispers, visibly wincing in horror.

'Don't make me come over there and make you, Wilkinson. If I have to sort you out, there'll be punishments your backside can't cash.' My voice drops down an octave and is the deadly kind of soft that you don't fuck with. Sure enough, Harper drops to her haunches without another word, and looks back at me nervously. She's good. I hate to think how much she's had to endure playing piggy-in-the-middle with her late husband and the asshole behind me.

Gabriel then decides it's his turn to have some fun. Harper's quite high up on the bed, near me, but he readjusts this balance by placing a hand around each of her ankles and yanking her downward, accompanied by a high-pitched yelp and some frantic clawing at the duvet, but she doesn't manage to stop her journey into his clutches.

'Mal, stop this!' she screams, but there's no conviction behind her tone. She knows this will play out exactly the way he wants it to, and she's already resigned to the fact.

While Gabriel pulls her body exactly where he wants it, raising her ass, I get into place in front of her face. Grabbing her hair in my fist I yank her head up until it's level with my cock, letting her get a good look at it. Meanwhile, Gabriel has his fingers between her legs, testing the waters.

'Is she ready?' I ask, unnecessarily. I know she is. I can see it by the way her pupils have dilated and by the rapid but shallow pounding of her pulse. Her excitement is palpable, even if it is coupled with fear.

'She's ready,' he affirms. 'Fuck she is so wet you could get two cocks in here at once. Want to try that, Brando? I've always wanted to try that.' I don't even want to think about trying that. My brain is exploding. One moment I don't want to touch her in front of Mal, and in the next I can't think of anything else. All the current in my body is short circuiting, and if I'm not careful I'm going to blow.

'One thing at a time, hotshot. Let's warm her up.' This is more for me than it is for Harper. I'm losing the plot. Can I do to this to her? Do I have a choice?

Bending over her I murmur, 'How much can you take? You're already pretty messed up, and I'm not sure if I can rein Gabriel in.'

'Don't even think about it,' she grits out just as quietly. 'I can take it.'

This is not what I want to hear. I want to protect her, not throw her to the wolves. What I need to do is speak to Gabriel and try to explain what's happening. If I can do that we can work something out between us.

'I'm going to alternate between fucking her pussy and ass. That about do for a warm-up?'

I don't respond; Gabriel's going to do his own thing anyway. I have to concentrate on my own game. There won't be any soft caresses or lingering kisses like this morning. We'll have to keep this impersonal. I wonder if Mal is going to kill me anyway. He found us in bed together, for fuck's sake. There are two indentations in the pillows, and I know the man isn't stupid. There's a chance he might buy the fact she's with me so I can torment her, but if I'm going to make him believe it, I have to sell it.

Fisting my cock in one hand I begin to pump, under the pretence of priming it. Believe me when I say it doesn't need any help in that department, but I need a couple of seconds before I go on the attack. My mind is blank.

Harper's eyes shoot daggers at me, thankfully spurring me into action. I get the message. I need to be the total jerk I've basically been since I kidnapped her. You wouldn't think it would be too hard, considering all the practice I've had in the last few days, but it is. She's been through too much, and I don't want to hurt her any more than she's been hurt already. If I do, I'm not sure I'll be able to live with myself when this is all over, although that might not be a problem.

My hands circle her throat while I lift her chin with my thumbs. It's time to see if I can supercharge my acting skills.

'Open those lips up nice and wide, Wilkinson.' Squaring my shoulders I do my best to go into bastard mode. She does as she's told without a moment's hesitation, but her eyes are not on me - they're on Mal. She's gauging his reaction carefully. I hope she knows what she's doing. If we hurt her she'll stand no chance against that monster.

'Ready, Brando?' Gabriel already has hold of her ass and is positioning himself for penetration.

'No, Mal, stop this,' Harper screams, but it's already too late, Gabriel is surging forward, pushing Harper's mouth onto my cock in a cocoon of heat that steals my breath away. I don't want to enjoy this, and throwing my head back I resist the urge to roar out loud.

'This is your chance to finally get your own back, Brando,' Gabriel says, with a wicked gleam in his eye. 'Try not to fuck it up. This girl is nothing but trouble, and everyone knows it.' He makes his point clear by hammering into her, over and over until my cock feels as if it's being sucked by a vacuum cleaner.

'Jesus, Gabriel. Slow down. If you're not careful she'll swallow the thing in a minute.' Grabbing a hold of Harper's hair once more I yank, in order to stop the poor girl being impaled on me. Gabriel just grins, but he does relax his pace a little.

'She's supposed to suffer, Brandt. That's kind of the idea.' He rolls his eyes. I know he's enjoying himself, but I also know he has one eye on Mal at all times. Gabriel is nothing if not careful.

'Yeah, but I don't want to suffer at the same time, asshole. If my dick is in two pieces at the end of this there'll be trouble.' More trouble than there already is, anyway.

'I wouldn't worry. I'm sure our friend over there can glue it back together for you.' Gabriel glances sideways at Mal and winks. Great. Now we're antagonising the beast.

'Focus, Gabriel,' I say. Harper is currently gurgling, trying to say something and failing miserably. It's probably for the best.

Mal isn't pleased with our performance and is quick to voice his displeasure.

'Gentleman, this is all very lovely, but I don't want 'nice'. If I wanted 'nice' I'd have got Tinkerbell the fucking fairy in to do the business. As it is I've got you, and I'm beginning to wonder why I didn't shoot you immediately. Do I need to take over and show you how it's done?' Mal's voice is dripping with sarcasm. He is not impressed with our antics, and he's not going to wait much longer. This is probably what Harper was trying to tell me. Looks like the warm-up session is over.

Gabriel grabs the whip and flings it my way. I catch it neatly in mid-air. 'Spice things up a bit, Brando. We've got an audience, don't you know.' The sarcasm is still there, and he's liable to get us both killed if he isn't careful. Pulling out of Harper's mouth, I give her a couple of seconds' breathing space as I figure out what to do.

'Do it,' she wheezes. Hell, the woman can barely breathe now, and she's asking for more? She's doing this to save my hide, and it leaves a sour taste in my mouth. I'd think I'd rather go down all guns blazing than serve her up for this sick motherfucker.

Gabriel's eyebrow slants my way and I know he's encouraging me to do something. Fuck this shit. Growling in the back of my throat I grab either end of the leather flails, and wrap them around her neck. Her eyes bulge, but as I haven't applied any pressure yet I know it's for show. Pulling her towards me, lifting her face, I spit, 'Think you can take this, my little whore? Think you can suck my cock while I drain all the air from your body?' My hands tighten and I hear her make soft gurgling noises. I can see Mal smile out of the corner of my eye and realise this is turning him on. I'm going to kill him. Maybe not today, but one day soon, I'm going to exterminate the fucker.

'Ready to take my cock again? Now that Gabriel's finished with your cunt, he's about ready to fuck your ass. Think you can handle both of us at once?' She's not got much choice, but she nods anyway. Yanking her head forward I watch her gag around me, and when I hear her squeal I know Gabriel is well on his way.

'That's more like it, gentlemen,' Mal enthuses. 'I knew you had it in you.' It's hardly the encouragement I'm looking for, but I need to find a way to talk to Gabriel to get him onside. We need to work together.

'Gabriel, what say we stand her up? One in front, one behind?' I raise an eyebrow and give him a wink. He takes the bait.

'Sounds like a fun idea to me.'

I pull until she's up in a kneeling position. Gabriel places his hands under her armpits, which is my cue to drop the whip and help him stand her up.

'Having fun, sweetheart?' Mal mocks.

'Go fuck yourself,' Harper spits, and if the bulge in Mal's pants is anything to go by, he's enjoying the show. Let's hope we tip him over the edge soon.

'So, which hole do you want this time, Brando?' Gabriel's fingers are fanning across her tits, the nipples standing like arrow tips. He gives them a vicious tweak at regular intervals, and I know he's enjoying the way her ass squirms against his cock.

'I'll take the one that's closest to me,' I say. I should probably offer to fuck her ass because I know I'd be a damn site more careful than him, but that's not what we're here for. Mal wants pain. Fuck, judging by the expression on her face, even Harper wants pain. It's hard to see her like this. Her eyes are filled with lust and there's a trail of arousal leaking down her legs. This is turning her on. There is no disguising the fact.

My hands drop between her legs and I work her clit.

'One...' Gabriel says. 'Two...' is followed by his fingers pulling her nipples as his teeth make their way to her earlobe. 'Three...' is accompanied by a squeal as he sinks his teeth and his cock into her at the same time.

'Shh,' I soothe into her other ear, the one that doesn't have the teeth of a madman clinging to it. 'I bet I can make you come in less than three minutes.' My cock is sliding forward, testing the waters, which seem to be very warm and quite deliciously wet. While I might be trying to add a little style and pizazz to the proceedings, Gabriel is moving like a battering ram. He should know by now that it isn't going to produce results quickly.

'Gabriel, let's get a rhythm going here.' I roll my eyes. He'll get with the plan in a minute. Gabe hasn't seen much pussy in the last few years, so he's easily excited.

'Good point, Brando, why didn't I think of that?' He raises his eyes in question as he waits for instructions.

'When I go forward, you pull back and vice versa. Let's see how that works. Then maybe we can work on getting them both inside her at the same time.'

Grabbing her hair I pull backwards until her neck is strained as she tries to keep her gaze on me. 'Would you like that, my little slut? Two cocks inside you at once?' She shakes her head, but I know differently. She is so aroused she'd come at the click of my fingers.

'Stop this, Mal, please stop,' she squeaks, but her gaze never leaves mine. Her eyes are deep pools of bottomless lust. Even her acting has its limits, apparently.

Mal doesn't say a word behind us. When I glance out of the corner of my eye I see his cock is in his hands, and he's fisting it slowly. We're on the right track. We just need to figure out a way to tip him over the edge. I'm pretty sure she can help with that.

Gabriel and I set an easy pace, pistoning in and out of her with slow, deep thrusts. At first I can see her eyes well up with tears as Gabriel sinks his cock deeper and deeper inside her. It's a vicious beast. I can sympathise.

'Concentrate on my fingers working your clit,' I murmur, tugging her hair gently to get her attention. 'Don't think about what he's doing behind you.'

'Easy for you to say,' she grunts, but I can see how close she is.

'Shall we try two at once?' I say to Gabriel. That should keep her away from the elusive pinnacle of pleasure she's been trying so desperately hard to reach.

'Thought you'd never ask, Brando. It's about time we showed her what we're really made of.' It's his turn to pull her hair and twist her head back.

Putting his mouth close to her ear, he says, 'I don't think you can handle both of us at once, do you?' When she tries to answer he sticks his fingers in her mouth, effectively silencing her. Her eyes darken and I want to tell him to pull them out, but before I get a chance she bites. Gabe pulls his fingers back as if stung and then slaps her. I grind my teeth in exasperation. Does the girl have a death wish or what?

'You'll pay for that!' he yells. She's already paying for it. We're sinking into her as fast and as deep as we can. But she's utterly lost in the moment, head thrown back against Gabriel's jaw as her fingernails scrape down my abs as if seeking something to cling to. Here I am thinking she's in so much discomfort she can barely breathe, when the reality is something else entirely. She's loving every second of it. She might not want to, but she is.

'Brandt, please,' she moans. My fingers are hovering, but they aren't about to deliver what she wants - not yet.

'You're not in a position to beg for anything,' Gabriel spits, abruptly pulling out of her. I pull back too, wondering what he's up to. 'Shove her up against the wall, Brandt. Let's see if we can get two cocks inside that pussy at the same time.' I don't get a say in the matter apparently because he spins her around and presses her into the wall.

'I've always wanted to do this,' he says, a wicked gleam in his eyes as he drinks in the sight of her. I want to punch him. 'Ladies first,' he says, spreading her for me. Now I really want to punch him, but I've got to the stage where I just want to finish this.

Sliding inside her again, I close my eyes as the tight heat of her sheath surrounds me. There is no way she'll get both of us inside. She's too tight. But Gabriel isn't the type to take no for an answer. He coaxes his cock against mine, inch by slow inch. I can't even begin to tell you what it feels like. Incredible. It is so much more than that, though. When we begin moving as one I come almost instantly, and he is only a few seconds behind me. Thankfully I had the foresight to put my fingers back on her clit before we began, and she's bucking in heat against it, Gabe's face tightening with pleasure.

We hear a roar behind us, and I guess Mal has emptied onto the floor, but a moment later I realise that is not the case. He's pissed at something. Before we know what's happening there's a loud bang and we're all cowering, wondering who the hell has been shot this time.

Chapter Four - Gabriel

The sound of a gunshot exploding deflates the high of my orgasm in an instant. One minute I'm up in the clouds, and the next I'm falling down to earth with no parachute. The landing is unpleasantly hard, as you can imagine. Pulling out of Harper my eyes dart around the room to see if I can spot who's bleeding out.

At first glance I can't see a thing. There's no tell-tale stain of blood on any of us, which is a good sign, so maybe Mal has just given us a warning shot. Sure enough, on further inspection I find little pieces of plaster on the floor, and when I look up it's to find there's a bullet lodged in the wall just above our heads. It looks like someone is on the warpath.

'I don't remember telling either of you to let her come. I'm the only one gets to do that.' Mal is advancing, waving his gun around, the expression on his face is predatory. One of us is in for the chop. This is Brandt's work. He let the bitch come. What is wrong with him?

'We didn't,' says Brandt, openly lying. 'She did that all by herself. She seems to like pain.' That stops Mal in his tracks. Now I'm not sure how closely he was paying attention to Brandt's antics, but there's a possibility he saw what was happening. Brandt is playing a dangerous game.

Mal gets in Brandt's face. 'Are you lying to me, boy? Do you think I didn't notice where those hands were?'

'Oh, I know you did,' Brandt says without a missing a beat, 'but I pulled them away before she came. I don't like her enough to grant her that kind of pleasure. She hasn't had an orgasm the whole time she's been here. Ask her yourself. Somehow she managed to carry herself over the edge without my help. Interesting trick, that. I'd love to know how she did it.'

Mal grabs hold of Harper and spins her around to face him. 'That true, princess?' His eyes narrow as he looks at her expectantly.

'Fuck you,' she spits, and she looks furious. It's obviously a look she's worn before because he smiles. 'Rubbing yourself up against the wall again, eh, 'Arper? What have I told you about that? It will get you into trouble.' He turns her around again and spanks her butt.

'Come over here.' He curls his finger towards Brandt. Stepping forward slowly, my ex looks rather apprehensive. I'm not feeling any better about this turn of events if I'm honest. Is he going to kill him? Does he know he's lying?

Mal hands his gun to him. Just like that. I'm pretty sure I can figure out what's going to happen next. He's is going to see where Brandt's allegiances lie.

'Kill her,' he barks, and Harper's mouth widens in a big 'O' that says she never saw this coming. Too bad. I did.

Brandt looks at the gun as if it's made of TNT. He looks afraid to touch the damn thing. Kill her, I silently urge. If you don't, we're all dead.

Finally he takes it and aims at her. I'm pretty sure he has no idea how to use the thing, so I don't know who he's trying to fool.

'What's stopping me from killing you with this thing?' he asks. It's as if the bloody man has a death wish. Just kill the girl, for fuck's sake.

Mal smiles. 'Absolutely nothing. But if you do kill me everyone else in this room will be dead a few seconds later. You're not getting past my boys.' He indicates the thugs standing at the back of the room. I suddenly feel sick. There is no way Brandt will kill Harper. He's half in love with her, so unless I'm much mistaken we're all going to be blown to smithereens because he won't man up to the job.

Snatching the gun out of his hands I say, 'I'll do it,' aiming at her forehead before the thing is yanked abruptly from me.

'Did I ask you?' Mal delivers a vicious backhander that sends me staggering. Clutching a hand to my injured jaw I groan. My mouth is now full of blood and it doesn't taste very pleasant.

He passes the firearm back to Brandt. 'Kill her,' he repeats. Brandt looks surprisingly cool, considering. He won't kill Harper, which will mean we'll all be dead very shortly. The asshole could at least look slightly guilty about that, but there's not a flicker of emotion on his face. I know that look well. I wear it often. On him, though, it's not something I see very often. What is going on here? What have I missed?

When he brings the gun up to Harper's head again my eyes follow every move he makes. Is he going to use that thing to shoot Mal? If so, the place is about to light up quicker than a war zone. But with Brandt anything is possible. There's still a person with morals and beliefs inside him. That part of me died a long time ago.

It's why I could happily pick up the gun and shoot her without a moment's pause. Brandt can't do that, though. Right now he'll be panicking. His blood pressure will be rocketing and before long his hands are going to start shaking. Mal is going to see through the act and bury us both.

When the safety is pulled back I wince for Brandt. There is no way he's going to do this. Any minute now Mal's brains are going to be scattered all over the floor and ours will follow shortly after. This pisses me off. I've just been released from a very long spell inside, and now someone's going to kill me? How's that for irony?

I stare at Brandt for the last time, as I watch his finger tighten on the trigger. It feels as if my retinas are trying to burn the image into my brain because time almost slows to a halt from which there is no escape. Life is so bloody unfair. I want to tell Brandt all sorts of things, but I can't open my mouth to say shit. For the first time in my adult life, I'm choked up. I do have a heart, after all. The gun is still firmly trained on Harper. What is going on? I can't believe he's going to kill her.

The gun clicks. I wait for the inevitable explosion of a bullet, but nothing happens. I wonder if I've entered a parallel universe. A really bizarre one.

For starters, the expression on Harper's face is so comical I want to laugh. She's got one eye open, one closed, her cheeks are scrunched up, and her teeth, for some reason, appear to be in mid-bite. It's like she's frozen in place with rigor mortis-like horror. Brandt, on the other hand, has both eyes open and the look of a killer within them. His shoulders are pulled back as if preparing for the gun's whiplash, his expression at first deadly, and then puzzled as he realises no one's died. The rest of the mercenaries in the room look shocked. We're all wondering what happened, and there's only one man with the answers.

Turning to Mal, I see he's the only one who isn't surprised by this turn of events. Then it dawns on me. This was never about killing Harper. He doesn't want her dead - at least not yet. He just wanted to see if Brandt would pull the trigger. I'm betting he was ninety-nine percent positive he wouldn't, so this must be an interesting result. I'm curious. Did Brandt know the gun wasn't loaded? I don't see how he could. That means he took a calculated risk - and a big one at that. Still, it might pay off if we're lucky.

'Didn't think you had it in you, pretty boy.' Mal plucks the gun from Brandt's fingers and then shoves a cartridge in it before placing it back in his pocket.

'What the hell was that all about?' Brandt asks angrily.

Mal's tongue gently strokes his upper lip as he raises his head to face him. 'Well, you didn't actually think I'd leave you with a loaded gun, did you? There was always a chance you'd shoot me, and I'm not about to take that risk. I just wanted to see if you'd actually do it. It was a test of sorts. If you weren't capable of pulling the trigger, you'd be of no use to me.'

Brandt seemed perplexed by the answer. 'Why didn't you give the gun to Gabriel? Why me?' he asks. I already know the answer to that question, but it seems my ex needs clarification. He shouldn't. He knows exactly what I'm capable of.

'Because, sunshine, I already know he's a killer.' Mal indicates me with a flick of his finger. 'You, though, I wasn't so sure of, and if you can't kill I don't have a use for you.' He sneers. 'I'm still not sure you'd be good for much, but I do have a job that needs sortin' out, and I don't have enough men to spare at the minute.' He looks at Brandt thoughtfully, but Brandt doesn't say a word. It's a good move. You don't want to say any more than you have to around this bastard. One word in the wrong place would be enough to hang you.

'Why? What's going on?' Harper has finally found her voice, which is quite surprising considering her near death experience. Most females would have melted into a little puddle on the floor right now, giving everyone an impressive display of histrionics. Not so our Harper. This one's as hard as nails because she's had to be, in order to survive. I almost feel sorry for her, even though she's in direct competition with me, so she's currently my enemy. Still, I work with the old adage: keep your friends close and your enemies closer. So she might come in useful at some point.

Mal tosses her one of Brandt's T-shirts he's found on the floor. 'Get dressed, princess. We're moving out.'

'What have you got planned?' she demands. She's not going to let this go. I swear she has a death wish. There's no way I'd mess with Mal, and I've only known him for half an hour.

He walks over to her slowly, grabbing her chin and pulling her to him. She doesn't even blink. 'Feeling nosey, darlin'?' he asks.

'You're going to kill me and these guys in less than a week's time. What harm can there be in sharing, *sweetheart*?' Her voice is dripping with sarcasm as she returns his endearment. Mal asking Brandt to put a bullet in her head has really pissed her off. Strange girl.

'You wanna get cheeky with me, sweetheart? You don't want to know what fun things I have planned for you when we get back home. Trust me.'

'Oh, I know exactly what you've got planned for me. What I want to know, is what are these two going to be doing? As I won't be alive long enough to tell anyone, you might as well share.'

'Who says I'm going to kill you?' He almost looks affronted.

Harper glares at him. 'I know how this works, Mal. I'm not stupid.' Pulling Brandt's T-shirt over her head, she looks him directly in the eye. 'Who's pissed you off lately? Maybe I could kill them for you?' Her hand reaches up to stroke the stubble on his jaw, and the action makes me shudder. She's like a mouse playing with a mountain lion. She doesn't stand a chance.

Mal smacks his lips together, and I watch him use his tongue to clean something from his left incisor. I'm feeling vaguely nauseous, and that can't be a good thing.

'You can't kill this one, princess. Everyone who's tried so far has ended up dead. And I don't want you dead because if you're dead...' He lets her finish the sentence for him.

'If I'm dead, you don't get to kill me. Must be someone big.' She sounds thoughtful. Maybe she's going through her databanks of drug dealers. Can she piece together who might be next to bite the dust with regard to Adley's world domination plans? Maybe she's trying to figure out if she can get us all out of this catastrophic fuck-up? I think that ship has sailed, but at least she's stopped him from killing us outright.

Mal clears his throat. 'It is someone big. I haven't been able to get anyone close to them, but Brandt over there, he might be able to.' He purses his lips. It's clear the cogs are turning, but he's a cagey bastard. I wonder if he's had this planned all along. Wouldn't surprise me. That way he has Harper in his pocket. She'll do anything he says if it means Brandt gets out of here without a bullet lodged in his skull.

'It's someone Brandt's father knows, isn't it?' she whispers. He raises his eyebrows, but he doesn't confirm her guess.

'You don't need to bother your pretty little head, darlin'. You just need to look cute and get ready to suck my cock. Believe it or not I've missed you. No one takes what I dish out quite as well as you do.'

'You mean no one else you hurt enjoys pain,' she clarifies.

He shrugs. 'Same thing.'

'Brandt and his father don't even talk any more,' she says. 'They've disowned him.'

Mal shrugs again. 'So? That will just make this all the more entertaining. Brandt will have to do some work for a change.'

'You're setting them up? You were never going to kill them, were you? You had this planned all along.' Her eyes have turned almost black. She is one pissed off little lady, and Adley seems to find it extremely amusing.

'Nah. I just wanted to see what you would do to save them. I can read you like a book, princess. I know you like him, even though you pretend to profess otherwise. Maybe I'll get someone to film these two twats as they try to play Bond. It'll probably give me hours of entertainment, and I'm sure you'll enjoy watching the footage with me. How long do you think pretty boy will last, Harper? Ten minutes? Half an hour? Won't be much more than that before the bodyguards mow him down. They won't even get close enough to wave at the bloke.'

Brandt and I risk a look at each other. Bodyguards? Who the hell is this fucker?

Harper shakes her head. 'You are one sick individual, Mal Adley. Was killing Alex not enough for you? Do you really need to stick the knife in and twist it?'

'Well, sweetness, you witnessed that murder. Although I admit it was kind of a joint effort, it still doesn't pay to have witnesses around. You knew this was coming. Don't play the wilting wallflower on me now.'

'A joint effort?' she says incredulously. 'Really? That's how we're playing this now? It was some joint effort, all right. One engineered by you from start to finish and filmed just in case I put a foot out of line. You and Alex were very similar like that, by the way. You don't like loose ends. People either do what you say or you kill them. It's no wonder you've got no pals, Mal. You're going to die all alone, without a single friend to mourn your passing. They'll cheer when they bury you.' Harper is foolishly winding him up, but she's sticking up for Brandt. Is this the part where I start to feel guilty for doubting her? She has been on our side all along. The part where she threw us to the dogs was to try and get Mal off our backs, not the other way around. I now realise that she's accepted the fact she's going to die, but she's trying her best to give us a chance out of this crap. I'm beginning to look at the waif in a whole new light. She's not the conniving whore I've always assumed she would be. Everything she's done, no matter how fucked up and twisted, has been to try and protect Brandt in some way. Harper may have got herself mixed up in the wrong crowd, but she isn't a nasty piece of work. She's just trying her best to survive, and I know from experience how hard that can be around creeps like Adley.

Mal grips her by the throat and bangs her up against the wall, knocking the air out of her. He continues with his vicelike grip until her head begins to roll on his fingertips. Brandt moves to get up beside me, but I slam him back down again with a fist in his gut. Now is not the time to interfere. We'll get to that part later, when we stand half a chance of rescuing her.

'You think I care about friends, cunt?' Mal's free hand slams against the wall beside her head. 'I rule the East End. You think I dole out drugs and run arms, but it goes much deeper than that. You have no idea what I'm involved in or how deep the hole goes. If you were a sensible girl you'd keep it that way. Now unless you want me to start chopping body parts off early, I suggest you keep that trap shut and get your ass out to my car. Remember, I still have the gun. There are so many ways I can make your life miserable, princess. I wouldn't push me. Nod if you understand.' He increases the pressure on her throat so she can do no such thing, before nodding her head for her. 'There, I knew you'd see sense.' Releasing her abruptly, she slumps to the floor gasping for air. He turns his back on her. Brandt moves to get up, and again I slam him down.

'Sit the fuck still,' I hiss from the corner of my mouth. What's with these two? Do they both have death wishes?

Mal turns to his mercenaries. 'Get her in the car and take her back to mine. As to these two, lock 'em up for the time being. Oh, and post a couple of armed guards. One of 'em might be harmless, but the other could be trouble, and no one wants that, do they?'

He strides out of the room without so much as a glance at anyone, while his lackeys scramble to obey orders.

Fucking hell. We're swapping one prison for another, and I have to confess, I'm pretty sure I'll like the other one a whole lot better than the new one I'm about to occupy. Why did I get involved in all this shit?

Three hours later we find ourselves locked up in some tin can shed in the middle of nowhere. The guards are taking no chances with us. We're both tied hand and foot with duct tape, so there go my filthy thoughts for the evening. I have no problem with Brandt being tied down, of course, but I take umbrage to being wrapped up in a butterfly-style cocoon. You think I'm kidding? Mal has us up in the rafters of his shed, and we're literally taped to the ladder-like rungs that line the top of the roof. If we move there's a good chance we'll hurtle to the floor, which will either entail us breaking every bone or dying instantly. Option two is preferable, but I'm not prepared to risk option one in the meantime. To make things worse, the fucker has taped us face down. A nice touch, I thought.

'You okay?' Brandt asks as soon as the thugs have finished their handiwork and gone. Thoughtfully, Mal has not taped our mouths shut. Maybe he finds the sound of screaming comforting.

'Yeah, I'm just peachy, thanks. Never been better, in fact. Had a top day, all things considered.' I get an eye roll for my troubles.

'He's just fucking with us. We'll be let down, eventually.' Brandt seems resigned to his fate. I am anything but.

'Do you think?' The sarcasm is pouring out of me, but I can't seem to stop it. I think it's the only thing keeping me sane. 'I have to agree it would probably be rather hard to kill people taped to the roof as we are. I'm pretty sure that running away after we'd done the deed would be a problem. As would holding a gun, standing upright, walking, or any number of other rather important things,' I add for good measure.

'Are you finished?' Brandt asks, as soon as my tirade is over.

I have to think about that. 'I'm not sure,' I confess. 'Are you going to say anything else that's completely and utterly stupid within the next ten seconds?' It's a reasonable question.

'Fuck off. I was just being nice. What else am I supposed to do? Yell 'we're all going to die' at the top of my lungs?' Brandt glances sideways and gives me a smile. I can't return the look. I'm not a fan of heights, and though I'm not scared of them exactly, I prefer not to be implicitly at their mercy.

'That might be more useful. You never know, someone might hear you and come to our rescue.' I am currently trying my best to avoid looking at the darkened floor below, but it's really difficult, seeing as how my head is pointed directly at it.

'For God's sake shut your eyes; you look scared half to death,' Brandt says. I resent that remark. I am scared half to death, there is no 'look' about it. 'It's nice to see that you do have a human side, you know. I thought you were invincible.' Brandt is really lucky I don't have the use of my limbs at the moment because if I did, he would be unconscious right now.

'There's no point shutting my eyes,' I grit out. 'I know what's beneath us and there's no 'unseeing' it. I can shut my eyes all I like, but that view will still be waiting for me when I reopen them. This is the stuff of fucking nightmares.'

'You were in a major nightmare for God knows how many years while inside. This is a piece of cake considering.' If he's trying to make me feel better, he's failing miserably.

'Then it's the shittiest cake I've ever tasted. Mal is setting us up. If we're not dead in the next couple of days he'll send someone in to finish the job.' That's another thing about me; I'm a realist. There's no point sugar-coating this crap. This is like falling into quicksand, while there's a tornado raging right above you. Any which way you turn is destined for disaster.

'Oh, ye of little faith. We just need to be smarter than he is.' Brandt is still sounding remarkably cheerful, considering. I wish his optimism was catching. In whichever direction I look the apocalypse is looming just around the corner, and our demise is almost guaranteed. I really don't want to die just yet. Brandt had better have something good up his sleeve.

'Then you'd better be Einstein because I'm not dying less than a week after I've got out of prison. You hear me?'

'I hear you.' Brandt's voice now sounds about as happy as mine because he knows as well as I do that it's going to be almost impossible to get out of this disaster without losing the contents of our bowels and developing a rather unpleasant blue tinge to our skin. Having said that, if anyone can figure a way out, it's him. As an added incentive, if he doesn't I'm going to be waiting for him on the other side with my pitchfork at the ready.

Chapter Five - Harper

As Mal pushes my head down into his car I resist the urge to angrily bat his hand away. All I will get is a slap for my troubles, and I'll be getting enough of those later.

'Who do you want him to kill?' I'm not sure why I need to know, but I do. As soon as he tells me, though, I'll begin hyperventilating about whether he'll make it out alive of whatever Mal has planned. The odds are firmly against it. The whole object of this exercise is for me to watch him die.

'Nice to see you, too, 'Arper. Did you miss me?' Mal sits back in the tan leather of his seat and grabs a lock of my hair, rubbing it together in his fingertips. He brings it up to his nose and breathes me in. I'm a weirdo magnet. It's official. First Alex, now Mal.

'We've already covered the pleasantries, I believe,' I snap. 'Now are you going to answer me, or are we going to play cat and mouse for the next few hours?' I can't deal with him right now. There is way too much going on in my head.

The car pulls away from the house with a burst of speed that threatens to send my spine bursting through my ribcage. What is wrong with Mal's lackeys? They're like animals. Perhaps that's a requirement on the application form. It wouldn't surprise me.

Buckling up my seatbelt because I don't trust our driver, I turn my attention back to Mal and wait for his reply. There's no guarantee he'll give me one, but I've got nothing better to do.

'You still love him, don't you?' It's just like him to answer a question with a question. The man should be a politician. If he's not giving me what I want, I don't see why I should return the favour.

Bringing my hand up to his stubbled jaw, I gently rub my fingertips across it. 'Still jealous? I hardly see the point as you're going to kill me in a few days' time.' Moving my lips to his jawline, I kiss it. If he wants to fuck with me, I can fuck with him.

As fast as a whip his fingers grab my chin and he tilts my face up to his. I can see the desire burning in his eyes. It's always pissed him off that the look is not reciprocated in mine. That's why Alex died, and it's why he wants Brandt dead. He's going about things the wrong way, though.

'It doesn't have to be like this, Harper. You obey, you get to stay in my world. Well, for as long as you can hack it. I can't be any worse than that bastard. You look like shit. What's he been feeding you?'

I almost laugh out loud. At least Brandt was nice enough to feed me. Mal didn't even give it a second thought. If he'd had his way I'd have starved to death already. The man is about as much use as the 'g' in lasagne.

'I'm not killing anyone else for you. I'm not putting anyone in prison, I'm not dumping drugs on your unsuspecting enemies, and I'm not going to be whored out to your friends. We've had this conversation before. I haven't changed my mind. You even try that shit and I'll squawk to anyone who'll listen.' My resolve is firm. It might not be when he's got the tube of superglue and a sledgehammer in his hands, but by that time I'll be a lost cause, anyway.

'Oh, I think you'll do exactly as I say,' he purrs. 'You can't handle the consequences.'

'Try me,' I whisper. Who am I kidding? We've already proved I usually fall at the first hurdle. Mind you, after last night with Brandt there's no way I can do the dirty on him again. I need to stand up and take responsibility for my actions, just like I said. On the plus side, there's one thing that stands in my favour. I like pain. I like even the really bad kind of pain. It's going to get me killed one day.

'Promises, promises,' Mal rasps, his fingers crawling between my legs. Fuck, what were we talking about again? It takes me a minute to get my head back in the game.

'Who are you getting them to kill?' That's the question I need answered. Clamping my legs tightly together until he plays ball, I clench my jaw and wait. As expected his next move is to pinch the delicate flesh of my inner thigh between thumb and forefinger. I grimace, but I don't budge. I know I'm going to lose this battle, but I need to learn how to put up a better fight.

'Open those legs for me, sweetheart. You aren't going to like the consequences if I have to part them with my gun.' I glare at him. Seriously? He's going there? And here I thought he was madly in love with me.

'Are you seriously going to waste a bullet on me? If I'm lucky I might bleed out, and then you won't be able to have lots of fun when you kill me later. There are some very important arteries in the leg.' From memory, I think they're femoral arteries and if you slice one open you probably won't be in good shape for a while.

Mal pulls his gun out of his jeans and slides the barrel up the valley of my thighs, so it's pointing towards my stomach. He then strokes the trigger with his index finger and everything in my body clenches.

'Open your fucking legs, 'Arper. If you don't, we'll have a banging little session where I'll show you just how good my knowledge of human anatomy is. I have studied it somewhat over the years, and occasionally I like to play with dead people.'

He likes to what? I don't think I want to know what that means. Does he cut them open? Does he... Oh God. I think I'm about to lose my breakfast - or I would, if I'd had any.

Opening my legs, a red stain of humiliation spreads across my face and chest.

Here we go again. One moment I think I can stand up to him, and the next I'm obeying every single word he says. This can't continue. A small part of me says I need to stay alive to see if I can help Brandt and Gabriel out of this terrible predicament, but how useful am I likely to be? Mal will have me tied up somewhere in his warehouse, and it will be a waiting game until he's got footage of their death. That's what he's after. That's what he wants to torment me with. It would be better if he shot me now. The trouble is, I know it won't be a kill shot. It won't even be a dangerous one. He'll give me something that smarts and a crack across the cheek, and I'll be his obedient little slut once again. I can't do this. I can't.

Feeling the butt of the gun crawl higher up my thighs, I feel a sense of impending doom hit me. I'm back in Mal's clutches, he has Brandt right where he wants him, and I'm pretty sure this is going to unfold like some kind of horror story. I'm Mal's next 'project' and he's going to enjoy making an example of me. If I don't play by the rules I'm going to suffer - in the most shockingly scary way possible.

The butt of the gun passes the hem of my T-shirt, burrowing between my legs. It doesn't stop until it rests against my pussy.

'Have you ever wondered what a bullet might do, if I shot it from here?' He inserts the tip of the gun inside me and twists it from side to side. The metal is cold and hard, the feeling unpleasant, to say the least.

'Can't say I have,' I whisper, not fighting his hands as they spread my legs wider.

'It would make a mess of the car, that's for sure.' It would also make a rather nasty mess of me, but no one cares about that.

'I'll have you back working within the week, 'Arper. I have so much shit on you, you won't dare put a foot out of line. I might even think about getting married. We could send some snaps to Brandt, after the event.'

'If you think I'm ever getting married again after what happened with Alex, to an even bigger monster than he was, you are much mistaken.' My face turns away from his to stare out of the window. I can't look at him. To do so would be to face my darkest fears, and I don't want to do that just yet.

Mal snorts. 'If I say jump, you say how high. That's what's so fun about our arrangement. You've never had a say in anything we do, and it will continue to work that way.'

'It won't,' I growl. 'Either kill me or set the cops on me. If you think I'm frightened of your bullets, you're wrong.'

'Don't even think of getting yourself arrested. I know people inside. You'll be dead within a day, two at the most. That is not your ticket out of this.'

'I know, I know,' I say with a bored voice. 'Alex already told me. There is no escape. I get it. You forget how alike you both are.'

Mal's hand snakes up to grab my throat, his face filled with fury. 'We are nothing alike,' he spits. 'You never respected that fucker and don't you think I didn't know it. Alex never really had you, did he?' He sits back from me, shaking his head. Thankfully the gun is also removed from between my legs, which at least allows me to suck in a small breath, although the surrounding air is now feeling particularly hot and unpleasant.

'He married me,' I say, when Mal's jaw tightens to near breaking point. 'If that isn't having me, I don't know what is.' I know it for a lie, though, as soon as I say it. Alex never had me, any more than Mal ever will. I didn't love him, didn't want him, and I sure as hell didn't respect him. Yeah, I found him attractive at the beginning but that waned quickly. As soon as I knew what he was capable of, I despised him with every fibre of my being. I tried to protect those around me, but when shit got personal I had to choose between protecting my friends or protecting myself. No one should ever be placed in that position, and yet here I am again with another sick asshole. Like I've said, I'm catnip for crazies.

'Nah, marriage means nothing,' Mal says, shaking his head. 'Marriage is just a little slip of paper with a couple of names on it. You can be married one day and divorced the next. That's not 'having' someone.' There's a dangerous glint in his eyes which I don't much like, but I'm going to ask the next question anyway. I know I'll regret it, but it has to be done.

'So what is 'having' someone, Mal? What exactly does that mean?' My face relays my vexation. I still haven't gotten the answer to my original question, and now we're back to the jealousy thing. I've had all I can take in the past few weeks. If he's going to kill me, I wish he'd just get on with it.

He twists his head and stares at me. 'That's what I mean. You don't know. But after an hour or two with me in the basement, you might. At the moment you're Miss High and Mighty, but I don't think that would last long when you experience my mean streak, and I know you've seen it, 'Arper. I made sure of it.'

'So you want me to be afraid of you?' That's not entirely what he wants, but I need to clarify it. Mal is well aware I was afraid of him from the moment I met him, and he took great care to foster that emotion. He wants something else, though. He wants to own me, like he mentioned before. The man wants to click his fingers and have me scurrying to do his bidding like a slave. I won't be that person and I told him so.

'I want you to worship the fucking ground I walk on, 'Arper. I need you to do everything I fucking tell you to the second I tell you - and you will, or you'll face the consequences.'

I won't. I'm done with this shit. Gabriel and Brandt will just have to look after themselves. I know as soon as I say it, though, it's a lie. If Mal will let Brandt live I'll probably do anything he asks, even if it's at the expense of my own life. If he knew, Brandt would kill me, but he'll never find out. The chances are we'll never see each other again. Still, I had my one night. It's something Mal can never take away from me, and the thought of us two being together will drive him crazy. It's small comfort, but I'll take it. I just hope those two make it out of Mal's clutches alive. I know he wants them both dead, and he'll take great pleasure rubbing my nose in their deaths, but there's a chance they might manage to slip out from beneath his clutches. Brandt's smart enough, and what he lacks in the violence department, Gabriel makes up for in spades. Together they'd make quite a pair if they could just get over their differences.

'What are you going to do to me?' I've changed tactics. There's no point asking any more questions about Brandt because Mal won't answer them. He has no intention of sharing whatever he has planned, and that's probably a good thing. I'm pretty sure I'd be horrified if I knew.

Watching the trees blur as our driver picks up speed, I'm not sure I want to know the answer. If Mal was mean before, he's going to be downright evil now, and judging by his past exploits I really don't want to be on the other end of anything he's dishing out. But it's not as if I have a choice. What are my options right now? I either play nice, and hope he takes pity on me, or I wait for the bastard to finish me. As I'm ninety-nine percent certain that's going to be the end result whichever stance I take, it hardly matters. It all depends on how much of a coward I am and how much pain I can take. As I sit trembling all over I decide I'm not feeling all that brave. I will probably do everything the bastard says to prolong my life for as long as possible. If a chance to escape presents itself I'll run, but that's unlikely.

'Anything I want to, and you'd better brace yourself because the thought of you sleeping with Brandt has brought out my nasty side.'

I look away from him, mostly because I don't want him to see the outraged expression on my face. He ordered me to sleep with Gabriel and Brandt and now he's going to get pissy with me? How's that for contrary? Still, there's no point arguing with the beast. It will get him riled up, and I'll suffer as a result. I might as well keep quiet and do my best to limit the damage coming my way.

I rub at my tired eyes. I didn't get a lot of sleep last night, mostly thanks to Brandt, and while I don't regret it for a second, I could do with a clear head right now. Every sense needs to be on red alert and I feel like I'm having an out-of-body experience. I'm jumpy, all over the place.

Who would Mal want Brandt to kill? Disjointed thoughts are coming at me from all angles and I can't piece anything together. It's obviously someone important. Someone who'll have security, or some kind of entourage. He said he thought Brandt would be able to get close to him, so it can't be anyone too famous. Brandt has connections, but he's not rich or powerful enough to be involved with royalty or major celebrities. It'll be someone connected to his father. I fail to see how he'll be able to re-enter that world now that his family has disowned him, but maybe Mal knows something I don't. There's always the chance Mal is setting him up for failure, knowing he'll be a laughingstock in that circle of familiar faces as soon as he shows up. Who is it likely to be? In the end, I whittle the possibilities down to either someone in a security capacity or local government. Maybe Mal's getting some trouble from the new Police Chief, or maybe he's being investigated. I can see how Brandt's family might have some influence there, although how much is questionable. Mind you, I guess all Mal needs is for Brandt to get an introduction. As long as he can get close to the guy, the possibilities for killing him are endless and Mal is nothing if not creative.

I wonder if Brandt will actually go through with it. I already know Gabriel will do anything to save his own neck, but Brandt has proven he does have at least some morals. I can't see him killing an innocent man, even if his life is on the line.

'Get on your knees and suck me off. I've been waiting a long time to be reunited with that filthy little mouth of yours, and the antics back there have left me with a pair of balls that are so blue you can almost see the ocean running through 'em.'

Mal reaches over to unbuckle my seatbelt, and before I can say a word I'm being hauled across the seat so that my mouth is level with his crotch. He runs a hand over his shaven head and settles back in his seat, getting comfortable.

'If you show me what that mouth can do, 'Arper, maybe I'll take pity on you when we get home. Show me a good time, baby, and we'll save the glue for tomorrow. How's that for a deal?'

He looks at me as if he's just given me an early Christmas present. Seriously? It's a crap deal.

'I'm waiting, 'Arper. You know I don't like waiting.'

Chapter Six - Brandt

I have no idea how long we've been up here now, but my stomach is making noises like an industrial boiler with an air leak. Gabriel isn't faring much better. At a guestimate we've been up here for a good twelve hours now, and the tape is beginning to cut off parts of my circulation. My whole body is protesting with pins and needles, and even if they did let me down now I wouldn't be able to stand. We'll be good for nothing when we're finally set free.

'How's the leg?' Gabriel is pale and sweaty. I'm not sure if that's down to blood loss or his fear of heights, and I'm not sure I want to know.

'To be honest, it's the least of my worries right now. My number one concern is how are they going to get us down from here? After that's sorted I'll worry about the leg. Thankfully it was just a glancing wound, and I know it's stopped bleeding so don't worry about me. We have much bigger things to worry about.' He's right, but I can't worry about something I know nothing about. As soon as Mal tells me what he wants us to do, then I'll worry. For now, I'm doing my best to stay sane. Every time I think about Mal I think about what he might be doing to Harper, and I can't bear the thought of her hurting.

'He's going to kill her,' I whisper. I can't help it, my voice gets all choked up, and if Gabriel wants to call me a pussy he can go fuck himself.

'She'll be all right. We'll get to her in time. Don't panic.' Gabriel's eyes are now open, but that's only because it's dark outside and he can't see the bottom of the shed any more. It's calmed him down somewhat and his voice is oddly gentle. It's a little disconcerting.

'I don't even know where he's holding her. How will we get to her in time? We don't know where to look.' So much for the not worrying part. Now that the words are being said out loud I'm freaking out. I'm never going to see her again, or if I do, it'll be on the front page of a tabloid with blood splattered about everywhere.

'Breathe. I know where he operates from. I used to deal, and I've known inmates on the inside who worked for him. He's in the East End, very close to where we are now if I'm not mistaken. He'll want to check in on us before he lets us loose.'

'I need to get Harper out.' I want to bang something, but that's not an option at the minute, so I settle for spewing out a string of expletives instead.

'You need to get yourself out first, and that's going to be difficult enough. When you've done that, I advise you run. Get out of the country and run as far and as fast as your legs will carry you. Then there's a chance you might live through the ordeal. If you continue on your path it's almost guaranteed suicide.'

'I can't leave her. Not with him. You of all people should know that, Gabriel.'

'She's poison,' he snaps. 'She put you away for five years, and maybe she'll try and put you away again before this is all over. Harper is going to do anything Mal tells her to.'

'And with good reason,' I snap right back. 'You heard her story. She'll be fighting for her life, and you'd do exactly the same thing if you were in her position.'

Gabriel just shakes his head and sighs. 'You'd be a fool to try and rescue her.'

This angers me no end. Although I know he is a cold-hearted bastard, I can't believe he'd happily leave her to the wolves. 'I couldn't live with myself if I didn't at least try. There are worse things than dying.'

He shakes his head. 'Not at the hands of Mal Adley there aren't. Your death could be strung out over several days while she watches. You have no idea of the amount of pain that asshole can inflict. If you go after her, you have to be prepared to suffer. The predicament we're currently in is particularly tame by his standards.'

'I'm not running. If you want to run that's your decision, but I can't do that to her. She's been through too much. If you and I thought we had it bad, we've got nothing on her. I've seen the marks. The woman has been through hell.'

Gabriel doesn't answer me. I'm not sure if that's because he thinks I'm a colossal idiot or because someone downstairs has switched the lights on. Either way, if we get out of this it looks like I'm on my own, which is fine by me. Seeing as how I'll probably get myself killed anyway, there's no point dragging anyone else down with me.

'Wakey, wakey, sleepy heads.' There's a man down there who looks a bit like a brick shithouse but bigger, and he's staring up at us. I already know, just from a glance, that I do not want to get on the wrong side of him. He is enormous. He also has a semi-automatic strapped to his back, which is another good reason not to cross him.

The bald muscle-head surveys us with amusement as a team of men file in behind. What's going to happen next? Is this the part where we die, or does that happen later?

'Evening gentlemen. I just thought I'd see if anyone wanted to get down from there? And if you do, let me know who wants to go first.' He's wearing this smile that says bad shit is about to happen, so I'm not eager to go first, but I know Gabriel is probably wetting himself because he's suddenly gone rather pale.

'Want me to go first?' I whisper.

'Yes,' he hisses.

'It might be better if you go first, then you won't know what's coming.' I don't mind waiting. My body is now pumped full of adrenaline, so I'm primed for whatever they're about to throw at me.

'You first,' Gabriel chokes.

That's fine by me. I hope he doesn't live to regret it, though.

'Yes, we'd like to come down,' I yell to the monstrosity below. He looks like steroids on legs. I wonder how much time you have to spend in the gym to look like that. Most of your life, by the looks of it. He's at least four times the size of me. 'I'll go first.'

'Well aren't you the brave one?' he replies, and before I get a chance to answer he makes a slashing downward sign with his wrist which has a thug to the left of him cutting a rope. Uh oh. I have a bad feeling about this, and sure enough, in the next instant the rung I am tied to goes hurtling downwards towards the earth and I have about two seconds to brace myself for instant death. I don't have time to panic. I don't have time to do anything, but inches before the floor hits me I shoot back up in the air experiencing a second or so of weightlessness before I shoot back downwards. It seems the ladder I'm on is connected to some kind of rubber cord. On another day I might have thought the whole thing quite good fun, but I'm really not feeling it today. I suspect the bastards just want to watch me piss my pants. By some miracle I haven't, and I feel quite proud of the fact.

'Get the other one down.'

When Steroids makes slashing motion number two Gabriel screams, 'No!' But he might as well save his breath. The rope has already been cut and he's in freefall. I wince as I hear him screaming at the top of his lungs. He is not going to be happy after this little stunt, but maybe that will work in our favour. If he gets a chance to take out any one of these bastards they'll be dead in a heartbeat.

Steroids pays no attention to the racket Gabriel is making. He and his men are concentrating on tearing the duct tape from all around me, and they are none too gentle about it. It feels a bit like I imagine waxing would, and I can't understand why anyone in their right mind would want to do that. Girls are really weird creatures.

'Don't even think about moving. You guys put one foot out of line and we'll make damn sure you don't move again.' Steroids barks the command like an army sergeant. I take the threat seriously, but just in case there's any doubt guns begin appearing all around us. Mal is taking no chances. Now I know that Gabriel and I are ex-cons, but we're not certifiable. I think he's giving us more credit than we deserve judging by the amount of firepower surrounding us.

Steroids chucks a cell phone at me. It takes me a moment to realise it's my own, which was confiscated as soon as they took me away. Why are they giving it back to me now?

'Well pick it up,' Steroids drawls. 'Don't you want to know how your fiancee's doing?' I blink. I can't think of anything further from my mind at the moment if I'm honest, and I have no idea where this is going. When a heavily booted foot connects with my stomach, though, I show a little more enthusiasm for the task.

'Absolutely,' I drawl right back. 'You want me to text her now? You want some sexting in there, too?' I get another boot in the rib for my troubles. Steroid's sense of humour appears to be very one-sided.

'Tell her you're going to come see her tomorrow night and that you can't wait to be married.' The man has got to be kidding. Is he serious? 'Do it now!' he yells when I make no move to obey. Okay. He's serious. I'd better get with the plan.

Reaching out for my phone I switch it on and key in my code. When it bursts into life I get beep after beep after beep as the messages rack up. They're all from Helena. I'm not sure I can handle this right now, but I scan through them all and summarise that the gist of them is wondering where I've got to. I'm kind of wondering the same thing. The last one is particularly pleasant.

Where are you, you piece of shit? If you don't get back to me within the next twelve hours you can find some other slut to marry. Helena

Well, at least she got one thing right. She is a slut. Frowning, I look down at my watch. It's been a while since that last text. Forget twelve hours and think more along the lines of twenty-four. It's more than possible she's deleted my number from her phonebook by now, and for that I would be entirely grateful, if some hulking great bloke wasn't waiting to shoot me. Hmm. Here goes nothing.

Sorry hun, I've been sorting out all the stuff in storage since I've been inside. I managed to lose my phone round Liam's, but I've got it back now. Did you want me to come over tomorrow? Brandt

I draw the line at leaving a fucking 'X'. The woman makes my skin crawl in the worst way, and I have no idea what I'm about to do to save my hide, but I really hope I don't have to marry the twat.

'It's done. She might not be speaking to me as I haven't texted her in quite some time, but that's your fault.' I give Steroids a shrug. I have to admit, I rather hope she isn't speaking to me. I have a feeling my life would be a whole lot simpler if that were the case. There is then a tell-tale ping that suggests otherwise.

Oh thank God. I was beginning to wonder if someone had killed you. Honestly Brandt, we're getting married in a few days' time. You need to get your ass down here ASAP. I'd thought for a moment we were going to have to cancel the wedding, and I can't cope with another scandal. This will all work out wonderfully. You'll see. Helena Xx

Jesus Christ. It's official. I now hate Mal Adley more than ever. 'Will that do?' I slide the phone back over to Steroids so he can take a look. For a second I almost wish we had sexted. I wonder if the big twat blushes?

Scanning the text, he takes a good look at it and grunts. 'That'll do for now, I suppose.' He then hauls me upright and barks, 'Follow me.'

My first step has my knees buckling and I nearly fall over. Shaking my legs out to try and get my circulation going, I try again with a bit more success. Walking slowly I turn back to Gabriel, but the men have closed ranks between us.

'Uh, uh, uh,' Steroids says. 'If you play nice and do what you're told you'll get your little buddy back. Until then he stays here for insurance purposes.'

'No way,' I snap, looking like someone's just punched me in the gut. 'Gabriel is the killer in this pairing. If you send me in on my own I'll be dead in seconds.' I mean every word I say. Prison might have taught me a lot of things, but it didn't teach me how to kill in cold blood. It didn't teach Gabriel that either; he knew how to do that before he went inside.

Steroids gives me a dark look. 'I think that's kinda what the boss is hoping for. So get your shit together and get out, unless you want to go back up there. Which reminds me, you can put him back now.' He makes a hand signal upwards and the men begin hauling on the rope that holds Gabriel.

'Oh no fucking way,' he yells. 'Brandt, you cannot leave me here like this. If you do I'll never forgive you.' He means every word and I don't want to cross Gabriel, but I don't see that I have much choice.

With this is mind, I do my best to reason with the big guy. 'I'm not doing this without Gabe. You might as well kill me now because I'm not setting a foot out of this door otherwise.'

Steroids grins, revealing a mouth full of fillings which suggests dental hygiene hasn't been big on his agenda for some time. 'You sure you want to play it that way? I really don't think you'll like the consequences.'

'Just for argument's sake,' I say, 'what are the consequences of me not doing as I'm told?' I think it's a fair question. Gabe might not like it, but I need to know.

'Mal told me you're smart,' Steroids says, with a bark of laughter. 'Okay, if you give me any trouble, I've got orders to get everyone in the joint to fuck your friend and then shoot him. Just so you know, they don't have an amazing bedside manner. If that isn't incentive enough, we can also fill Harper or yourself with bullet holes until that gets the job done. I'm also allowed to be more creative, with various kinds of torture if necessary. But it's not going to be necessary, is it?' Steroids has his hands on his hips, and I swear the fabric of his T-shirt starts to tear as his biceps flex. Forget being between a rock and a hard place. I am in the middle of a full nuclear meltdown.

I shake my head at him. 'No, that won't be necessary,' I say quietly. Shit. What do I do now? The only thing I can do for the time being, I guess. I need to try to stay alive.

'Gabriel, you're on your own!' I call out as I'm manhandled out of the door. Doing my best to ignore the string of expletives that exit his mouth, which have a lot to do with fucking and my mother, I really hope he isn't serious about all the lovely things he wants to do with me when or if we finally get out of this mess.

Chapter Seven - Brandt

Several hours later I'm being driven to Helena's house at roughly the speed of sound. Mal's goons have no respect for any of the speed limits imposed by the UK's Road Traffic Act, nor do they care that I'm about to throw up if they don't slow down. I haven't eaten in hours and I'm feeling nauseous enough as it is without this added to the mix. There's no point moaning, though. I'm going to be the last person they listen to. Still, if I heave all over the new suit they've just bought me, with any luck Helena and her family will send me packing.

When we get to the Foster-Lyle residence I can't get out of the car quick enough. While Helena and her parents may be unpleasant at best, they're a lot friendlier than Mal, and in this instance it's better-the-devil-you-know. Slamming the car door as hard as I can on the thugs inside, I press the bell and wait to be embraced back into the fold. The men don't wait to see if I do as I'm told. They have Gabriel and Harper. And I'm sure Mal has a backup plan if that isn't enough.

'Brandt, oh my God, what happened to you?' Helena looks at my bruised face in horror. She's dressed up to the nines in a black evening gown and sporting half the Tower of London's Crown Jewel collection. Diamonds glisten around her neck and adorn her wrists and ears. She looks like a Christmas decoration. Should I feel honoured?

'Ah, I had a bit of a run in with something nasty,' I offer. Now is probably not the time to announce I'm friendly with one of London's worst gangsters.

'The wedding is in a couple of days' time, Brandt. What were you thinking?' She's talking to me as if I'm an idiot and I really don't appreciate it, but an argument is not going to solve anything.

'I didn't really have much choice in the matter, Helena, believe me.'

She steps backward and sighs.

'It's our engagement party tonight, Brandt. I did try to ring you but you weren't picking up, so I texted instead. Wherever you were it must have been a really bad signal.' She examines my face more closely. 'Good God, they really did a number on you. Still, I guess it's nothing that a bit of make-up can't fix.'

Fuck, I really cannot handle this tonight on top of everything else. I haven't had any sleep, I haven't eaten, and now I need to make idle chitchat with a bunch of people I can't stand while looking all loved up.

'Oh, Jesus,' I say, making a show of patting down my jacket, looking for the cell phone that has once again been confiscated. 'Where's my phone? The thing has a life of its own, darling, and I can't seem to keep track of it. Life has been hellishly busy these past couple of weeks. Forgive me? Do you need me to change, or will I do?'

I assume Mal's thugs read the message which is why I'm dressed in a suit rather than more casual attire. At least I won't look like a complete jerk. I'm not sure why I even care about it, but I do.

'Brandt, you're worse than a girl and you think I'm blonde. No matter. You look perfect, sweetheart. The guests aren't arriving for another half-hour, so if you want me to cover those bruises there's plenty of time.'

Flinging my arm around Helena's shoulder, I pull her close to me. 'That might be a nice idea. I'd also love a cup of tea, if you don't mind. For some reason I've forgotten to eat and drink for most of the day.' I place a soft kiss on her forehead. If Helena is surprised by my change of heart regarding herself and the wedding, she makes no mention of it. She must think I'm nuts. I have my reasons, though. If I want to get through the next couple of days alive I'm going to need some allies. My soon-to-be wife needs to be one of them.

'Seriously? How can you forget to eat? I wish I could. There's no way I'm going to lose any weight before the wedding.' Helena rolls her eyes at me as if this is the worst thing in the world.

I can't help my horrified expression. 'You're pregnant, sweetheart. I think losing weight would be bad for the baby.' I bite my lip to stop myself from saying something snarky. What is wrong with the woman?

Helena shakes her head, as if she's trying to remember something, and then smiles. 'I know. I wasn't actually thinking of losing any. It's just that every girl wants to look perfect for her big day.'

I let that wash. Something doesn't add up somewhere, but I have too many other problems to worry about it.

'Have you decided on what type of suit you'd like to wear for the wedding?' Helena looks up at me expectantly. Uh oh. I wasn't supposed to have needed to figure that out. Now I've been put on the spot. Shit. Mal can't really expect me to go through with this, can he? Of course he can. He knows my wedding will be splashed all over the tabloids and that it will hit Harper right where it hurts. He's going to use it to try and turn her against me because he wants her for himself. It's all beginning to make sense. After we're married, I'll then be tasked to kill whoever it is Mal wants silencing, and no one will care too much when I'm killed straight after. Harper will be forced to stay with Mal, and he'll torment her to the end of her days. Wearily I run my hands across my eyes. I can't think straight.

'Brandt? Did you make a decision on the suit, or did you want me to pick for you?' Helena leads me through to an English country-style kitchen and sits me down on top of an oak bar stool at the island in the centre. There are pots and pans hanging above my head, and an array of herbs in a long black planter in front of me. It makes me think of home, and it's the last thing I want to think about.

'Sorry, Helena. I didn't. Give me a minute. I can't think on an empty stomach.' That much is true at least.

'Oh, goodness, forgive me. Let's get some food into you.' Helena busies herself by switching on a metallic cream kettle, where she sets the water to boil at precisely ninety degrees centigrade. It makes all manner of weird bleeping noises that are extremely irritating, before she then goes over to raid the fridge, which is in the exact same shade of cream as the kettle. Meanwhile, I try my best to consider which type of suit I'd like for my upcoming sham of a wedding. I know she isn't going to let up about it, so I may as well get it over with. If or when I get married for real, I want a fairly casual suit and setting. The last thing I want is a society wedding, but that's exactly what this is, even though Helena and I are both lepers skirting the very outskirts of that term. People will turn up to watch us tie the knot, but more as a kind of freakshow performance. Either that, or they'll be there for the free food and drink. Anyway, seeing as how I have little choice in the proceedings, I might as well go all out and dress in something ridiculous. Maybe I'll let Helena pick it, after all. That would probably be fitting. A horrendous suit to go with a perfectly horrendous day. Marvellous.

'So, what have you being doing with yourself since the last time you saw me?' As Helena places a steaming hot mug of Earl Grey beside me, and finishes putting a plate of cold cuts together, I find myself nearly spitting out my mouthful of tea.

Hmm. What have I been doing? Fucking another woman? Oh, and another man. Then you can add a bit of torture to the mix. I've also been knocked around and abducted, blackmailed and shot at.

'Oh, nothing much, really,' I reply. 'Just sorting out a few odds and ends. How about you, darling? What have you been up to?' I need to keep the woman talking. That way she won't have time to fire questions at me.

'Oh, we've been visiting hotels, looking at menus, sending out the invitations, checking out some fabric swatches for bridesmaid dresses - that sort of thing. It's been a lot of fun, really. It's just a shame you weren't here, Brandt.'

No, it wasn't, but smiling sympathetically I make all the right noises.

'So, who's going to be here tonight?' I really don't want to know the answer, but it will keep the conversation flowing in the right direction. Now that a plate of food has finally landed in front of me I have an excuse not to talk, and I intend to make the best of it.

Helena shrugs. 'Pretty much everyone my parents could get hold of at such short notice. We'll have a fairly sizeable amount of glitz and glamour in attendance. Dad's work colleagues, some of mum's friends, a few minor celebrities, some stuffy old officials, and your friends, of course. I rounded up everyone I could think of.'

I look up and finish the mouthful of quiche I'm chewing. There's one thought at the back my mind which has my body tied up in knots. 'Are my parents coming?' I ask eventually.

Helena gives me a pitying smile and shakes her head. 'I'm so sorry, Brandt. We asked them, but they refused.' She gives my shoulder a reassuring nudge. 'They will forgive you. They just need time.' Bollocks. They've had five years to forgive me. If they couldn't figure it out in that time, I don't see why another five should make any difference.

'No matter,' I say lightly enough. It would have been nice to speak to someone in my family before I'm buried six feet under, but that doesn't look likely now. I'm not exactly surprised. I've known the score for a while now. 'Tell you what, Helena. Why don't you pick out my suit for me? I know you'll pick out something nice.' My words make her face light up and somewhere inside me something dies. I am going to lie to the woman and hurt her. I will marry her, and a few hours later I will either disappear or be dead. The woman is pregnant, she's counting on me to save her sorry ass, and I'm not going to be there for her. I should feel guilty. She'll be jumping from one scandal straight into another, and she'll have to pick up the pieces all on her own. Still, what choice do I have?

Helena rattles on for the next ten minutes about how the preparations for the wedding are going. I listen half-heartedly and make nods at appropriate intervals. I don't give two flying fucks about the wedding. What I need is time to think about how I'm going to get myself, Harper and Gabriel out of this mess. Currently I don't have any bright ideas, nor do I have anyone I can turn to for help. I'm on my own, and since I've been in jail for the past five years, there isn't anyone around I can lean on.

It would help if I knew who Mal wanted me to kill. Then I could start making some kind of plan. Mal's not stupid, though. He's going to keep me in the dark until the last possible minute. That means I need to figure it out myself. It feels like I'm trying to find a particularly small needle in a haystack the size of London. It's not going to happen. And when I solve that problem I have a dozen more that need attention, but at least I'd have something to go on.

'Looking forward to meeting our guests, darling?'

'Absolutely,' I lie. Making nice with London's elite is not high on my list of priorities, but on the upside, at least I'm not in Mal's shed. Things could be worse.

'Fabulous,' Helena trills. 'Before we greet our guests, though, would you do me the honour?' She places a small red velvet box beside my hand, and I know what's expected. Even so, it makes my stomach crawl. If I ever lay hands on Mal Adley again, he's going to pay in spectacular style.

'Of course, sweetheart. Would you like me to get down on one knee?' It's a rhetorical question. There is no doubt in my mind that the answer to my question is...

'Yes!' Helena giggles. 'Would you mind, darling?' She tips my face up with a finger underneath my chin and gazes at me adoringly.

'Not at all.' All of a sudden I'm back in the past, being the suave, sophisticated man of my youth, but this time around I have a few years of experience under my belt. The innocence that was once prominent in my eyes has been replaced with cynicism for the world at large, and any semblance of respect for the people I am now about to meet has long since vanished. I know what these lawyers and law makers are capable of. I know how they work the system. I know how utterly unfair it is. If I was a smart man, I would know how to take advantage of that fact. Am I a smart man?

Getting down on one knee, I take the little velvet box and flip the lid. I'm curious as to who bought the ring inside it, but not that curious. I'm just glad it wasn't me.

'Darling,' I purr, taking Helena's hand, 'would you do me the great honour of becoming my wife?' I look at her expectantly, even though this is a done deal, and raise my eyebrows. If she wants the act, she might as well get the whole damn charade.

There's another giggle as Helena puts her hands over her lips, and then she nods her head. For some reason I appear to have rendered her speechless, and that can only be a good thing. Plucking the ring out of the box, noting an impressively large emerald-cut diamond, I slide it gently upon her finger. It sparkles like shards of glass in sunlight, and I almost feel like it's laughing at me.

Squealing, Helena places her arms around me and plants a kiss on my lips. Thankfully it's a quick one. She obviously doesn't want to ruin her make-up, and unless I'm much mistaken, that's the sound of the doorbell I hear. It looks like it's time for my debut performance as a soon-to-be-husband. Shit.

The guests at our engagement party are, for the most part, exceedingly dull. We've got a couple of councillors, a few doctors, one or two police officers of varying seniority, a couple of band members, some paramedics, and lots of scientists. Apparently that's Rupert's field, although I haven't worked up the courage to enquire as to what it is he actually does. If I play my cards right this evening I'm pretty sure I'll find out anyway, whether I want to or not. On the female side, there's a few more doctors, a veterinarian, the deputy mayor, two prominent authors, a couple of celebrity bloggers, someone who's been on Strictly Come Dancing, a firefighter and all manner of delightfully sparkling and coquettishly elegant socialites. The firefighter is hot, by the way.

'It's quite a crowd here this evening,' I whisper to Helena, when I can get a word in edgeways. Presents have been delivered by the droves, and by the time we've greeted everyone I already feel exhausted.

'Oh no,' Helena whispers. 'This is just who we could gather together at a moment's notice. At the wedding there'll be at least ten times this many.' I fail to see how that can be possible, seeing as how we're only giving them a couple more days' notice, but I refrain from mentioning this to my fiancée. The last thing I need is an argument, and I've read somewhere that pregnant people get very emotional.

'Is there anyone in particular you'd like me to speak to?' I ask. I'm sure she's got a few people she'd like to impress. Helena always struck me as someone who wanted to move up the social ladder, but alas, she's probably got to put those plans on hold. I wonder if she realises she will never be accepted now? All her fluffy little dreams have been dashed for a stupid petty crime and a romp under the sheets with someone unsuitable. How terrible.

'Yes, darling. Mingle with everyone. Impress them all. Show them how wonderful we are.' Helena stands up and twirls around in her black evening gown, the ends of which sparkle with sequins. She nearly loses her balance for a second, and I catch her before she totters on her heels.

'You haven't been drinking, have you?' I frown at her for a moment, but she pinches each of my cheeks with her fingertips and shakes my head in her hands.

'Only a tiny glass of champagne, darling. It is my party, after all. Which reminds me, you need one, too. Did you know it's rude not to drink at your own party?'

I didn't, but I do now.

'Okay sweetheart, I'll grab a glass and go talk to some of our guests. Will you be all right on your own?'

Helena looks at me as if I'm a little green alien from outer space. 'Of course, darling. I've known these people for years. Go have fun.' She gives me a peck on the cheek and shoos me away. Suits me.

Plucking a glass of champagne from a wandering waiter's tray, I take a sip as I wonder who I should talk to first. I've already figured out there's a reasonable chance that whoever I'm meant to kill is here tonight, although it's possible they might only turn up to the wedding. Still, I'm here, so I might as well try to find out what I can.

Who would be Mal's most likely targets? Someone in a position of authority, perhaps? Does he need them out of the way? Is he killing them in order to replace them? I need to consider all the possibilities, and quickly. Time is something I don't have much of.

With that in mind, I begin doing the rounds and flirting the ass off any piece of skirt that comes my way. I dare say my fiancée is going to be roaring mad by the time I've finished, but she's about to learn she's not the only one who can manipulate people. It's been a long time, and I'm out of practise, but judging by the looks I'm getting I might actually be quite good at this. Being inside has taught me a few things, you see. Never trust anything you hear at face value, and the best secrets will only be spilled one of two ways. If you can figure that lot out, to the victor go the spoils. Although it's unclear what I'll be winning if or when I manage to figure this little puzzle out, I might as well enjoy what little time I have left, while I can.

Unfortunately, this means I can't start with the hot firefighter. I fail to see what Mal could possibly gain from killing her, unless she's killed someone he knows, and if she had, she'd already be dead. Whoever I need to kill will be either difficult to corner on their own or there will be major ramifications for killing them - which Mal wants to distance himself from. Squeaky clean Mal. He wouldn't want to get his hands dirty, now would he? Mind you, what's the point when you can get a patsy like me to do the deed for you? That way you don't lose any men, and you get to show your girlfriend what an incredible catch you are. Yeah. About that.

Anyway, it's time to get to work. Do I start with the women or the men? I decide to go with the men. The women will give me something to look forward to later. I immediately head towards the law enforcement guys, as I figure they're probably an obvious choice. After that, I'll do the rounds with the officers and officials, and maybe even add the odd doctor into the mix. I might chat up the Strictly girl, too. It depends on how much time I have. If Helena has a spike anywhere, I guarantee my head is going to be on it by the time this evening has finished, but at least it'll make for an exciting life. Besides, it's about time I showed her who's boss.

Chapter Eight - Gabriel

The fucking bastards drag me all the way back up to the top of the rafters, only to let me drop again. Then, they do it again, and again. Obviously this is quite a fun game, and it doesn't take me long to figure out that they enjoy the sound of my screaming.

Somehow I have to figure out how to shut my cake-hole without swallowing my tongue, and then hopefully they'll become bored rather quickly. I know how these thugs think. When I eventually manage to accomplish the task, the game finishes abruptly. With any luck they'll hurry up and kill me now. If they don't, they're about to have the contents of my stomach decorating their shoes. It will be a fitting end to my miserable excuse of a life.

'Get him down,' Steroids yells, when everyone stands there gawping at me. This is when I begin to wonder if I wouldn't have been better off left back up in the roof. It's more difficult for them to hurt me up there. It's not that I'm a coward, but I'm not very fond of being beaten to a pulp, either.

'If you're going to kill me, can we go with a headshot? I'm not especially bothered how I'll look in my funeral casket, mostly because there won't be anyone there to see it. Just make it quick.' I give Steroids a decent pleading look and wonder if I should blow him to seal the deal. He looks like a homophobe, so I don't think there's much point, and it probably won't do my chances of a quick death any good if I piss him off.

He shakes his head at me. 'Oh, we're not going to kill you just yet. Where would the fun be in that? Besides, we need you alive just in case your mate gets cold feet. That's where we tie you up and start cutting things off. A severed finger or toe usually makes sure the job gets done, but if not we can always film you begging for your life as we poke holes in you with a big knife. That usually does the trick.'

My stomach does a dry heave, but it's been well-trained. I hold half a ton of bile back while I consider how pretty it would look decorating Steroid's face.

While the boys rip the tape off my body, my gaze continues to focus on him. He seems to be the ringleader here, and the one to watch.

'Where are you taking me?' It's a reasonable question. I probably won't get an answer, but it doesn't hurt to try.

Surprisingly, the guy is generous enough with the details. 'Back to Mal. He wants to watch Harper and you together again. He'll probably film the shit and send it to pretty boy. He likes screwing with people's heads.'

Yeah, I'd noticed that. 'Lovely,' I remark, with what I hope is enthusiasm. 'I'll look forward to that.' If I have to do a threesome with Mal, I am going to bite that man's dick off in two places.

'I doubt it. Mal doesn't like it when his *friends* enjoy themselves too much. I don't think you're going to have a lot of fun in the next couple of days.'

Honesty. It's so refreshing among thugs, thieves and drug lords. I can't resist a quip after that. 'Thanks for the heads up. I'll pretend she's the worst shag I've ever had then.' I get a cuff around the ear for my troubles, which almost sends my head off its hinges. Ow. Steroids knows his stuff.

'If I were you I'd keep quiet. You might live longer that way.' I'm grabbed by the scruff of the neck and frog-marched towards the door. I'm not sure whether I should be rejoicing the fact that I'm now on solid ground, or shaking in my boots. I can't think that spending any time with Mal is going to be good for my life expectancy, so I hope Brandt is on top of this crap. If he isn't, I'm pretty sure I'm going to suffer a long and painful death, and I suspect Harper won't be far behind me.

Steroids bundles me in a car, with a thug on either side of me, to make sure I behave. As I suspected earlier, we don't need to travel far before we reach the boss' headquarters. Everything is in darkness, and there's no sound bar the noise we're making. Maybe I'm in luck. Maybe Mal is otherwise occupied. That thought, unfortunately, is short-lived.

Steroids raps on the door, and a few seconds later Mal answers. 'Put him in the room at the back,' he says, 'and make sure you tie the fucker up. That one's dangerous when left unsupervised. I'll have one in the back of the 'ead before I blink.' He's right, but he underestimates me. If I get the chance the last thing I'm going to do is shoot him. I'd have to like him in order to give him a clean death. If I get the chance to kill him, he's going down slow, and he's going to scream the whole way. He's not the only one that can inflict serious pain around these parts.

Unfortunately, that's not going to happen tonight. I'm shuffled off to the back room as ordered, and when I get there someone pushes me to the floor and pins my arms behind my back. There's no point struggling, so I don't bother. There are four guys surrounding me and Mal's out back. My chances of success are slim, and if I fail, I won't be alive to tell the tale. I need to bide my time and pick my moment. Mal isn't someone you mess with. I'll only get one chance to end the bastard, so I need to play this very carefully.

After they've finished tying me hand and foot, leaving me flopping about in the middle of the room like a wet fish, the guys file out letting the door slam behind them. That's when I look up.

'Long time no see,' says Harper, with a rather resigned look on her face. This might be because she is dressed in nothing but a pair of stockings and high heels. It might be because of the evil black eye and red lump she is sporting across her cheekbone, or it might be because she is tied hand and foot like me, but this time in an 'X' shape across the wall. More than likely, it's probably due to all three.

'I would say it's nice to see you again, but I'm really not feeling it,' I reply. 'Who gave you the black eye?' I already know, but I have to make sure.

'Who do you think? He's pissed that I slept with you guys.' Harper gives me a wry grin. I'm just beginning to understand what this woman went through while Brandt was inside. Hell doesn't even begin to describe it.

'Let me get this straight. Even though he ordered you to sleep with us, and you initially refused, he's upset with you?' Forget slow, I'm going to drag his death out over several weeks and carve him up piece by piece.

'He's sweet like that,' Harper growls angrily, looking up at the ceiling. This gives me ample opportunity to check out the rest of her body for bruises, but mostly just because I want to. The woman is hotter than a jalapeno's backside and twice as fiery. I want to fuck her every which way under the sun and come back for seconds.

'Brandt's okay,' I say. I know she'll be wondering, and it would be wrong of me to keep that from her. Besides, she's not the enemy any more. Mal has taken top spot and until he's dead, I haven't got time to hate anyone else.

Harper's gaze slowly lowers down to mine, and though she is smiling, the smile is lopsided. 'Yes, but for how long? He means to kill him. We need to get out of here and help him.'

Tell me something I don't know. 'Well off you go then, Houdini. You do your stuff.' I look at her expectantly and sure enough I get a reaction.

'You're the one who can pick locks, asshole. This is your area of expertise.' To be fair, she has a point, but she's forgetting a few things.

'While I admit I have a talent for getting out of tight spaces, Miss Wilkinson, it's hard to pick a lock when you've been tied up, rather than cuffed.' Wriggling about on the floor to test out how tightly I've been tied, I am rather dismayed to find they've done a reasonably decent job of restraining me. This does not look good.

'Well you'd better get good at it, pretty damn quick. After one night with him you won't want to stay here for another, trust me. Mal has a way of making you wish you had never been born.'

I don't doubt it, but that still doesn't help me at this moment in time. There is no way I'll be able to get those cuffs off Harper in my current predicament. I'll need to find another way.

'Do you trust me?' It's a stupid question, and deserves a stupid answer.

She snorts at me, as expected, and shakes her head. 'I wouldn't trust you if you were the last man on this earth.' Yeah, that's kind of what I expected, and it has to change. We need a truce.

'We're on the same side here, sweetheart. We'll need to work together if we both want to get out.' A bout of screaming from inside the workshop makes us both stiffen, and we remain quiet until it subsides. I have no idea who's out there because it was dark when I entered, but it's obvious Mal has found someone to play with. Let's hope whoever it is keeps him busy for a while.

'You must be mad. Don't think I don't know you were going to kill me. You told me so yourself. Nothing's changed. You want him. I want him. We're not going to be friends in this lifetime, *sweetheart*.' The sarcasm dripping off her tongue is endearing. I like a woman with a vicious sense of humour.

'We're going to have to figure out some kind of truce, or we'll die here. Is that what you want?' I like to point things out in black and white, just so I know where I stand.

Harper glares at me. 'Yes, dying is preferable to being idiot enough to trust you.' She looks all righteous fury as she stares at me, her indignation worn like a burning badge upon her chest. I want to drink all that anger up and channel it into something useful - preferably our escape plan.

'You know I like to fuck angry women, don't you?' I grin at her. 'Angry blokes, too, for that matter.' Brandt was an incredible fuck when angry. I wonder if Harper would be as good. My cock is already stirring just thinking about it.

'You know Mal likes to kill people that fuck me, don't you?' Touché. Little Miss Firecracker is making my dick hard. There is then another scream from outside, and it sounds much worse than the first one. So much for my horny thoughts. I think Mal's getting a little carried away out there.

'I fucked you a few hours ago and I'm still alive.' I'm losing the circulation in my wrists, but so far everything else seems to be working.

'You won't be for much longer, so don't get comfortable.'

There's little chance of that. 'Does Mal like men?' I feel the need to get the question out there before we begin. I like to know what I'm up against.

'Don't you want to leave that as a surprise? You sure you want to know beforehand?' She gives me a sassy little grin. How the hell has the woman stayed alive this long? If she were mine, I would have killed her years ago.

'I'm a masochist. I need to know these things.' Why I want to know whether I'm about to get fucked in the ass is beyond me, but maybe it's so I can brace myself in advance.

'Liar. You like inflicting pain just as much as Mal does. You're just as much a monster as he is.' She gives me a knowing look, but she's wrong and I have to set some things straight.

Looking up at her, my lips tighten. 'Mal and I are nothing alike. Sure, I like kinky

44

shit, and I have fun controlling people, but my end result is pleasure not pain. Brandt may hate me, but it's not because of the sex or what happened between us. It's about what happened after. I never meant to hurt him. I'm in love with him, and you know it.'

'You've killed people. You'll kill again. Give me one good reason why I should believe a single word you say?'

'Because as I said before, we're on the same side. We both want Brandt, and if he's dead neither of us wins.' I'm exasperated, but it's not her fault. I'm not getting through to her. I can see it by the way she's looking at me. I need to try harder.

She makes a funny little squeaky sound in her throat. 'We're not on the same side. If you get a chance to kill me you'll take it. Then you'll have Brandt all to yourself. Call me a liar.'

Damn it. This one is not as stupid as she looks. Trust Brandt to want a woman with brains. It's no good, though. I'm going to have to come clean with her. If I don't, neither of us are getting out of here with a heartbeat.

'Fine. At first, I wanted you dead. I was jealous, and yes, I do want him back. He doesn't want me, though. You may have noticed. If we manage to get out of here alive, and Brandt wants you, I won't stand in your way. I give you my word. That's one way I differ over Mal. My word means something. Yes, I've killed people, but I won't kill you. We'll need each other to get out, and besides, Brandt would never forgive me. That boy is in love with you, however much he wants to deny it.' There. I've said it.

'And I'm just supposed to believe that? You'll let me ride off into the sunset with your ex and you'll never kill anyone ever again? You must think I was born yesterday.' She growls in frustration, pulling at her shackles, and at the same time there's another scream from outside. The effect is quite eerie. I do not want to know what is happening out there, although I have a bad feeling I'm going to find out, whether I want to or not.

'Never kill anyone again? You must be fucking joking. The first chance I get that idiot out there is biting the dust. I've never killed anyone for sport before, but Mal is going to be my first. He's going down slow and painfully. That's a promise.' Jesus Christ, I've made two promises to Harper in less than ten seconds. This is a record for me. I must be desperate.

She looks at me suspiciously. I've not won her over - not yet. She's been through too much to just start trusting people at the drop of a hat. That's going to take time - time we don't have. How can I convince her? Dammit. Where do we go from here? She's probably going to ignore me for the foreseeable future, and I can't say I blame her.

'What did you do to him?' Her voice is low and quiet. She doesn't want Mal to hear, and I can't say I blame her. The last thing we want is for him to come rushing in and gag us. Things are bad enough as it is, and they're only going to get worse. I've got one thing to be thankful for, though. She is speaking to me. Curiosity has got the better of her.

'I did something stupid.' Actually, I did something really stupid, and I haven't stopped regretting it ever since.

'How stupid?' As I've just answered that question in my head, I sigh. Still, she deserves the truth. If I tell her some of my secrets, perhaps she'll tell me some of hers.

'You can probably already guess what I did.' It's not hard to join up the dots and as I've already mentioned, Harper is a fairly intelligent lady. Mind you, she's not that bright. She ended up with two psychopaths for partners, one of which she married.

'You slept with someone,' she murmurs.

'I did. I slept with someone.' Even now it hurts to talk about it. I didn't think it would. I thought I'd forget about him ten seconds after the deed was done. How foolish was I? Still, it taught me a valuable lesson. Never shit on your own doorstep. You'll end up putting your foot in it at some point.

'Why? You loved him. Why would you do that?' Harper's looking at me as if I have two heads, and to be fair, she has a point.

'It doesn't matter,' I say, evading the question, but it's too late. Memories are already coming back to haunt me.

She twists her head, trying to get a closer look at me, but it's my turn to look at the floor. I don't want her to see me now. 'You didn't think he'd find out,' she whispers. She says it, like I committed the worst sin in the world, and to some, maybe it is. In prison, though, it's a way of life. It opens doors, it procures goods, it lets you in on secrets, and it gets you places. It's a necessary evil if you don't want to spend your life rotting in a cell.

'No, I didn't think he'd find out,' I growl. Hopefully she'll get the hint. I do not want to talk about it.

But Harper has no intention of leaving it alone. She can see I'm in pain and she wants to twist the knife. 'Was he prettier than Brandt? I find that hard to believe. Was he better in bed, perhaps? Again, hard to believe. I know there are anatomical differences between us, but he's pretty talented under the sheets, isn't he?'

Oh, you have no idea. There are things we've done together that would have to been seen to be believed. I decide not to answer. She'll get bored with this conversation, eventually.

'Look at me, Gabriel.' For some reason, I obey. I look up at eyes that are almost as dark as mine, and equally as beautiful, albeit in a different way. Mine are hard and only flames of obsidian can be found in their depths. Harper's are a deep, rich sable. They are the colour of dusk, upon mountains of fiery sand dunes. They change every time you look at her. They are as unique and unfathomable as she is.

'Why did you stay with him?' I ask. If this is twenty questions, I don't see why I shouldn't have a turn. 'You're not afraid of dying. I can see it just by looking at you. In fact, you'd welcome death, wouldn't you?'

'Stop trying to change the subject,' she bites back, although her voice is soft. There is no sound outside now, which means Mal has either taken a break from his fun, or he is listening in on us.

'I'll answer you, if you answer me.' Besides, I'm curious. I think I'd have rather killed myself than put up with Adley's perversions day after day. What hold has he got over her? Brandt. Mal controlled her by using him.

46

I can already see the cogs in her head turning. There are wheels between wheels, but she'll figure out what she needs to.

'You weren't betraying Brandt, were you? You were getting yourself out of there. What did the fuck pay for? A lawyer's visit? Some fresh evidence? And he never let you explain, did he? He wouldn't give you the chance.'

I smile grimly. Harper has obviously had a lot of practice at this. She's far too clever for her own good. 'It paid for some evidence to disappear, actually, but it had the same effect. I knew Brandt would get out well before me, and I didn't want to be stuck rotting behind bars while someone else took my place. I always knew he was in love with you. It didn't matter how much he tried to hate you, every time I talked about killing you he'd clam up like a constipated hippo. I wanted to get to you before he did.'

'I'm not a threat to you,' Harper whispers. 'You're beautiful and deadly. Who can compete with that?' Her eyes begin welling up with tears. I don't know if it's because of the situation we're in or because she thinks Brandt is still in love with me, but I can soon put that notion to rest.

'You're right, you're not a threat to me, mainly because you've already won. You've blown me out of the water. Brandt only has eyes for you.' It's the truth. I know he still cares about me, but it's not in the same way he cares about her. That's when it comes to me. There is a way to win back his affection, and the way rests between the girl's legs. Well, that's possibly oversimplifying the problem. I'll need to get under her skin first.

'If you'd explain why you did it, he'd forgive you.' She looks away as she thinks about what I've told her, biting her bottom lip in the process. She looks adorable. I want to suck that lip into my mouth and bite it - hard - but there's no chance of that at the moment.

'I would never explain myself. Firstly, it makes me look weak, secondly, he doesn't want to hear it, and thirdly, he wouldn't believe me anyway. That ship has sailed.' It doesn't mean I can't board another, though. Whether I'll get the chance is a different question entirely.

As if to echo those thoughts the screams from the other room begin again, and this time they are much more frenzied than before. Then they end abruptly, before the door to the little bedroom flies open and Mal storms in, looking very pleased with himself.

'That little snitch won't be talking to anyone in the near future,' he comments, placing the cap back on the little tube of glue he's holding. I close my eyes. I wonder if I've got that to look forward to in my imminent future. I really hope not.

Mal's feet walk towards me until they're planted in front of my face. 'I'm thinking of training you up to do this shit for me,' he comments, as he places the tube of glue back in his pocket.

'Always happy to help,' I grunt. I've done worse things. What's a few more evil deeds between friends?

'Good. We'll get Harper to watch. She loves that sort of thing.' Judging by the expression on her face, she's not quite as enthusiastic as he thinks she is, but I'm not about to tell him.

'Right, after a hard day's work it's time we had some fun,' says Mal, rubbing his hands together. He bends down, and just when I think he's about to kick me in the stomach, he begins slicing through the rope that holds me.

'I want you to hurt her, Gabriel, and I want to watch. Think you can do that?'

I nod and give him my best smile.

What else am I supposed to do? I could pretend I'm not going to enjoy this, but that would be a big fat lie. As long as it's just me hurting Harper we'll be fine, but when he starts taking his temper out on me things will change. As it's only a matter of time before that happens, Harper and I need to bash our heads together and come up with a way to get rid of the evil asshole. That's not going to be easy. If we kill him, someone's going to kill us. This is a dog-eat-dog world. It's the nature of how things work around here. Once you've seen inside this world, you don't generally get the chance to talk about it. You're either useful or you're not. I need to become useful.

We have to find a way that will prevent Brandt from killing someone, while trying not to get killed ourselves. But from where I'm standing that looks almost impossible, and it's a fairly depressing thought.

Chapter Nine - Brandt

Our engagement party is a huge success. I make it my mission in life to ensure that everyone has a drink in their hand before I do my best to charm the pants off them. I used to be particularly good at making women lose their panties, but now I've progressed to men as well. I am on fire. Not all men swing that way, though, so I have to do my best to entice information out of them by whatever means necessary. That's where the alcohol comes in. So far it seems to be working fairly well, but I've yet to learn anything particularly interesting.

Helena is doing an equally good job at keeping our guests entertained. She looks like a little starlet in her slinky black dress, and she's not showing at all beneath its seductive curves. I wonder if she's wearing one of those silly corsets. Nothing would surprise me where Helena is concerned. She needs to think of the baby. That should be her main priority now.

When the evening finally comes to a close and we both head upstairs, Helena links her arm around mine. Is she about to offer me a reward for a job well done? I hope not. The thought of sleeping with her makes me ill. If I have to do it, I will, but I don't think we've reached that stage yet.

'Did you enjoy yourself this evening?' she purrs as we walk up the grand wooden staircase, heading for what I sincerely hope is my bedroom. If I'm sharing hers, we will need to have words.

'I had a wonderful time.' No falser words have been spoken. With the exception of the hot firefighter and perhaps one of the doctors, the evening was about as much fun as contracting the bubonic plague.

She smiles, like a little child, her eyes sparkling with happiness. When we reach the landing of her parent's house she leads me across the hall to one of the rooms furthest away. I take this as a good sign. When she opens the door, I turn to her to say goodnight, fully expecting her to walk away. But instead, she sails straight past me.

'You're sleeping with me. This is my room.' Without warning she begins unfastening the neck of her gown, and before I've had a chance to say a word she's peeling it down to reveal a pair of naked breasts. Considering I've been inside for the past five years, it should have me champing at the bit, but I find I have nothing but mild disgust for the girl.

'I'm not sleeping with you, Helena. It's too soon. Go put a gown on. We can discuss this when we're both a little less drunk.' Is this the reason she's made sure my glass has been topped up all evening? Was she hoping to get her wicked claws into me? That's too bad. I've got more important things to worry about.

'Brandt, don't be so silly. We're going to be married in a few days' time. We may as well get to know one another.' Strolling towards me she places her arm on mine, but I begin walking backwards quickly. This is not happening.

'If you don't have a spare room I'm happy to sleep on the couch, darling. If we've waited this long, I'm fairly sure we can wait until the day of the wedding.' I know damn well they've got more bedrooms than the Hilton in this place, but if Helena wants to play nasty, I've got news for her. I don't care. There's only so far I'll go to further this little charade. I don't want to piss her off, but I'm not going to whore myself out either.

'Oh, Brandt. You're not going to be stuffy are you? I thought you'd have been desperate to get some action after having spent so long inside. Why wait? I'm desperate for you to be inside me, darling.' She pouts.

Yeah. So desperate she was fucking someone else a week ago. She sways from side to side, heavily intoxicated by alcohol. I want to shake her and tell her that she should be thinking of the baby, but I do no such thing. It's not my baby, and it's not my body. I don't even know the woman well enough to scold her. If she's stupid enough to have such disregard for her unborn child, I'm glad I'm not going to be around her long.

'I'm really not in the mood this evening,' I say, shaking my head. I won't be in the mood any other evening, either, but she'll find that out soon enough.

'Come on,' she almost slurs, 'I saw you smiling at all those other women. You were trying to make me jealous, weren't you, Brandt? Am I no longer attractive now I'm pregnant?' The last word ends on a hiccup, before she dissolves into tears. Oh fuck. Now what have I done?

Backtracking fast, I say, 'No, that's not it, Helena. You're a very attractive woman, and I'm sure you already know that. This isn't about that. We still don't know each over very well, and I'd like to wait until we've rectified that. What's the hurry, sweetheart?'

She sniffs and wipes frantically at her eyes. 'I'm going to be big and fat soon. You won't want me then. I want to make love to you before I look awful.' More tears follow. I can't help it, I walk into the room and put my arms around her, even though the woman is half-naked. She sniffles for a bit, but eventually quietens.

'It's late, Helena. We're both drunk. This can wait a couple of days. It will be better if we wait.' The door closes behind me as she brings her hands to her eyes to wipe the tears away. She then smiles. It's an odd sort of smile; one that suggests the tears were never real to begin with. Something is very wrong here.

'I've waited a long time for this, Brandt. I'm not waiting any longer. Take your clothes off.' Her tone is frosty, but I ignore it. If she thinks I'm sleeping with her she's gone soft in the head. I've had enough of this. Immediately turning around to reach for the door handle I twist it sharply, but nothing happens. What the fuck?

'It's locked, darling. I just needed you to come through it. You aren't getting out of that in a hurry. Feel free to yell all you like, by the way. The walls are soundproofed and my parents are in the opposite wing. If I decide to make you scream, no one will hear it in this household. Now get naked.' The edge of her voice has now been honed with a slice of cold, hard steel. It's like she already knows she's won, but nothing could be further from the truth. There is no way I'm sleeping with the bitch. If I have to stay in the room all night repeating that fact to her, I will.

'I am not going to sleep with you, Helena. Locking me in this room will not change my mind on the matter.' What it will do is make me very pissed off, which she is about to find out if she doesn't give me the key in the next thirty seconds.

'You're not going anywhere, Brandt, and you are going to sleep with me. In fact, you're going to do everything I tell you to for the foreseeable future, and you've got a very long night ahead of you. I've wanted you for a long time, Brandt. You're going to fulfil all of my fantasies this evening.'

There's the sound of a rasping zip and the rest of jet-black gown drops slowly to the floor. Helena is standing there naked, dressed in nothing more than a sheer black thong. God give me strength. Has everyone gone mad? Maybe it's in the water. I make another mad grab for the door handle before remembering it's locked.

'Let me out, Helena. I can get a taxi and find a hotel. For the very last time, I am not sleeping with you. We barely know each other.'

'You weren't planning on sleeping with me, were you? You were hoping you could get out of this wedding and then skip the country. Even now, you're thinking that if you do have to marry me, you won't have to stick around long after the deed is done. Isn't that right, Brandt? Even though I'm standing here right in front of you, your mind is on that little gutter rat, Harper. If I were you, I'd get with the here and now. Harper isn't going to be alive much longer, darling.' Helena begins walking towards me, her hips swaying seductively.

I barely notice. My jaw is visiting the floor while all the air in my body evaporates as I try to process what Helena has just said. How does she know all this? What the hell is going on here?

'Have you figured it out yet, Brandt? You're a smart boy. I'm confident it won't take you long.' While I'm stumbling around my brain with a white stick and a golden retriever, Helena is unbuttoning my shirt. I barely even notice. It isn't until the cool night air hits my chest that I realise what is happening.

Her fingernails scrape down my abs, teasing my nipples, but I'm already pushing her away. 'Please tell me this is not what I think it is,' I whisper. It can't be anything else, though. I've been well and truly had.

'Poor baby,' Helena croons. 'Don't you hate it when someone gets you by the balls?' To emphasise her point she grabs my crotch, and I shoot upwards as if stung.

'Take off your clothes or I will ring Mal Adley and get him to hurt your precious little whore, or your boyfriend, whichever works for you because I'm not entirely sure.' She begins to unfasten my belt, and slips it slowly from the belt loops, obviously practised in the art. When her hand slides across my cock, reaching for the zip, the traitorous bastard rears up for attention and she laughs. 'I think you protest too much, Browning. I think you like this more than you are letting on,' she purrs, rubbing my cock up and down with unconcealed glee. I want to murder her, but I want to murder Adley even more.

'What's stopping me from strangling you?' My fingers whip around her neck, digging into the soft flesh beneath her chin. I'm not pressing hard enough to cause her any pain, but that might change.

'You wouldn't strangle a pregnant woman, would you? You don't strike me as the type. Besides, you're going to enjoy this. Trust me.' My fingers tighten. Once upon a time I had a conscience, but these days it's a bit hit and miss. I have five years in prison to thank for that.

'Try me,' I grind out. She is not doing this. I won't let her.

'Really, Brandt?' She struggles to get the words out as I'm crushing her windpipe, but even now she isn't worried. There is still smiling light in her eyes. She is not afraid of me. That means she has other things up her sleeve; things she can use to control me.

My fingers tighten, until I have virtually stopped the blood flow in her neck, and she makes cute little gurgling noises as she fights for her life. I don't think she counted on me being a killer. Neither did I, but a lot has happened in the last few days and I don't think much of being crossed.

'If anything happens to me,' she gurgles... she can't get the rest out. My grip is too tight. If I continue she'll be dead inside a minute. The idea is tempting - too tempting - but I release her suddenly, pushing her away from me, watching with horror as she gasps for breath. Oddly, I remain calm. I don't want her to see me flustered. I'm not sure why, but it'll come to me before long.

'Jesus,' she spits out when she's able to talk again, 'you could have killed me!' Her eyes are wide and scared. She's invited a viper into her nest and now she's scared she can't control him. Too bad.

'The idea had crossed my mind,' I confirm, raising my eyebrows so my icy blue stare catches her head on. I want her to know exactly how unimpressed I am by all this nonsense. I have enough on my plate without having to deal with more crap.

'If you kill me Adley will kill your friends,' she stammers, rubbing her neck while giving me a wounded look. Too bad. If she was worried about her safety she should have thought twice about marrying an ex-con.

'So you say. Maybe I don't give a shit about either of them. Five years inside is a long time. A man can grow cold. He learns how to live without friends.'

Helena backs away from me, but the fear in her eyes has disappeared, replaced with anger. My mind fights through the alcohol I've consumed in order to work out what's happening. There's a picture forming in my head, and I don't much like it.

As she nears the back of her bedroom she pulls a chair out from under a lavishly carved gold dressing table. The legs, drawers and stool have all been inlaid with mosaic-style mirror, in a middle eastern design. Various pots and glass jars sit atop it, as well as a massive vase containing half a dozen sunflowers. It is a little too much for me, but I'm sure she doesn't care a whit for my opinion.

'You're in league with Adley.' I don't know why I feel the need to state the obvious, but I do. I have no idea why she would do such a stupid thing, but it's the only reasonable conclusion.

'Took you long enough. Of course I'm in league with Adley. Now get your clothes off.' Her fire is back. Interesting. I nearly killed her not ten seconds ago. Why does she think she is suddenly back in command of the situation?

'For the last time, Helena, I am not sleeping with you.' Shaking my head I advance towards her. If she wants another lesson in obedience I'm happy to give her one.

She laughs at me and picks up her cell phone, which resides on the edge of her dresser. Its design is also gold in colour, so it blends almost seamlessly with its surroundings. It's an amateur mistake. I should have spotted it immediately. I'm better than this. How many glasses of champagne have I had?

'What's stopping me from calling Adley and telling him to kill your little friends?' She holds the phone up in front of her as if it's a shield that will protect her from me. I have news for her. She'll need to do better than that. I might be slow, but I'm not that slow.

'Nothing,' I remark glibly. 'If you think you can call Adley faster than I can get over there and spread you across my knees, then you go for it. If you fail, Helena, I will not be gentle with you, nor will I show you any mercy. You won't sit down for a week, and as we're getting married in a few days' time, that could be rather awkward.' It's the alcohol talking. I feel the need to unleash some of my temper and taking it out on her seems like the perfect solution. I feel like I've been boxed in on all sides. I'm guessing it's a lot like drowning with a lead weight around your leg. You can see the light above you, and you know where the air is, you just can't get to it. Maybe it would be easier if I killed myself now.

We stand facing each other. Helena's eyes are on me, and mine are on the phone she holds in her hand. Several questions run through my mind. The first is how quickly she can dial out. There's a good chance it's password protected, but it could just as easily require a fingerprint. From there, how quickly can she find his number? Does she have him on speed dial or will she have to look through her address book? I'm betting I can get over there and knock it from her hands before she has a chance to do anything. So, am I going to make the first move? Damn right I am.

Jumping over the bed I grab the wrist holding the phone, which clatters to the floor. She looks up at me, horrified.

'Not expecting that, huh?' Tightening my hold on her wrist I use my foot to grind the phone into the floor. With a bit of pressure there's a nasty crack which indicates she won't be calling anyone for a while. 'So, Helena, I'm curious - what's your next move?' I may not be able to get out of the room without her help, but now I have the upper hand I don't feel quite as bad about it.

'Let go of me this instant, Brandt. Get out of here.' She tries her hardest to shake off my grip, but I'm a big guy and she's going nowhere.

'Which one is it, Helena?' I ask, giving her a mocking look. 'One minute you want me to take my clothes off so I can fuck you, and in the next you want me to go away. Was it something I said?'

She screams. 'Get off me now, Brandt, or I swear it will be the worse for you as soon as tomorrow dawns.' I have no idea what's going to happen tomorrow, nor do I care. I've had it with taking orders from people.

'Oh, I don't know,' I say, 'I don't think it's going to be a very pleasant day for you either, sweetheart. I think you'll be bruised in some very important places.' Very bruised, as it happens.

'You wouldn't,' she starts to sob, and tears begin to fall. If she thinks I'm falling for that act twice she isn't as smart as I thought.

'That's not going to wash this time around,' I feel the need to state, though she should be able to figure that out all by herself. 'You wanted to be fucked, right? Well, I'm going to make sure you are, in all the places that count. You'll also get the spanking you deserve, pumpkin. My only question is, are you going to lie there and take it like a good little girl, or am I going to have to tie you down?'

She shrieks and makes a mad dash for the door. Excellent. That's just what I was hoping for.

Chapter Ten - Gabriel

When Mal has finished sawing through my restraints, he holds out his hand to help me up. It's a bit like accepting help from a rattlesnake, but I do it anyway. There is nothing to be gained from antagonising him just yet. I am wondering if I can take him out, and as I get to my feet I feel my body poise for action.

'Don't even think about it. I have ten guards stationed outside, and they have orders to kill you if you prove difficult. Either you cooperate, or you and your friends will die. Which is it to be?' He raises his eyebrows as he waits for my response, but he already knows what my answer will be. He holds all the cards, but if or when that changes, he'll know about it.

'I'll cooperate.' The words are succinct. I'm not going to say any more than I have to. Words can get you into trouble, and we're in enough trouble as it is.

'I was hoping you'd say that. I want to see if you can be useful around these parts. If so, you might get to live. Follow me.' He begins striding off outside, so with a last look at Harper, who's face is even paler than normal, I shrug my shoulders and do as I'm told.

When we get outside there's a man tied to a chair in the middle of the warehouse, and he's been beaten bloody. He has a black eye, a fat lip, a broken nose, and his jawbone doesn't look great. Mal has gone to town on him. He's unconscious, but I suspect he won't be for long.

I want to ask what he's done, but I don't. Mal won't like questions. He wants robots who follow orders. The less people know, the less likely he is to get into trouble.

I wait for instructions. I already have a rough idea of how this will work. He'll want to see that I'm not squeamish and that I'm capable of doing what I'm told. A smart man would also film it, so he has leverage over me. That way, if he ends up killing both Brandt and Harper, he can threaten me with the prospect of going back to jail if I don't play nice. In his world, I'm only useful if I'm a monster.

We both stand in silence, looking at the mess before us. This is foreplay for Mal. He enjoys it. He knows I'm uncomfortable, and he's waiting for me to speak first. I'm not going to. I'll stand here all night if I have to.

When the silence stretches on for what seems to be a lifetime, he finally gives in.

'You're a tough one to crack, aren't you?' he says.

'That could be why I was in a top security prison,' I remark flippantly. If it earns me a smack around the head, it's a small price to pay.

'Good point. How did you get there?' It's a rhetorical question. He already knows. You don't get into a position of power like he has without knowing all there is to know about everyone around you. Some battles he fights are silent, but just as deadly.

'I killed someone. Killed a few more while I was inside too, but I got better at covering my tracks.' I'm about to kill again, too. That's why I'm here. I'm not bothered by this prospect. I've known it was coming. I can torture, kill or maim, and not lose a moment's sleep over it. I know I should, but I don't. The difference between Mal and me is that I do it for survival, not for fun. I don't get turned on by it, and I don't want power. Lust for power will always bite you in the ass, eventually. Mal just doesn't know it yet.

He pulls over a black plastic chair and sits on it back to front, his gaze on me the entire time. He doesn't trust me an inch. I feel similarly conflicted, but I need to keep my gaze forward and concentrate on what I'm supposed to do. There's a good chance I'm not going to like what comes out of his mouth next, and sure enough, I'm not disappointed.

'I want you to pull his fingernails out one by one until he squeals.' I remain expressionless, even though I want to sneer in distaste. I know there are cameras trained on me, and that Mal will take great pleasure in watching this little episode later. I've said I'm a killer, now I need to act like one. Torturing people is not something I enjoy unless I know they've earned it. Fighting Mal's battles is not high on my to-do list, but that doesn't matter right now. Staying alive does.

'What happens if he doesn't squeal?' The guy in front of me doesn't look that tough, but I would be the first to admit that looks can be deceiving. Take Harper, for instance.

'Then you're not doing the job right. In any case, do what you want to him, but you need to get results. You're not leaving here until you do.' Well, that told me.

'What do I have to work with?' If it's just my fists it will take longer. If I have some tools to play with I can probably finish up inside of five minutes, although I won't. Mal wants to have some fun. As I'm at his mercy, I'm not going to piss him off just yet.

He comes around to stand in front of me and puts his hands in his pockets. He's relaxing. That's probably because he's got men stationed all over this place.

'Whatever you can find. He's tied up. He's not going anywhere.'

'And what do you want to know?' I'm not sure I'm going to like this, but I ask anyway.

'Who he snitched to. I just want a name.' Well, that's simple enough at least. Now I've just got to wake the poor bastard up.

Getting straight down to business, I give the guy a backhander that sends his chair rocking. His eyes bug open and he blinks at me stupidly.

'Sorry mate,' I say unapologetically, 'but nap time is officially over. I'm cutting your fingernails off in a few minutes, from the root, and I'd like you to be awake for the experience. Normally I'd ask if you've got anything to say before then, but that would spoil all the fun.' He blinks at me stupidly, probably wondering where the hell he is and what's happening to him. He'll remember in a few seconds.

'Oh God,' he splutters, when he finally comes back into the land of here and now. 'No, no, no, this can't be happening.' I have news for him, it is. He begins trembling like a leaf, and I wonder if he's going to throw up all over me.

'Okay, I'll just go and find a pair of pliers, and then we can begin. I'm afraid I haven't been given very much notice for this gig, so you'll just have to bear with me.' Mal's workshop looks fairly well equipped, so I'm hoping he'll have what I need. If not, as Mal says, I'll have to improvise.

'I didn't say anything,' scared man says to my back as I begin wondering off. 'I swear it. I haven't talked to anyone.' There's conviction in his voice, but I don't believe him. Dying men will say all sorts to save their fragile little necks.

My eyes scan the contents of the warehouse, trying to see if I can find what I'm looking for. If I'm not mistaken, this is a cut and shut shop - or at least a front for some kind of car body repair. There are paint sprayers, panel beaters, trim and spoiler kits, pipework and heat lamps, among other things. What I can't find, however, is a pair of pliers. There must be a toolbox around somewhere.

A thorough search of the premises reveals there are hundreds of tools stashed away in drawers under thick wooden countertops. Hammers, saws, chisels, pliers - everything the average torturer could want. If I get bored with those there is an array of battery-powered power tools that can get the job done in half the time. Let's see how much patience Mal has. While I know he'll want a show, he won't want me to take too long because Harper is waiting for him in the bedroom. It's hard to resist a beautiful, naked woman who's chained to your wall. I haven't been able to get the image of her body out of my head, so I'm pretty sure Mal hasn't. We're out here for a spot of foreplay, and then he'll get his rocks off by tormenting her. He is good at games. He keeps his empire under control by making sure all his men fear the consequences of disobeying him. So far he's doing a pretty good job if the poor bastard behind me is any example.

Grabbing a few tools that might come in handy, I make my way back to the poor schmuck that has earned Mal's displeasure. This isn't going to be a fun day for him. But that's not my problem. Grabbing another plastic chair I sit on it sideways so I'm facing my victim, while laying out the tools I've chosen on my legs. I've collected a pair of pliers, a small handsaw, and a chisel. Torture is ninety percent intimidation, and ten percent actual effort - provided you're doing it right, of course.

Both of the poor guy's eyes, which are almost swollen shut, open as far as they can before his body starts trembling again.

'I've told you, I don't know anything,' he groans. He's obviously trying to protect someone. The trouble with this game is that he dies whether he tells the truth or not. He'll just die quicker if he talks. If I'm in his place, the only reason I wouldn't talk was because I really liked the other person in question - and I mean really like.

'What's your name?' I ask him. I don't give a shit what he's called, but it's going to make talking to him easier if I have a name. That way, when he's close to passing out, I can yell at him. People generally respond to their name being yelled at top volume.

'It's S-S-am,' he stammers. Well, that was easy enough.

'Right, Sam,' I say, looking him square in the eye, 'do you want me to start with the pliers or the handsaw? I have no preference really, so I'll go with whatever you decide.'

The question is a no-brainer. All I'm doing is wasting time until the main event.

'I don't know anything,' Sam pleads. 'Please, you have to believe me, I didn't do anything.' He begins struggling on his chair, as if the thick rope binding him will suddenly magically disappear.

'Fair enough, I'll choose for you,' I say brightly. 'I think I'll go for,' I pretend to look at the various tools on my legs, considering my options, before saying, 'the handsaw. The blade looks quite sharp. It should melt through flesh in no time at all.'

Sam goes a rather unpleasant shade of green and tries his best to move words past his trembling lips. Meanwhile I've got the saw and I've grabbed his hand, making sure his fingers are nice and straight on the arm of the chair.

Sam finally finds his voice. 'No, no!' he shrieks. 'Pliers. Can I go with the pliers?' I sigh and frown at him as if this is a major inconvenience, but then I shrug my shoulders. It's all part of the game. Replacing the handsaw, I pick up the pliers and get ready to do some damage. I think my eardrums are about to take a pummelling, so maybe it's best to ease them into the screaming gradually. Chopping fingertips off has to be far more painful than pulling out fingernails. These are assumptions, of course. I've never had to test the theory, thank God.

'Pliers it is then.' Sam looks visibly relieved, which is almost laughable. There is no scenario under which he is getting his ass out of here alive, and although we're now starting with the pliers, we'll get to the handsaw soon enough. He's just delaying the inevitable, but I have to confess I'd do exactly the same thing in his shoes.

Grabbing a finger and holding it steady, I watch while Sam decides what to do next. He knows he can't go anywhere and that resistance is futile, but I think this inaction will change in a few minutes. At the moment he's thinking how much can the loss of a few fingernails hurt? He has no idea.

I let the pincers of the pliers grip the fingernail of his middle finger, and I yank hard. There's no benefit to drawing it out. The more pain I dole out, the more likely I am to get answers. While I'm in no real rush to get back to Harper, where I'm sure I'll be greeted with more nasty games, I don't want to crucify the poor bastard either. I need to look reasonably capable, or Mal will put a bullet between my eyes.

Sam doesn't think much of my approach. Screaming for all he's worth, he begins bucking violently back and forth on the chair. I'm ready for him. Discarding the bloody nail I've just pulled out, I already have the next finger ready, and with another yank we're two down, with eight to go.

'Still don't want to talk?' I ask. I've seen men bigger than him squeal like a baby when faced with a little pain. Everyone copes with it differently. I don't think he's going to last too long, but then, what do I know?

'I told you, I don't know anything.' He looks at Mal pleadingly. He's well aware that I'm not the one calling the shots, but he's wasting his breath. Mal is barely human, like me. There is no compassion riding in the depths of those slate-grey eyes. It's like trying to reason with a man who only speaks Japanese. It's not going to happen.

Yanking out the third fingernail, I don't give him a chance to talk before I begin taking fingernails four and five. The thumb gives me a little trouble, and it takes several tugs before the nail comes free. Sam is openly sobbing now, but he still makes no move to give us the name we want. He's obviously trying to protect someone - but who?

Mal sighs. 'Move it along, Rodriguez. We haven't got all day.' What he means is that he's bored of watching the tame stuff. Now it's time to get messy.

Sam jumps as I toss the pliers away over my shoulder, which bounce off the floor with a loud clatter. He then watches as I pick up the handsaw again, and a little sob leaves his throat.

'I think it'll be quicker to saw them off, don't you?' Waving the tool about in the air, I watch as Sam's about to lose the contents of his lunch. He gives one dry heave, but manages to hold himself together. Unless I'm much mistaken, it isn't going to be long before he throws up everywhere. My fingers are crossed it isn't over me.

'This is really going to hurt, Sam. You sure you don't want to talk?' Just get it over with for Christ's sake, I think, but the idiot obviously can't read minds because he shakes his head. Here we go again.

Grabbing the other hand, his left, I place the saw just below the knuckle of his little finger. I then settle the saw atop it.

Bracing myself, I begin sawing, and things progress rather quickly once I get to bone. Sam yells every swear word under the sun at me, before screaming and struggling as violently as he can while tied to a chair. When that doesn't stop me he vomits all over me. All manner of stuff is coming out of his mouth, but none of it is what we want to hear. When the fingertip finally comes off and falls to the floor I want to tell him not to be such an idiot. But instead I grab finger number two, and that's when the guy goes into shock. He begins shaking like a damn jackhammer, making it difficult for me to hold his hand still. I'm going to be lucky not to cut myself at this rate. Sighing, I use my body weight to hold him down, before I start slicing again.

Another fingertip hits the dirt, and we are no further forward than before. There is blood everywhere, and if I'm not careful the guy will bleed out before we get our answers. Feeling Mal's stare burning into me from behind, I wonder what I should do next. And when Mal begins to tap his foot impatiently I know I need to do something pretty drastic. What will get Sam to spill the info in the quickest possible time? It doesn't take long for an idea to form.

'Wait there, Sam,' I say, smiling brightly as I decide to go for a little walk. What I need is a half-decent power tool. The circular saw I spotted earlier will be just the job.

'Hurry up, Rodriguez, you're running out of time,' Mal says to my retreating back. Charming bloke, Mal. Here I am doing his dirty work for him and he's giving me abuse about it.

Retrieving the saw I test it works. Nothing worse than looking like an amateur in front of your victim. Walking back to Sam, who I'm sure has heard the rattle of the saw, I parade it in front of his eyes. Revving it a couple of times for effect, I watch as he shrinks back on the seat, his eyes wide as he takes in the whirring metal of my little beast. I think it's a bit more intimidating than the pathetic little handsaw, but what do I know?

'We're on a schedule here, Sam,' I remark, not unkindly. 'We have people to see, places to go. You, on the other hand, only need to worry yourself about one thing. Do you want to die fast or slow? Fast is generally preferable. Slow is messy and unpredictable, and very painful.' I allow him a moment or two to process this.

'If you want to go down the slow route, that's really inconvenient if I'm completely honest, but I'll make an exception for you, just this once.' Sam nods, but I'm not sure he's really hearing what I'm trying to say. I think he'll hear my next sentence just fine, though. 'So, Sam, here's what's going to happen next. I'm going to saw through your chair, which will melt like butter under this baby, mostly because it's the easiest way to reach your balls. Then I'll hack through your cock, and I'll keep going, severing as many internal organs as I can, until you decide you want to talk, and I'm pretty sure it won't take too fucking long.' I give him my scariest face as I say it, the one that has death written all over it, and without any further warning I begin sawing away at the thin plastic. I get no more than two inches before Sam goes nuts.

'Stop, stop! I'll talk! I'll talk! Please stop!' I decide to go another inch for good measure, watching him freak out big time, before stopping about a centimetre shy of his balls. I don't want him to change his mind, do I?

Pulling the saw away and setting it down beside me, I say, 'Talk, and remember this is your last chance. Next time my saw isn't stopping until I've chopped you in two.' I sit back, cross my legs and wait to see what will happen. The bastard had better talk. I have no desire to get soaked in blood from top to toe, but once you've made a threat you have to go through with it, else no one will respect you. Mal needs to see I'm not a fucking pussy.

'It was my brother, Tommy. He snitched. He's working for the police department. They got him on a drugs bust, and if he doesn't snitch he's going down for life.' This explains why Sam was so reluctant to talk. It's never nice to drop family members in it.

'Foolish boy,' Mal comments slowly behind me. 'Life imprisonment is a picnic compared to what happens when you annoy me.' He passes me his gun. Very trusting is our Mal. 'Shoot him,' he says.

There's no point pissing about, so I do. I shoot him right between the eyes and put the poor bloke out of his misery. He doesn't get the chance to utter a word before his face goes slack. Poor bastard. I don't even want to think about what's going to happen to his brother. Sighing, I wipe my blood-spattered hands down my jeans and try to ignore that I smell like an abattoir. And there will be worse smells around than me in a few minutes.

'Good work; you pass with flying colours,' Mal remarks dryly, holding his hand out for the gun. I wonder what's to stop me from shooting him right here and now. Oh, I know I'll die shortly afterwards as the men behind me come running, but it might almost be worth it.

'I wouldn't try it if I were you,' He says, intercepting my thoughts. 'There was only one bullet in that gun, and it would be a shame to put an end to such a promising relationship.' See? I knew there was a reason I should just hand the thing back.

Placing the pistol carefully in Mal's hands, I watch as he reloads it and places it back in his waistband.

'You need a shower before we continue,' he remarks, pointing to the small bedroom where Harper remains tied to the wall. 'Oh, and take the pliers and saw with you. They have possibilities.'

They have what? Now I really don't want to know what's going to happen later this evening. If I have to use them on Harper, Brandt is going to take me apart piece by piece. Jesus Christ, what is wrong with this man?

Picking up the tools I begin walking away, trying to put as much distance between me and Mal as I can.

'I didn't mean the handsaw,' he says to my retreating back.

Chapter Eleven - Brandt

Helena doesn't make it to the door before I'm on her. Whipping one hand around her neck I crush her to my body, so she can feel the weight of my erection against her naked body. She started this. Now she can have a taste of her own medicine.

'Let me go!' she shrieks, pounding her fists again my chest. Grabbing them both with one hand I twist them to the side, gripping her chin with my other hand so she has to face me.

'There is no baby, is there?' I whisper. Now that I'm beginning to calm down my brain is once again trying to function. It's not the easiest with a beautiful naked body pressed against me, but it's a challenge I feel sure I can overcome. When Helena doesn't answer I shake her so hard that strands of her elaborate hair-do unravel.

'Answer me!' I bark when the room goes silent. But she does no such thing. Instead she looks at me with venom and shakes her head. So, the woman has secrets. This should be interesting.

'Do you really want to go down this route?' I ask. It's a pointless question. I already know the answer because I can see the excitement in her eyes. The woman wants to know what I'm made of, and I'm about to show her.

Not bothering to give her an opportunity to answer I pick her up and throw her on the bed. I sling her over my knees and press the back of her head into the champagne rose-covered bedspread. She starts struggling, but when I press her face into the soft mattress she stops almost as quickly. I could smother her with virtually no effort, and she knows it.

'Want to die, Helena?' I push her face harder into the mattress. I want to scare her - not too much, but enough.

'You wouldn't hurt me,' she pants, when I let her up for air. She's wrong. I'm quite happy to hurt her, and I'm almost looking forward to it.

Raising my hand I let it swoop down hard on her ass cheeks. There is no warm-up. I want to let her know exactly what she is dealing with. Another ten swats follow, all in quick succession. I'm not feeling very patient. It takes another ten before I know I'm getting somewhere. That's when her ass starts to redden, and her little squeaks of displeasure turn to groans of pain.

'Let me know when you're ready to talk,' I say amiably. 'I'm in no hurry. I can quite happily do this all night.' I'm not lying. I could do this all night, but I won't have to. Harper's fragile body is far stronger than this one will ever be. Helena isn't used to pain. She hasn't had a proper taste of it, but I'm about to give her one.

'Fuck off, Browning,' she shrieks. 'You have no idea what you're dealing with. When I tell Mal he'll cut your pretty little princess in two. Don't think I don't know you've got the hots for her. Anyone with half a brain could see you looking. She's white trash, Browning, and soon enough she'll be right back where she belongs. Mal has plans for her.' The last sentence ends on a squeak as I pummel the hell out of her ass. My hand slams down so hard the bed shudders.

'So what am I dealing with? Why don't you enlighten me, darling?'

Unfortunately for Helena, she can barely speak at the minute. Until I let up on the demanding rhythm of spanks I'm hammering down on her ass, she's going to find it rather difficult to concentrate, and I'm damned if I'm going to do that for the next five minutes at least. I'm enjoying myself far too much to stop now.

The redder her ass gets the more frantic her struggles become. It doesn't bother me. She can struggle as much as she wants; there's no way she's getting away from me. She earned this, and she is going to feel my displeasure. When the tears come a few minutes later, just as I expected they would, I don't feel an ounce of guilt. Anyone who can sell me out to Mal Adley is not to be pitied. If you're in league with the devil, you need to make damn sure you can handle the heat.

'Stop, stop,' she whimpers, mewling and snuffling and clawing at the sheets. But I'm not stopping; not until I'm good and ready. 'I'll talk. I'll talk. Please stop.' This doesn't sway me either.

Eventually, when she gives up pleading with me, and when my hand stings like a bastard, I end on a catastrophic smack that sends her whole body reeling. She shrieks like a banshee but says nothing further. At this moment in time she couldn't string two sentences together, even if she wanted to.

She tries to get up immediately, of course, but I don't let her. I'm going to keep her right here, with all her juicy little bits exposed, until she gives me what I want. I'm not entirely sure what that is, but I'll figure it out as I go along.

Giving her a few minutes to calm down, I wait until the tears disappear. There's no point trying to have a conversation through them. It will take forever. Besides, I'm locked in the room with her until morning, so what's the rush? I might as well have some fun. When she finally stills underneath my hands, I begin talking once more.

'There is no baby, is there?' I repeat.

She doesn't make the mistake of trying to evade the question twice.

'No,' she whispers, shaking her head. Her breathing is still fast but she's not taking the gulping breaths she was before. Her pulse rate is another matter, however. She's scared of me.

'And the shoplifting?' I prod. I have a feeling that was staged for my benefit, too.

She nods. 'It was done to lure you in. Mal thought you'd take pity on me. He wanted us married.'

'Why?' Things are making more sense now, but I don't have all the pieces of the puzzle to hand. I still have no clue as to why Helena and Mal are working together. What on earth possessed the woman to get involved with a gangster?

'He wants to destroy Harper. He can do that by taking you out of the picture.'

My stomach clenches at the ease in which she recites that sentence. I wonder if she'll be the one to kill me? I don't think I want to know, so I don't ask.

'What hold does he have over you?' I'm curious to know what persuaded her to drop all her morals and take up a life of crime. It must have been something good. Maybe Mal has caught her doing something naughty? Maybe she's one of the biggest drug addicts London has ever known, or maybe I don't have a clue.

Helena stills beneath me. Her breathing has slowed down, and I can only feel a slight rise and fall of her chest as she manages to get herself under control. Her delay in answering me tells me that her next words will be lies.

'Brandt, why don't we just stop all this nastiness? Forget Harper. Forget your friend. He's an ex-con, for Christ's sake. We could put all this behind us and start afresh. Mal won't be a problem, and if he is, we'll go live somewhere else. Somewhere no one can touch us.' She tries to get off my lap again, but I press a hand into her neck to hold her down. She is going nowhere for the time being.

Perhaps she is not as smart as I thought. There is no escape from Mal once you're on his payroll. You do as he says, or you die. Anyone with half a brain could see that, so why can't she? What am I missing?

'What hold does he have over you? Please tell me you aren't dealing drugs for him. You are not that stupid, surely?' There are no guarantees on that score. The woman has proved she can be exactly that stupid when it suits her.

When she doesn't answer I decide it's time to remind her why she started talking in the first place. Kneading her raw backside with my hand, I smile when she jumps and yelps.

'Want me to start again?' I don't want to slam into her ass again because my hand has had enough, but I will if that's what it takes.

'No. What's my reward if I play nice and answer all your questions?'

I can't believe she's just asked that. This isn't a game. I don't think she realises what the stakes are, but I guarantee Mal will make them clear in short order.

'You get to live,' I say darkly.

'You're not going to kill me,' she fires back. 'If you were you'd have done it by now. Anyway, you're not the type.'

My lips tighten. Am I that easy to read? I don't think she knows how much I've changed since I've been inside. I'm not the carefree young lad she used to know. I am thousands of miles away from that person now, and there is no going back.

I decide to meet her halfway. 'Out of curiosity, what do you want?' I suspect I will regret asking, but if it gets me answers it may be worth it.

Helena pretends to consider my offer, but I know she's already decided exactly what she wants. If I were a mind-reader I'd say it had something to do with sex, judging by the amount of squirming that went on in the initial stages of our spanking session.

'Hmm, let me think,' she purrs, drawing out the process.

'I wouldn't think too long if I were you,' I grunt. 'I'm tired. If you haven't decided in the next five seconds I'm going to bed, after I truss you up, of course.' I'm not taking any chances with her. If she's the enemy, she'll be treated accordingly.

Helena is quick enough to speak after that. 'I want an orgasm,' she pleads. 'That's not too much to ask, is it?' Her voice is a seductive whisper. I don't want to be aroused by it, but I am. Attractive naked bodies do that to me, even though I sometimes wish they wouldn't.

'Agreed. Where are my answers?' I give her ass another squeeze to hurry the process along.

She twists her head to frown at me, pushing straggly wisps of long blonde hair out of her eyes. 'You don't play fair, Brandt. You were always such a nice boy. What's changed?'

I twist her head back to where it should be - looking down at the floor. 'Life has changed. Now are you talking or am I going to find more inventive ways to cause you pain?' To be honest, I haven't got the energy to do much else, but she doesn't know that.

'Money.' The word is short and to the point, but I need more details than that.

'As in you owe him?' If she's borrowed money from that thug she'll be in it up to her neck, but I don't understand how that could happen. Her family is rich. Why didn't she go to a bloody bank?

'Yes, but now I'm making money. Lots of it.'

'Please tell me you're not dealing drugs for him?' I want to smack my hand against my forehead. How thick is the woman?

'Yes, among other things.'

'You don't need money. Your family is filthy rich. Whatever possessed you to do something so stupid? If they catch you they'll throw you inside for even longer than I was.'

'I'm well aware of that, but they're not going to catch me. I'd be the last person on their suspect list. Everyone thinks like you do. I've got loads of money, so I have no need to do something that ridiculous.' She shrugs.

'That might have changed after the shoplifting incident,' I comment dryly.

'Nah,' she replies. 'They think that was just a stunt - a way to attract Mummy and Daddy's attention.' She then visibly deflates.

'Why do you need money, Helena?' I can't think of one good reason she would pair up with a shark like Mal. Whatever she's got herself into she's now desperate, that's for certain.

'I made a few silly mistakes,' she says reluctantly.

That sounds like the understatement of the century, so I immediately press for more details.

'What did you do?' I might as well know what we're dealing with. I'm in shit up to my neck, so what's a little more between enemies?

'I made an error of judgement,' she says sullenly. That could mean anything. I need specifics.

'What kind of error?'

'A gambling error.'

Oh, fucking hell. 'What kind of money are we talking about here? Fifty thousand? One hundred?' If I know her, it will be a lot.

'Five million.'

I can't say anything for a minute. Helena's family may have plenty of money, but they couldn't bail her out of that one. That's an incredible sum. What the hell was she doing? Scrap that. I don't even want to know.

'So you decided it would be sensible to source a loan from one of London's biggest crime lords? Smart move. All those years of private schooling went to good use.' I shake my head in horror.

'Come on, Brandt. No one else would have lent me the money. You know that.' I do know that, but I also know you don't bet that kind of money if you don't have it. She'll never walk away from this. She'll either end up inside or dead. There is no middle ground.

'You're an idiot.' I want to say a lot more, but my tongue is still in shock.

'I'll find a way out.' Helena's voice is firm and confident. She might believe what she's saying, but I don't.

'You won't. Take it from me. The best thing you can do is pack your bags and run. If you don't you'll be his lackey for the rest of your life.'

'Then I'll find someone to kill him.'

I snort. I can't help it. 'Like that'll save you. The next person who takes his place will come for you instead. There's a certain honour code among thieves. If his men are loyal, they'll finish his dirty work.'

'I'll find a way.'

I'm pretty sure she won't, but I don't see any point in hashing this mess out further. That reminds me.

'Do you know Mal wants me to kill someone?' My fingers find her cunt, mostly because she'll be a little more pliable when she's aroused. I, unlike most of the people I meet, keep my word. Even when I find it extremely distasteful to do so.

Helena almost purrs beneath my fingertips, squirming excitedly. I'd have thought the spanking would have put her off me for life, but that doesn't appear to be the case. I know she doesn't enjoy the pain - not like Harper does. Her cries were those of torment, not desire. Maybe she just hasn't had any attention in a while.

'No,' she moans eventually, 'but it wouldn't surprise me. He always wants someone or other dead.' Helena is trying her hardest to grind her cunt into my hand, but I don't want her to come just yet; not until I'm finished with her.

'I have a feeling it's going to be someone at our wedding party.' I need to get that out there. If Helena has any objections she'd better voice them now.

'It had better not be my parents,' she remarks, which makes me wonder if there is something still human inside of her. 'I'm not all that fond of most of my relatives, but even so, if Mal starts putting holes in my family I am not going to be impressed.'

'With all due respect to your parents, I'm not sure they're important enough to kill.' I'm not joking. While her parents aren't short of a bob or two, they aren't the kind of people you'd bother to get rid of. Father is a scientist who studies molecular biology, and mother does sweet FA, bar chair a few charities in order to make her husband look good.

'Probably not. Well, as long as it's not a family member I don't mind who you kill, so long as you don't get caught.'

'Oh, Mal won't let me get caught, so you can rest easy on that score.' My fingers begin moving more quickly over her clit, and I smile as I hear her breath hitch. It is quite possible she will be the last woman I ever bring to orgasm. Maybe I should savour this moment, but I'm not that desperate yet. I may be in a day or two, but not yet.

'What's that supposed to mean?' she squeaks, and they're the last words she utters for some time. My fingers are slipping inside her, rubbing that sweet spot that drives all women wild. That's one of the few things Gabriel taught me. That, and never let your enemy think they're your enemy. Always keep them unbalanced. Sex is a weapon. I didn't learn it until I was on the wrong side of a set of iron bars, but I learnt the lesson well.

'It means I'll be dead,' I say softly. 'On the plus side, you'll be able to have the marriage annulled. It will be a short but sweet affair, mon petite.'

Dragging out her orgasm for the better part of half an hour, I finally let her come, but only after she has begged me incessantly to do so, using every fucking swear word under the sun.

It feels good to reduce Helena to her base desires, much like an animal. Now she knows what I feel like. Now she knows how much it hurts.

Chapter Twelve - Harper

I can hear the screams through the thin wall, which is all that separates me from Gabriel, Mal and some poor sod who will never live to see the light of day again. The victim's screams won't haunt me, though. Once upon a time they would keep me awake for hours on end, but I've become anaesthetised to them over the years. Now all they produce is a wince and a shudder, mostly because I'm more concerned about what's going to happen to me once the noises stop. They always stop eventually. Mal never lets one live. No one tied to his chair walks out alive.

I know Gabriel is out there being manipulated by Mal, and that he'll do everything he's told. I know this because I would, too. You obey, or you die. I'm getting tired of obeying, though. I know dying will be messy and painful, but life under Mal won't be much different, and at least dying will eventually put an end to the pain. How long could Mal drag my death out for? A week, maybe two at most? I shudder. I don't want to think about it. I'm fairly certain it will be far worse than I could ever imagine, and I can imagine a lot.

The sound of a gunshot from outside makes me jump, as it always does, and straight after my heartrate rockets. It will only be a matter of minutes before Mal and Gabriel are back here, and then it will be my turn to suffer. Except I won't get the release of knowing a bullet in the brain will be waiting for me when it's all over. My death won't be that easy.

Tipping my head up, so that my eyes rest on the yellowed, smoked-stained ceiling, I wonder if Gabriel would kill me if I asked him nicely? The idea has merit. He doesn't want me around because he's worried I'll take Brandt away from him, and with me out of the picture who will stand in his way?

I don't get to examine the thought further because Gabriel bursts in, and I want to retch just looking at the blood-soaked state he's in.

He doesn't say a word, just flings a pair of pliers and something else that looks dangerously electrical on the bed, before heading straight for the bathroom. He doesn't look at me as he stalks off, which tells me all I need to know. Things are about to get messy, and I'm really not going to like it. Now I have two men who can't stand me, and they're both ganging up to see who can cause me the most damage.

When Mal saunters in he has a smug smile on his face. It's a look I know all too well.

'Looking forward to this evening?' he comments, carefully looking me up and down. I suspect he's planning what he's about to do next in glorious detail.

'Can't wait,' I reply. I might be about to die sometime in the next couple of weeks, but I don't see why I have to go quietly.

'Why can't you just do as you're told?' Mal stops walking when his face is about two inches from mine. It's far too close for comfort, but I don't shrink away from him. We've been doing this dance for years.

'You'd have got bored with me almost instantly, if I had,' I reply. It's the truth. Mal's had a lot of women in his life, and out of all of them I've lasted the longest. Mainly because I wasn't his to begin with. I proved a bit of a challenge, and he likes that. He likes crushing things, breaking their spirit and walking all over them. He wants to feel powerful and unstoppable. He's just a controlling asshole.

'Maybe. Maybe not. We'll never know now, will we?' He slides his head forward until I can feel his breath on my lips. I want to recoil, but I don't. There's no point angering him. I'll hurt enough if we're on good terms, I don't want to think about what will happen if I get him mad.

'Why don't you just finish this now? Get rid of me and start afresh. Find someone who'll enjoy working for you as well as crawling all over your cock and obeying your every sordid little command.' My lips reach out to brush against his as I say it, and taunt him with a soft puff of breath.

'I've already told you that would be too easy, pet. I like to watch things suffer. You haven't; not nearly enough. Soon, though. Don't worry, you've got yours coming. I've put a lot of effort into making sure your last few days are going to be spectacular. I'm fairly certain you're going to enjoy every second of it.' He takes my top lip between his teeth and bites. I don't give him the satisfaction of hearing me whimper. I'll be screaming later whether I want to or not, but for now he can deal with my utter contempt. My eyes relay the loathing and hatred I feel as I stare at him with ill-concealed disdain. He can go fuck himself. I'll get a slap for my troubles, but I don't care. At least it will be a warm-up for the slaughterhouse act to follow.

It never comes, though. Gabriel breaks up the tension as he slams the bathroom door behind him and Mal releases my lip as his head snaps around to make sure no one's coming for his throat.

Gabriel isn't that stupid. He's dressed in nothing more than a white bathrobe, and while it shouldn't look sexy, it does. That's mostly because I know he's completely naked underneath it. Tonight's bloodbath will be easier than normal. I only have to look at that man before my panties melt right off my body, and any pain I take for him will be all the sweeter for it. I decide not to mention this to Mal, though. I don't want him to kill Gabriel as well. Brandt will need a friend when this is all over. At least, I hope he will.

'What do you want me to do, Boss?' Gabriel stands there, his arms crossed, looking expectantly at Mal. He stays a safe distance away for the moment, almost as if he knows he makes Mal nervous. Interesting.

'Good question.' Mal turns to me. 'What would you like him to do to you, darlin'? Any requests?'

'I'd like him to do whatever pleases you, darling.' This is an old game. If I stick to the script there's a chance I'll leave the room with all my bones intact. If not, it will be the worse for me. The good news is that I'm used to playing by the rules.

Mal's chest puffs out in pride when he hears me speak. He looks like a proud little peacock. Oh, if only he could see Gabriel's face right now. The rage that sits below his furrowed brow is quite a sight to behold.

'See how well I've trained her, Gabriel? It takes years, that does. You have to get them young and beat it into them, bit by bit. Most of them don't put up much of a struggle for long. Not if you do it right, anyway.' Gabriel's face darkens, but he doesn't say anything. He's a man who knows when to speak and when to stay silent. I don't think we'll get much out of him while Mal's around, and that's a fairly sensible move. Brandt was lucky to have found Gabriel while he was inside. Without him, I suspect there was a good chance he would have died.

Mal gets impatient as the silence stretches. 'Well, that's quite an invitation, isn't it? What would you like to do to her?' Mal turns around to examine Gabriel's face, but his expressionless mask is now firmly back in place. He can change moods faster than I can click my fingers. One might almost wonder whose side he's on. It wouldn't do to trust him in a hurry, but he's Brandt's friend, so that must mean something. At least, I hope it does.

'Hmm.' Gabriel appears to be thinking Mal's request over. Approaching us slowly, he then says, 'May I?' He's looking at me as he says it, and I feel every limb in my body tighten. A burst of energy surges through me, but there's no chance of running. Mal has me trussed up tighter than a pig at a luau. Escape has never been an option for me. I generally settle for survival, and even that's been a stretch lately.

'Of course. Check out the merchandise. See if anything creative springs to mind. I need a drink anyway, and we appear to have run out of Jack. I'll be back shortly. Don't do anything stupid while I'm gone, though. I'd hate to have to tie you to my chair tomorrow evening.' As far as threats go, it's as good as it gets. I hope by now that Gabriel realises who's he's dealing with, but if he doesn't, I'm going to let him know shortly.

When the door closes Gabriel is on me in an instant. 'He wants me to hurt you,' he whispers fiercely through gritted teeth. I can see rage in his eyes again. He looks like he's about to explode. You can only bottle that stuff up for so long. If he's not careful he'll go pop.

'That's the name of the game,' I whisper. 'You hurt me, I scream. You can do that, can't you? Give it a go. You might even enjoy it.' I'm not sure why I want to get a rise out of him, but I do. Maybe I'm just trying to figure out who's side he's really on.

'I'm not fucking joking,' he bites back at me. 'There's a pair of pliers and a circular saw on the bed. He wants me to use them on you. This isn't a bit of slap and tickle. At best I'll scar you for life, at worst I'll kill you.'

'And here I thought you wanted me dead.' My smile is bittersweet. I wonder if Gabriel will manage to get Brandt back when I'm gone? If he does, he's a lucky bastard. Waking up to Brandt every morning is my idea of heaven.

'That's not even funny. Brandt will kill me if anything happens to you. Besides, I don't want to kill you any more. At first I wasn't sure I believed your story, but now I believe every word. That man out there,' he points behind me, 'is a monster.

He needs to be eradicated from this earth by any means necessary. All I want to know is, are you going to help me?' He sucks in a breath, as if trying to control himself from lashing out, and he stands there, his body rippling with tension as he waits for my reply. Now I know Mal is dangerous, but Gabriel is in another league entirely. Mal is only dangerous because of the people that surround him and the gun he carries. Gabriel, on the other hand, is a walking, talking, killing machine. He has a finely honed edge that only prison can teach a man, and Mal lacks his precision and grace. They are both deadly, but in different ways. If I had to pick one to have on my side, I'd go with Gabriel. I'm counting on the fact that he isn't as fucked-up as Mal. It's a long shot, but I'll take it.

'I'll do anything I can to put that man down, and that includes killing myself,' I whisper back as my face clouds with rage. 'He's tormented me for years. You can't even begin to understand the hatred I feel for him.' This much, at least, is true.

'Maybe not, but I'm beginning to.' He brushes a hand across my cheekbone. It's a gentle touch, and I don't expect it. Gabriel unnerves me in the worst way. I never know quite what to expect when he's around.

'Do whatever Mal tells you to,' I say, trying to take the sting out of this awful situation. 'Don't worry about me. I can take it.' I've been taking it for years. What's a little more of the same?

He shakes his head. 'Not this time, you won't. He means for me to start cutting into you. You'll be screaming within seconds. I meant it when I said it will leave permanent scars, and they might not all be physical. Does Mal have any drugs around here? Anything you can take for the pain?'

'No.' Mal would never dream of making my life easy like that.

'Fuck.' Gabriel locks his jaw as his eyes penetrate mine. Light dances in them, and for a second I find myself entranced in that beautiful face. I know tonight will hurt, but I also know it could be worse. Mal could be doing it, for starters. With any luck I'll get away with a quick blowjob after this is all finished and then I can slink away to bed. Sleep seems to be the only respite I get these days, and even then there's a chance that the nightmares will be almost worse than the real thing. How I long for oblivion - the long, unending, buried under six foot of dirt kind.

'Just do what you have to do to get yourself out of here. If I die I'm not going to come back and haunt you. I promise.' I accepted the fact that my life would be short a long time ago. To be honest, I've lived far longer than I thought I would.

'That's not even funny. While there's breath in my body you will live, you understand me?' His eyes eat mine alive, burning them from the inside out. My head wants to leap back, to escape that gaze, but there's only cold, hard plaster behind me, and I'm going nowhere. When there's no response from my lips, Gabriel hisses, 'Nod your head.' I do. I'm too scared to do otherwise. 'Good. I'm glad we understand each other. Tonight I will try my best to do you the least amount of harm possible and you, in return, will scream like I'm frying you alive in oil. That should keep him at bay. If I find a chance to escape I'll take it, but I'm not holding out much hope. Mal seems far too careful.' The light in his eyes extinguishes. He looks worried, and I can see the pain in his eyes. He's thinking about what will come next. He's the lucky party. I'm the one who will bear the brunt of this.

I nod. I will do anything I can to lessen the ordeal I'm about to face, and I'm happy to obey him to the letter. I'm not sure there's much he can do to stop the carnage that's about to unfold, but I'm not about to tell him that. He'll figure it out.

I wonder if he can read my mind because he grabs my hand, squeezing it tightly, and says, 'We will get out of this, Harper. I promise. I've been taken by bigger thugs and been in worse situations, trust me. I always find a way out. You just need to be strong. Do you think you can do that?'

'I can do that,' I say. At least, I hope I can. I have a bad feeling my limits are about to be tested, though.

'Good,' he whispers. 'We'll beat this bastard together, I promise.' They are the last words he gets to utter because the doors behind us crash open and Mal storms in waving about a full bottle of whisky.

'Anyone want a glass?' he asks. He is high. I can tell by the sound of his voice. While he's been gone he's taken something or other. I wouldn't like to speculate what, but I hope it doesn't make him any more aggressive than he already is. We've got problems enough at the moment.

'I'll have a glass,' says Gabriel, amenably. He's probably figuring that the more whisky Mal gets down his neck, the easier he'll be to control. That's not necessarily the case. It just depends on his mood. I cross my fingers that he's in a good one.

'Harper, you want a glass?' Mal calls out across the room. I want to slap him. How am I supposed to drink anything with my hands tied up like this?

'I'm good thanks,' I say quietly.

'Nah, she'll have a glass,' Gabriel interrupts. 'Don't be a party-pooper, Harper. We're all out to have a good time tonight, right?' He gives me a look that says my life won't be worth living if I disobey, so I smile tightly and acquiesce.

'Whisky sounds good,' I say, trying to inject some enthusiasm into my voice. I have never liked whisky. The stuff makes my throat burn and my nose vomit, but I said I'd do as I was told, so I'm doing it.

While Mal busies himself pouring out three glasses of whisky my thoughts get darker by the second, and when Gabriel finally lifts a glass of amber liquid up to my lips, I'm ready to spit it back at him, but he says, 'Drink.' It's a command rather than a request, and I obey instinctively. He softens the order by murmuring, 'It will help lessen the pain. Swallow as much as you can, no matter how much it burns.' I do as I'm told. As Mal isn't paying us much attention at the moment I manage to drink the whole glass, and most of Gabriel's. Given how little I've eaten, in a few minutes the stuff is guaranteed to have me high as a kite.

'Time to get this show on the road,' Mal says as he sinks down on the bed, getting comfortable. 'What say you start with the pliers?'

My heart sinks as Gabriel walks over to where Mal is sitting. Bending slowly, he retrieves and twirls them over in his hands.

'Do we have any rules here?' he asks, and turns towards me, pretending to check me out from head to toe. His perusal should fill me with disgust, but it doesn't. Slow, curling tendrils of heat begin to lick up my body, making me clench in all the right places. Although I have a feeling this will be one of the worst evening's

I've ever had, at least I'm not with Mal on my own. It's small consolation, though.

'No rules,' Mal confirms, lacing his fingers underneath his head as he lies back on the bed. 'She's going to be dead in a couple of days, so have fun. Just make sure she's in a good enough condition to finish me off when you've had enough.'

Gabriel looks sideways at me and I have to resist the urge to roll my eyes in answer. I'm on display at the moment and I have to be careful.

'No rules, huh? This should be interesting then.' Moving towards me with cat-like grace, Gabriel opens the jaws of the pliers while his index finger caresses the cold, hard steel. 'Do you like pain, Harper? Would you like me to mark that beautiful, porcelain skin of yours? Make you cry out in agony while you beg for mercy? Is that the kind of thing that turns you on?' He shrugs himself out of the bathrobe, revealing a pair of tight black briefs underneath. My eyes immediately dip toward them, wondering if he's aroused by all of this, and sure enough, his cock is standing proudly to attention. It seems I'm not the only one who enjoys fucked-up shit.

'Like what you see?' He's noticed the direction of my gaze, and while I should be embarrassed, I'm not. I've gone past that. My eyes travel slowly up the black-inked skeleton abs, before resting on his beautiful face. If someone's got to kill me, I wouldn't mind so much if it was Gabriel.

'Not particularly,' I comment. I'm lying. This is for Mal. From this point forward we need to be enemies, and I need that rage if I'm going to get through the next few hours of pain. Without it I'll break down, and if I cry I'll never stop. Besides which, I don't want to give Mal the satisfaction of tears. He doesn't deserve them.

Gabriel's head twists to the side as his eyes flicker up to mine. 'That's too bad. Here I was hoping we could both be friends.' Before I know what's happening he's got two fingers around my nipple, and he's pulling it painfully towards him. Biting on my lower lip, I try my best to prevent the gasp that wants to escape.

Bending his head towards me, he whispers, 'Lash out at me. Get rid of all that anger. Do whatever you have to in order to stay sane because this is going to hurt.' He places the pliers where his fingers have been, and it doesn't take me long to discover he's not lying.

'Stand back,' Mal commands when I suck in a sharp breath. 'I want to see her face. There's nothing better than watching a woman's face as it twists in pain. Wouldn't you agree?'

Gabriel moves back but makes no comment on Mal's statement. Instead, he lets the pliers hang from my left nipple and the pain is simply indescribable. They are so ridiculously heavy I want to wail.

'Scream for me,' he says, grinning at me as my mouth hangs open in shock. I don't know if the smile is for me or Mal, who has a look of utter fascination in his eyes, but I do know that I am going to kill Gabriel when this is all over.

Tears spring from my eyes as the weight of the pliers begins to take its toll.

'Isn't that beautiful?' Gabriel muses. His fingers caress the underside of my breast, making the pliers jiggle around, and that hurts even more. My wrists are pressed tight to the cold metal cuffs that surround them, and for once in my life I wish someone would burst in to save me. If there's no happily ever after coming for me, I don't want to go on any more. I can't.

'Very, but it would be even more beautiful if you put it on her clit,' Mal says, and I think my eyes try to burst out of their sockets. It hurts enough where it is, so I can't even begin to imagine what that would feel like down there. If I'm not lucky it'll tear the bloody thing off. Maybe that's all part of the fun.

'I'm going to work up to that, one step at a time. When we get there I want everything to hurt so bad she'll be sobbing her little heart out.' Gabriel's words are so cold my body begins to tremble. He's on your side, I try to remind myself. But I still don't trust him. That's the trouble; I keep wondering whether he'll turn on me.

'I can't see,' complains Mal. Gabriel rolls his eyes and I release a breath I hadn't realised I'd been holding. He is still on my side, for the moment, at least.

With his back to Mal he says, 'I'll move in a minute, but I need to see what I'm doing here. Just a sec.' He moves in closer to me, squeezing my right nipple, getting me all nice and prepped for round two.

'I'll put one of the handles between your legs and you hold it in place. It'll help keep the weight off your clit. Scream like your life is ending, but do not let go of that handle. If we're lucky and you're a good enough actress, Mal won't notice.' He steps back quickly, allowing the bastard behind him to take his fill.

On the bed, Mal is happily sipping his whisky while he watches my face with interest. He's yet to break me, but I have a feeling that's coming soon. Up until now I've had Alex as my back-up plan. If anything happened to me, Mal would have been held accountable. No such plan exists now. Getting rid of me, a girl with no family or friends, is almost too easy, and he knows it.

'Let me go, you bastard!' I howl. I'm only half acting. 'Kill me now and have done with it. Go get your glue, you fucker!' If I'm going to die anyway, I see no need to prolong the agony. I figure I might as well ride head-on into the storm.

Mal strokes his cock through his jeans. From the way his face darkens it is clear he's unimpressed with my outburst. 'Shut up, or I'll gag you,' he growls. He then necks the rest of his whisky and pours himself another glass. Yet again, he is growing impatient.

'Get a move on,' I whisper to Gabriel. 'If we're not careful he'll get a knife out and start stabbing holes in me.'

As he yanks the pliers off my nipple I let loose a low growl. The resulting throb builds in intensity until I almost see stars, but in reality I know this is nothing compared to what's coming. When the cold metal jaws come for my clit I almost have a meltdown, but somehow I hold it together.

'Eyes on me, Harper,' Gabriel says in a soothing tone, and somehow I summon up enough courage to look at him. I don't want to. I know what's coming next.

'I can't do this,' I whisper. For the first time in my life I'm ready to throw the towel in. I have no fight left in me. Mal has pushed me to my limit and I want out. I don't want to have to endure another second of this shit. I've had more than anyone should have to take, and my mind is cracking.

'Trust me, I'll get you through this,' he whispers, placing two fingers on my clit.

'I can't,' I whisper as my body twitches underneath his hand, my pussy clenching tightly with need. When he's so close all I can think about is sex. Maybe it's hormones or pheromones or whatever, but Gabriel is as intoxicating as Brandt - probably more so. I just have to look at him to want him. It doesn't matter that the man is as evil as sin because that face would be the downfall of any woman on the planet. No one is safe around him. No one.

'You can. I told you I'd get you out of this and I will. Don't give up on me. We can't let him win. We won't.'

As far as pep talks go I'm not sure it boosts my spirits any, but when those pliers come for my clit I have bigger problems. The first is that my whole body now feels like it's on fire with adrenaline thundering through my veins, and the second is that I'm so damn aroused I could cry. Tears form, but I blink them back. Gabriel is right. I'm stronger than this.

When he lets go of the pliers he wedges one of the handles between my thighs as he promised, and I hold them tightly in place. It doesn't stop the pain entirely, but it's nowhere near as bad as it could be.

'Very nice,' Mal comments, his eyes scouring my body up and down like he hasn't had a fuck in years. I know differently. The man can't go more than a few hours without giving his sorry excuse of a cock an outing.

'How about we speed things up a little? Get the saw started, Gabriel. I want to see how much she can take.'

A solitary tear dribbles down my cheek. While my eyes might be spitting fire, there are some things I can't control. Weeping uncontrollably is one of them. I'm about to lose the plot, and I don't mean I'm about to have a mental breakdown. My mind is going to up and leave whatever's left of my body, and I don't think anyone will be able to do much with what's left. On one hand, it will be a relief, on the other, it will mean the end. I haven't got the strength to care either way.

Chapter Thirteen - Gabriel

I'm losing her. I can tell by the look in her eyes. Yesterday there was nothing but fire and ice in those irises. Today there is nothing but defeat. When I first saw her I thought a stiff wind would blow her away. Then I spent some time with her and changed my mind. Now I'm worried. She must have some kind of shell she retreats to when something like this happens. Some kind of happy place? I have no idea how she deals with it, but she needs to deal for just a little while longer. How do I bring that out in her? What can I do to make her fight this?

'You stay with me, you hear?' I want to shake her but I daren't; not with Mal watching.

'What's the point?' she whispers. Her eyes dip towards the floor, like a true submissive, except that she isn't. She's survived this long by fighting everything that man throws at her. If she gives in, she's lost. He won't want to play with a doormat. I've seen his type before. He's only stayed interested in her this long because he doesn't have her. Once she buckles she'll have a bullet in the middle of her forehead in two seconds flat.

Obviously I'm not going about this the right way. She doesn't need words or platitudes. She's not used to them and she isn't listening. I need to give her something that will catch her attention.

Working the handle of the pliers out of her thighs, I let the beast drop. That should focus her attention a little, and sure enough I hear the hiss of an enraged woman. Good. Her fire is back. We've gone from defeat to anger. I can work with that.

Mal's phone chooses that moment to ring, and as far as messages from above go, I'll take it.

Swiping it out of his pocket he looks at it and frowns. Good. That must mean it's important. Let's hope he has to take it in private and that it's a very long call.

He looks at me and rolls his eyes. He throws me the handcuff keys and I catch them neatly mid-air. 'Duty calls. Get her down from there, wake her up, and get her ready for when I get back. Think you can do that?'

I nod. We've gone from violence to sex. That works for me. 'Sure thing.'

As soon as he's left the room I rush to get Harper out of the restraints.

'Are you okay?' I ask. It's a stupid question. She is not okay. If I'm not careful she is probably about to tear my balls off, if she's got any energy left for that.

'I'm fine.' Her eyes are now wide open, staring into mine with unconcealed lust. That's the last thing I need.

'Stop looking at me like that.' I can't think when she's doing that, and I need to think. Freeing her left wrist I move over to her right.

'Looking at you like what?' She blinks and flexes her freed wrist. It must be sore. Pretty much like the rest of her body.

'Like you want to eat me.' Her other wrist pops out easily as soon as the key is turned and she slumps forward, unable to support herself. I catch her easily. 'Whoa there,' I say, gently popping her body back upright. 'Take a minute, okay? You must be exhausted. Just lean on me for a second. When you feel better I'll free your legs.'

'My saviour.' She giggles and I find her gazing at me with those big sable eyes. My cock rises to a stiff, flag post position, and I clench my teeth as I try to ease the tension in my boxers, but now her attention is solely focused on my cock. Oh my God. This isn't happening. My pulse is beginning to hammer in my veins and a buzzing sound is erupting somewhere in my ears. I want to fuck the woman so bad. What the hell is wrong with me? Since when have my allegiances turned? I seem to be a bit flaky all of a sudden.

'Can I let you go now?' I ask. 'Think you can stay upright while I free your legs?'

'I'm fine,' she says, when she must be anything but. Taking her at her word, however, I release her legs and help her out of the X-frame contraption.

'You have got to play with me, Gabriel,' she says. 'If Mal gets back in here and I'm not wetter than a North Sea storm, he's going to take it out on you.' Her voice is pleading.

'You're already soaked, princess,' I say, knowingly. 'My playing with you won't make any difference. All it will do is make the next hour or two with Mal that much worse.' I don't want to get too near her. I'm in dangerous territory. If I do something Mal doesn't like, I'm likely to get tied to his chair while he cuts chunks out of me. There's also the very real possibility I'll get carried away. I can't think clearly when Harper's around.

'Please Gabriel,' she whispers, staggering over to the bed. Just the sound of her voice gets me going, but I ignore it. Striding off into the bathroom I try my best to push all thoughts of sex from my mind. The trouble is, I've already had a taste of Harper Wilkinson, and I liked it far more than I should. Now I want a replay.

'What's he going to do to you?' I have no idea why I'm asking a question I don't want to know the answer to, but I do it anyway.

She lies on the bed and doesn't look at me as she says, 'Hard to tell, but it will be nasty, degrading and utterly humiliating - especially with you watching. Don't sweat it. I've endured his hands on me hundreds of times before, so once more isn't going to make much of a difference.' She's already resigned herself to what's about to happen, and that, for some reason, makes me really mad.

Her eyes catch mine, and she looks at the little red pack in my hand. 'There's no real point in taping me up until he's finished with me. He loves blood. You're going to spoil his fun if you do that, and he doesn't take kindly to anyone who tries to interfere with his whores.'

'Don't call yourself that,' I bark, annoyed that she thinks of herself that way. Is this what years of conditioning have done to her? I hope not.

Harper sighs theatrically, but she does as she's told. 'Patch me up when he's finished,' she says. 'He'll be in a better mood then.'

I don't give a fuck about his mood. All I care about right now is forming a plan that will get us both out of here with our hearts still beating and most of our limbs intact. At the moment, it's looking like a long shot, but I'm a reasonably resourceful kinda guy. I'll come up with something... or die trying.

Chapter Fourteen - Brandt

The day of my wedding dawns with a thick blanket of cloud and lashings of wind and rain. It is so gloomy not a single flower in the Foster-Lyle's perfectly manicured gardens has dared to open. Helena is going to go mental, but that's her problem.

In my humble opinion, it's the perfect day for a disaster of grand proportions. If possible my mood is even blacker than the weather and people would do well to stand as far away from me as they can. Not even the vicar is safe, and that's saying something.

My thoughts are everywhere and nowhere all at once. Is Harper still alive? Is Gabriel? Will I live to see the end of today? Am I going to kill someone? Will I fuck up my fake vows in front of hundreds of people? Actually, I don't even care. If I'm only going to be alive for the next twelve hours or so, worrying over my lines isn't worth my time or attention.

The only blessing today has provided so far is that I will not be seeing Helena until we walk down the aisle. She's a stickler for tradition, apparently. Highly odd then, that she has virtually steamrolled me into marriage by claiming to be preggers several weeks before the event. Traditions must have changed somewhat since I've been inside.

Pacing up and down in my hotel room, I keep staring at the suit in the wardrobe. It is dark grey and comes with a white dress shirt that has been starched to within an inch of its life. It is accompanied by a gold waistcoat and cravat. I hope someone can help me with the cravat. I have no idea how to tie the thing.

Looking down at my watch, I realise I have just half an hour until the wedding car is due to pick me up. Christ, I'd better get dressed. The last thing I need is for the soon-to-be in-laws turning up while I'm running about in my boxers.

Pulling on my pants, I wonder for the one millionth time who it is that Mal wants me to kill. I have my theories, but as yet that's all they are; theories. I'm no closer to unravelling this mystery, and that can only be a bad thing. How am I supposed to do it, anyway? Am I going to have to shoot someone? Strangle them? The thought of killing someone is so abhorrent I'm not sure I'm going to be able to get through the day without puking. There are two types of people in this world - those that can kill and those that can't. So far, I've fallen into the latter group. I haven't got the stomach for it, and my conscience would eat me alive after the event. Am I prepared to kill someone to save Harper and Gabriel's life? Will Mal even keep his word if I do? He's a thug, for crying out loud. He tortures people for a living. I have about as much chance of seeing my friends alive again as I do of meeting the Dalai Lama.

There's a sharp knock on my door. It makes me jump. I already know it's not room service because I ate breakfast over an hour ago, so I think I can safely assume that it's someone who wants to drag me to my impending nuptials. Grabbing my shirt, I button it up as quick as is humanly possible and drag some socks on. Looking almost presentable, I then open the door.

'Well, look at you,' says a fat bald guy dressed in a very bad suit. Mind you, it's still better than the ridiculous attire I'm in, so I'll keep quiet.

Raising my eyebrow expectantly, I wait for something bad to happen. I'm fairly sure this guy is one of Mal's meatheads because the Foster-Lyle's wouldn't be seen dead conversing with the likes of him.

'Yes?' I ask, after we've been standing and staring at each other for what seems like an hour.

'You Brandt Browning?' bald guy asks.

'Yep, that's me.' Shoving my hands in my pockets, I wait patiently for whatever is about to happen next.

'Good. Let's go inside.' He indicates the interior of my hotel room.

'Oh, I don't think so,' I say, shaking my head. The last thing I need is to be trapped in a small space with one of Mal's goons.

'I don't think you understand; that wasn't a question,' bald guy says, and there's then a bulge inside his very unflattering suit jacket, which suggests I should obey unless I want my guts splattered all over the insipid magnolia walls that surround me. What an asshole. Doesn't he realise this is supposed to be the happiest day of my life?

Throwing the door wide open and plastering a monstrously fake smile on my lips, I let the twat inside. To be fair, it's unlikely he's going to kill me; I won't be able to do Mal's dirty deeds if I'm dead, will I?

Closing the door as soon as he's inside, I turn around. 'Any chance you know how to tie a cravat?' I ask.

Bald guy spins around and grabs me by the throat. 'Do I look like the type of guy who gives fashion tips for a living?' Getting his gun out of his jacket he begins waving it around. This is exactly why I didn't want to let him in.

'Good point,' I reply. 'So, what are you here for?' I figure we may as well get this over with.

'To tell you who you've got to kill this evening,' he says, quite happily. He even smiles as he says it. Where does Mal get these people from?

'Well, let's get on with it then. I have people to see, places to be.' I look at my watch meaningfully. I've got less than half an hour before I need to be out of this place, and I still haven't figured out how to tie a cravat.

'So I hear,' says bald guy, his sickly grin still firmly in place. I want to punch my fist straight through his face, which I'm fairly sure would wipe it off in an instant, but I figure that would be unwise. Grabbing my suit jacket, I shrug it on and go hunting for my shoes. If bald guy wants to drag things out, that's his problem, but I'm damned if he's going to have my full attention while doing so.

Bald guy loses his enthusiasm for tormenting me as soon as he sees I've lost interest in the game.

'Their name is Frankie,' he says, as I'm busily shining my shoes with the hotel sponge. While this day might not be the happiest of my life, I have certain standards to maintain.

Frankie. Is that a man or a woman? It would be hard enough for me to kill a man, but almost impossible if I have to kill a girl.

'Who are they?' I ask. Maybe if they work for the Inland Revenue or something I won't feel quite so bad about all of this.

'You'll figure it out. Mal says you don't need to know any more than that, so my job here is over.' Bald guy's eyes are currently glued to my shoes, and while I have to agree they are so damn shiny you could almost see your face in them, he needs to get out of here.

'Wonderful. Now if there's nothing else, I have a wedding I am going to be later for...' I leave it hanging. In case he's almost as stupid as he looks, I eye the door behind him for clarification.

Thankfully he gets the message. 'Right ho. I'll be seeing you later.' The man then strides out of the door without a backward glance, and as soon as it shuts behind him there's another knock.

He's probably forgotten to give me a gun or something. Fantastic. This is all I need. So dragging the door open wide I say, 'What the fuck do you want now...?'

Two seconds later Rupert Foster-Lyle comes in. Shit. I cannot deal with my life right now.

'Do you want to try that again, son?' he asks, in what is a rather frosty tone. Can't say I blame him.

'I'm so sorry, Sir,' I say, trying my best to think of a way to backpedal out of this as quickly as possible. Thankfully it doesn't take long for something to come to me. 'The last person to knock had the wrong room number, and I thought he was going to demand I up and leave right away. I can't cope with that right now. I think I have these pre-wedding jitters. Even my hands are shaking. And to make matters worse I cannot, for the life of me, figure out how to tie this damn cravat.' I throw my hands up in exasperation. Rupert smiles. There is a God.

'I can sort that out for you, son. After that, we'd better get a move on. The cars are waiting downstairs. It wouldn't do to be late.'

The wedding goes off without a hitch, despite everyone getting torn to bits by the weather. I don't fluff my lines, Helena looks beautiful even though she's a traitor, and no one kills anyone. Yet. Even the bridesmaids behave themselves and considering not one of them is above the age of six, that's a result in my book.

So far I have no idea who Frankie is, or how I'm going to kill them, but I hope that will become apparent as the day wears on. If I get desperate, I'll just have to ask Helena the names of all of our guests. Knowing her she'll love that. She hasn't stopped gasbagging since we got out of the church and her constant drivel is beginning to drive me nuts. If I had to stay married to her for any length of time, I'd go insane.

Our reception is being held in a hotel which, whilst not one of the glitziest hotels London has to offer, still oozes five-star luxury and charm. Quite honestly, I'm surprised we weren't banished to a bed-and-breakfast or something. I'd thought Rupert and Julia would probably want to hide us away, but that doesn't appear to be the case.

When we enter the reception room, the blinding white walls around me nearly dazzle my retinas. Everything is white, except the silverware on the tables, and the mass arrangements of pale pink peonies that sit in clear glass bowls as the focal centrepiece. Even the chairs are upholstered in thick white leather, and the lamps strategically set around the room are also of monochrome design.

'Don't you just love it?' Helena squeals. From my point of view it's a bit like white torture, but I am wise enough not to mention this out loud.

'It's stunning, darling,' I say tactfully. The last thing I need now is drama or hysterics. This is Helena's day, and she can have whatever she wants, whenever she wants it. I just need to get through it in one piece - preferably without killing someone.

In fairly short order we are handed a glass of champagne while trays of canapes are draped in front of us, one by one. I don't have much of an appetite for anything, but I try my best to appear as if I'm enjoying myself. Normally this would involve drinking, but today that could be dangerous, so I need to be careful.

It isn't long before the first guests begin to arrive. Then we are stood alongside Helena's mother and father while we welcome everyone inside. It doesn't take me long to realise that this is an excellent opportunity to learn everyone's names. As each couple is introduced to us, my eardrums are on red alert for the name Frankie, but no such name is announced. Typically everyone is announced formally by their first and last names, just to make my job that little bit trickier.

In the end I narrow it down to three possibilities. We have a Franklyn, who's at least seventy years of age and a lover of tweed, a Francis who is in his mid-forties at a guess and accompanied by his pregnant wife, and a Francesca. Francesca is just a young girl, but devilishly attractive with black hair and startlingly blue eyes. When she directs her attention to me my wife immediately stiffens, but manages to suffer through some polite niceties until the next couple comes along. This is interesting. I'll have to ask her about it later, when I get a chance. All I can do for now is commit the three faces to memory. I'll have to ask my questions later and draw my conclusions from whatever I can learn then. I'll also have to figure out if I'm prepared to kill someone to free my friends. If there was a guarantee of them being released, I have a feeling I might, but there is no such guarantee. Mal is unreliable at best, and it would be wise for me to remember that.

The day drags on with speeches, toasts, food, wine and dancing. I have no appetite for any of it. My focus is on working out which one of the three Frankies I'm going to have to kill and trying to learn everything I can about them. It's not until it's time to dance that I finally get my bride's attention all to myself. Prior to this we've been sat around our table, making polite conversation with guests.

'What can you tell me about Franklyn?' I ask her, as the dulcet tones of *Somewhere Over the Rainbow* begin. The song makes my skin crawl. This wedding is entirely Helena down to every last horrendous detail, including my gold suit, but as it's a sham that is unlikely to last for more than a day, there's no point in complaining.

'Is that who you're supposed to kill?' Helena asks with a puzzled frown.

'Why?' Her face tells me that Franklyn is about as threatening as a kitten.

'He works with my dad. He studies molecular biology. I can't think why Mal would want him dead. Besides, he's likely to die of natural causes within the next five years. He's already had two stokes, and he's not in the best of health.'

I mentally cross Franklyn off my list. If Mal is targeting pensioners, he's getting desperate.

'Who's Francis, then?'

Helena gives me another odd look. 'Mal hasn't told you who you've got to kill? You've got to figure it out for yourself?' It seems she can be intelligent when it suits her.

Shaking my head, I say, 'No, all he's given me is the nickname, Frankie. There are three people here who could possibly have that nickname, which is making life a little difficult.

'He didn't give you any more than that?' Helena looks surprised. Clearly she hasn't seen Mal's sense of humour in action. The man lives to torment people. And now I've got out of prison he's got a new idiot to play with, although it doesn't look like he intends to drag our relationship out for long.

'That's all I've got. Does he do this kind of thing often? Maybe he doesn't get out much, and he has to get his kicks where he can?' Hell if I know.

'I just ferry drugs for the man. We don't chat. He's not my type.' Interesting. Mal can't get enough of Harper, but he has no interest in Helena. Maybe we do have something in common, after all.

'He's not come on to you sexually at all?' After what she's just said I'm pretty sure the answer's no, but I have to check.

Her eyes flicker away from me. 'God, no. That would be the end of us, if he did.' Wrong answer, I think. That would be the end of you.

Changing the subject back to the original one I ask, 'So who is Francis? Is he worth killing? Does he do something illicit or illegal for a living? Maybe he works for law enforcement?' Who would a drug dealer hate? Someone who would get in his way, I'm guessing.

'Brandt, for God's sake, kiss me. They're all waiting for that photo. Don't drag it out.'

Shit, I hadn't even noticed the crowd around us. Everyone is staring as though we're the entrée in their seven-course dinner, and they are expecting big things. They obviously haven't seen my dance moves. These poor people are about to be sorely disappointed. Giving it my best shot, I dip Helena towards the floor as the song comes to an end and cover her mouth with my own. A dozen camera flashes go off at once as our guests fill up their memory sticks.

Picking my wife up, I then waltz her around the dancefloor to the next song, and thankfully we're joined by a few others this time. I don't have to feel quite so conspicuous now.

'Francis,' I repeat. 'What do you know about him?' Thankfully this number is a slow one, so we've got plenty of time to be up close and personal while whispering sweet nothings in each other's ears.

'You taste like strawberry pavlova and Sumatran coffee,' Helena purrs, licking her lips. We're going off topic again.

'Answer my question and you get another taste,' I say, hoping that might motivate her to speak.

'I'm your wife, I'm going to get plenty of kisses.'

'Fine, play it your way.' Pushing her away from me I grab the nearest single woman and spin her around. That will piss my wife off. Sure enough, we haven't done two turns around the dancefloor and I can feel daggers slicing into my back. My little kitty has claws, but tonight I'm going to use them to my advantage. After the next song has ended I graciously dance with my mother-in-law to the delight of all our guests, before picking up the hot firefighter I met at the engagement party. Unless I am much mistaken, Helena's patience is about to come to an abrupt end any second now.

Sure enough, the next words I hear are 'Can I cut in?' Helena is standing between us, staring at my dance partner as if she has just grown horns. Hot firefighter blinks, and then hurriedly makes her excuses. She's a sensible lady.

'Don't play hardball with me,' Helena snipes as her claws sink into the tender flesh of my neck. I don't even blink. On the pain scale it barely registers these days.

Placing my hand on her ass and squeezing cruelly, I figure I'll return the favour. When her mouth opens to squeal in protest I cover it with my own. By the time the camera flashes have finished with us, she isn't squealing any more.

'Francis,' I repeat, as if we'd never left each other's arms, and when her face clouds over I give her a gentle nudge. 'Remember where we are. This is the happiest day of your life darling. Don't let them take a photo of that frown.'

She takes a breath and then gives me her most dazzling smile. 'Francis is an accountant. Happy now?' I nuzzle her neck while I pretend she is the most amazing woman on earth.

'Happier,' I confirm. 'What field? Tax, financial or management?' Does Mal want me to get rid of an accountant? It seems unlikely.

'Tax, I believe.' The lights dip above us and the music speeds up. More guests pile onto the floor, and all of a sudden we are crammed in a sea of gyrating bodies. The evening is wearing on and my time is running out. Still, I'm on the right track.

'Good girl,' I purr. 'See, that wasn't so hard, was it?' My hands feather over the back of her shoulders as they pull her closer to me. We might as well look like we're having fun.

'Do good girls get a reward? Can we work under an incentive scheme here?' Helena grinds herself up against me like a cat and though sex is the last thing on my mind, I need to keep her sweet.

'Sure. You scratch my back and I'll scratch yours, sweetness. What do you want in return?' I don't care what she wants. I'm not going to be alive long enough to deliver it, so she could ask for the moon and I'd say yes.

'I want to come with you when you do it.' Now there's a cerebral landmine.

'You want to what?' I heard what she said but I need it repeated, just to make sure.

'I want to watch. I've got a vested interest in you doing this right. If you fuck up I stand to lose you moments after I'm married. Fuck that.'

'So you want to get yourself killed at the same time? I don't think so. Think of something else.' It seems I was wrong about the moon part.

'But—'

I cut her off immediately. 'It's non-negotiable and there's nothing you can say that will make me change my mind. There are a million and one other things you could ask for, pick one of them.'

Helena stares at me, her arms stiffening around my body, before she once again relaxes. She's decided this isn't a war she needs to fight and thank God for that.

'Fine. Just keep me in the loop, okay?' That I can do. Mostly because she's going to be my eyes and ears for this operation anyway.

'Agreed. One more question.' My hand reaches up to brush against the underside of her breast and she gasps. Thankfully no one can hear her over the loud roar of thumping bass, but I can feel her body tighten in desire. In another lifetime it might have been reciprocated, but she's from a life I've long since left behind. I no longer remember the person I was way back then, and I think she's coming to realise that.

'Fire away.' Helena's voice is raspy now, and she feels like liquid in my arms. Her body does exactly what I tell it to do, as if it has no will of its own. She can't be in love with me because we don't know each other that well, but she certainly feels something for me. I haven't been immune to the looks I've been getting since I got out of prison, so I guess there's something about muscles and tatts that turn women on. Even Harper looks at me differently. She's always had those faraway eyes that look at me as if I'm a God, but now the desire I see there is my undoing. Every time I look at her I want to sink every part of my body inside her. It's a primal feeling. I know what lust is, but what I share with her is something more. It's something that can't be replicated with anyone else. Unfortunately for Helena, she comes in a very poor second. If I saw her in the street I wouldn't even give her the time of day.

'Tell me about Francesca.' I've purposefully left the elephant in the closet until last. It's obvious Helena doesn't like Francesca, and now is the perfect time to find out why.

Pursing her lips, my darling wife draws back from me. 'She's a viper.' When she makes a move to escape me I capture her wrists and drag her back into my arms. When she's so close that no one can see what's going on between us, I tweak her nipple beneath the thin lace bra she's wearing.

Circling the little nub around and around, until it makes a pretty little point beneath my fingertips, I bend my head close to her ear. 'And why do you dislike her so much?' I don't let her answer my question immediately, choosing to return my lips to hers, to keep her off balance. I want the truth. I don't want her to think too much. When I finally pull my mouth away she is breathing hard and her lips are glazed. She's also a little unsteady on her feet, but I pretend not to notice.

'God, you do that well,' she chokes out. I resist the urge to tell her Gabriel taught me everything I know. She is not someone I want to share my past with.

'Francesca?' I prompt, keeping my hands moving across her body. 'Is she anyone of importance?'

'Not really,' she says with a sneer, 'although she likes to think she is.'

'So she can't be the one,' I say, with a sigh of relief. The last thing I want to do is kill a girl.

'I wouldn't be so sure,' Helena replies, shaking her head. 'While Francesca is just a little tramp who likes to whore herself out to anything that moves, her daddy is well-renowned in these circles for being the boss of a string of designer clothing boutiques.'

I give Helena an odd look. Mal is unlikely to want the daughter of a shopkeeper dead. I can't think he's looking to compete in that industry. The idea is almost laughable.

'Well, that settles it,' I say. 'It's got to be Francis.' Somewhere in the back of my head, though, I remember Mal saying something about bodyguards. Accountants aren't that important, are they?

Helena shakes her head. 'I don't think so. Francesca may not be anyone of note, but her old man is. Daddy is also the head of one of London's biggest crime families and is probably Mal's arch enemy these days. It looks like Mal wants to send a message.'

Oh shit. Oh fuck. He wants me to kill a mobster? I am never getting out of this hellhole alive. They'll have to scrape me up off the damn floor, piece by piece. That's if there's anything left worth scraping, and I suspect there won't be.

Chapter Fifteen - Brandt

The one good thing about your own wedding is that you get to leave early, and I am itching to ditch mine. Doing the rounds one final time, my bride and I thank everyone for coming and say our goodbyes. We are subjected to lots of rowdy claps and cheers as we head up the stairs to the honeymoon suite, and I do my best to ignore them. At the back of my mind, the whole way up those stairs, I am thinking that in a few minutes I will have to murder someone.

It's the perfect setting, really. Everyone's high on alcohol, there's loud music thumping away which might muffle any screams or gunshots and by the time I get out there again, everyone's getting tired and will be off their game. Who kills people at a wedding? You've got to be a pretty sick individual to do something like that.

Helena babbles on about something or other all the way back to our room. She doesn't seem at all bothered by the fact that I'm about to become a murderer, and instead she waxes lyrical about the highlights of our day. Seriously? I'm going to be dead in a couple of hours and all she can think about is how fabulous her cake was? Normally I'd probably have yelled at her by now, telling her to shut the fuck up, but nothing is normal about this evening. The last thing I need is her wailing and screaming, so I keep quiet and ignore her. If she's bothered by my lack of response, she doesn't mention it.

When we get to the room I pull the key card from my pocket and after the beep, push the handle inwards. There's an overpowering scent of lilies as I enter the room, and it seems the hotel has gone all out and put a massive bouquet of them on a black lacquered table in the middle of the hallway. It's nearly enough to give me a headache. Heading straight for the minibar, I grab the biggest bottle of water I can find and neck it in one go. While I'd dearly like to drown my sorrows in a mountain of alcohol, I don't dare. Very shortly it could mean the difference between life and death.

Meanwhile, Helena's heels come skittering towards me, sliding across the marble floor as she kicks them off one by one. There's then the rasp of a zipper and a frustrated mewl.

'Would you help me, darling?' she purrs. 'I can't seem to get this thing off.' Sidling up to me, she turns and rubs her body against mine. This is the last thing I need. Sex is most definitely not on my mind. But I guess I can help her out of her dress. At least it's not her wedding dress. After dinner she changed into a simple gold satin ballgown that hugs her figure in all the right places. A lot of men's eyes lingered on my bride, and I didn't feel the tiniest jot of jealousy. In fact, she could go and sleep with one of them now, and I wouldn't give a damn. Actually, she could sleep with ten of them, and I'd be glad they were taking her off my hands.

Lowering the zipper slowly, making sure I don't tear the fabric, I breathe a sigh of relief when the task is over. With any luck she'll want to go take a shower, and leave me to be miserable in peace.

'Where shall we make love, darling? You wanna do it on the bed, or try out the hot tub?' She then flings her naked body around me and attaches her lips to mine. Oh, God. This isn't happening. I don't push her away, not immediately. I know that however I handle this an argument is about to ensue, and I want to employ some damage control. While there is no way I am sleeping with Helena, ever, she doesn't need to know that. For now a decent excuse will do, and I have the perfect one.

'I can't Helena, not right now. I've got to go out there and kill a girl in a few minutes' time, and that's all I can think about.' I'm not even lying. Kissing her forehead, I gently push her away from me. Hopefully there won't be any screaming or slapping. I'm nearing the end of my tether as it is. All I can think about is Harper. What is Mal doing to her right now? Is he torturing her? Fucking her? Killing her? What if I can't hold up my end of the bargain? What then? *You'll be dead, idiot, and so will she.*

Helena pouts and gives me the wobbly lip, which means hysterics are about to follow unless a miracle happens. For a second I almost wish I was back in jail. Things were a lot simpler inside.

A sharp rap on the door wipes my darling wife's drama queen face clean off, so I guess miracles are real. In any case, I'm extremely thankful that we've delayed the bedroom chat until I'm more able to deal with it. Shooing Helena away to the safety of the bathroom, I stride forward to open the door.

Bad Suit Guy resides on the other side. He's looking considerably more rumpled than he did this morning, and he smells worse, too. Inwardly, I sigh.

'Can I help you?' I ask, trying my best to keep my temper under wraps. While this is a welcome intrusion, I suspect he's not here to give me any good news.

'No, but I can help you.' He hands me a bulky manila envelope, which weighs a ton, and says, 'Have you figured it out yet?' He can only mean one thing, so I don't bother to beat around the bush.

'Francis, the accountant?' I say, a little too optimistically.

Bad Suit Guy blinks at me. 'Mal said you were intelligent,' he says, frowning. Probably wondering how he's going to break the news of my new target to me.

'You want me to kill Francesca, the girl, right?' I decide to put him out of his misery. The longer he's here, the more chance there is of us being seen together.

He nods, obviously relieved.

'That's the one. They have a car coming for them at midnight. Make sure the job's done before then. Understood?' He turns around and walks away without waiting for confirmation.

'Is there any chance there's a getaway car waiting outside for me when this is all over?' I know there isn't, but I feel the need to get the last word in.

'No fucking chance,' is his quick reply, and in the next instant he's rounded a corner which pretty much puts an end to that conversation. Looks like he got the last word in, too. Fuck it.

The manila envelope contains a gun. A Beretta, according to the wording above the trigger. Staggering to the nearest sofa, I nearly fall into it as I realise how tonight is going to go down. God damn. What Mal failed to factor into this little equation is that I have no idea how to use a gun. I have no clue how to aim one. Yeah, I know you point the barrel at your target, but I figure you need a bit of practise to shoot someone where it hurts. If the little lady I'm expected to kill has bodyguards, the first shot has to count. If I miss, I'm not going to get a second chance. Perhaps this was what Mal had been hoping for all along. The likelihood of the rich kid falling at the first hurdle is almost guaranteed. Then he can break the good news to Harper.

When I hear the sound of the shower running full pelt in the bathroom, I am relieved to find my wife is occupied for the time being. Turning the gun over in my hand, I wonder if I'll actually be able to use it. Is the thing even loaded? I assume so, but have no clue how to check. I might need a five-minute tutorial to get to grips with the thing. As it is, it feels like dynamite in my hand. I don't want to touch it, much less use it, and I need to get over it. Yes, the girl is a kid, but she's part of a crime family that extorts money and kills people for a living. They pump the streets full of drugs and put knives and guns in the hands of dangerous people. I'll actually be doing society a favour. Yeah, keep telling yourself that, Brandt.

The shower stops and Helena walks out, her eyes zeroing in on my present.

'Wow.' That wasn't the word I'd have used, but I'm not going to contradict her. 'It's a nice piece, that. Have you used a Beretta 92 before?' She walks over to me, wrapped in nothing more than a towel, and sits down in my lap. The woman doesn't seem at all bothered that I'm holding a gun. If the situation had been reversed, I'd like to think I might be a bit more concerned.

'No, have you?' I'm guessing she isn't completely clueless as she spotted the brand and make of the gun from halfway across the room.

'Yes. Obviously not in the UK because they're banned over here, but my cousin owns a ranch in Texas. He taught me how to use one. I didn't fire it at anything other than tin cans, but I do know how it works. All I've done here is clay pigeon shooting.' Helena is one step ahead of me then.

'Great. So show me how to use the thing.' I hand her the gun.

She then proceeds to show me how to make sure it's loaded and how to aim by lining up the sights. Bar pulling the trigger, this is all I need to know, she tells me.

'Seriously, this will be a piece of cake, Brandt. We'll shoot her and get the hell out.' Her fingers find the nape of my neck and she curls her hands around me, before kissing me on the lips. I let her; we're on the same side for the moment.

'There is no 'we', Helena. You are staying here.' She pulls away from my lips before giving me a mulish look. She then shakes her head at me.

'If you think I'm staying here while you—'

I cut her off.

'Promise me, Helena.' There is no way the two of us are going down. It's bad enough that I've managed to get myself into this mess in the first place. There's no way she's getting involved too. I've accepted the fact that I'm not coming out of this alive, but I'm sure as hell not taking anyone with me.

'Brandt, I'm part of this too. You need to let me—'

'Promise me.' I'm not taking no for an answer. If I have to I'll tie her up and leave her here, but there's no way she's following me.

Helena looks at me, and something in my eyes must convince her I'm serious because she backs down. 'Okay, fine, I'll stay here, but please be careful. Those guys don't mess around. You need to get the girl first time and run.' She isn't telling me anything I don't already know.

'I'll be fine,' I say, lying.

'I know you will,' she says, gazing at me adoringly. 'There is no way you're dying on me before we've even been married a day.'

That's where she's wrong, but I don't contradict her. What I do need to do is get away from her ASAP.

'Right. I'd better get moving. The sooner this is over with the better.' Gently depositing her on her own two feet, I decide I'd better get dressed. I'm going to be a little bit conspicuous in my wedding attire.

'Don't you think we ought to consummate the marriage first, sweetheart? You don't have to go down straight away. Why not take a moment to enjoy yourself first? They'll still be there in an hour.' Helena moves towards me once again, but I am already striding past her.

'I can't concentrate on anything else until this is all over, darling,' I say, quite truthfully as it happens. There's also the matter that I don't find my new wife in the least bit sexually appealing, but now is not the time for that conversation. Anyway, given my updated and much decreased life expectancy, I figure it's not going to be a problem for too much longer.

'Brandt, why don't you just grab a drink and relax for a minute?' The pout is back but I'm having none of it, so I shake my head.

'I'm going to get showered and changed, and then I'm going downstairs. The sooner this is over, the better.' I mean it, too. I'm sick of waiting. I just want this over with.

Heading straight for the shower, I don't give Helena a chance to try and change my mind. Thankfully there's a lock on the door, and the next ten minutes are mine and mine alone. I need this time to get my head around what's coming.

When I'm finished I go straight to my suitcase and take out a pair of black pants and a white shirt. I want to blend in. If anyone mistakes me for the wait staff, so much the better. There's a good chance someone will recognise me, but you'd be surprised how you suddenly become nearly invisible when you're one of the hired help. To aid with my transformation I don't gel my hair back, but leave it brushed forward over my forehead. I'll still need to stick to the shadows, but I don't intend to mingle. Besides, by this point most of our guests will be too pissed to notice anything. The Queen of England could waltz in and no one would be any the wiser. By the time I get downstairs I'll be lucky if some of them aren't already passed out on the floor.

Helena, who's been strangely quiet since I've come out of the shower, suddenly pipes up.

'You'll need a bowtie if you want to pass for one of the waiters.'

Dangling a black one from her fingertips, she sashays over. The woman is now dressed in a negligee, if you can call that dressed, and nearly any other man on the planet would give his eyeteeth to tear it off her, but honestly, I don't think of her that way. There's only one woman on my mind, and I'll be lucky if I ever see her again.

'How did you get that?' My brow furrows as she winds the silky fabric around my neck, fastening it with swift, deft moves. She's clearly done this before.

'I always come prepared. Know your enemy and all that.' She winks at me. 'You'll do.'

For the first time since we met at the airport I give her a genuine kiss of affection, although it's only on her cheek. Helena's stupid, vain, often annoying and a vicious snob, but she's not a bad person. I don't know exactly what circumstances have led her to get tangled up with Mal, but I hope she manages to get out from under his clutches.

'Wish me luck?' I smile at her and take a deep breath.

She shakes her head and smiles back. 'You won't need it,' she says confidently.

That's where our thoughts differ. I have a feeling I will need it - and lots of it.

Three-quarters of an hour later I am down in the hotel lobby, staying close to the shadows as I try to work out where Francesca is. The gun is burning a hole in the inside pocket of a jacket I stole from the staff room not moments ago. While I was there, I also grabbed a big silver serving platter that I try to keep in front of my face whenever I can. As the staff are currently walking around with plates from the evening buffet, I should fit right in.

I'm petrified. The last thing I need is to be recognised. Mind you, maybe that's what Mal wants. Maybe he wants my face plastered all over the papers as this evening turns into a monstrous mess. It wouldn't surprise me. As I walk around the hotel, my eyes scanning everywhere for the girl I'm about to kill, all I want to do is scream. Can I do this? I don't know if I can, even if it is to save Harper and Gabriel. I don't know if I'm that kind of person. *You've got to try. You won't know until that gun is in your hand, pointing directly at your target. Remember, she's not an innocent party in all of this. She'll grow up to be a sleazebag, just like her father. She'll be pedalling drugs and assaulting people before you know it. Will she though? She might just be an innocent bystander who never gets involved in any of this.*

Filled with all sorts of misgivings I continue my search for Francesca. It will probably be a blessing in disguise if I don't find her. If she's disappeared I can't kill her - problem solved. Somehow, though, I suspect things aren't going to be that easy. When I find the dancefloor I'm grateful that the room is so dark you can barely see a thing. Most of our guests are now staggering about, lurching from side to side as they expel some of their alcohol calories. Most will be lucky if they don't spend half the night doubled over in the bathroom. I'm almost jealous. These people don't realise how lucky they are. I don't remember the last time I felt like I had a carefree existence. All I do know, is that it was a very long time ago.

My eyes scan the floor, carefully assessing the crowd. I was almost positive she'd be on the dancefloor, strutting her stuff, but there is no sign of her. Where's a teenage girl likely to be at this time of night? Damn it. Putting my tray in front of my face once again, I walk as fast as I can to the bar and the tables beyond. No one is going to stop me, if I have anything to say about it. In my head I'm currently trying to figure out all the places she could be. Bar, lobby, toilet, or maybe she went back to her room? Who knows?

In the lobby I spot her father. He's sprawled on a leather Chesterfield sofa and he's talking animatedly on his cell. He has two men sitting beside him, who must be bodyguards, but there is no sign of his daughter. I wait around for a few minutes, hovering in an empty hallway, wondering if she'll come back to join him soon. Ten minutes pass and there's still no sign of her. It appears Daddy has left her to her own devices. Just as I'm about to turn around and go back to the dancefloor someone bursts in a set of double doors, sending a freezing draft of air in with them. The area beyond is lit up with fairy lights, and leads out to a courtyard garden. Maybe Francesca has gone outside to cool off. It's a possibility.

Shoving my serving platter down on an empty table, I make my way outside as quickly as possible. From the corner of my eye I spy someone putting a hand in the air, trying their best to attract my attention, but I concentrate on walking straight past them. The last thing I need is a request for two gin and tonics and three pints of beer. My fingers are firmly crossed that they do not come running after me, so I move as quickly as I can.

The night air greets me like a bucket full of water - quite literally. The rain around me is lashing out in driving waves of malevolence, and the air is about as frigid as a woman who's been dumped by her partner for her best friend. When I step outside it almost feels as if someone's dropped two tonnes of snow down the back of my neck, but it doesn't put me off. I need to know if she's out here. If she is, the girl is damn stupid and will probably die of hypothermia before long, but teenagers aren't known for their common sense. Maybe she's been partying hard and needed to cool off? Stranger things have happened.

The terrace is surrounded by topiary trees, in rectangular oak planters that are covered with hanging ivy. There's a wooden pergola above my head, where more ivy hangs, as do a myriad of plain white lightbulbs. Tables are dotted under angled, white canvas panels that are currently sagging with rainwater. No one is sitting at them. When I look over them I can see the hotel floors stretching high above me, one by one, blotting out the sky. A few lights are on inside the rooms, but not many. Most of the guests haven't gone to bed yet. London is still in party mode.

Turning around to go back inside, I stop when I hear a squeal - a female one. Frozen to the spot I look all around me, but I can't see anyone. I stand there for two minutes, wondering if I'm going crazy, and finally I decide I am. Maybe I imagined it? Just as I'm about to head indoors there's a giggle.

'How did you give your dad the slip?' This time it's a young male voice, and I think it's coming from a small wooden shed to the side of the garden. It's difficult to tell with the rain still pelting down.

'I told him I was off to the ladies. He doesn't send the goons with me if I'm off to the toilet. The hotel has CCTV everywhere, so he's not worried about me in here.' There's more giggling, and it's definitely coming from what I suspect is a storage shed, so I shift on over.

'How long do you think we have?' There's another squeal, and I'm guessing the little tyke has just copped a feel.

'Not long. Ten minutes, fifteen at most, before the BFGs come looking for me.'

The young man snorts. 'You call your dad's bodyguards BFGs? Ouch.'

'You talk too much. Shut the fuck up and get on with it. I may have mentioned we don't have much time.' I can hear slurping, so by the sounds of things he's taken her at her word.

When the guy comes up for air, he asks, 'You really want me to do it here?'

I've heard enough. All I really need to do is confirm that the girl is Francesca and then shoot her. It's a bit annoying that she has a bloke with her because it's extremely likely that I'm going to have to shoot him too. Oh well. It could be worse. If we were inside the hotel, with the BFGs, it would probably be mass murder on a grand scale.

Pulling the gun out of my pocket I glare at it, as if it's about to blow my hand off. Mal hasn't provided me with a silencer, which is telling. When I pull the trigger, this thing is going to announce my presence to half of London. I've already figured that Mal wants me to go down noisily, probably so he can show Harper the news report of me being led away in cuffs - or being shot. The latter is more likely. When those bodyguards hear the noise they'll be out here faster than a rocket with lightspeed turbo-boosters. Okay, maybe not quite that fast. What is wrong with me? Just get on with it.

Edging around the side of the shed I note that the door is open. The two lovebirds haven't bothered to close it, probably thinking that no one would be stupid enough to follow them out here in the rain. Normally they'd be right. Unfortunately, tonight is not their night. Craning my head around to the entrance, I try to keep most of my body behind the shed while I peer inside. One quick glance is all I need. It's Francesca. It couldn't have been anyone else, really. Pulling my head back around, so I can stay hidden, I lean against the side of the shed with my chest heaving. The gun is shaking in my hand. What the fuck am I doing?

More squeals and giggles are coming from inside as the two kids continue making out, and I am standing there shivering, my hair plastered to the side of my head, frozen to the spot. She's just a girl. It doesn't matter which way I paint this, I can't justify shooting a child. If Mal had asked me to shoot her father, that might have been different, but I can't do this. I'm not made that way. My hands are shaking so hard I won't be able to aim the gun anyway. This isn't happening. No way. If I have to sacrifice Harper and Gabriel in the process, so be it. I'm not a child killer. Fuck this. Fuck my life. And while I'm at it, my death had also better be fucking quick. Putting my face in my hands, I try my best not to scream out loud.

Two shots ring out in the darkness, startling me so much I nearly drop the gun. They weren't loud, but you couldn't mistake them for anything else. It looks like someone has beaten me to it, and they've hired a professional. What do I do now?

If they find me they're going to kill me too. Oh Jesus. What a fucking evening.

'For crying out loud, Brandt, you look like a ghost. They're dead. Breathe.' I know that voice. Oh. My. God.

'Helena? Is that you?' It's a stupid question. I know it's her. I just can't believe it.

'Get in here and put these on. We don't have much time if we want to get out of here alive.' She yanks on my arm, pulling me into the shed where I come face to face with Francesca and her buddy, who now have matching holes in the middle of their foreheads. It's an image I'm not going to be able to unsee for quite some time. By some miracle I don't retch all over the floor in front of me, but it's a close-run thing.

Helena is thrusting a pair of black jeans and a black shirt in front of me. I grab them instinctively, not really knowing what I'm doing. Thankfully she seems to be on top of things. She's wiggling out of the black catsuit she's wearing and removing a black scarf from her hair. Stepping into a pair of blue jeans, she then pulls a cream jumper over her head.

'Didn't you hear me? Hurry the fuck up. They'll be out here before we know it.'

That finally spurs me into action. Changing into the jeans she's just given me, we stuff our old clothes into a bag she's carrying.

When I've finished Helena is already back out in the garden. 'Follow me,' she says, and I do. Even I'm not stupid enough to wait around. All hell is about to break loose, and I want to be as far away as possible.

Helena strides off ahead, but she doesn't go back through the bar area. Instead she heads for a fire door which is situated at the back of the courtyard, and by some miracle it happens to be open. Pushing through it we head through a darkened corridor at the back of the staff quarters, which leads around to the front of the hotel. At this time of the evening it's empty, and I am glad of the fact. We've barely gone twenty metres when all of a sudden we're in the bright glare of the hotel reception, coming in through a side entrance. Helena is still marching onwards, heading for the revolving doors which lead outside to freedom. Surely it cannot be so easy, can it?

It is. When we get to the steps outside there's a car waiting for us, and we jump inside. I have no idea where we are going, and I don't care.

Chapter Sixteen - Gabriel

'Here, have mine. I'm not hungry.' Pushing my plate of stale pizza towards Harper, I watch as she shakes her head. The action maddens me. She's sick. She's needs to eat. There is no convincing her though. It's like she's already accepted the fact she's going to die in here. I'm not having it.

'Eat,' I threaten, almost growling at her. I can't watch her starve herself to death. She looks bad enough as it is.

'No.' She pushes the plate back at me. 'You need it more than I do. If we stand any chance at getting out of here, it will be because of you. Keep your strength up.

I'm used to being hungry. This is no big deal for me.' To make matters worse she then pats me on the arm, encouraging me to go ahead and eat the damn thing. I want to scream. The girl is so selfless and unassuming that I just want to wrap her up in my arms and tell her everything will be okay. I don't, because I don't like lying. At the moment there is no guarantee of anything at all.

Picking up a slice of pizza that's seen better days, I split it in two and hand her half. 'Eat. If you don't eat yours I won't eat mine.' This tactic has worked for me before, and my fingers are crossed that it will work again. 'I mean it,' I add when she looks ready to argue.

She sighs but accepts the offering. We both then bite into the cold dough and grimace. It's unpleasant, but it's some kind of sustenance, I guess.

Mal's kept Harper and I locked up for days inside this pathetically tiny room. Sometimes he remembers to feed us, sometimes he doesn't. We're lucky there's a bathroom, else we'd probably have died of dehydration by now too.

And speaking of Mal, the bastard is on his cell phone outside. I swear he should have that thing glued to his ear. Mind you, it's probably the only thing keeping him from spending all day in here with us, so his phone is a godsend.

'Are you okay?' I've been awake for hours, but Harper is sleeping longer and longer. Her body is weak and it can't heal itself, not without proper nourishment, and she's not going to get that here. We both know we're not leaving here alive - which is why we can't stay here much longer. It will only be another day or two before Harper is unable to walk, and I'm not leaving her here. I can't leave her with him. Even though I'm already going to hell, the devil would have a special place for me if I left this poor girl here with that monster. There are no words for what he does to her. No. Fucking. Words.

'I'm fine,' she whispers. It's a standard response. She's not fine, and she hasn't been fine for a long time. I have no idea how she's managed to last as long as she has, but I'm praying she can last just a day or two longer.

'Hang on in there. We will get out of this,' I whisper, squeezing her hand tight. I'm working on something. At the minute there are a few holes in my plan, but I'm ironing out the wrinkles. I just need a decent distraction. Then we're good to go.

She nods, but I can tell from the look in her eyes that she doesn't believe me. She thinks this is a one-way street from which there is no escape. I refuse to believe that. I've been in tighter situations, and I'm still here to tell the tale.

'Can you handle him tonight?' I already know the answer to that, and it's a no. Harper's reactions are getting slower and slower, mostly because she's sick, and Mal's patience is wearing thin. She needs to be at the top of her game when he's in the room, and at the moment that just isn't possible.

'Yes,' she whispers. It's a lie, but she says it with such conviction. How is it possible that such a small girl can possess such strength? I have no idea, but I wish I had half of what she does. I know for a fact there's no way I'd have lasted this long under his hands.

When Mal comes back in from his phone call, he is in a bad mood. He doesn't say anything, but I can tell from his wooden movements and by the way his jaw has hardened. I'm good at reading people like that. Perhaps someone has stiffed him on a haul, perhaps he's caught someone dipping their fingers in the till, or perhaps one of his rivals is trying to expand their territory - whatever it is, Mal's long face says it all. He's going to take his ill humour out on us, and by 'us,' I mean Harper.

Walking over to the half-opened bottle of Jack, he pours himself a generous measure of whisky before his glance then flicks over Harper's massacred body. He then smiles, obviously deciding life isn't all that bad. This doesn't bode well.

'Miss me?' he asks, when Harper glares at him.

'Go fuck yourself,' she replies, and her dark sable eyes spit fire in his direction. This turns Mal on. I can see it from a mile away. If I were her, I'd play the meek little pussycat because he's intent on putting her through hell. Takes one to know one.

He slowly circles her, admiring my handiwork, while he swirls his whisky around in the glass.

'You're not still counting on Brandt coming to your rescue you, are you?' A hand comes down to squeeze her ass, and she yells out loud. She's got good reason to. I've caned that ass to a pulp at Mal's request and it's black and blue, along with every other colour of the rainbow. I wince for her.

'I'm not counting on anyone coming to rescue me,' she says feebly. 'I'd given up on that idea a long time ago. Why don't we just stop this nonsense? Let Gabriel go, and then you can concentrate on killing me. Let's just get on with this.'

Mal shakes his head. 'Oh, I don't think so, 'Arper. I've got big plans for us and I don't intend to rush 'em. In fact, I've got a little video I want to share with you, as it 'appens.' He pulls an iPad out of the bedside drawer and switches it on. He then passes it over to Harper, who is so sick she can barely lift the thing. In a few seconds the sound of bells can be heard - wedding bells. Oh fuck. I know what he's showing her. The man is such an evil fucker.

Harper's eyes are glued to the screen, and Mal watches her face with glee. He wants to hurt her in any way he can, and on the physical side of things he's running out of time. She bounces in and out of consciousness at the moment. He's becoming frustrated that she isn't more responsive. If he fed the poor girl it might help. She was already half-starved before she got here. There's only so many ways you can torture someone, and he's going to run out of options soon.

Mal cares about none of this, of course. He's just interested in digging the knife in, as far and as deep as it will go. As Harper continues watching her fingers tighten around the screen. Her hands begin shaking as she realises exactly what she's watching. Mal doesn't say anything, he just drinks in her expression of pain. When the video clip is finally over he decides it's time to hammer his point home.

'See how much your precious man cares about you? After he left you, it took him less than a week to move on. Seems he's really cut up about you, Harper. Looks like he's missing you dreadfully.' He's trying to make her believe that Brandt never cared about her. What he's failed to factor into the equation, is that Brandt had already told her he was being forced into marriage. While it might not make what she's watching any more palatable, she will at least understand it.

'What a bastard, eh?' he sneers. 'Do you think we should kill him? I'd do that for you, Harper. I'd put an end to that miserable little shit. All you have to do is ask.'

I now understand his game. He wants to kill Brandt, but he wants Harper to think it's her idea. It's going to backfire on him. I'm ninety-nine percent certain she's not going to play his game, which means he'll revert to Plan B, whatever that might be.

'Finish me, Mal. I don't want anyone else killed. Brandt was never mine in the first place. We would never have worked. I told Alex this years ago, and you know it.' She lays the iPad back on the bed and pushes her head against the pillows, lost in thought. I suspect none of them are pleasant, but there isn't much I can do for her at the moment.

Mal stares at her, and he looks like someone has just yanked the jam from his donut. He was almost positive she'd ask him to kill Brandt, and that hasn't happened. Poor baby. Score one for Harper.

'Don't you have any pride?' he whispers. He can't understand why she's not mad as hell right now. Considering all the time they've spent together, he has underestimated the girl big time.

'No. Alex took it away a long time ago, and you haven't done much for it since. I'm not mad. I'm not bothered. Finish this, Mal.' Her last words have bite. She's had enough, and I can't say I blame her.

'You're still holding a candle for the guy, aren't you? Even after all these years, you still worship the fucking ground he walks on, don't you?' Mal is angry and has started pacing. It's clear today hasn't panned out the way he hoped it would.

Harper doesn't say anything; she just looks at the floor, which confirms everything he's thinking. She should be denying this shit, if only to placate the bastard, but she does no such thing. I'm losing her. She can't even be bothered to play the game any more. I hope this doesn't backfire on her. Mal will want to hurt her even more after this, and I'm not sure I can beat the shit out of her again for his amusement. I might have to kill him. Yeah, we'll both die, but at least we'll go down quick.

'What do you want from me, Mal?' she whispers. 'You made me watch while you killed my husband, and then you decided you'd take his place. Did you expect us to be best buddies after that? I'm broken. I'll always be fucking broken. Just because you picked up the pieces that were left, it doesn't mean you can figure out how to put them back together again. End this. I'm sick. I'm tired. If you don't end it soon, I'll die on you anyway.' Harper then picks up the iPad once more and throws it at him. She can't throw it very hard or far, but it does hit him before crashing to the floor. The splintering sound suggests that Mal won't be using it to show her any videos in the near future.

His face darkens at her outburst. 'You aren't going anywhere unless I allow it!' he yells. 'I own you. If you don't want to take care of Brandt, that's your problem - but I'm going to.' He sits on the bed beside her and runs a single finger down her bruised body. Some of that work is his and some of its mine. I'm going to have nightmares about the stuff he's made me do to her, and I've never lost a day's sleep over anyone in my life, so that should tell you something.

'Leave him be. He's suffered enough. Wasn't putting him in prison for five years enough for you? What more do you want?' I can see Harper's chest heaving as she struggles for air. Arguing with the monster is taking more energy than she's got to spare. She isn't going to make it through the evening. I need to get us out of here.

Mal's finger digs between one of her ribs, making her gasp.

'Remember that gun I had you plant on him, along with the drugs? Although his fingerprints were on it, they couldn't tie it to a crime at the time, could they?' His fingers are now running around in circles over her right breast, and I have a bad feeling about where this conversation is headed. 'That gun was used to kill someone, Harper. All it would take is a quick conversation with a copper, and they'll be able to find the body and bullet. Forensics will do the rest. Five years is nothing compared to the amount of time he'll spend inside for murder, especially as he'll be reoffending this time. It's awfully easy to kill someone when they're on the other side of those metal bars. I've already given the nod to one of my contacts. As soon as he's back inside, he's dead. Say your goodbye's, princess. He's not long for this world.'

Harper comes to life pretty quickly. Jumping off the bed she stands in front of him and her fists pummel at his chest. 'No. You promised. You said you wouldn't hurt him. I've done what you've asked. Leave him out of this. He has nothing to do with it. What are you going to do, kill every damn bloke I take a glance at?' One of her fingernails scratches his cheek and he grabs her wrist in a vicious, vicelike grip. There's a scream, and for a moment I think he might have broken her arm. Thankfully she drags it away from him, so at least I know she's still in one piece.

Mal doesn't take kindly to being pushed around though. He slaps her across the cheek with so much force she goes staggering backwards, and I'm tempted to dart halfway across the room to try and catch her. I don't, but it's only because I know I'd do her more harm than good.

'If that's what it takes to make you see sense, precious, then yes. That's exactly what I'll do.' Mal puffs himself up like a lilo and sticks his chest in her face. Harper doesn't back down. I don't know whether to smack her upside the head for her stupidity or applaud her bravery. She's endured years of this. Anyone else would have gone stir crazy long ago.

'You gonna kill him too?' Harper sticks a thumb over her shoulder my way. I look taken aback, but it's all an act. I know damn well Mal's going to kill me. Actually, let me rephrase that. I know that Mal wants to kill me, and he's going to give it his best shot. I'm going to do my best to get the hell out of here before it comes to that.

'Yes, of course I'm gonna kill him. I'm hardly likely to keep him around for a souvenir, am I? Why? Please don't tell me you like him too?' Mal's face darkens, but Harper throws her hands in the air and screams again.

'What is wrong with you?' She sits back down on the bed. 'Fine, if you want to be an asshole you go ahead. I don't like the fucker anyway.' I don't take this as a personal insult. I know she's just trying to protect me. But she's wasting her breath. If Mal wants to end me, no one is going to get in his way.

'Good. But I'm not going to kill him until we watch the footage of Brandt being arrested. Maybe I'll even drag it out until I put an end to the rich kid. They were friends, after all.'

Those words make me want to wrap my hands around his neck and squeeze for all they're worth, but I continue to lean nonchalantly against the wall, as if I haven't a care in the world. This is how Mal runs his empire. Intimidation and his ever-worsening reputation are the way he gets people to do his bidding with no questions asked. The more crazy-assed shit he pulls, the more his guys are scared of him - so it's a win/win as far as he's concerned. I know the score. It's not too different in prison. The stakes are higher here though. There's lots of money to be earned, and you've got to try your best to remain on the right side of the law if you want to enjoy your spoils. That generally involves more money, and quite a bit of corruption. I wonder who the bastard has screwed over in order to get where he is? There'll be a lot of people on his payroll, that much I know for sure.

'When you die, I hope someone drags it out for the longest time possible,' Harper says sourly. Fuck. She's not even worried about getting into trouble now. The woman seems to be actively courting it. I can only limit the damage of what I do to her so much. Every time Mal makes me do his dirty work things get progressively worse, and I can't take much more of it. I'm amazed that she's still speaking to me as it is. If I'm honest, I'm amazed she's still alive, full stop.

Mal stands in front of her, fuming, and then slaps her around the face again. 'When are you going to learn a little respect, darling? Why do you need to do everything the hard way?' It's a good fucking question. I wish she'd shut the hell up. I could use a break.

'I'm bored with this, Mal. Had enough of the whole fucking deal. There's only so many times you can torment someone with the threat of death. I'm over it. I want to die. In fact, I'll beg you to end me on my knees if that'll get you excited. Just let me know.'

His face tightens, his expression a black cloud of fury. Jesus Christ, what has she done now? I can't do damage control if she's pouring gasoline on the fire. Just gimme a fricking chance, woman. The way she's going there'll be nothing of her body left but ash.

Mal spins around to face me. 'Get her on her knees. On the floor. Now!' He can barely talk with rage, and I don't make the mistake of disobeying him. Hauling her off the bed, I make it look like I'm slamming her into the concrete floor, but in reality her landing is a soft one.

He walks around the bed until his shiny black loafers stop in front of her nose. I can see the tension vibrating through his body, and I'm desperately thinking of a way I can get her out of here without being shot. This is coming to crunch point. The trouble is, one wrong move on my part could end everything.

He grabs a handful of her straggly brown locks and pulls her face up to his. 'Apologise for being a naughty girl, Harper, or I promise you won't like what comes next.'

There's a period of horrible silence in which I pray with everything I have that she does as she's told. I don't want to be a party to this. Unfortunately for me, though, I'm an atheist and no God worth his salt is going to listen to my prayers very carefully.

When she finally speaks her voice is reed thin. 'Fuck you. Hurt me already. It's what you do best, Mal. We both know that's what you live for. Isn't it a crying fucking shame that the first girl you fall in love with can't love you back?' Just to make her point clear, she spits in his face.

Holy hell. That cat has some scary-as-shit claws. There's no way he's going to take that lying down. What is she playing at? If she gets me killed I am never going to forgive her for this. I only just got out of the clink for crying out loud.

In response Mal uses her hair to shake her head. He won't let this go. No way. Releasing her hair and throwing her head back to the floor he says, 'Now, now, now,' in a condescending tone. He looks like he's calmed down, but I know that is not the case. This is the eye of the storm and the shit is about to hit the fan. Sure enough, the man keeps going. 'You're going to pay for that little outburst, sweetheart. Remember how I make you pay when you really upset me? We haven't done that for a long time, have we? Maybe it's time we revisited that little number.'

She seems to come around then. Her head snaps up to look at him, and she almost cowers backwards as she says, 'No, you promised.' Her words are a mere whisper.

'My promises don't mean shit any more,' he retorts. 'If you don't play nicely I'm not going to play nicely. Simple as.' He dusts his hands off in front of her. Harper immediately begins shaking.

'No. I can't go through that again. No. No, no, no. I'll do anything you want. Name it.' She hunkers down on the floor in a small ball, as if that is somehow going to save her. Something is freaking her out. The question is: what?

Mal's attention is no longer on her though. It's on me. What does he want now?

'Tie her to the bed!' he barks. I want to roll my eyes. The poor girl has spent most of her time here tied to the bed while I've spanked, whipped, caned, flogged or paddled her. She hasn't made a single complaint. Sure, she's screamed and cried like a baby, but not once has she uttered a word to try and stop me. Mal always finishes the evening off. Sometimes he lets her come, and she does - like a fucking steam train, over and over again. Other times he leaves her sobbing for release. When the lights go off and he's long gone, I sort her out. It's not much, but it's the least I can do to make up for the hours of torture I've put her through.

Hauling her back on the bed, which isn't the easiest as she's now a dead weight, I carefully cuff her hands to the headboard. Her wrists are already ringed with bright pink sores from where she's pulled against them.

'That's it. Do her legs too. You need to make sure she's firmly secured. She's going to thrash around like crazy in a minute. Trust me.' My back is to him, and I swear my eyes light up like the fires of hell because Harper looks at me and smiles. She smiles, dammit, like I'm about to read her a bedtime story. Fuck it. I can't take much of this.

The next thing I hear is the door slamming, and at least I can breathe a little easier for the moment. I have no idea where Mal's gone, but he'll be getting something nasty - guaranteed.

'Do you want me to take him out? I can do it in less than ten seconds. Boom. My foot will crack that asshole's skull in two, and yeah the goons will come running but there's a chance we might make it. I can't keep hurting you like this. I'm starting to get acid reflux at the thought.'

Harper snorts as if this is funny.

'I'm serious,' I say. 'Either three-day old pizza is giving me indigestion or I'm developing a conscience in my old age. I'm hoping it's the former, otherwise I'm losing my touch.'

'As if you could. You just have to look at women to melt their panties right off them. Yeah, you like to play the tough guy, but inside you're all gooey marshmallow really.' She bites her lip as she speaks. She obviously finds the conversation amusing. How she can find humour in this situation is beyond me.

'Fluffy marshmallow, huh?' My expression is wry and she snorts again. 'You'd better have a good explanation for what you just pulled back there, or I will show you what I'm really made of, and you won't like it much.' I raise my eyebrows and give her a look that makes men twice my size wobble at the knees. It does fuck all to Harper, of course.

'Oh, ye of little faith. We need to get to Brandt before Mal does. If he gets that thing to the police he'll be inside for twenty years or more. We're running out of time. You wanted a distraction, right? Well, Mal's about to bring a shit load of psychotropic drugs in here. Your job is to shove some of those into his bottle of Jack. It only came to me a moment ago, but it's the only thing I can think of so let's run with it. You'll still have to deal with the goons outside, but hopefully we'll figure something out.'

I only hear half of what she's just said because I'm focusing on the 'psychotropic drugs' part. 'He's going to slip you something nasty?' I want to know what we're dealing with.

She nods. 'Yes. He used to do it to me a long time ago, when he was trying to get me to kill Alex. The stuff is awful. It causes me to hallucinate something wicked, and I'm going to get freaky on you.' She shrugs. 'The good news is that I'm a ninety-pound weakling. Mal might be more difficult to handle, and I won't be able to help you. Just make sure you kill the fucker. If you have to leave me here, fine; but make sure he's dead. Promise me you'll go get Brandt.'

I do no such thing. 'You're coming with me. There is no way I'm leaving you here, and that's the last I want to hear about it.' When she bites her lip and gives me a mournful look I nearly lose it. 'I mean it; not another word.' My face goes hard and she gets the message. 'I don't care if you scratch my eyes out after taking whatever shit he's going to give you or if you try to hit me with all you have. I'll drag you out of here kicking and screaming if I have to, but I'm not leaving without you. Brandt would kill me.'

'Fine, have it your way,' she says, batting her eyelashes and rattling her handcuffs theatrically, 'but you should know you're not going to look so pretty tomorrow morning.' She sticks her tongue out at me. Honestly. How can she make jokes at a time like this? There is no doubt in my mind she is the strongest woman I know.

My tongue is firmly in my cheek as I answer her. 'It's doubtful, seeing as you're rather tied up at the moment. But if you do manage to lump me one, you'll be doing me a favour. It's a pain having women draped around my shoulders everywhere I go.' Hey, if she can joke, I can too. I don't smile though.

'Poor baby,' she coos. 'If it's any consolation, I'd still sleep with you even with the black eye I am almost certain to give you.'

This time I do smile. Squeezing her tiny bicep, I say, 'I'm not convinced your right hook is up to much, but you can try, sweetness. You can try.'

Chapter Eighteen - Harper

Gabriel and I know it's crunch time. If we don't get out of here soon Brandt will go down for yet another crime he hasn't committed, and he'll be lucky if he's not claiming his pension by the time he comes out. If he comes out. I can't let that happen. This is all my fault. How can I have been so stupid?

When I planted that gun and those drugs on him five years ago I knew bad things would happen, but I never expected them to be this bad. I thought his parents would bail him out with the best legal eagle money could buy, which would result in nothing more than a firm slap from the judge, followed by six months of community service. That was what I had been told when I asked one of the college lecturers for some friendly advice. He said that leniency would probably be given as he was a first offender and provided he showed remorse his sentence wouldn't be too onerous. How wrong was that guy? The judge in question virtually threw the book at him, and I see no reason to believe that this time will be any different. Brandt's parents haven't spoken to him since he's been released, so any help from them is out of the question. There is a chance Helena's parents might bail him out, but I don't want to risk another disaster. It seems like Mal has it in for Brandt, and if he knows the judge, then anything can happen. I'm not the naive girl I was five years ago. I've seen too much since then. We need to stop this before it blows up in our faces. Once it's exploded, there will be no going back. If I screw up Brandt's life any more than I have already, I will go crazy. There are no two ways about it.

'What's he likely to give you?' Gabriel is looking at me with those dark-as-fuck eyes, and all I can think about is sex. For the last couple of day's he's been horribly tormented by the shit Mal's had him do to me, but for the most part I've enjoyed it, if you can call being in a constant state of arousal enjoyable. There is a definite possibility I could fall in love with the man, but I won't let myself. It would be too dangerous. I've been around men like Gabriel all my life, and it never ends well. If I get through this alive and want a chance at happiness, I need something in-between. Someone who can hurt me but knows when to stop. Gabriel is not that man, even though the thought makes me want to weep. What is wrong with me, anyway? My hormones have gone into hyper-drive just lately. The Gabriel and Brandt mix is enough to push any sane woman into meltdown.

'Probably Zyprexia or Seroquel, though I don't know for sure. The man has access to just about any pharmaceutical under the sun. He's also been known to mix them.' I don't really care what he gives me. I just want Gabriel to stop him from ruining Brandt's life. If he can slip him some of what he's giving me, we're in with a chance.

'Can you handle that? You've barely eaten for days.' There is concern floating in his eyes, and it's ridiculously touching. A week ago the man couldn't stand me, and now look where we are. He's seen what I've had to go through at Mal's hands, and I don't think even he realised how sick and twisted the jerk is. He does now.

'I'm used to going hungry. This is no biggie, trust me.' It is a biggie, but he doesn't have to know that. It'll only make him feel bad, and I hate seeing the tough guy brought low.

The last time I took this stuff was years ago, and on a full stomach. It was pretty damn scary then, and I can't think it will be any better now.

Gabriel gives me a funny look. 'Why is it I think you're lying to me, little lady?' Hey, this guy is good. He can spot a lie from a mile away. Now it's time for deflection.

'We're never getting out of this alive, are we? Even if you kill Mal and all the guards, we'll be dead before the week is out. He had friends everywhere. What are we thinking?' All his men know my face. I've been around too long. There's a chance Gabriel may manage to get out of here, but he won't if I tag along with him. 'You have to leave me behind,' I repeat. 'There's no way you'll escape if I come with you. Taking me will be like painting a target on your back.' I mean it. There is no future that has me in it. He has to realise that.

'We discussed this earlier; I have a plan,' Gabriel says. 'Just concentrate on not getting yourself killed and I'll do the rest, okay?' I can't argue with him again because Mal strolls back in.

He has a bottle of pills in his hand. I have no idea what they are because I can't read the label from here, but they're nothing pleasant, that's for certain. He'll chuck them in some whisky and force me to drink it. It gets into the bloodstream quicker that way, or so I'm told.

'You wanna know what I'm going to do to you, after you've taken these?' Mal asks me.

I shake my head. I don't want to know. If he keeps quiet there's a chance I won't remember either, which would be ace.

'Don't be such a spoilsport, darlin',' he says, pouring a glass of whisky. He then shakes out three pills from the plastic bottle and pulls them apart one by one, letting the powder sink into the drink. I try my best not to watch. I'm not sure how much he should be dosing me with, but that looks like too much. With any luck I might OD on the stuff. Gabriel doesn't look happy either. I can see his jaw tightening.

'Isn't that too much? She'll be out of it if you overload her system.' This is new. Gabriel doesn't usually say a word around Mal. He's worried.

Mal ignores him. He's completely focused on me. 'I think it's about time I got my tube of glue out, don't you, sweetheart? You've seen me work often enough. If you can't play nicely, why shouldn't you suffer a little? If I cut off a couple of fingers and toes, and stick them somewhere else, maybe you'll be a little more amenable next time I ask you to perform. What say you, sweetheart?' My eyes bulge. I hadn't expected him to start this so soon, but to be fair I have been asking for it, in a roundabout kind of way. Oh shit. This is really happening.

'Well, I was wondering when we'd get down to that, darling,' I purr, with my eyes flashing like a Siren's. Watching him swirl the amber liquid around in the glass, to dissolve all the white powder, my legs go to jelly beneath me. Toughen up, girlie. I'm not going to cower in the corner. If he wants a piece of me he can take it, but I'm going down fighting.

It helps that Gabriel is already moving silently behind us. He knows Mal's attention is elsewhere. This is the perfect time to strike, but he needs to act fast. As Mal holds the glass to my lips I tip my head back and drink. There's no point fighting him on this point. If I defy him he'll only pinch my nose until I'm gasping for breath and then shove the contents of the glass down my throat, or even worse, find something he can inject. I'll take my meds like a good little girl, but everything after that is up for discussion. I'm not sure what I can do with my wrists and arms handcuffed to the bed, but I'm willing to explore all possibilities.

Swigging the whisky down with a grimace, I check on Gabriel from the corner of my eye. He's already opened the bottle of pills Mal's left on the table, and he's emptying as many as he can into the opened bottle of Jack. There's a good chance he'll kill Mal if he necks a glass of that stuff, but perhaps that is his plan. I'm not against the idea, but I was hoping for something a lot less quick and far more painful. Maybe I'm joining the dark side in my old age.

When Mal pulls a knife out of his pocket I recoil instantly. It's a military-style hunting knife, and it looks evil. The blade has been freshly sharpened judging by the edge I can see, and for kicks and giggles there's a serrated part to the knife at the rear. I'm about to be cut into ribbons. I've seen him use these too many times before. While I always knew this day would come, now it's here I'm trying really hard not to freak out. I know he wants me to lose it, and that's why I'm not going to.

'Can you feel it yet?' He's not talking about the knife on my body because it's nowhere near me. he wants to know if the drugs have kicked in. He needs me a little unbalanced and unhinged before he begins. The dance is more fun that way.

'Nope. You got to give it a couple of minutes,' I say, slowly and carefully. I'm lying, but I'll use any delaying tactic I can to avoid that knife for as long as possible. In reality I'm beginning to feel a little lightheaded and woozy, and I'm pretty sure my heartrate has rocketed, though that might have something to do with the knife.

Mal flips it in his hand, catching it expertly by the handle. 'I think you're lying,' he says, bringing the knife down to my stomach, where my flesh is already bruised and abraded from his previous games. My body does its best to sink into the mattress, trying to get as far away from that blade as possible, but it follows me with the greatest of ease.

'Well since you know what I'm feeling, why bother to ask?' Gabriel will swear at me for backchatting, but I'm doing him a favour. While Mal's attention is on me I'm giving him a chance to reseal the pill bottle and reposition himself to where he was before Mal's attention was diverted. Besides, the damage is done. This is happening whether I like it or not. My fingers are crossed that Mal has a glass of that doctored whisky sooner rather than later. I don't particularly want any of my fingers or toes cut off, if I can help it.

The knife moves to a spot just under my breast. I hiss in trepidation. Mal, on the other hand, looks like we've just had a Hallmark moment. His face is in raptures. He loves to sit and look at the destruction he wreaks upon others. I think it makes him feel powerful. It's either that or he has mental health problems. Actually, it's probably a mixture of both.

'Tell me you love me, Harper. Tell me you love me, and I'll stop all this nonsense.' His grey eyes are burning like smoking charcoal, and they try their best to scorch a path through me. I've got news for him. His X-ray vision isn't up to much.

Sighing, I say, 'We're not playing that game again, are we?' My head may feel a little fuzzy but I'm not stupid. Alex and I played the cat and mouse game too. As soon as he got what he wanted he lost interest. He didn't want to finish me though. But this time the game has new stakes. There's no real point in giving Mal what he wants either, because as soon as I do I'll be dead. Wait a minute... this might actually work in my favour.

'Tell me,' he repeats, the knife scratching a delicate path down my midriff, 'tell me what I want to hear.' He grabs my jaw in his hand and shakes me. Alex and Mal both became frustrated with me for the same reason. They knew I'd never love them, not the way I love Brandt. That's why he was such a sore point between them. I'd happily lay my life down for Brandt, and they both knew it.

'Tell you what; I'll tell you what you want to hear if you release Gabriel and promise me a quick death. A bullet to the brain is all I ask. You give me that, you get your words.' Shit, I've begun slurring. This does not look good. How much shit has he given me?

Mal is quick to respond. 'There's no way you're spoiling all my fun like that, 'Arper. No way in hell. Besides, you'll give me what I want soon enough. If not now, perhaps after I've cut a finger or two off you might be more friendly.'

'I doubt it,' I say, and I mean it. I'm also counting on Gabriel getting me out of here before I bleed to death.

In the background I can hear a glass of whisky being poured. It looks like my saviour is taking matters into his own hands. Good for him. Let's get this show on the road.

My body is wrapped in soreness, blood, bruises, pain... and heat. There is so much heat inside me I feel like I'm burning up. I'd love to say it was the effects of the drug, but I'm not so sure. I'm a bizarre creature like that. Mind you, the drugs are helping. Mal is counting on them to wear down my defences, and he may be right. Give them another half hour to work their way into my system, and I may tell him anything he wants to hear. I haven't in the past, but I haven't been this weak before either. I'm on my last legs, and we both know it.

'Have a glass, Mal.' Gabriel sets down the whisky beside him, and I do my best not to look at it. I keep my eyes firmly on the monster in front of me. Mal makes no acknowledgement of Gabriel's offer; just continues his intimidation play by letting the knife score a path along my flesh. I'd like to tell you it hurts, that I struggled and writhed like a wildcat trying to get out of my restraints, but I'd be a liar. I watch the knife with delicious anticipation and wonder where it will go next. It doesn't matter that I hate the man in front of me with everything that's holy because I'm now under his spell, and he knows it.

'Tell me, Harper. Tell me what I want to know.'

'Since when has it ever been that easy? Aren't you supposed to be chopping off some fingers or toes?' I hear Gabriel's intake of breath behind me, but he doesn't know how this works. I do. I need to get him mad. Then he might take a swig of that drink Gabriel's just left him. We're a little desperate here. Something has got to give.

'Haven't the last couple of days taught you anything?' Mal roars. Score one for me. The beast is not happy. It seems he thought I'd just roll over and die. Well, guess what? He's gonna have to work for it. Now it's time to push my point home.

'The last few days have taught me that Brandt is fucking marvellous in bed, and that you're still the same sicko you always were. Do you need me to elaborate?' I pucker my lips for a kiss, just to show him the kind of crazy he's dealing with. Yeah, some of it's the drugs which are beginning to do all kinds of funny things to my system, but most of it is me. I should have done this a long, long time ago. Why has it taken me so long to grow a pair of balls? I have no idea, but I've decided they look good on me.

'Did you want me to take over for a bit, Mal?' Gabriel pulls a chair around for Mal and holds his hand out for the knife. It's a bold move on his part, but not unwarranted because Mal normally likes to watch while Gabriel does his bidding. Tonight, however, is not one of those nights. This evening two is company, and three's a crowd.

'Fuck off.' Slamming his arm into Gabriel's chest, Mal pushes him backwards, telling him in no uncertain terms that his presence is not required. Gabriel is not going to be able to save me this evening. My knight-in-shining-armour will just have to take a backseat for a change and enjoy the view. He'll need to do his part soon enough.

Mal eyes the bedside table and for a moment I think he's going to take a slug of the drink. I find myself holding my breath for a second, but then he picks up his cell phone and examines it quickly, before setting it back down again. He's obviously due an important call. I wonder what's gone wrong now. Will this mean we have another victim next door to us this evening? I could do without all the crying and screaming, if I'm honest. It's hard enough as it is to get any sleep in my state.

'Am I interrupting something important, darling?' I slur lazily. At this stage I'm not sure whether I'm the brave one or whether it's the drugs talking. Judging by the rapid blinking of my left eye and the pins and needles that are beginning to work their way through my entire body, something is definitely afoot inside me. My thoughts are getting jumbled up inside my head, and it's an effort to push words through my mouth.

Mal shakes his head and gives me the eyeball. 'Since when are you in a rush to have your fingers cut off?' The evil smile that has haunted most of my nightmares these past few years starts to dance in front of my face. Oh God. He has no idea how much I hate that face. If I could snap his head clean from his neck right now I'd do it, and I'd smile.

Leaning over me, he releases one of my hands from the restraints. Oh shit. If possible my heart speeds up a little faster. My body is getting ready to implode, if my pulse rate is anything to go by. What the hell has he given me?

'Such pretty 'ands, 'Arper. You sure you want me to mutilate 'em?' Rubbing his fingers up and down the length of mine, he looks at me intently. I try to speak, try to push words past my lips, but my tongue feels like it's glued to the roof of my mouth. Speaking of mouths, it feels as if someone has lit a fire inside mine and then blown it out, leaving nothing but cinders and ashes in its wake. I am so thirsty I think I could cry.

'Can't...' I whisper. It's all I can get out, and that's a monumental effort in itself.

Mal laughs. 'Such a shame, baby. What a pity you can't do this one little thing that would stop me from massacring this pretty little hand. Still, it's your call.' Picking up his knife, he begins to circle the index finger on my right hand with the blade. The really important one that you use to write with, eat with and point with, amongst a hundred other things. Why couldn't the bastard start with my little finger?

'Should I sever it quick, sweetheart, or do you want me to draw it out? I know how much you like pain, and I have a feeling this is going to blow your mind.'

Hah. That's where he's wrong. My mind has already been blown. Now if I could just find that spare fuse I have lying around...

'Got nothing to say to me, 'Arper?' Mal shakes my head until the damn thing rattles. I have a feeling I passed out on him, but I can't be sure. Maybe he's already cut my finger off. Maybe that's why I fainted.

'Mng. Nng.' I'd like to say I know what that means, but I have no idea. My brain cells are mush and my vision is all blurry. Jesus. I feel awful. A quick glance down to my hand reveals that every finger is still intact for the time being, but there's a ring of blood around it from where he's been toying with me. I suspect it's not going to be in one piece for much longer. When is the bastard going to neck his fucking whisky?

'Want a drink before I chop it off?' Shit. Mal can see that my eyes have landed on the whisky glass. The drugs have made me slow and stupid. My head sways sluggishly from side to side as I try my best to say no. If I drink that whisky I'm a gonner. 'Painslut forever, huh? Why would you want to dilute that little bite of ecstasy? What a girl.'

By now the drugs inside me are taking off, big style. My head is a swirling void of lights, colours, and the odd flying elephant. Mal's face is changing shape regularly, morphing into Gabriel's and then Brandt's, before changing back again. I have no idea what's real and what's not. It's probably a good thing.

Mal doesn't care about my woes though. With no further warning he takes hold of my hand, slams it down on the bedside table, and putting an enormous amount of pressure on the tip of the blade, cuts my finger clean in two.

There is some mind-bendingly cruel pain involved with slicing through a bone.

This is the type of pain that even I don't enjoy, although I know it will leave an unpleasant residual burn when the throbbing dies down. For now it is more than I can cope with. The last thing I remember is watching my finger bounce off the table to the floor, as blood pours from the wound. Rivers of the stuff leak everywhere, staining everything around me, and my world goes a nasty shade of red. Thankfully I don't stay around to enjoy the party after that.

"Arper. Wake up.' The phrase is repeating over and over in my head. I want to tell Mal to shut the fuck up, but my voice is not my own. Neither is the rest of my body if I'm honest. My limbs feel weak and stiff, my stomach feels like someone has pummelled their fists into it, my whole body is now trembling. Am I going into shock?

'Say it, 'Arper. Say you love me.' We're back to this again? Seriously? Mal chops one of my fingers off and wants my undying love in return? I wonder how many women that trick has worked on in the past?

'Nnng,' is the closest to 'no' I can manage, but just so the bastard doesn't get the wrong idea, I shake my head loosely from side to side. He'll figure it out.

'You want me to chop 'em all off? This is how you want to go down? Maybe I should just cut both your hands off at the wrist and save us all some time.' Mal yanks my hand toward him, and my other hand that's still cuffed to the headboard protests painfully. 'Or maybe I should chop one of Gabriel's fingers off instead. Maybe that would inspire you to behave? What do you think, 'Arper?'

Oh, you fucking monster. This is between us. Except apparently, now it isn't.

Chapter Nineteen - Harper

'Come here, Gabriel!' Mal yells, thumping his fist against the table. In the other hand he is still holding the knife, which has my blood on it.

One glance at Gabriel tells me that this is the straw that will break the backs of a whole desert full of camels and probably a handful of coyotes too. There is no way he will take this lying down. Mal has finally gone too far.

Surprisingly enough, though, Gabriel does as ordered. Standing beside us, he waits to see what will happen next.

'Put your hand on the table,' Mal orders. Even through the vicious pull of the drugs I can see he's twitchy. His eyes are moving back and forth too quickly, and he seems on edge. I don't know what went down today, but something tells me it wasn't good.

'The right or the left?' Gabriel's voice is low and soft. You wouldn't know there was danger there, unless you'd had the privilege of being on the wrong side of him before, and I have. I know exactly what that voice means, and if I were Mal I'd get out of here.

'The right one. Now.' Mal bangs the table-top with his hand again so hard it jumps, anxious to get on with his dirty deeds.

'Of course.' Gabriel puts his hand on the table as ordered, splaying his fingers wide. Oh my God. I cannot look. It's bad enough when it's happening to me. It's ten times worse now that he's threatening to do it to someone else.

'Say the words, Harper, and this all stops.' My monster waves the knife around, which is my cue to lie my ass off. I can be the tough gal when my life is on the line, but I can't watch someone else be tortured. He's won this round. I can't fight this.

'F-fine,' I stammer. Thankfully my voice is coming back. I don't know whether the drugs are wearing off or whether adrenaline has jump-started my system, but for whatever reason I'm grateful.

'Say it!' he barks, losing patience with me.

Opening my mouth, I get ready to say the three little words he's so desperate to hear, even if they will be the biggest, fattest lies I've ever told. I can't do anything less. Gabriel will still lose his fingers because that's the way Mal works, but at least I will have tried. I owe him that much.

Looking into those cold, dead grey eyes, I feel my head swim with undercurrents that can't be controlled. What was in that drug cocktail? If I live to see tomorrow morning, I am going to have one hell of a hangover. Meanwhile, the knife hovers above Gabriel's hand, the blade glinting viciously in the artificial light. *Say the words. Let's get this over with, Harper.*

'I...' I don't get the chance to finish the sentence because Mal's cell phone begins ringing and vibrating. Snatching it off the desk he rises to his feet and strides away from us, out of the room. That's when I notice something important. Looking at Gabriel, who's still hovering over the bedside table, my eyes dip down to the glass of whisky that was full the last time I looked at it. Now it's empty.

'Did you drink that, or did Mal?' I'm almost afraid to ask. If Gabriel has just swallowed that we can kiss goodbye any chance we have of escape. In less than five minutes Gabriel will be about as useful as Long John Silver's second boot. Oh shit. This cannot be happening. I want to cry, but that's not going to be very helpful either.

Gabriel grabs my cuffed hand, and producing some sort of metal pin he starts to work on the locking mechanism. 'Relax. Your BFF drank it all up a couple of minutes ago, and he had a free refill. I'm just biding my time. Can you hang in there for me?' He presses his forehead into mine as the cuff around my wrist breaks open. I suck in a breath and squeeze back. I can do that.

'I swear 'hang in there' is my middle name,' I grumble. 'I've been hanging for years.'

Gabriel squeezes my hand again. 'Will you be able to walk in a few minutes?'

That's a good question. I have no idea. My head is a little less woozy than it was, but I'm still seeing shit that's not there. You would not believe the stuff that is going on in my brain. It's like a full-on Ibiza dance party back there. But at least I'm not getting violent. It could be worse.

'Yes, I think so.' I'll crawl if I have to, but one way or another I will get out of this place.

'Good girl. Won't be much longer now. I promise.' Gabriel pulls me into a great big bearhug, and for a moment I am almost conned into thinking everything might be okay. The man has that effect on people. He also makes my pulse pound, so at least that should help me try to get my toxicology stats lowered. I'm going to need all the help I can get if I'm supposed to try and run in a minute.

'Do you need me to do anything?' I'm not going to be useful for much, and I'm still seeing carousels and flying elephants spinning in my head, but I'll try to help where I can.

'No. Just sit tight. I've got this. I just need to get close enough to him. He'll be feeling pretty unsteady on his feet right now, so I'm going to meet him head on.' Gabriel walks towards the door.

'They'll shoot you,' I whisper, my jaw hanging open in horror. There are at least four guards out there. There's no way he'll come back alive if he goes out unarmed.

'Relax. I'll think of something. I'm good like that.'

I'm just about to tell Gabriel that he is one screwball short of an ice cream, when there's a loud bang. I have no idea what it is, but it doesn't sound good. We both look at each other. I'm mentally saying goodbye, and I have no idea what Gabriel's trying to say, but he's clearly not fond of long farewells because the door flies open and he's gone.

More gunshots follow. Shutting my eyes tightly I cower on the bed, wondering what on earth is going on out there. Whatever it is it does not sound pretty. All I can do is pray that one of them finds Mal as a target and that all the bullets magically miss Gabriel. I haven't got a hope in hell, have I?

My body decides that now is the time to start having violent tremors, and as I lean against the side of the bed I can feel my forehead banging against the wood. I am so hot. I feel like my body is melting from the inside out. I want to crawl towards the door to see if I can help Gabriel, but I am too weak to manage even that small action. Since when did I become such a pathetic creature?

I don't get more than halfway to the door before I vomit all over the floor. *Keep moving.* Somehow I make it to the door and with a burst of almost inhuman strength, I manage to swing it open. The sight that greets my eyes is like something out of a horror movie. There are five men in the room, six including Gabriel, and everyone is armed. Three guards are already dead on the floor and the remaining men are circling around each other. Mal, however, is nowhere to be seen.

Someone fires and my head snaps over to Gabriel who is holding his gun like a pro. His body twists as he's hit, and I watch him fall to the floor with an air of impending doom all around me. But what happens next isn't what I'm expecting. As the guards come closer to inspect their kill Gabriel springs up and picks three of them off before anyone can manage to get a shot out. He would have managed four, but a tell-tale click reveals he's out of bullets. When the remaining two realise what's happened shots begin to rain like hailstones, but Gabriel isn't anywhere near them. He's dived towards the guard nearest to him, feet first, and brings him down swiftly. The guard's gun is knocked out of his grip by the hard impact with the floor, and the two grapple with each other. It takes seconds for Gabriel to wrap his hands around his head and twist it sharply. There's the sickening sound of bones snapping, and it doesn't take a genius to figure out that he's dead. Then before I've even managed to blink Gabriel grasps the gun which was skittering across the floor beside him and he's pointing it upward towards the remaining guard, who is towering above him.

They both aim their weapons at each other, fingers on the trigger, both breathing hard and wondering whether they really want to die.

'You don't work for Mal,' Gabriel pants. He's suffering, as he still has the weight of the dead guard on top of him and he can't move for fear of getting shot.

'You're not as stupid as you look.' The guard, who is around six feet six inches tall and at least two times the size of the average male, smiles. 'You do know you can't stay under him for long if you want your lungs to remain intact. Give it up, tough guy.'

Uh oh, that's like waving a red flag to a bull. There's no way Gabriel will go down that easily.

'Who do you work for?' The Mexican standoff continues, with the two men trying to size each other up. I'm not even sure who has the advantage. It won't be the easiest firing a shot into Gabriel as he has a dead guy for a human shield. On the other hand, standing on your own two feet without a dead weight on top of you has to be a bonus.

'Markovich. Who else?' Tall Guy shrugs. He thinks he's got this in the bag.

'Ahh, you want Mal's territory. That's what all this is about. Did you get the bastard?'

Gabriel seems remarkably calm for someone on the receiving end of a gun.

'No, he sprinted off before we could pepper him with holes, and his men protected him. You're all stupid fucks. If you don't know he's on the way out, you will soon.'

'I don't work for Mal. He's been keeping us captive in his back office these past few days. You've just done us a massive favour.' Gabriel looks behind Tall Guy, his eyes resting on me.

'Us?' Tall Guy grins. 'There's no way I'm falling for that line.' He doesn't even bother to survey the room. I've had hold of a gun for the past few minutes now, courtesy of another dead guy I found just outside Mal's bedroom door, so I fire it. Tall Guy's head snaps around in panic as the shot echoes around the room. The thing makes a colossal bang and ends up smacking me in the face as it recoils, which gives me cause to swear. As if I don't have enough lumps and bumps already. For fuck's sake. Anyway, the long and short of the matter is that I don't actually hit anything. How could I? I'm in cloud cuckoo land with the fairies and I'm seeing pixie dust at every turn. I never meant to hit anyone, either. All I needed to do was give Gabriel a distraction, and a beautiful one it was too. When he fires again he doesn't miss. Tall Guy now has a big hole between his eyes, and the expression he's wearing on his face is priceless. I shouldn't find this shit funny, but I do. Collapsing on the floor in hysterics, I wonder what life is going to throw at me next. When life throws you lemons...

'Wake up. For Christ's sake, Harper, wake up.' I don't wake up because someone is calling my name over and over again. Even though it's really irritating, I could probably sleep through that. No, I wake up because some cretin is slapping me about the face, and I take exception to that, especially considering what I've just been through.

Grabbing their wrist, I open one eye groggily and do my best to bite their finger off.

'Oh, thank God,' they say, which is really weird because it's not the kind of thing you say when someone has their mouth around your finger. I stop going Hannibal Lecter for a moment, to fasten my eyes on the annoying person who seems desperate to disturb my sleep. Blinking, I discover it's a bloke and I'm fairly sure I know him.

'Wow, you're pretty,' I say. I can't help it. I have no control over my mouth right now.

'You're still high,' Pretty Guy says, shaking his head.

'So sue me,' I reply, shrugging my shoulders.

'Do you know who I am?' he asks.

'You're pretty and unbelievably sexy, in a this-is-my-dreamworld-and-everyone-else-can-fuck-off kinda way. Have we had sex before?' My mouth is like a runaway train that thinks it's in an episode of Lost Girl - which basically means it's uncontrollable and up there with the fairies. Fuck. This is not cool.

'If we haven't we definitely should,' Tall, Dark and Handsome says. Oh God. I so need sex right now. I have no idea what's happened to me, but everything hurts and if that isn't a good enough reason to have sex, I don't know what is.

'I like pain. Did I mention I like pain in any previous encounters?' Clapping my hands over my mouth my eyes stare on in horror. It's a sure sign someone, somewhere is trying to tell me to shut up.

'Perhaps that's where I've been going wrong all this time.' My angel grins, and I'm sold. Whoever this other worldly being is, I want to be inside his pants inside of a half-hour. In fact, half an hour is too long. Five minutes sounds better. My eyes shutter closed because as much as I'd like to fuck the guy, I am way too tired to do anything. I have a feeling I may regret this tomorrow though.

'Wake up, Harper. We need to move.' The angel is slapping my face again and I have a feeling I'm going to have to demote him from his position of higher moral authority. Things are beginning to come back to me now.

'I crawled out here on my hands and knees in order to save your ass. I couldn't move another inch if this place was on fire. Go save yourself. I'm done.' I wave him away. 'Oh shit.' I then remember that Mal cut my finger off. 'I need to get to hospital,' I howl. 'Did you find the finger he cut off?'

'What finger?' Gabriel looks at me like I'm crazy. I shake my head, trying to clear away the lingering cobwebs. Bringing my hand up to my face, it's then I find that my finger is still there. My mouth opens and closes as I try to process this. Don't get me wrong, Mal has hacked into it pretty badly, but he didn't cut it off. Jesus. What else have I imagined? It doesn't bear thinking about. Anyway, that's just brightened up my day.

'If Mal's not dead, toss me a knife on your way out, darling.' I mean that too; Mal is not getting a second chance to dismember me.

'Tsk, tsk, tsk.' Gabriel shakes his head at me. I don't care. He can shake his head all he likes, I'm still not moving. I stick my tongue out at him. I actually stick my tongue out. I hope I don't remember any of this tomorrow. I want this to be a black hole of Star Trek proportions in my memory. I don't ever want a whisper of it to come back to me.

When Gabriel doesn't move, I decide to reiterate my position. 'I'm not moving. Go do your thing. Kill people. Take over the world. Save Brandt if you're feeling generous. Sort out world peace, yadda, yadda, yadda.' I wave my hands in the air. They make pretty patterns, even if they are covered in blood.

Gabriel rolls his eyes. 'I am going to save Brandt but I'll need your help, so get your skinny butt up of the floor and start walking towards the shower. We cannot go out looking like this.'

'I'm not moving. There isn't anything you can say that would make me change my mind.' I am exhausted beyond words, and while there is someone, somewhere that is yelling at me to hurry up and get the hell out of here, the rest of my body couldn't care less. I'm going with the easy option.

Gabriel is currently wrestling with a dead guy's jeans. They've got a bullet hole through them, but I guess it's better than walking around half naked. If he's not careful he might even set a new fashion trend. When he's finally yanked them off the poor guy and found a passable T-shirt, he drapes them over his arm and walks towards me. I stare at the ceiling. I am not playing any more. I've had enough.

'You're right,' he says, squatting down next to me. 'There isn't anything I can say that will make this go away.' He proceeds to sweep a couple of strands of hair away from my forehead with a gentle caress, as those wonderfully dark eyes attack mine. In the next minute he is straddling me, his hands sliding firmly under my neck.

'There is, however, something I can do,' he whispers, before his mouth attaches itself to mine like a heat-seeking missile bent on destruction of great magnitude.

Men are such utter bastards. One moment you're happily staring at the ceiling, waiting for death to come and claim you, and in the next you're in an adrenaline and pheromone-laced overload, thinking you can take on the universe. It wouldn't be so bad if he weren't so good at this. Every twist of his tongue ignites a line of flames in my body that sears me to my very core, and those lips need an insurance policy of their own. Within seconds I am lost. My hips are dancing upwards to meet his and they are in full-on party mode.

When Gabriel lets me up for air I can barely breathe, and what's more - I don't care. Oxygen is highly overrated. My hands are tangled in his mop of curly black hair and they are holding on for dear life. Mal has strung me out to dry for the past few days, with little hope of release, and now it seems to have hit me full circle. I. Need. Sex. Now.

Gabriel can see it, too. Gripping the back of my head he pulls me back towards him, so close our lips almost touch. I try to close the distance, but he's not having any of it. The asshole is going to string me along, I just know it.

'You want some of that, kitten? You wanna get your rocks off with me?' he purrs. No. Yes. Oh fuck, what is happening here? It's wrong and I shouldn't want it, but

I do. I want it so badly I could almost cry.

'Please,' I whisper. I can't say anything else. Gabriel's kiss has rendered me virtually speechless.

'Good. Now I'm going to get you showered, and dressed, and then we're going to find a hotel. You're going to let me take care of you and feed you. Do you understand?' I look up at him in a daze. There is no way I'm going to be able to do all of that. I can barely crawl.

Looking up at those lips and eyes, I almost sob out loud. 'I'm on my knees here, Gabriel. Don't get me wrong, it sounds tempting, but I have no idea how I'm going to put one foot in front of the other. I'm all over the place. You should get out while you still can.' I look pointedly towards the door. Mal could come back at any moment. Why is he risking his life for me? The man's an idiot.

Gabriel smiles. 'Good job I don't need you to put one foot in front of the other, then,' he says, pushing his arms underneath me before he hauls me up over his shoulder. I grunt and swallow my gasp of pain. My body is so bruised and battered the smallest amount of pressure on my skin is agony, but I like that kind of thing. I'd like it a whole lot more if I had the energy to enjoy it, though.

The next hour goes by in a pain-induced fog of tormenting heat and white-hot passion. Gabriel is using my body against me. He knows exactly how to manipulate me into doing what he wants, and I don't have the strength to resist him. The man is full of contradictions, too. In the shower he washes me infinitely slowly, with such care and tenderness I wonder if I might cry. When it looks like I'm about to pass out he slams me into the wall, his teeth biting into my bottom lip with a vice-like grip, the other hand cupping my sex while his fingers pump into me. There is no thinking when I'm held like that - none at all. Whatever reserves of energy my body has left, they are beckoned forward by his touch.

'Stay with me, Harper. This will be all over soon. I've got a car coming for us. Stay with me.'

The bastard keeps me in limbo with his talented lips and hands, as he finishes washing and drying me. Somehow he then finds me some clothes, although they're way too big for me. I don't protest when he puts them on me, but I want to. Thankfully the hum of pain is all around me now, its insistent throb bleating all the way through my body, from the top of my head all the way down to the tips of my toes. Whoever pulls those strings owns me, and Gabriel knows it.

When we make it outside, maybe ten minutes later, there is already a car waiting for us.

'How did you manage this?' I ask, as I slide into the comforting leather seat of the taxi that is idling on the roadside.

Gabriel shrugs his shoulders. 'I snatched a dead guy's phone.' He pulls out a black iPhone from his back pocket and waves it at me. 'He won't be needing it any more.' Barking some instructions out at the taxi driver, I can feel the car move as it pulls away from the curb. Gabriel then looks back at me, and I take the opportunity to pass out cold. Again.

Chapter Twenty - Brandt

'Why did you save my ass?' That question has been bugging me. I still can't figure out why Helena would murder someone, putting her own life and freedom at risk, in order to get me out of that mess. The woman must be all sorts of crazy to do something that stupid.

'Well, you were never going to do it, were you?' She rolls her eyes at me, which are currently lined with masses of black kohl, making her look like a throwback from the Addams family.

'That didn't mean you had to step in.' Sitting down heavily on the bed in our ridiculously expensive hotel, I tug my jeans on angrily. 'If you get caught you'll go away for a very long time. Let me be the first to tell you prison isn't half as much fun as it sounds. Why would you get yourself involved in this?'

She throws a pillow at me. 'I'm getting involved in this because you're my husband now, and I don't want to have to sort out your funeral the day after I've got married. It's going to look weird.' She drags her attention away from the episode of Gangs of London she's watching and reaches for me. She's naked of course, her tits spilling all over the pristine white sheets, but I do my best not to look. This annoys her no end, but that's too bad.

'This isn't your problem. Don't you ever do something like that for me again. Do you hear? If you end up in jail I will never forgive myself.' I mean it. Even though I'm not Helena's best friend, there's no way I want to see her go to jail. She just killed a girl, though. Oh God, I can't wrap my head around this.

'Relax. The gun's untraceable and there were no cameras anywhere near the area. I checked. No one is pinning anything on me. I'm smarter than I look.' Helena licks her ruby-red lips and pouts. 'Brandt, we've been married two days and we still haven't consummated the marriage. Give a girl a break. Let yourself go. I'm pretty sure I can make you feel much better if you'll just give me a chance.' Her lithe, tanned arms reach out to grab my shoulders, and she pulls me towards her. She's tried this approach before. It didn't work then, and it's not likely to work now.

'Fuck off, Helena. I'm not in the mood. I need to get to Mal. Tell him the job's done. I won't be able to think straight until I have.' We went to his warehouse yesterday, but it was deserted. To make matters worse, there were dead bodies strewn all over the floor. My heart was in my mouth as I walked around the place, and I kept seeing Harper and Gabriel's face on each body we passed. Thankfully they weren't there, but it didn't make me feel any better. What has the bastard done with them? Where the hell is he keeping them? I fulfilled my end of the bargain. Kind of. Now where the fuck are my friends?

Helena rolls over in the bed, taking half the sheets with her as she snuggles up close to me. 'Can't you just call him? I know his number if you don't have it.' This isn't helpful. No, I can't just call him. He has both of my friends trussed up and is probably cutting them to pieces as we speak. It's not going to be a social visit. I'm not going to mention this to Helena, though. She's not Harper's biggest fan, and she's going to think even less of Gabriel the ex-con. Actually, they have a few things in common now. Maybe they'll hit it off. Then again, maybe not.

'No, I can't just call him. I need to find him.' There's a raw urgency in my voice that even she can't miss. My nerves are strung out like tensile steel rods. The type that hold up massive bridges that span miles of water. That's the kind of pressure I'm under right now. I feel like I'm going to break at any moment.

'You can't trust that fucker as far as you can throw him. It looks like he's already double-crossed you. If I were you I'd walk away.' Her fingers tiptoe up my leg before they try their best to dive under my shirt, but I stop them before they get the chance.

'I am well aware of that, but I still need to find him.' Returning her hand to her she pouts at me, but she doesn't back off.

'Tell you what, Brandt. You get these sheets tangled with me, and I'll show you another of his hideouts. Maybe he's there. He has a few boltholes dotted around. He's probably licking his wounds after this mess, trying to figure out who crossed him.' She slips a leg out of the duvet and rubs it up and down my back. This is the last straw.

'This isn't a fucking joke,' I hiss, my body already on top of hers with my hand circling her neck. I squeeze cruelly, letting her know I am deadly serious, and I don't stop until her eyes bulge and she starts struggling beneath me. I then relax my hold a little, knowing I have her rapt attention.

Leaning close I bend down until all she can see is me. My face is now entirely blocking her vision of everything else, and my eyes are fucking scary. Gabriel taught me this look, and it hasn't failed me yet. Now is the time to spell out who calls the shots around these parts.

'This was a forced marriage, and it has consequences you can't even begin to comprehend. The last thing on my mind right now is sex, Helena. If you have any idea where Mal is, you need to tell me. Now.' My eyes flare. I'm not kidding. If she messes me around I'm about to go supernova.

'You're no fun. You know that, right?' She moves to get up, and I let her. I can't bear the sight of her anyway. If she pisses me off much more she's liable to get it in the neck, and there's been enough killing around these parts. 'Give me twenty minutes to get dressed, and then we'll be on our way. That work for you?' She tries to act as if the last five minutes haven't happened. I get a cheery wave and a wink as her ass sashays into our walk-in wardrobe, without a hint of animosity in sight. I just tried to kill her, for fuck's sake. What is wrong with the woman? Mind you, I'm not about to look a gift horse in the mouth. If she's going to take me to some of Mal's hiding spots, I'm prepared to play nice for the time being. Not as nice as she wants me to play, but I'll make an effort. Jesus. I'm fucking married. When did life get so damn hard?

Helena takes forever to get ready. Apparently it is impossible to leave the hotel without applying mascara, especially when you're consorting with one of London's biggest criminal minds.

'I don't think he'll care if you forget the mascara just this once, babe,' I call, after I've been looking at my watch for the past twenty minutes. As we're probably going on a wild goose chase I fail to see the importance of a full face of make-up, but apparently Helena wouldn't be seen dead without it, which is a distinct possibility if we encounter Mal, so I let her get on with it.

When the woman is finally ready and we set foot outside our hotel room, I don't know whether to laugh or cry. It's entirely possible my friends are no longer alive, in which case I am probably walking to my death, but I can't leave them there. I know Gabriel would do the same for me, and while he's a lot of things, he's not a coward. If he's stolen my bloody girl while I've been gone, though, I am going to wring his miserable neck.

Helena looks like she's just stepped out of the cover of Vogue as she walks down the hotel corridor. She's got a Dior bag arranged 'just so' over her shoulder and a pair of oversized sunglasses that make me think we're heading for somewhere exotic, like Tahiti, but somehow I doubt it. Maybe she's just being sensible and trying to disguise her identity. Why didn't I think of that?

We haven't walked very far when she comes to an abrupt halt. We're still miles away from the elevator, so I nearly knock her over when I topple into her.

'Helena, what the fuck? Give a guy some warning why don't you?' The woman totters on her four-inch spike heels, but by some miracle manages to remain upright. Thank God. I can't take any more drama.

My wife doesn't even bother to respond. She turns around, examines the number on the hotel door, and then knocks. I want to scream. Can my life get any more surreal? I doubt it. If this hotel room is one of Mal's hidey-holes I am going to eat my non-existent hat. Is she double-crossing me? The hell if I know. Right now I'm not even sure I care.

'Helena, what the hell are you doing? We need to get a move on.' I'm pretty sure Mal's not in a hotel room right next to ours. Grabbing her by the scruff of her neck I ignore her shocked gasp of indignation and begin to propel her towards the elevator doors. I have no patience for her antics. We need to get moving.

'Wait. Just wait,' she chokes. My tight hold around the collar of her sheer white blouse is not doing much for her vocal cords, and I can't say I'm overly concerned. 'Stop,' she hisses again. I ignore her. If she's not careful I'm going to snap.

I then hear the sound of a door opening and a familiar voice calls out, 'Brando. Thank God. When Helena said you were alive I almost didn't believe her. Get in here.' I almost drop Helena, spinning around to confirm what my ears are hearing. It's Gabriel's voice, but I need to make sure with my own eyes. When I see him I break into a run.

'Gabe. Thank God. I thought you were a gonner!' Gabriel looks pale and thinner than when I last saw him, but at least he's alive. Wrapping one arm around his neck I pull him into me and give him a solid pat on the back before releasing him. Words cannot express how relieved I am, but that doesn't change the fact that I'm still worried sick about Harper.

'Do you know where Harper is?' I whisper. My sentence is cut short as a weak groan comes from inside the room. I'm pretty sure I know that voice, and even though I don't dare hope it might be her, I need to see to make sure. Trying to push past Gabe, he stops me in my tracks.

'She's not in good shape, Brando. You'd better brace yourself.' He then opens the door wide enough, so that I can step inside.

Harper is lying on the bed, fast asleep, and she looks like a ghost. Her skin is almost translucent, and she's lost even more weight. If Mal has fed her while she's been gone, he hasn't fed her much. When I get my hands on that fucker I am going to tear him limb from limb.

Grabbing her hand, I sit quietly by her bed in an upholstered armchair. I'm guessing Gabriel's been watching over her while she slept. On the desk by the window there's a glass of water, the remains of what must have been room service, and several packets of tablets.

My head turns as Helena and Gabe walk back into the room. 'What did he do to her?' I whisper. I don't want to wake her; Gabriel is right, she doesn't look good. She should be in a hospital, probably wired up to all sorts of bleeping machines. If I lose her I will never forgive him, even though this isn't his fault.

'He hurt her - a lot. Sometimes on his own, sometimes he got me to do it for him, but it wasn't pretty, Brandt. She refused to go to the hospital, but she needs to. Perhaps you can talk some sense into her when she wakes up.' Gabe has dark circles under his eyes and his cheeks are sunken. Rage flies through me when I think of him hurting her, but I know this was not his fault. He would never do something like that unless his hand was forced. Gabriel is many things, but he isn't a complete monster. He'd kill her in a heartbeat if he had a mind to, but he wouldn't torture her unnecessarily. It isn't his style.

'What did he make you do?' My voice is barely a whisper, hiding the fury that resides within me. My teeth grind together as I imagine what she's been through.

'You don't want to know, Brandt,' he says, just as quietly, but he isn't getting off that easily.

'Tell me, or I'll kill you right now and I mean it.' I might actually be able to do it for a change, too. The man in front of me looks like he's been through hell. Once he's had a couple of decent meals down him and a good night's sleep, I'm sure he'll be right as rain, but at the moment the poor bastard looks defeated. I'm fairly sure I don't want to know what Mal did to them, but I have to know.

Gabriel sits down slowly on a couch opposite me, then puts his head in his hands, which I'm fairly certain is not a good sign.

'I can't,' he whispers. This is a first for him. I've never heard that phrase from his lips.

'It's that bad?' Now I really don't want to know.

'It's that bad,' he confirms. 'She needs to be checked over in a hospital. She went into meltdown yesterday when I suggested it, but you need to get her seen to. She won't listen to me, but she'll listen to you.'

Harper chooses that moment to sigh, and we both look towards her. She's looking up at us, her eyes blinking in the light, and she smiles weakly when she sees me.

A ball of painful emotion expands in my stomach, and I am so grateful that she's alive I can't even begin to put it into words. I stand there, with my tongue stuck to my throat, willing myself to say something. Harper beats me to it.

'Brandt,' she whispers. 'Thank God you're okay.'

'I'm fine,' I whisper, squeezing her hand, 'it's you we're all worried about. You need help. Gabriel tells me you won't go to hospital.'

She shakes her head and frowns at me. 'This is nothing. I've been in much worse shape than this before. Nothing is broken. I'll heal. I just need food and rest.' She then stretches out on the bed and winces.

'We'd all feel better if a doctor checked you over, sweetheart. You don't look so good. Will you go, if I come with you?' Rubbing the pad of my thumb over her hand gently, I silently urge her to do as I say. There's no way I'm going to argue with her, but if she says no I'll just wait until she's asleep and take her there myself.

She shakes her head. 'I don't go to hospitals. Mal can find me there. You have to tell them your name.' If possible, the lump in my throat gets bigger. Jesus Christ, what has the bastard done to her? She's even too frightened to get medical attention.

'I'll get a doctor to come and see you, then. The hotel probably has one downstairs. We won't give him your real name. Will that work?' The only perk of being married to Helena is that I still have money. I have done what my parents have asked, which means a generous allowance will still be paid into my bank account on a monthly basis.

Harper's eyes are tearing up as she stares at me. I don't think I can look at her without breaking down myself, but I do my best to keep it together. If we both dissolve into tears nothing will get done. She suddenly grabs my arm.

'You need to get out of here,' she whispers. 'Mal is setting you up. Remember the gun I planted in your room, along with the drugs?' I nod. It's a part of my life I'd sooner forget, but I remember all the details of my trial very vividly. 'He still has it. He says he's going to send it to the police in connection with a crime that will get you put away for years.' Her eyes are scared. I look to Gabriel to see if he'll confirm what she's saying, and he nods. I sit there, incensed for a moment, my anger simmering over into an explosive boil. What have I ever done to the bastard? He's put me away for five years, and now he wants to send me away for murder? Then I realise something important.

'There won't be any fingerprints on that gun. I never touched the damn thing.'

Gabriel shakes his head at me. 'Makes no difference, man. You could have cleaned them off straight after the crime. If ballistics can connect a bullet from that gun with a crime, it'll be pinned on you.' I already know this. It was a stupid thing to say.

'Why doesn't he just kill me and have done with it?' I moan, pushing my fingers into my forehead to stop the pounding that's beginning to hammer behind my eyes. I am so sick of these games.

'He likes to play with people,' Harper whispers. She's not telling me anything I don't already know. I also know that he wants me out of the picture so he can have her all to himself, even though he wants to kill her. Yeah, he's that kind of jealous bastard.

'I love you,' I whisper. If I'm going back to jail or worse, I want her to know that. We've been through too much for me not to be honest with her.

'I love you too,' she replies, smiling up at me. 'I think I've always loved you, little good that it did me.' I smile at that. In the beginning my parents stood between us.

I couldn't defy them. Now, nothing stands between us but Mal, but he is a much bigger obstacle than they ever were. Why didn't I put two fingers up to my family years ago? We could have been happily living together in a two up, two down, with three kids in tow by now. None of this misery would have befallen us, and while we might not have been rich, we would have been happy. Harper would have seen to that. I'm an idiot.

Helena clears her throat. I'd almost forgotten she was in the room, but she strides towards us with a decidedly disgusted expression.

Standing over us with her hands on her hips, she says, 'Touching. Oh, how touching, Brandt. When Mal said you were in love with her I didn't believe him and had to see for myself. I thought you'd have far more sense than to fall for a tart like her, but it seems he was right. What little brains you had left you lost as soon as you stepped out of that jail cell. Such a shame. I thought we could have made something of ourselves, but it seems it's not to be. Too bad.' Her pouting lips are mocking. 'It seems you will have to go back under lock and key after all.' She strides back towards the door and throws it open wide.

'Helena, what the fuck?' I hiss. What is she up to now? Gabriel is as shocked as I am and jumps to his feet almost instantly, as if sensing danger. It looks like his sense is bang-on, too, because in the next instant the room fills with thugs. This cannot be happening. Not now. Now after all we've been through.

It is, though. Guns are aimed all around us, and even Gabriel doesn't bother to fight back. We know when we're beaten.

Helena strides back into the room and pulls two more guns out of her bag. 'Hold that for me,' she purrs. I do no such thing. I have no idea what she's up to, but it cannot be good.

'Fuck you,' I spit, backing away from her.

'Oh, Brandt,' she says, her voice dripping with sarcasm. 'Don't be like that.' She then proceeds to place one of the guns at my temple, while thrusting the other one towards me. 'Hold the fucking gun, or I'll blow your brains all over the place. There's no coming back from that, darling. If I were you I'd take my chances in jail. Your choice, though. I don't particularly care either way.' The other gun is then thrust into the middle of my face, dangling off her index finger by the trigger guard, taunting me. Grinding my teeth together I pick it up gingerly. I know what's about to happen next. I can see it play out like a movie in my head, and it's not one with a happy ending.

Helena looks pointedly at the gun. 'Place your finger on the trigger, darling, there's a dear. That way we can pin Frankie's murder on you as well, even though you weren't capable of such a thing. You're a pathetic asshole, really.' Yep, this is what I was expecting.

'And if I don't?' It's a stupid question, but I could accept my death over the next forty years in prison. There are other consequences I'm less accepting of though.

'I'll put a bullet through Harper's forehead, and then Gabriel's. You've got to the count of three, dumpling. One, two...'

She doesn't get to three. I do as I'm told. The gun that was used to kill Frankie in the Langdon Hotel now has my fingerprint all over the trigger. This, in combination with the other weapon, should ensure I never see the light of day ever again. The plan is genius.

'There. That wasn't so hard, was it?' I get another mocking frown, and I've never wanted to punch someone so much. How did I not see what a vicious little bitch she has become?

'Was planting the drugs and gun in my room not enough for Mal? Five years in prison is a mere paltry sum in his world, right? Now he just wants me to rot in there, to make sure I never go near his girl again, huh?'

'I'm his girl now,' Helena barks back. 'He's going to kill Harper later today. You're not going to live, either. He'll just arrange for someone on the other side to slice your throat. Better say your goodbyes now while you still can, sweetheart.'

I don't say a word. I am not saying goodbye to Harper again. She is not going to die while Gabriel and I still have breath left in our bodies.

Placing the gun in a plastic bag, Helena turns to one of her underlings. 'Take him to the nearest police station with this. Now they'll be able to connect him with two crime scenes.' Thrusting the plastic bag at one of her thugs, two others step behind me to make sure I don't try to escape.

'No!' Harper screams behind me. 'Take me. Leave him out of it.' The sound makes my stomach clench. She has been through so much. If Helena sends her back to Mal I won't be able to live with myself.

Turning to Gabriel, before I'm frogmarched out of the room, I say, 'Don't do anything stupid just yet, and keep her safe. Just give me a few hours, okay?' He nods at me, but there's a look of desperation in his eyes. It worries me. Gabriel isn't a quitter, but he isn't the type to flog a dead horse either. Still, he values his own hide, so maybe they'll be alive for a little longer yet.

Helena, meanwhile, is smiling smugly. Gesturing to Gabriel and Harper she says, 'Take them both out back and dump them in the SUV. I know someone who's going to be very pleased to see them.' It doesn't take a genius to guess who that 'someone' will be.

Considering I thought spending five years in prison was my worst nightmare, I decide I have greatly underestimated the level of bad shit I would have to deal with this year. Nightmares have nothing on my life.

Chapter Twenty-One - Gabriel

Everything around me is spinning out of control. What the fuck just happened? We've been double-crossed by Brandt's new bride? I have to admit, I never saw that coming. So, it seems the woman's been working for Mal all along. What's her problem? Whatever it is, it doesn't matter. We're fucked. There is no getting out of this mess.

From where I'm standing, Brandt's just been gift-wrapped for the Met police, and we're about to go back to finish the ending of a horror movie that's worse than anything I've seen on TV lately. Harper isn't going to make it past a day. They're pulling her up off the bed, but she can't even stand on her own two feet. The girl is all over the place due to Mal's mistreatment of her, and the only good thing about that is that at least she won't have to endure too much more. I, on the other hand, could be there for weeks as he picks me apart piece by piece. I'm almost tempted to go gung-ho on them now, consequences be damned, but Brandt has just pleaded with me to behave myself for a little bit longer, and I probably owe him that. But I have no idea why he wants to drag this shit out. There is no way he can get out of this, of that much I'm certain. He might be the brains of this outfit, but things are way out of control here. There's no coming back from this. I'm not watching us both die a long, slow and torturous death under Adley. If things go pear-shaped I'm taking matters into my own hands, and that's that. He'll understand. Actually, I don't care if he doesn't because I'll be dead.

Harper and I watch as Brandt is basically dragged out of the room. His eyes are wild as he looks back at us, and I suspect he's thinking what I'm thinking: that there's a good chance we'll never see each other again. It's hard to believe that we both got out of prison a few weeks ago, only to find ourselves on death row before the month is out. How's that for irony?

Once Brandt is out of the room Helena turns on us. Striding forwards on her ridiculous heels, with a pair of massive sunglasses perched on her nose, she tries her best to look down on me, even though I am several inches taller than her. The woman is trying her best to let me know who's boss, not that I give a shit.

'Mal never told me you were attractive. Fancy that,' she purrs, while her viciously long nails snake over my face.

'I bet there's a lot of things Mal didn't tell you about me,' I reply, smirking. I'm fucked if I'm going to bow down to her. If she wants me on my knees she'll have her work cut out.

'Such as?' her voice is a throaty whisper as her hands move lower, checking out the line of my abs through the thin veil of my T-shirt.

'My cock is as big as a firehose, darling, and I enjoy waving it around.' If there's one thing I've learnt during my time in prison, it's that sex can be an excellent weapon if used correctly. Brandt had to learn that one the hard way. I smile as I think about it, and what do you know, Helena thinks the smile is for her. The next thing I know her hand is all over my junk. Thankfully it's hard as I've been thinking about Brandt because I find her about attractive as a garden slug. This is coming from a man-whore, by the way. I can fuck anything, take my word for it, but I'd have to use my imagination with the viper standing in front of me.

'Good to know,' she purrs. 'Maybe we can find out if that firehose feels as good as it looks later. Mal just wants you dead, but I don't see why we couldn't drag it out for a bit. What do you think, sweetheart? Fancy being my fuck-toy for a bit?'

I recoil inwardly, but you wouldn't know it to look at my face.

'Always happy to oblige, princess. You tell me when and where, and I'll be there.' I gently remove her hand from my crotch. Gun or no gun, she's not getting her hands on my dick unless I'm naked and have no other choice in the matter. To soften the blow, I lift her fingers up to my mouth and gently kiss her hand. She is my captor, after all, and I can play nice when needs be.

117

'Well, well, well. Perhaps I'll have more fun this evening that I thought. You are intriguing, Mr Rodriguez. I look forward to seeing you later.' She slides her wrist out of my hand, flicks back her blonde mane, and then motions for her goons to get me and Harper out of the joint.

I can't help a sigh. Round two, here we come. Let's hope I play this hand better than the last one.

Less than an hour later we are back at the warehouse where it all began. As we are ushered inside it's hard to believe anything has happened here. All the dead bodies have been cleaned up and there's not a speck of blood in sight. Was the shootout we witnessed before staged? Were we meant to escape so we could witness Brandt being arrested? It's a possibility. It's also possible that Mal has neutralised whatever threat there was on his life, and now that the problem is taken care of, business can continue as normal. My money's on the former, though.

The ride over is not pleasant. Harper is shaking like a leaf and there's little I can do to console her. She cannot go through this again. To have a taste of freedom and then for it to be whisked away from right under your nose is more cruelty than most people can handle. This is probably why Mal did it. He wants to crush her flat like a used aluminium can. He won't be happy until there's nothing left of the poor girl. I won't let him. If it comes to it I'll end us both, because there's no way he's torturing her more than she has been already. Yes, I'm in love with her. Yes, I need a fucking lobotomy and yes, I know this won't end well. The trouble is, I couldn't pick a side even if I wanted to. Yes, I still love Brandt, but the emotions are different. With Harper, I want to caress her, protect her and worship her. With Brandt, I want to slam the man into next year, torment him and make him worship me. If circumstances were different I'd probably want them both the same way, but they're not. At the moment Harper's like a precious Ming vase balanced precariously on the edge of the table. One wrong move and she's never going to be the same again. Brandt is just being stubborn, but he has every right to be. I was a class-A shit. I don't deserve to be forgiven, and once he finds out I'm in love with his girl, he's probably going to get me a tombstone for my birthday present. With any luck I won't have to worry about it. I can't believe I just said that.

When we get to the warehouse Mal is waiting for us, and let's just say he's not standing there with open arms. The man is dressed from head to toe in black and he has a face as long as my arm. Things obviously haven't gone quite the way he planned. I have no idea what's up with his dream of world domination, and I think it's better not to ask.

'Afternoon Mal,' I say cheerily when he stands there looking at us, much as you would a prized painting in an art gallery. Now don't get me wrong, I know we're pretty, but we ain't that pretty. Unfortunately I get a thump in my gut for my troubles. Trying to draw in breath through my ass, Harper wobbles on her feet beside me.

'Get her inside now!' Mal thunders, looking up and down the street to make sure no one is witnessing this little exchange. There isn't a soul about, lucky for them, because if there was they wouldn't live to tell the tale.

A couple of the guys take Harper by the arm, and she has to lean heavily on them as they walk her inside.

'And him?' One of the remaining guard's points to me and Mal's head swivels round as he examines me with narrowed eyes. For a minute I wonder whether he's going to order them to shoot me on the spot, and my heart accelerates like a McLaren MCL35.

Then his hand flies towards the door and he says, 'Put him inside with her for now. Maybe we can kill him later while she watches.' His smile is nasty. It appears we're done playing games. This is the last leg of the journey and it's a one-way ticket to hell.

I don't say a word as I'm led inside. There's no point. You can't reason with Mal's thugs. The penalty for disobeying him is a rather painful and drawn-out death, and that's a good enough deterrent for just about anyone. I've already come to the conclusion that we aren't getting out of here alive unless a miracle happens. The only decision I have to make is how we want to go down.

The guards thrust me back in the little room at the back of the warehouse. Harper is already sprawled on the bed, and she's shaking so hard I fear the poor girl is going to fall apart. Sitting down gently beside her, I grab her hand and say, 'Breathe. Just breathe.' She needs to calm down, else she'll pass out. Actually, that might be the kinder option.

'Kill me,' she whispers. 'Just get it over with.' I can tell she's deadly serious. I've seen that look of desperation before. But I shake my head. While a part of me wants to put both of us out of our misery, another part is going to give Brandt a chance. I keep trying to tell myself he's a smart guy, but brains or no, I don't see how he can dig himself out of this. Still, he's surprised me on more than one occasion, so I owe it to him to drag this out a little longer.

'No.' My voice is gentle but firm. When she grabs my hands and places them around her neck, I have to swallow down the tennis ball that has lodged inside my throat. She is going to make me cry, and I don't cry - ever.

'I need to give Brandt a chance,' I whisper. 'If things look like a lost cause, I'll take care of you. I promise. Trust me?' She shouldn't trust me. No one should, but she nods anyway. It's probably because she doesn't have the strength to argue, which is just as well.

We don't get a chance to talk any further because Mal comes storming in.

'Sweetheart,' he croons, walking towards Harper's prone form, 'you don't look so good. See what being apart from me does to you?' He sits down on the bed causing me to jump up off it, and he runs a hand over her face. I watch as she flinches. She's not strong enough to hide her reactions now.

'You've got what you wanted, Mal. Brandt's inside, I'm dying, and you're ruler of the fucking underground. What more do you want? A four-piece quartet advertising your victory? Kill me and get it over with. Enough already.' That's my girl. She may not be able to control her reactions, but she doesn't pull any punches with her words.

Mal picks up her hand and squeezes it so tightly she gasps. 'I don't think so, darling. Especially not after your pal over there drugged me. It took me a full twelve hours to recover from that shit.'

'Welcome to my world,' Harper says dryly. 'While we're at it, if you have anything half-decent, I wouldn't mind some. I could do with something to take the edge off.'

What the hell is she saying? She can't handle anything right now. Her body is shutting down. Any kind of drug in her system is likely to kill her off and she knows it - which is probably why she's goading him.

'Oh, I don't think so, sweetheart. Not this time. No, no, no. This time you need to be at the top of your game for what happens next.' Mal pulls his gun out of the back of his jeans and I fight the urge to take cover, but he uses it to scratch an itch on his back before placing it back where it belongs. Jesus Christ. My nerves are shot.

'So, what do we do now then?' Harper says resignedly. Now I know she is scared because I'd be shitting my pants right now, but you wouldn't know it to look at her. Hell, she's braver than most blokes I know and that is saying something considering where I've been.

Mal doesn't say anything, he simply pulls a tube of glue out of his back pocket and waves it in front of her. His cell phone then chooses that moment to ring, and he snatches it out of his pocket and frowns.

'You,' he swivels around to point at me, 'tie her to the chair. I'll be back in ten.' Don't hurry on my account, I feel like shouting after him, but think better of it.

I have to carry Harper to the chair. She's so weak she can't stand on her own. It makes my blood boil. I keep asking myself over and over if I'm doing the right thing. This would be the perfect opportunity to break her neck in two, and I could sort myself out seconds later by having a go at one of the guards he's got stashed outside. There are even more here now, so Mal isn't taking any chances. Maybe he's worried Markovich will come back?

As I place Harper in the chair she starts sobbing. I didn't think I could feel any worse than I already do, but something inside of me breaks.

'Look,' I say, as I sit her down, 'Brandt asked me to give him a few hours. I figure I owe him that. I have no idea what he has up his sleeve, but I think we should give him a chance. The trouble is, I owe it to you not to let that bastard take chunks out of you. I'm in love with you, Harper. If you haven't figured that out in the past few days, you know now. When he hurts you it feels like he's physically ripping me to shreds. Now I've seen a lot of shit in my time, but nothing has ever affected me this way. If I can find a way to get him to leave you alone for a bit, could you hang on for me? I have no idea if Brandt will come through for us, but if there's a chance we might make it out of here alive, I'm willing to give him a couple of hours. Are you?'

When she gives me a look which says I must be going crazy, I shake my head. 'I won't let him hurt you. If it comes to that, I'll kill us both. Hang in there for me. It won't be for much longer now.'

'You're crazy,' she whispers, wiping away her tears. 'There's no way this can end well.' She sniffs and looks up at me. 'If you think there's a chance, I'll wait.' There's a sad nod before she holds her head up high, all business again. The fighter I know and love is back. 'Go on, tie me up.' Placing her hands behind the chair, she indicates with a flick of her head that I should get on with things. 'If you don't finish this before he gets back he won't be happy.'

Harper is still dressed in the oversized T-shirt I put her in when we left here. Mal will be able to rip it off without a second thought. It's riding up her legs so most of her thighs are exposed, and I can see the cuts and bruises that cover her. I put most of them there. I should have ended this long ago. I cannot watch her being hurt again. What am I letting myself in for? What if my plan backfires?

Picking up the reel of rope that rests on the concrete floor, I begin winding it around her wrists. I make sure it's not too tight, mostly because her wrists are still red raw from his earlier mistreatment. Besides, she's not going to fight him. She's not stupid. This is bullshit. Still, I have to try for her sake.

'What's the first thing you're going to do when we get out of here? Go find a house and move in with Brandt?' I don't know why I'm torturing myself with this, but the small talk passes the time and stops me thinking about... other things.

Harper snorts. 'We aren't getting out of here.' She seems quite convinced of the fact. I hope she's wrong. I can't bear the thought of Adley winning this round. Anyway, I'm not letting her get away with that defeatist attitude.

'Just supposing we do. What's the first thing you're going to do?' I walk back around the front so I can see her. My eyes are drowning in hers like a lost puppy's and they are taking their fill. I have no idea how much time we have left, so I'm going to make the best of it.

'Grab a decent meal.' She laughs bitterly, but then she smiles and continues. 'I want three kids, maybe four, a house near the sea, and someone who'll love me. That's all I've ever wanted. It's not too much to ask, is it? I'm not greedy. The trouble is, nobody loves me. I'm unlovable. People treat me as a possession, not a person. They want to walk all over me. They want to own me. I never wanted that.'

Her comment takes my breath away. Is that what she really thinks? Oh my God. She doesn't realise how beautiful she is. These men have stamped all over her self-esteem until there is nothing left. I daresay Brandt and his fucked-up family didn't help with that, but it had nothing to do with Brandt not wanting her. I can't think there are many blokes who are immune to her, and he's not one of them.

'It's not too much to ask, no,' I say. 'And as to the other matter, you are not unlovable. Your trouble is that you are too beautiful. Everyone wants you, and some will go to extraordinary lengths to have you. If you had family, they would have looked out for you. On your own you were a sitting target for every mad man out there, and oh boy can you find them. You've just been unlucky, Harper. You're all too easy to love, trust me.'

She doesn't get a chance to respond because Mal comes storming back into the room, and he looks pissed. Great, that's just what we need. I take a moment to think about that. Hmm. Actually - that's probably exactly what we need. This might work in my favour.

Mal turns to me. 'Get the whip!' he barks. 'Might as well make a mess of that T-shirt as I'm going to be ripping it off in a few minutes.'

I cross my hands over my chest. 'Nothing doing,' I say. 'I'm not hurting her. She's close enough to death as it is. You can do your own dirty work for a change.' I mean it, too. I'm done here.

Mal gives me a sneer. 'Do as you're fucking told, or you'll regret it,' he barks. Of that I have no doubt, but I'm not changing my mind. We stand there, giving each other the eyeball, as Harper watches on. This time I'm not backing down. If Mal wants to give it to me, I'll take it. I'd much rather he focused his energy on me than her.

'You sure this is how you want to play it? Is she really worth getting yourself killed over?' Mal pulls his gun out of the back of his jeans.

Harper yells from behind us, but it's too late for that.

To add fire to the flames I say, 'She is. So do your fucking worst, Adley.' I'm kinda counting on him not to shoot me. If he shoots me we've had it, but everything leads me to believe he'll play with me first. This is what I'm hoping for. Actually, hope is the wrong word, but you get the idea.

Mal's face darkens. I can tell he's angry by the way his jaw hardens. I hope Brandt has something good up his sleeve, else my last few moments are not going to be very pleasant. I must be mad.

'You're going to regret that, Rodriguez.' He moves forward, crowding me out, and I let him. As long as the focus is on me I'm buying us a little time. It won't be much, but anything is better than nothing.

'Kill me, asshole. I've had just about enough of this shit anyway. You'd be doing me a favour.' That's a lie, and if his trigger finger even thinks of squeezing I am diving for his ankles, with the hopes that he doesn't hit anything vital in the meantime.

Tense seconds of silence follow. Mal doesn't relax his hold on the gun, but he doesn't fire it either. Interesting. Where do we go from here?

'Who said I was going to kill you? I have another fucking chair, asshole. Why don't you take a seat?' He steps back a few feet to reveal another plastic chair, and with his foot, he slides it forward. 'Sit,' he barks. Now there is no way I want to sit on that chair, but if the alternative is to watch him cut Harper up, I guess I'll take it. So I sit down on the hard red plastic.

He beckons several of his thugs over. They stand behind him, training their guns carefully on me. I grin up at them. I'm buggered if he thinks he's going to intimidate me.

'Ah, tough guy, is that it?' Mal stands in front of me scrutinising my expression. I'm not going to give anything away, and if he hopes I'm about to burst into tears, he is much mistaken.

'Not particularly.' I run a hand through my hair and debate my next choice of words carefully. I should keep quiet, but I don't think I'm going to. 'But I do know that when I love a woman and she doesn't love me, it's time to move on. You're flogging a dead horse, Mal.' That's not far from the truth.

He doesn't respond. He simply shoves his booted foot between my legs and presses so hard my eyes begin to water. It looks like we've finally dispensed with the chitchat.

'Want to know the first thing I'm going to do to you?' he asks.

'Not particularly,' I admit. 'In fact, I'd rather you kept it a secret. It kind of spoils the surprise, otherwise.' Yeah, I'm playing with fire, but if you're going down you might as well do it in style.

Mal shakes his head at me. 'Oh, Gabriel,' he says, with mock concern, 'and I had such big plans for you. I thought you were going to fit into my little world quite nicely. Your friend was hopeless, so I'm going to have him killed, but you? Well, you had promise.'

'Yeah, I know, I'm such a big fucking disappointment. Story of my life.'

He continues as if I haven't spoken. 'The first thing I'm going to do to you is glue up that smart mouth of yours. When I've done that I'm going to glue all of your fingers together, because it will make them much easier to chop off. I can do a couple at once that way. Then I'm going to glue your eyes together because that will make the next part much more fun. Now ask me what's the last thing I'm going to do to you?'

I answer in a bored fashion, knowing it will piss him off. 'As I've said before, I like surprises.' I have no idea what he plans to do for my grand finale, but I don't think I'll like it much. Brandt had better come through for me. Once my eyes are glued my options are severely limited. Ideally I want to be dead before that part.

'And don't think I've forgiven you for that last cocktail you served up in my whisky,' Mal continues. 'I was lucky you didn't kill me.' The aim had been to kill him. I put enough drugs in that whisky to kill a horse, but somehow the bastard is still here. Bloody man is a bit like a whack-a-mole. You bang him over the head, and he keeps bouncing up again for the next round.

'That would have been terrible,' I say, twiddling my fingers - the same ones that are shortly going to be removed from my body. I'm quite attached to them. The thought of them decorating Mal's floor is not a pleasant one. One or two I could cope without, but it sounds like he's planning to take them all. Still, I'm going to be dead when all of this is finished, so who the hell cares?

Pulling his tube of glue out of his pocket, he waves it at me. I don't flinch. I refuse to give him the satisfaction.

'Think you're a tough guy, Rodriguez? We'll see soon enough. It doesn't usually take me long to make grown guys scream, and I have a feeling you won't be any different.' Hah. That's where you're wrong, I think. I've had years of practise of not screaming. I'm a street rat. We learn the hard way that life isn't fair, and I didn't learn to fight without taking a few punches in my time.

'Are you still talking?' I waggle my fingers at him. Sometimes when you anger the beast you get them to do stupid things. That's when they slip up. Yes, I'm certifiably nuts, but at least Mal's attention is fully on me. I'm going to pay for my outburst, but it will be worth it. I think he's forgotten Harper's still here.

A fist flies in my direction, aimed at my jaw, and while I could avoid it I don't see the point. He'll just keep going until he's done some damage, and sure enough, that's exactly what he does.

All the while this is happening Harper is screeching behind us, but neither of us pay her any attention. Mal doesn't because he's too focused on making a mess of me, and I don't because there's no way I want this shit happening to her. I do have a conscience, after all. Who knew?

The fists keep flying, and I take them all. I'm going to have one or two wobbly teeth when this is finished, but that's the least of my problems. When the glue comes back out of his pocket and he takes the top off, I know I'm really in trouble. The fun and games are about to begin.

Chapter Twenty-Two - Brandt

You don't learn much in prison. Letting go of control is probably the first thing you come to terms with, swiftly followed by the second, which is to trust no one and keep your head down. When you find yourself behind bars, the last thing you want is to be the centre of attention. You also discover that there are consequences for every action you make, and to mitigate the effect of this, you learn to become very observant.

When Helena told me she'd become involved with Adley to pay back her gambling debts, I naturally didn't believe her. Oh, I looked like I believed her, and I nodded my head and said all the right things, but the cogs were turning. Helena's family has money. Even if she'd done something really stupid, they'd have bailed her out one way or another. Some people might have been too proud to go to their parents, but not Helena. She's smart. She knows how to play people. Sure, she can act the clown, but behind the bleach-blonde hair there are plenty of brain cells calculating how to do a hostile takeover of your brain, without you actually realising it. Unfortunately for her, I spotted her game a mile off. It helped that I have a friendly private investigator, the same one I used to find out Harper's whereabouts, and I used him to track down all the information he could find on her. As it turns out, there's quite a lot.

For starters, there is no gambling debt. Helena fell in love with a bad boy, plain and simple. No surprise there. What is it with women and bad boys? Maybe she just wanted some filthy sex, or maybe she wanted to piss her parents off - whatever the reason, she's been in league with Adley for a while. To make sure, my PI hacked into her phone. It was full of cute little love notes from Adley, if you can call extreme sadism that, depicting exactly what he was going to do to her if she was successful in setting me up. He also bet her fifty-thousand pounds in cash to sleep with me within three days of the wedding. There was no way she was going to win that one in a hurry. Anyway, to cut a long story short, I knew she was going to set me up.

Normally, in that situation, the best thing to do would be to run, but that wasn't an option. Harper and Gabriel were being held hostage, and besides, this thing had gotten personal. Adley had preyed on Harper for years, and there has to be some kind of payback after something like that happens. If there was any chance of a future for us, Adley needs to be out of the picture - permanently, if you catch my drift.

Trying to find a way out of this mess has been almost impossible. Whichever way I looked at it, we'd have to spend the rest of our lives running. Even if we kill Adley, his replacement would never let us live, and there is always a replacement. That's another lesson prison taught me. You can kill someone, but it doesn't get rid of the problem. I've pondered this for a while, but I think I've come up with a solution, although I'll probably get a broken nose for my troubles.

On the drive to the police station the thugs don't say a word, and I'm not in a particularly chatty mood either. I'll give my voice a rest until I'm assigned an arresting officer. Boy, is he going to have a field day with me. At the moment I'm just thanking my lucky stars I haven't been searched. If Mal had caught up with me I would have been. But Helena is nowhere near as smart as she thinks she is, and for that I can be grateful.

The four blokes take no chances with me. They stop right in front of the police station, have a word with the station chief, and I am then handcuffed and led away. Believe it or not, I am relieved when this happens. I stand a chance here. If I'd been taken back to Mal's the only thing being dealt up there would be death.

'I need to talk to someone urgently,' I tell the female officer leading me to one of their holding cells. 'I have crucial information that will help you break up a drugs gang.' This is the one area I am uncertain of. If I don't get the police to Mal's ASAP, Harper and Gabriel will be dead. There's the added worry that Gabriel will take matters into his own hands if he thinks the situation is hopeless, and from where he's standing it is. This is why I can't wait. I want to send Mal down, but it will be a horribly hollow victory if Harper and Gabriel aren't around to share it with me.

'You think you're special, huh? You and everyone else in this joint.' The officer looks at me with disdain and then jerks my body forward painfully. She's heard all this before. I need to say something that will get through to her.

'I'm not kidding. I know where the guy is right now, and he's just had a fresh haul of heroin in. Someone needs to get out there, before it's gone. I'll happily tell you all the details, just get me someone who will listen.' This is all lies of course, but when they arrest Mal, Harper can tell them everything else they need to know which should get them what they want; a high profile arrest. My dad will be very happy with that, I should think, now that he's the Mayor of London. Think of that. The black sheep of the family will be doing him a favour.

'Save it, kiddo. You'll get seen when you get seen. Let's hope you get lucky and we don't have a busy day. For now, get your ass in there and don't give me any trouble. We clear?' I nod because there really isn't anything else I can do, but there's a look of desperation in my eyes. This could all explode in my face if I'm not seen quickly, and I'll never forgive myself if that happens.

My cell is a tiny, white square box with a concrete bed and a plastic mattress. This is just like old times. Sitting down gingerly, I try not to think about what might be happening while I'm here twiddling my thumbs. I couldn't have played this any other way, I try to tell myself. If Mal had been suspicious he'd have run, and if the police don't have him, Gabriel, Harper and I will never be safe. We need him either dead or under lock and key. I'm partial to the former if I'm honest.

Time moves slowly in a cell. I alternate between imagining worst-case scenarios and best-case. It doesn't do much for my blood pressure. Every time I hear a pair of footsteps go down to the corridor I almost jump up and hammer on my cell door, but even I am aware of the futility of that. I have to be patient. Someone will get to me in time, they have to.

I am left waiting for what must be hours. Even the footsteps up and down are getting less frequent, and I'm beginning to wonder if they've forgotten about me. It would be just my luck if the Met were short-staffed today. Try to stay positive. That's easier said than done. I haven't even begun to explain what I need to in order for them to get out and go do something. Meanwhile, Harper and Gabriel are out there taking everything Mal can dish out, and I'm well aware that it isn't going to be pleasant. Come on, people. Someone give me a break. Placing my head in my hands I nearly give in to screaming out loud, when there is a sudden rattling of my cell door.

I don't dare hope that someone has come to question me. I suspect it will be some lackey who's come to throw food at me, following government protocol, but the door opens and an officer is standing before me.

'Brandt Browning?'

'Yes,' I whisper. I wonder if he can see the desperation in my eyes, because the man then smiles.

'I hear you have some information for me that might be useful. Most people who say that are wasting my time, so you have three seconds to give me a name before I move on to someone more interesting.' There it is. Short but sweet. Let's hope I can impress him.

Clearing my throat I say, 'The guy's name is Mal.' God, I hope he's heard of the bastard or I'm in deep trouble. If he walks away from me I'm liable to commit a real crime and it won't be pretty.

The officer's head snaps back as if in shock. Is that a good thing or a bad thing? It'd better be a good thing.

'Mal Adley?' His mouth is now hanging open.

Of course, Mal Adley. How many people named Mal can be running drugs in London? I decide not to let my mouth run off. I don't think that would be the smartest move here.

'The one and only,' I confirm instead.

The officer nearly yanks my arm off, dragging me out of my cell. 'Why the hell didn't you say something earlier? We've been after that bastard for years. Do you have something concrete for us? We're not interested unless you can give us something solid. He's as slippery as an eel. Most of the city is in his pocket.'

I did say something earlier, but no one was listening. Arguing is hardly going to be productive, though, so I get straight down to facts.

'I have something concrete.' At least, I hope I do. They took it off me when they were processing me, so my fingers are crossed it's still there. If it's disappeared I have nothing.

'Then you are my new best friend,' the police officer says dryly. 'So, I suppose we'd better go find an interview room.'

Ten minutes later, over a cup of coffee that is only slightly better than prison

126

coffee, I tell my sordid, sorry little tale, including as many details as I can think of, and elaborating where needed. The heroin bust he thinks he's going to stop isn't real, but if he gets Mal he'll be able to find out where it is, along with a hell of a lot more.

I rattle on with my story as fast as I possibly can, and when finished I for some reason feel exhausted. I shouldn't be because my backside has been stuck to a plastic chair for the better part of an hour, but it's been a rough week, and sleep hasn't been a big priority. Anyway, right now I have to figure out a way to get this officer to jump all over the case ASAP. I have a feeling that telling him Mal has two of my best friends in tow and is planning to kill them won't sway him much. If I tell him he's about to skip town and kill a load of people, however, that might make him move. It's worth a shot.

'How much heroin are we talking about here?' Officer Biggs asks me as he finishes up his paperwork. I've finally taken the trouble to read his name badge. Seeing as how we're hopefully about to become friends, I think it appropriate that I at least know how to address him.

'He's one of the main dealers in the East End of London,' I say. 'How long is a piece of string? If we hurry I can give you his girlfriend too. She'll tell you all of his inner dealings. You'll be able to nail him for everything, but we have to hurry. Once he's skipped town you've lost him.' I'm beginning to wonder if any real police work ever gets done in these parts. I know they have to do their job, but seriously, how many of these fuckers slip through their fingers while they're filing reports?

'You realise that if we find you're lying to us you'll go down for a very long time.' Officer Biggs is trying his best to make sure I'm telling the truth. He's probably been on quite a few wild goose chases in his time, and I can appreciate that it's probably not a fantastic way to spend your evening.

'I'm telling the truth,' I admonish, waving my hands around in the air animatedly for effect. I'm telling the truth on at least seventy-five percent of my tale, anyway, and they'll get the rest later.

After we go back and forth a little longer, as he checks my earlier statement to make sure I'm not lying, he eventually seems satisfied by my story.

'Right, I think I've got all I need here. Is there anyone you'd like to call?'

I don't want to call anyone. I want to head straight out to Mal's and rescue Harper and Gabriel before it's too late.

'I don't suppose I can come with you, can I?' I already know the answer to that question, but I ask it anyway.

Officer Biggs thinks it hilarious, and that is all the answer I need, unfortunately. I don't even bother to argue. There is no point.

'Yes, I'd like to call my lawyer,' I say. This time I'm going to hire a decent one. Hopefully I won't need them, but I'm not taking any chances.

'We'll sort that out for you. If your story checks out, though, you won't need one.'

For my story to check out I need Harper alive, and if this guy doesn't get his arse in gear there's a distinct possibility she won't be.

'Just hurry,' I say. 'Please hurry.'

Chapter Twenty-Three - Harper

I know what Gabriel is doing. He's distracting Mal so he can take the focus off me. While admirable, he's a fool. If he'd have left Mal to it, only one of us needed to die. Now, it looks like we'll both go down the same way and I want to scream. Scrap that, I am screaming - but no one is paying a blind bit of attention to me. This is the last thing I want to happen. I don't need anyone to save me. This has been coming for a while, and now it's here I just want it over with. All Gabriel is doing is dragging the damn saga out, and I can't watch Mal hurt him. Maybe this is punishment for all the crimes I've committed in the past. If so, it's brutally effective. If you'd shown me how my life would end five years ago I would have moved heaven and hell to make sure I never stepped a foot down this path. It is far too late for regrets though. I swear my life is going to haunt me long after I'm dead, too.

When Mal starts using Gabriel as a punchbag I go mad. This is not his fight. I tell this to both of them in no uncertain terms, but no one is listening. It's as if I am suddenly invisible. Since I've been invisible most of my life, I have no idea why this should be such a surprise to me.

Don't get me wrong, I should be grateful for what he's doing, but I am just so tired. I need this to be over. All this will do is draw things out and make the beast in front of us angry. He's bad enough at the best of times, but when he's angry you don't want to be anywhere near him.

I do my best not to watch as blood and spittle go flying everywhere. The sickening sound of Mal's fist crunching into bones does funny things to my stomach, and it's not in a very stable condition as it is. Gabriel doesn't make a sound. His face is knocked this way and that, and I'm pretty sure he's lost a tooth or two, but he's as silent as a tomb. But he won't stay that way for long. Mal will make sure of it.

When the tube of glue comes out I nearly lose the plot. It doesn't help that I've seen this so many times before. I know how it works, I know what he does, and I know how it all ends.

'Gabriel!' I scream. This is code for 'you are not going to sit there and take this for me'. If I say what I really mean Mal will tie him down, and that's the last thing we need. Mind you, as soon as his eyes are glued shut it's game over anyway.

When Gabriel doesn't make a move to do anything I yell again, but he ignores me, so I start bouncing up and down on my chair. It doesn't make any difference, but at least I feel better.

Actually, I don't. I have to sit there and watch while two of Mal's men hold Gabriel down, so they can glue his gob shut. Mal then proceeds to pull a pair of black latex gloves on, in order to ensure he won't get any glue on himself.

'Are you watching, Harper?' he goads, looking straight at me. 'When this is all over I'm going to chop his cock off, fry it, and feed it to you - piece by fucking piece.'

I don't vomit. There's nothing left in my stomach to bring up. Besides, I wouldn't give the bastard the satisfaction. Thankfully I can't see Gabriel's face from where

I'm sitting, but the poor bloke must be close to losing it as Mal spreads the glue over his mouth. The thing about superglue is that it sets really quickly. Mal just has to close his lips together for a couple of seconds - and voila - the job is done. If Gabriel tries to pull them apart he'll end up tearing half his skin off. Besides the fact there's no point, because Mal will just glue him back together again.

'Doesn't look like you'll be licking any cunts in the near future, Rodriguez,' Mal says, laughing as he looks him over. This is typical Mal style. Once he has them helpless before him, that's when he really sticks the knife in, quite literally, unfortunately.

'Leave him alone!' I yell. 'You've got me. I love you. I love you. I LOVE YOU. Jesus Christ, Mal, I'll say any damn thing you want me to, just let him go. This is between us. It has always been between us.' I'm trying to think of something that will appeal to whatever sliver of conscience he has left, but I'm pretty sure I'm wasting my breath. My tormentor is playing out his fantasies, and it looks like he's enjoying himself immensely.

'Too late for that, 'Arper,' Mal says, without looking at me. 'We're officially past the point of no return. 'Ave you got any last words for Gabriel? If so, you might as well get them out of the way. He's not going to be breathing for too much longer.'

I can hear Gabriel trying to speak through his glued lips, but I can't make out a word he's saying. The sound is soul-destroying. I can't take this on top of everything else, but it's not as if I have a choice. What is Gabriel waiting for? Brandt isn't coming. This needs to end. He promised me.

That's when I start rocking on the chair, while I do my best to break out of the rope that holds me. It's not a good precursor of mental health, and unfortunately, I suspect there is worse to come. I can't think straight. I hate this building. I hate everything it represents, and everything that has happened here. I wish I had tried to claw Mal's eyes out while I still had the chance. I've been thinking about killing him for years. You wouldn't believe the amount of times I've dreamed of pulling a gun on him and blowing half his head off. There's no question he deserves it. The trouble is, I'm too much of a coward. I also know that if I somehow missed or didn't go through with it, we'd be back to where we are now. God. The walls all around me are darkening and thickening, and I feel like they are sprouting arms. All of these arms have long, pointy fingers which want to rake at my flesh, tearing me apart piece by piece. Normally it takes a lot of drugs to induce these kinds of hallucinations, but not today. Today my brain is in freefall, and Salvador Dali has nothing on me.

'Last words, 'Arper?' Mal's reminding me that I'm supposed to be saying goodbye. I'm not going to, though. Gabriel will get his goodbye when he wraps his hands around my neck in a few moments' time. Then I will smile at him and say thank you, and I will mean it. If he can take me out of this world and keep me out, then he'll have my gratitude.

Mal waits patiently for my response, but I give him nothing. Am I dragging this out in the hopes that we will be rescued? It seems doubtful. I gave up on fairy tales a long time ago. What is wrong with me? One moment I want this all to be over, and the next I'm using delaying tactics. To add insult to injury my throat is dry, my head is spinning, and I have a cracking headache.

When Mal gets bored of waiting he fills in the blanks for me. 'Seems she's got nothing to say to you, Rodriguez. Maybe she doesn't love you after all. You know, just because you fuck 'em, it doesn't mean they fall for you. 'Arper's strange like that.' He clears his throat and rubs his gloved hands together as he gets ready to torment his victim. Sure enough, the next words out of his mouth are, 'Which finger do you want me to cut off first, Rodriguez? Any preference?'

Gabriel has given up trying to speak. I should think breathing is his number one priority right now. Sucking air in through your nose isn't quite as efficient as breathing in through your mouth. Mal's tested the theory on several people numerous times, and most ended up hyperventilating. I can't imagine Gabriel having a panic attack. He always seems so calm and confident, but I wouldn't blame him if he did.

'Cat got your tongue?' Mal chuckles. 'That is a shame. I'll just have to decide for you, then.' Tilting his head to the side, he pretends to think about this. I know he has already decided exactly what he wants to do, but he's going to drag it out. He likes to see his victim's sweat, but I have a feeling Gabriel isn't going to give him the satisfaction. I'm not exactly sure what he's hoping for, anyway. The poor bastard can't speak with his lips glued together. Maybe he's hoping Gabriel is going to come at him, so he can mow him down, but that would spoil his fun.

"Arper? Do you have any thoughts on the matter?' Ahh, so that's his angle, is it? Cute. I shake my head. My voice is AWOL and besides, he's never listened to me in the past, so why should he start now?

'I'd speak up if I were you, sweetheart. If you don't I may decide to do them all at once.' He grabs Gabriel's left hand and begins to glue each finger to the next one. Strangely enough Gabriel lets him. I have no idea what's going through his head, but if it was me I'd be leaping off that chair and going out with a bang. My head drops towards the floor with despair as I begin to wonder what dying will feel like. Yes, I've already given up, and yes, I don't care. Someone's had it in for me the moment I set foot on this earth, and as I get older life gets worse, not better.

'I can't hear you, 'Arper.' Mal sing-songs my name, and the sound makes me wince. Do something, Gabriel. I have no idea what he's waiting for, but it had better be good. Meanwhile, all the fingers on his right hand are now stuck solid.

When Mal still doesn't get a response he decides to take matters into his own hands. Approaching me he grabs my face, pulling it upwards so I have to look at him. For a minute he doesn't say anything, but my eyes must be rolling about in my head or something because he then slaps me. It shocks me out of my stupor, if nothing else.

'Focus, 'Arper. It's not your turn to die, yet. Tell you what, why don't I let you cut some fingers off? You can show lover-boy over here what you're made of.' He goes behind me and begins untying my hands. By now my body is trembling so hard I feel like the chair has taken on a life of its own.

'No,' I whisper. 'No, no, no.' The sound is so soft he can't hear it. Nothing works any more. I can't speak, can't think, can't breathe.

'Don't worry, sweetheart. He won't hurt you. I've glued those 'ands up good.' Mal thinks I'm scared of Gabriel, in the same way that I am of him. Perhaps I should be, but I'm not. While Gabe has his issues, he is not Mal. There is a beating heart inside him. I know because I've seen it.

The rope falls to the floor, the soft thud echoing in my ears. This isn't happening. I haven't recovered from Alex. The guilt still eats at me, even though the man was a monster. I can still remember Mal's hand curling around mine as he aimed the gun at my husband's forehead. The utter shock and horror that he actually expected me to do something like that. I remember screaming as I tried to pull away, but Mal wasn't going to let me escape that easily. His finger tightened on the trigger, and so did mine. It makes me a killer. I murdered my husband. Yes, I might have had help, but that's what happened. I'm going to have to live with that. Gabriel has his demons too, but he seems to have made peace with his. If we get through this, maybe I'll ask him how he did it. If we get out of here and live to tell the tale, that is. If, if, if. So many ifs.

Mal squats in front of me and brings my trembling hands up into my lap and holds them there, trying to calm me down. He can forget it. We're past that. I'm a nervous wreck and I need somewhere with padded walls. All I want to do is lie on a nice soft bed and sleep forever.

'Get a grip, 'Arper.' Mal thrusts a Swiss army knife into my right hand, flicking the blade up for me. My first reaction is to let it drop to the floor, but he closes his hand over mine and shakes his head. I'm not going to get away with it that easy. Looking at the knife with terror, I shake my head. No, no, no.

Gabriel turns around to look at me. My eyes are drawn to his lips, which are cracked, bleeding, and covered in glue. His face is all bruised and swollen, he has one black eye, and blood is dripping from his nose. He looks like something from a horror movie. He eyes the knife in my hand and nods his head. Mal can't see this because his back is towards him. It's just me and Gabe, and it's like he's telling me that this is okay. This is not okay, though. It is anything but okay. My eyes can't hold his and my lashes drop back down. I want to tell him that I love him, that I'm sorry I got him messed up in all of this, and that I wish we could turn the clock back. I can't utter a sound, though.

Grab the knife, Harper. Stick it through Mal's chest. That's what his eyes are telling me. If I did that this could all be over in a heartbeat. The surrounding mercenaries will then shoot, and that will be that. I can't do it though. I'm not a killer. Even though I've been tormented beyond what any sane person should ever have to endure in a lifetime, I can't finish him off. I could hurt him, but that wouldn't be enough. Mind you, perhaps that's all I'd need to do. Gabriel doesn't need his hands. He's still got his feet. Maybe it's time I took a chance. Taking a deep breath, I let my fingers close around the smooth plastic of the handle. Looking up at Mal, I nod once. That's all he needs from me.

His face lights up as he says, 'Fuck, I knew you'd do this for me. I knew it, 'Arper. You do love me, don't you? Alex told me you'd never fall for anyone because you were set on that rich kid, but I told him he didn't know shit. I was right, wasn't I?'

Is it me, or are we going around in circles? Why won't Mal take no for an answer? I seem to be a homing beacon for psychopaths.

His question hangs in the air between us like an STD, because Mal's sure he's got it, and I sure as hell don't want to touch it. I don't have the energy to lie to him any more, either. Still, I guess I can give him a weak smile. Sell the lie, Harper. Sell it good.

My hand tightens on the knife as my gaze wanders down over my once white T-shirt.

'Rodriguez, get over here.' Mal thumps the back of his chair, and there's a distinct pause before I can hear the metal legs scraping as he pushes it back behind him. There's then the slow thud of footsteps before he's standing tall before us.

Mal spins his chair around so he can sit in front of us. Always the thoughtful one, our Mal.

'Put your hand on the table,' he instructs sharply. Gabriel looks at me, raises his eyebrow, and then places his left hand on the table. He isn't shaking like I am. He is all tightly controlled energy, coiled like a spring, ready to pounce. Even Mal can see it because he chooses to pull his gun out of his jeans. Gabe is making him nervous. Even with his fingers glued together the guy looks dangerous. Mal thinks the guards dotted all over the place will ensure he will stay still, but I know better. Maybe Mal does too. Maybe he just wants to make a mess of him. That would be right down his alley.

As I move to get into position for what I'm about to do, I have several decisions to make. The first one is figuring out where to stab Mal. I am not in the finger chopping business. That is not my style. When I use the knife I am going to sink it in somewhere deep and twist the fucker, before I pull it out and begin all over again. Maybe I am a killer after all. Maybe everyone has a killer inside them somewhere. I guess I'll shortly find out.

Mal isn't one for patience, so I lift the blade and let it hover above Gabriel's hand. Mal takes a step back. He's making sure he's out of my reach, so I can't go and do something stupid. He's one step ahead as usual. I don't even look at him. I'm too good at this. I've had years of practise.

'Not going to beg me to take pity on your sorry ass?' I ask Gabriel, giving him a mean grin. The fighter in me is back. He should be pleased.

As if to answer he does his best to grin right back at me. He knows where this is going, and neither of us are in any hurry to see each other die.

'So which finger should I cut first?' It's another delaying tactic. We won't be allowed to get away with them for much longer because Mal is not known for his sweet, caring side. He's an impatient bastard who loves blood, depraved sex, and screaming - not necessarily in that order.

Gabriel leans forward and points to the skin between all his fingers on his right hand. He then makes slashing movements which tell me all I need to know. He wants me to cut through the glue.

'You sure?' I ask loudly, followed with a whispered, 'That's going to be messy.' Gabriel nods quickly, as if to say 'get on with it'.

Mal studies us, wondering what I'm whispering about. He's getting suspicious and there is no time to argue.

'Good choice,' I say quickly, and lowering the knife I make swift incisions to separate his fingers. It's not clean and I do slice into some of his skin. It can't be helped. Then I press the knife's handle between them and pray for a miracle because I have a feeling that's what we're going to need.

Gabriel immediately begins screaming through his nose. It's a smoke screen. My head is leaning over the table at the minute, so Mal can't actually see what I've done, but we need to make him believe we are playing along. To add to the commotion there is then a big crash from somewhere in the warehouse and shots are being fired off left, right and centre. Are Mal's men turning on him? Who knows? Right now I don't care. Mal has his gun, and if we're not lucky we'll both be rather cold and looking a very attractive shade of blue this time tomorrow.

Gabriel's head spins around, with his arm already in motion. The knife is thrown with meticulous accuracy, considering the state his hand is in, and hits its target with unerring precision. Obviously this isn't the first time Gabriel has done this, but it is still breathtakingly impressive. One moment Mal is standing there in his freshly-pressed black suit and pristine white shirt, and the next his chest has a bloody knife sticking out of it while he clutches at his throat for air. I hope the knife has managed to nick a lung or something because I really need the asshole to suffer.

With a swift lunge of his leg Gabriel knocks Mal to the floor, and the bastard lies there, wondering what the hell has just happened. To be honest I'm kind of in the same place. Gabe then waves his hand in Mal's direction, as if encouraging me to do my worst.

I need no further encouragement. Kneeling down slowly over Mal I grasp the knife that's embedded in his chest and twist it slowly. The sound of his screaming, after all these years of being his bitch, is a sheer joy to behold.

Gabriel heads for the medicine cupboard in the bathroom, while I kneel beside Mal's body. He is still screaming as I twist the knife, and I have to confess I haven't gotten tired of the noise. After a couple of minutes Gabe comes back with lips that are cut and bleeding but are at least two parts of a whole. He holds up a razor blade and smiles.

'Happy birthday, sweetheart,' he says.

If this was a birthday present, it would be the best I've ever received and I'm very grateful. Hopefully my smile of appreciation conveys this.

'You okay?' I ask. The poor guy looks a mess, but I think everything should heal given a week or two. But if Mal had messed about for much longer that might not have been the case.

'I'm fine. The glue is annoying, but I can get rid of most of it with acetone later. As to the bruises, I've had worse. How are you?'

'I'm feeling much better, funnily enough.' That reminds me, we shouldn't still be alive. 'Where are all the guards?' The place should be crawling with bad guys by now, but we're still alone in here. I can't work it out.

'Oh, don't worry about them. I'm staging a coup. I asked Markovich if he wanted to join forces, and it looks like he's come to my rescue. I didn't think he'd go for it, but perhaps my reputation has preceded me.' Gabriel looks thoughtful.

I don't even pretend to understand. It goes over my head the same way water travels across a duck's back. I can mull it over later. All my thoughts are focused on the evil bastard lying on the floor. He's barely bleeding, but I figure I can do something about that.

Gabriel changes the subject. 'By the way, there's nothing sorry about my ass,' he says, deadly serious. He obviously hasn't forgotten my comment from earlier. 'A lot of hours' work went into that ass. Women faint at the sight of it. A few men, too, come to think of it.'

I roll my eyes. The guy is one arrogant-son-of-a-bitch, but he's not wrong. He's got the face of an angel and the personality of a dirty politician. For some reason I find it an irresistible combination, but that doesn't mean I'm going to let him get away with it.

'How would you know? Have you seen it? Besides, you've been inside for the last God knows how many years and women are as alien to you as a voting booth. Your ass could be downright awful.'

'It isn't,' he states confidently.

I sigh. 'It isn't,' I confirm. The damn bastard smiles again.

Pointing to Mal he says, 'If you need a hand with him, let me know, and try not to kill him. I don't mind if you stab him and chop little pieces off, but it would be a shame if he died too quickly. I have plans for him once you've had your fill. Leave me something to work with, okay?'

Gabriel walks towards me before sliding his hands, which are still rough with superglue, over the back of my neck. It's as if he's encouraging me to do my worst.

'Thank you,' I whisper, suddenly feeling all choked up.

He laughs. 'You can thank me by making that bastard suffer. Go do your worst, Wilkinson. Show me what you've got.'

'For a mere slip of a girl you'd be surprised at what I've got.' Pulling the knife out of Mal's chest, I press my fingernails into the wound sharply and relish the screams that accompany it.

'Well, I'm not easily surprised,' Gabriel remarks, peeling his bloodstained shirt off as he pulls up a plastic chair to watch me work.

Gods, that man is a distraction. He grins evilly, as if he knows exactly what he is doing to me, even though I haven't got anywhere near enough energy to take him up on it. That reminds me, there is something I need to say, and it can't wait any longer.

'I still love Brandt, Gabriel.' I bite my lower lip as I confess this and wonder whether he's about to go apeshit on me.

He simply nods his head. 'That makes two of us, sweetheart,' he says. 'That makes two of us.'

Chapter Twenty-Four - Brandt

You hear things on the inside. There was a sting operation at Mal's warehouse after I'd spilled the beans, and Mal was found. He'd been dead for at least five hours before anyone got there, along with quite a few other people. I have no idea if those included Harper and Gabriel, and I have no way of finding out. The police are only so helpful. They did tell me he wasn't in a good way. Someone had gone at him with a knife, a pair of pliers, a circular saw, and an orbital sander. One of the officers told me they'd never seen anything like it. That's what keeps me hopeful. It sounds like Gabriel's work. If he's alive there's a chance Harper is still around, and however slim that chance might be, I'll take it.

Unfortunately, though, this means they can't get any information from Adley, which they weren't too pleased about. Everything now rides on either Helena or Harper. Happily they have managed to pick Helena up. She was still staying at the hotel in the room we'd booked together. She didn't suspect a thing, so the woman is nowhere near as clever as she thinks she is.

I'm already thoroughly sick of being back behind bars. At the moment I'm not really in jail; I'm more of a grudging guest who's thinking about long-term stay options. I can't say I'm up for another round, though. The first time was bad enough. Besides, I've got someone to look out for now.

'This is a mess.' My lawyer looks at the paperwork before him and winces. The police aren't sure what to do with me, and the poor guy is quite frankly horrified that I've already spilled my guts to them without his say-so. He mutters something about leverage and the fact we'll need all we can get if I don't plan on hanging around. Yeah, I've already thought of that.

'They won't put me inside,' I say, shaking my head. The look he gives me is withering.

Straightening his navy silk tie he says, 'You're an ex-con, who's been released mere weeks ago. They'll put you away again in a heartbeat. They have a murder weapon.'

'They have a murder weapon without my prints on it. I know the real murderer. I've already given her to them.' There are several ways to disguise your fingerprints, as it happens. I thought I'd take a leaf out of Mal's book and cover them with superglue. It was entirely possible that Helena had cleaned her prints off the gun before giving it to me, in which case I have plenty of audio, recorded on my new mobile phone. I also have her phone, which contains all her conversations with Mal. A friend stole it for me shortly after she left the hotel. I have quite the network of talented friends these days.

'And the other murder weapon you mentioned? The one that might be connected with another crime?'

'Oh, that one,' I say, waving my hand in the air. 'That one has gone missing. Trust me.' He eyes me warily, but doesn't say a thing. Remember what I said about friends? Gabriel has lots of friends, and it is quite frankly astounding how many people owe him favours.

'That still doesn't mean you'll be able to wriggle your way out of this mess,' he warns. He's only doing his job. Things often don't go smoothly once you're behind bars, and I know that from experience.

'It does if I've already made a deal with the cops. They were more than happy to cooperate once I told them I could hand them Mal Adley and show them the whereabouts of the labs. You're just here to complete the paperwork and make sure I haven't missed anything.'

My lawyer blinks but doesn't miss a beat. 'Are you happy with the deal you made? If you aren't, now is the time to mention it.'

'I'm happy. I get to walk. They can't actually hold me, anyway, as I haven't committed a crime, but if anything does turn up with the other murder weapon, they're prepared to look the other way as long as all the other testimony adds up.'

Snapping open his briefcase, the man pulls a shiny silver pen out and begins filling in my paperwork. He tells me that he should be able to get me out of here, barring any other incidents, in the next few hours. It isn't soon enough, but there is no rushing the process, so I sit back and try to calm myself down.

Gabriel assured me everything would be okay. He was in on our last little meet in the hotel room. I told him everything that was happening, but I didn't like the way that meeting panned out. I hadn't discovered Helena intended to have me arrested from her phone, so she must have decided to do that after a meeting with Mal. If I'd known that things would have gone down differently. Thankfully, I did know she intended to frame me. I also discovered a lot more things about her that I never really wanted to know.

When all the relevant paperwork has been filled and filed, things start moving. I am duly processed, and my watch and belt are finally returned to me. They're keeping hold of my cell phone for the time being, and they're welcome to it.

Stepping out once more into the broad light of day, I wonder what I should do next. That's when I see my father waiting for me. The Mayor has come all the way down here to watch his son's walk of shame? Surely not. He made it very clear that he wouldn't give me the time of day the last time we spoke. Pretending I haven't seen him, I stride off in the opposite direction.

'Brandt, if you'd just give me a minute...' He sounds awkward. We haven't spoken in forever, so I guess that's how he should sound.

'Fuck off, Dad.' I have nothing to say to him, so I continue walking. I'm in no mood for a fight right now. I suspect he's going to speak to me about my actions, telling me how damaging they are for his career, but I couldn't care less. I have bigger things to worry about.

Dad doesn't stand there on the sidewalk, as I expect him to. Instead he comes rushing over. 'I need to speak to you. It's about Mal.'

That captures my attention quickly enough.

'What do you know about Mal?' I ask, whipping my head around so violently I nearly give myself whiplash.

'Mal was the reason we haven't spoken to you. He threatened to kill you if we came anywhere near you.' Dad's hands are shaking. I've never seen him like this. He is genuinely distressed.

Ping. A massive lightbulb switches itself on above me and everything falls magically into place. Oh. My. God.

'He controlled you through me, didn't he? He got you to look the other way as soon as you were elected. You did his dirty work for him, didn't you?' This is not the conversation we should be having outside a police station, and when dad's eyes flare and he points to his car, I decide I'll give him the chance to explain. If this goes the way I expect it to, he may not be a monster after all.

We don't speak again until the car starts moving. Dad is looking at me, his face devouring mine, and I can tell he is close to tears. He usually isn't one for outward displays of emotion, but today appears to be different.

He looks pained as he tries to figure out what he needs to say, but eventually he manages to spit it out.

'Adley knew I was going to get elected. He had this planned from the start. He has half the city on his payroll and everyone lives in fear of him. I'm so sorry, son,' he whispers, grabbing my hand.

Turning to face him I say, 'Are you in trouble, Dad?' If one of Mal's goons has taken over the business, it's entirely possible that he's still between a rock and a hard place. I'm not exactly sure how this kind of intimidation will work if I'm not behind bars, but I'm guessing they'll just use someone else as leverage. Hopefully not another member of my family, else I will lose it.

'I don't know,' he murmurs. 'I guess it depends on who takes over the business.'

'If they have footage of you with Mal, you're going down,' I whisper.

'I know.' His lower lip wobbles and for a moment I think he's going to break down on me. 'Your mother and I have missed you so much,' he eventually says, changing the subject. 'We thought you were going to die. We had to abandon you, but everything that was done was because we feared he would get to you. No one is safe around him. He killed two of my colleagues a week after I'd first met him. The man scared me witless.'

'He told you that you couldn't help me with my legal counsel, didn't he? He wanted me inside.' I shake my head. Adley, you sadistic son-of-a-bitch, it's a good job you're dead. I hope you suffered horribly.

Dad nods. 'We heard stories of what happened to you inside, every time something happened that Mal didn't like. It drove your mum insane. We've been living on a tightrope these past few years. She was admitted to Redgrove last month, and she's still in a bad way.'

Redgrove is a psychiatric hospital about ten miles away from home. Oh God.

'And Zeb, is he okay?' I don't know if they've managed to keep this mess from my brother, but they would have had to have told him something.

'He's okay. He misses you. We've tried to keep what was happening from him, but I'm pretty sure he's figured some of it out.' Dad chews his bottom lip.

'You didn't ask me to marry Helena, did you?' I know who did.

Dad shakes his head. 'No, that was Mal. He got hold of Simmons and orchestrated the rest. He said that if we even thought of going near you, someone would get hurt.'

'You don't mess with Adley,' I say, unnecessarily.

'I am so glad you're safe,' he whispers. 'I know I've been hard on you over the years, but that was because I wanted big things for you. I thought if you followed in my footsteps you'd have everything you'd ever want.' Dad rolls his eyes skyward as he looks away from me.

'Didn't turn out that way, huh?' I let out a small, bitter laugh.

'You have no idea. I'll be lucky to get out of this mess without going to jail as well - and I thoroughly deserve to, if I'm honest. I'm a corrupt politician who's made a mess of everything. I'm resigning my position as of this afternoon, and I'm never setting foot in politics ever again. While I don't expect you to forgive me, I hope you'll go see your mother and brother. They've been so worried about you. They both miss you terribly.'

I lean over to take his hand, which is still shaking, and I grasp it firmly.

'I know what Adley is capable of. You didn't have a choice. There is nothing to forgive.' Now I'm choked up and my voice is tight in my chest. Then we both try to speak at once.

'God, you've changed so much, son. What did they do to you in there?'

'I thought you'd abandoned me. I couldn't believe you'd do that.'

We both stop short, wondering who should go next.

'Let's go to dinner,' Dad says eventually. 'We have a lot to talk about.'

It's amazing how much I've missed since I've been inside. My brother has graduated from university and now has a job as a statistician. He was always good at maths. Zeb also has a steady girlfriend, a new passion for downhill skiing, and he is the life and soul of every party, Dad tells me. The last part is not news to me. He always was the party animal.

'And Mum?' I know she won't be in a good way. She was always nervous and anxious about things, and this will have nearly killed her.

'She's not good,' Dad admits, 'but she'll be better once you speak to her.' He grabs his diary from his pocket and writes a number down, before tearing out the page and handing it to me. 'She hasn't been the same since you left. This mess has been eating her alive, and six months ago she nearly lost it. Be gentle with her.'

I nod. As if I could be anything else. This is not her fault.

Dad finishes the steak in front of him and wipes his lips with his napkin before placing it on the table. 'Will they be able to charge you with anything? Are you in trouble? Do you need help?'

'I don't think so. Adley tried his best to pin a few things on me, but I think I've wriggled out from his clutches by the skin of my teeth.' The thought of spending twenty years inside makes me feel queasy. I couldn't go through that again.

'Good. If you need any help, let me know. I know I didn't help you the first time, but it wasn't because I didn't want to. Now Adley is not around, we can throw all the lawyers in London in your corner if need be.'

I smile. 'I don't think that will be necessary, but if I need help you'll be the first person I call.'

'Are you sure you're okay, Brandt? You don't look okay.' Dad keeps looking me up and down, and I'm beginning to wonder if he can read minds.

'It's the tatts, isn't it? You don't like them. You think they make me look like a thug.' I'm still going to be the black sheep of this family, but I can cope with that.

Dad rolls his eyes. 'I can cope with the tattoos. I have seen them before, Brandt, and that's not what I meant. What's wrong?' Mum was always the intuitive one, but it looks like he has some skills of his own.

'It's a girl,' I admit. 'She's tangled up with Adley and I don't know whether she's still alive.'

Dad folds his hands together on the table and looks serious. 'You don't mean Harper?'

I almost recoil in shock. 'You've met her?'

'I've met her,' he confirms. 'Adley must have beaten her up the last time I saw her because she looked black and blue.' This isn't news to me, but it still hurts.

Dad must be able to see the look that crosses over my face because he adds, 'You're in love with her, aren't you?'

I nod slowly. I do love her, and I'm shit scared that she's dead. If she is I won't be able to forgive myself. I'll end up in the same place Mum is because it will eat away at me until it drives me crazy.

'Then you'd better go get her. Let me help,' he says.

I speak to my mother on the drive down to dad's office. At first she wonders who the hell I am, but then the penny drops. Her son is back. The danger has passed. The nightmare that has been plaguing us all for so long can finally disappear. It might take a few years, but I hope that will be the case, eventually. This is all a bit too much to process for my poor old Mum, though.

At first I get two or three-word sentences, but when she realises this is not a joke, she finally opens up. She starts crying down the phone, and I want to cry with her. This all seems so surreal. I thought they both hated me, and now I find out it's all Mal's doing. Any moment now I'm going to wake up and find myself back in prison. That's how unreal this feels. While I know that Mal was one of the East End's biggest criminals, I had no idea how far his reach extended. In the end no one would dare defy him, except perhaps for Harper. God, Harper. She is all I can think about right now. What if she's dead? I daren't linger on that thought.

When we get to City Hall the place is buzzing with activity. It takes a few minutes to get me signed in, but after that Dad is all business. This is how I remember him. He's always been very focused, and he can usually charm the pants off anyone. Anyone bar Mal, of course.

Dad makes some phone calls and leans on some people to get us some CCTV footage near the crime scene. The area directly outside Mal's warehouse is a blind spot, and for good reason, but we hope to find something nearby either directly before or after the event. But finding any trace of either Harper or Gabriel's whereabouts is virtually impossible. With the help of the city's CCTV footage and some of Dad's contacts we scour hours of feed, and look through numerous police databases, but nothing crops up. They haven't been found dead, which is something, but that doesn't mean they aren't. They could be resting in an unmarked grave, fed to pigs, dissolved in lye or lying in an empty dumpster somewhere. We have no way of knowing.

'Do you know who killed Mal?' Dad finally asks, and I'm surprised it's taken him this long.

'No.' This is true. I'm hoping Gabriel or Harper has, but I don't know for sure.

Dad takes two cups of coffee from a guy that looks like he left school yesterday and hands one to me. 'There's usually always someone waiting in the wings, ready to take over when this kind of thing happens. Doling out drugs is a multimillion-pound business. We could both be targets when the new guy takes over.' Dad's face is pinched. Judging by the black circles under his eyes, he's not slept for some time.

'Could be a girl,' I say, to fill in the silence that resumes.

'I doubt it. They don't normally have the stomach for it, but yes, it's possible.'

'Maybe everything will die with Mal,' I say optimistically.

'Unlikely,' is my father's reluctant reply. He gives me a tight smile. 'It's possible that the next guy to step up will choose his own contacts and ignore those that have gone before. It depends on how closely he worked with Mal. What is far more likely is that we're going to be preyed upon by his successor very soon. I don't want that to happen.' He takes a large slug of coffee and grimaces. 'No sugar,' he says by way of explanation.

I roll my eyes. 'I don't see how you can stop it. They'll kill you if you interfere. Even if you have resigned.'

My phone begins to vibrate in my pocket. It's the first time it's rung since I've got out, and I'm not sure whether that's a good or a bad thing. When I look down at the screen I see Gabe's name, but I don't get my hopes up just yet. This could be Mal's replacement, and I can't say I'm looking forward to that conversation.

Considering I've just made amends with most of my family, I will not be amused if someone starts threatening to kill us all again.

Chapter Twenty-Five - Gabriel

'I'm not going to kill him.' I hear Brandt suck in a breath on the other end of the phone, and I know he's wondering if I'm speaking to him from beyond the grave. I can't help but find this funny, so I laugh.

'I'm not dead, Brando. The reason I know what you're talking about is that Mal has your dad's office bugged. It's amazing how many bugs that asshole has stashed around the city. You'd be impressed.'

'You're alive,' Brandt breathes. 'Oh my God, you're alive. Is Harper there with you?' I hear the note of despair in his voice and immediately feel guilty. I should have rung sooner, but I've been a little busy on my end. After our 'ordeal' Harper went into shock and needed medical attention. I didn't want to take her to a hospital as Mal's old contacts might still have been hanging around, so I had to get her some help privately, and while I've been doing that, I've had other things to sort out too. In a nutshell, I've been a very busy boy.

'She's okay. She has her own doctor, and he's got her stable, but she's not going to be in tiptop shape for a while. Poor girl is lucky to be alive, and it amazes me that she's still holding it together, considering what she's seen.'

'Did you kill Mal?' Brandt already knows the answer to that question, he just wants it confirmed.

'You think anyone else could have done that to him?' I feel affronted. Sometimes the fact that I'm bordering on psychotic is a blessing. I messed that fucker up bad, and I'm quite proud of the fact.

'That's a good question. What did you do to him? I overheard a copper telling someone that the body was virtually unrecognisable.'

'At least the copper got his facts straight,' I say smugly. 'That fucker superglued my mouth together, before gluing my fingers to one another, and then he was going to do the same to my eyes. I was a little pissed, Brandt.'

'Oh my God,' he says, trying to take all of that in.

'Then he threatened to cut my cock off.' I hear Brandt choking and someone asks him if he wants some water. Too funny.

When he can finally talk again he says, 'If that's the case, I'm surprised there was anything left of him.'

'If I'd had more time there wouldn't have been, but there were things that needed to be done. Harper wasn't good. She managed to stab him once or twice, but then she sunk to the floor and started sobbing. I think she was just relieved that it was all about to be over. Anyway, suffice to say, I made sure the fucker suffered as much as possible in the time that we had.' I was efficient, if nothing else.

Thankfully Brandt doesn't ask what that means. I'm pretty sure he doesn't want to hear all the gory details.

'I'm just glad you got out of there okay, and that you're both still alive. You've given me nightmares, Gabe. Never do that again.' The boy sounds close to tears.

I ignore that comment. I'm not much for emotional outbursts, so I immediately change the subject to something much safer.

'Are they going to charge you with anything, or did you manage to get away with it?' I know Brandt is going to get away with it, but like I said, we needed a change of scenery.

'I don't think so. So far, so good. I'll be fine until Mal's replacement comes looking for me. Actually, you need to be careful too. If they suspect for a second that you killed him, you're next in line for a long lie down in a big black car.'

'About that.' I pause as I try to put this into words. Shit. This is going to get messy, and he's not going to like it, but he's had to deal with worse.

'No one's going to kill me, Brando. That's why I did such a nice number on Mal. Actually, no, that's a lie. I quite enjoyed everything I did to Mal, and I'd do it again, given half a chance.' I'm not lying. Watching the light die out in his eyes is going up in my personal hall of fame for feel-good moments. Yeah, I know I'm a psychopath. We enjoy that kind of thing. Luckily, I seem to be able to turn it off and on. If I was a serial killer we'd have problems.

'That would be tricky, considering he's dead,' Brandt says slowly. He's got a good point.

'Anyway,' I say, 'no one is coming after me, you, Harper or your family - or anyone else for that matter. Relax. I've sorted the problem out.' That reminds me. 'Oh, and Harper says you need to speak to your family. They haven't abandoned you. That was Mal's doing. He threatened to kill you if she told you. I figure you know that part already as you're with your dad in his office. My bad? You have no idea how much I'm looking forward to Mal's funeral. I'm going to stamp all over that fucker's grave.' I'm changing the subject again. I'm feeling a little bit nervous about where this conversation is headed and how it's going to end. I even begin to fiddle with the black shirt I'm wearing (it's one of Mal's), and I never do shit like that.

'How do you know no one is going to kill us?' So much for my changing the subject. I need to work on my technique. Maybe I need a better subject.

'Did I mention Harper is doing well? The doctor reckons she'll be back to eating solids tomorrow. Her stomach is still a little sore, but at least the bruises are fading now.'

'Gabe. Answer the fucking question.' There's the sound of a hand slamming down on a desk and I know that my boy is not happy. Looks like it's time to 'fess all. I need to take a deep breath and just say it. Air goes in, air goes out. Fuck.

'I know because I've taken over from Mal, Brandt. I am now king of the East End. All hail the new god of London.' There. I've said it. That's the first thing I had to get off my chest. Only one more to go.

'You what?' I don't think he could have sounded more shocked if I'd told him aliens had abducted me and were going to use me to breed a new super race of little green men. Actually, that's not a bad fantasy if they all have tentacles. Might need to come back to that one later.

'You heard. It's not forever. It's just to take the heat off you guys. As you know, I had to pay for several favours to make sure your sorry ass didn't go to jail, and I need to pay those men off somehow. Besides, now that we're ex-cons I need to make a little retirement money if we all want to sail off happily into the sunset.'

'I have money,' Brandt points out.

'It wouldn't be any use to you if you were dead.' I may just have pointed out that I've done something chivalrous for the man I love. It feels weird. I've never done anything like this for anyone before. I'm going to try and not make a habit of it.

'You can't do this,' Brandt whispers. 'You're sacrificing your life for ours. That's not the way it works. We could have figured this out together.' He's nearly at the breaking down stage. I can hear it in his voice. Shit. I can't deal with this.

'It's too late. I did it. I'm running the gig now. I'll get out in a year or two's time and fake my own death. In the meantime, I plan to kill everyone who's ever pissed me off, and the list is fairly long. I'm going to have such fun. Oh, and I can get high whenever I want. Did I mention that part? Don't feel sorry for me, Brando. I'm going to be having the time of my life.'

'No, there has to be another way,' he insists. 'I'll do it. Sign me up instead. I can't let you do this for me.'

I nearly laugh. 'Brandt, you wouldn't last a day. You have to be a scary-ass fucker to do this job. You have to know something about drugs, too. Oh, it also helps if you've got 'murderer' somewhere on your CV. I'm sorry mate. You can't have the job. Maybe if you go off the rails and do something really bad I'll let you take over in a couple of years.'

'That's not funny.' Brandt is clearly appalled.

'I know it isn't, but I've got this. Try to make sure your dad doesn't arrest me within the first month though. It's not going to do much for my reputation if I'm back behind bars in a few weeks.'

There's a sigh on the line, and Brandt makes me wait for what he's about to say next. He's going to regret this, but I'm going to let him do it anyway.

Another few seconds go by, but he finally gets it together. 'I love you, you know. Even though you're a shit. Even though I don't want to, and even though you're a pain in the ass.'

My blackened heart swells a little. 'I love you too. I just realised it too late. The only reason I slept with Shaney was because he had evidence that helped get my sorry ass out of prison. Maybe I should have told you that first. I don't expect you to forgive me, but I didn't do it for any reason other than that. I just couldn't rot in jail when I knew you were going to be outside.'

Brandt roars over the phone. 'Now you fucking tell me? If you were here I'd break your nose!'

'Nah you wouldn't,' I say. 'But you might after I told you I'm in love with your girlfriend.'

Chapter Twenty-Six - Harper

I am so happy. Unbelievably happy, in fact.

If anyone had told me how much my life would change in two short years, I wouldn't have believed them. If I had to go through every awful moment my life has held in order to get here again, I'd do it without question.

This kind of happiness is a once in a lifetime deal, and you don't get a second chance at it. They say everything comes at a price, and I really hope I have paid mine. What I suffered under Mal and Alex's hands will always be one of the darkest points in my life, but as time passes the nightmares slowly recede. My psychiatrist tells me they may eventually even go away entirely, but I think she is being too optimistic. If she isn't lucky she'll be having nightmares too, by the time I've finished with her.

Brandt and I are currently living in Cambridge so we can be close to his family, but now that they're settled we've decided to try a three-month vacation in Sydney, Australia. I've always wanted to go, and when I foolishly mentioned it to Brandt, he jumped all over it. I am so spoilt. Brandt gives me everything I could ever possibly want and more. The man brings tears to my eyes nearly every single day, and they are the good kind. For a girl who's learnt the hard way how to school her emotions twenty-four-seven, it's a bizarre about turn, but I'm getting used to it.

I still remember when he first set eyes on me after Mal's death, striding through the halls of the Johnson clinic, looking anxious as hell. I'm not sure if he expected me to be cut up into bits, but he breathed a massive sigh of relief when he found out I wasn't.

'Oh God, Harper. I've been worried half to death. Gabriel only just called me, I thought you were dead. Are you okay? Have they been taking care of you? Jesus, I've missed you.' The words tumbled out, one on top of the other, as he stood there looking adorable in a pair of ripped blue jeans and a black hoodie.

I remember him rushing over to my bedside as he gathered me in his arms. A bit like that scene from *An Officer and A Gentleman* but with a hospital bed and the smell of antiseptic everywhere.

'Ow, ow. Gently.' I laugh as he hugs me a bit too tightly. When he looks at me with a worried frown, I say, 'I'm fine. I'll heal. It'll take a few weeks for the bruises to fade and I'll be left with plenty of scars, but at least I'm alive.'

'Fuck that bastard,' Brandt says. 'If he were still alive, you don't want to know what I'd do to him.'

'I'm kind of glad Gabriel got that job,' I say, not unkindly. 'He deserved a violent, messy and excruciatingly painful end. It's more Gabriel's field. By the way, he did a mighty fine job. You would have been proud of him.'

'So I heard. Did you know he planned to take over from Mal?'

'He what?' This is the last thing I want to hear.

Brandt nods. 'In order to stop Mal's replacement from rushing out to kill us, he's decided to take over the reins.'

My eyes well up with tears. 'Since when did he become so noble?' I shake my head, sniffing, and do my best to hold the floodgates at bay. I can't bear this. I am toxic. I heap misery upon everyone I come into contact with. This shit is never ending.

'He also told me he loves you. Do you love him back, Harper?' Brandt looks at me with sympathy, and for some strange reason that hurts even more. Then the tears begin to flow, and I can't say a word. All I can do is hiccup and take in great, gasping breaths that obviously make me look like I'm dying because Brandt calls for a doctor.

'It's okay,' I wheeze. 'I'm fine. I just can't believe he'd do that.'

'That he'd rescue us both? Try to let us enjoy a little happiness?' Brandt tries to wipe my tears away with the pad of his thumb, but he's wasting his time; there's plenty more where they come from.

'Well, yes. The guy is a colossal asshole. Let's not forget that.' I try to sound as if I mean it.

'But you love him anyway?' Brandt gently smooths a few strands of matted hair away from my face and waits patiently for my answer.

I can't lie. 'Yes, I do,' I admit. 'He protected me in there. He did his best to make sure I didn't get too messed up, and we were locked in a small room for days on end with virtually nothing to eat. Anything we did get he'd give to me. He even patched me up when I got hurt. It's hard to hate someone who's looking out for you. He would have died for me in there.' I'm not entirely sure how I know that, but I do. Thankfully he didn't have to, but the alternative he's facing isn't much better.

Brandt smiles and grabbing the jug by my bedside, pours a glass of water. Handing it to me he says, 'Don't feel bad about it. Everyone falls in love with Gabe. Even those who electrocute him and try to take his head off with an iPad.' He presses his lips together and tries not to grin. Yeah, I did that, didn't I? I'm amazed Gabe didn't kill me there and then.

'Do you still love him? He slept with that bloke to get himself out of jail. You can't blame him for that.' I tip the glass up to my lips and drink. I can feel a headache coming on.

'He was still unfaithful.' Brandt looks thoughtful as he speaks, not angry. I wonder what this means.

'You'd have done the same thing to get out of there,' I point out. I know I would have.

'You're probably right. Anyway, it doesn't matter now. He informs me he's going to have the time of his life over the next couple of years, getting high on anything that's going.'

I roll my eyes. 'I can imagine him saying that. Will he come and find us when his time is up, do you think?' I want him to. I don't want this to be the last we ever see of him. I think if Brandt were honest, he'd say the same thing.

'Who knows?' He shrugs his shoulders. 'Right now we have to concentrate on getting you better, so we can get you out of here. As soon as you're up for it I'm taking you to meet my parents. There. That'll encourage you to eat your greens, won't it?'

I snort with laughter. I can't help it. Then a thought occurs to me.

'Oh shit. I meant to tell you. Mal has your parents...' Brandt cuts me off mid-sentence.

'I know. That's why you are going to meet them. It wasn't a joke.'

'Oh.' The 'O' sound goes on for quite a long time.

'Do you love me, Harper? Think long and hard before you answer because there is no going back from this. I'm going to take care of you, whatever the answer, but I need to know the truth.'

I blink. He needs to ask me? After all this time, he's still not sure? Men. They really are from a different planet. Taking his head in my hands, one on either side of his face, I give him the brightest smile I've ever given anyone.

'I've always loved you, Brandt Browning. You were my first love, you will be my last. I've daydreamed about you for years, convinced myself I'd never have you, and cried over you. I've tried to forget you, tried to ignore you, and tried to distance myself from you. None of it worked. Alex knew it, Mal knew it. The knowledge drove them crazy. Even if you walk away from me now, I will always love you. I can love you from afar. I've had lots of practice. You are up here, and you always will be.' I tap my forehead a couple of times. 'You were the only thing that got me through the last five years of my life. I am so sorry for what I did to you, and I would do anything to make it up to you. Anything. You just have to say the word.' I mean it, too. I would walk on water for the guy. Probably dance over it, too.

'Well, thank fuck for that. Will you move in with me, Harper Wilkinson? Will you let me take care of you? I've been in love with you for years, I was just too much of a pussy to stand up to my parents. You should have told me what an idiot I was. You are the only woman that could ever make me happy and I want to spend the next fifty or sixty years proving that to you. Will you let me? I might drive you crazy, but please say yes.'

I'm crying again. I don't cry for years and then I'm waterworks woman all of a sudden. What's with that? 'Yes,' I sob. I can't say anything else. The thought of waking up to Brandt every morning makes me want to sob all over again, harder and with much more enthusiasm. Poor Brandt obviously thinks I'm a loon because he then picks me up and carries me out of there.

For the next eight weeks, through my slow and cumbersome recovery, he won't take his eyes off me, but that's okay, because I can't take my eyes off him either. I am treated like a princess, albeit one that's made of spun sugar, and for the first time in ages Brandt has a genuine smile on his face. We drown in each other at every opportunity, sharing all our hopes and dreams, and amazingly enough, they are relatively similar. We both want to travel, figure out some kind of fulfilling career that isn't illegal, and hopefully start a family one day. For now, though, we're taking it one step at a time.

Sydney, Australia

'Either you get your ass down these stairs immediately, Harper, or I'm coming up and I'm going to spank the living daylights out of it.' Brandt sounds exasperated, as well he should. We're supposed to be meeting friends for drinks in just over an hour and it's a forty-five minute drive to the restaurant in Darling Harbour, which is just minutes away from the Opera House. I love Australia. Everyone dines al fresco out here because the weather is always fantastic, and the seafood is to die for. The shellfish here are literally double the size of anything you can find in the UK. I don't know what the Aussies are feeding their fish, but hot damn, it must be good.

Standing at the top of the stairs dressed in something expensive, slinky and revealing, I say, 'Has that threat ever worked for you before?'

Brandt grins. 'Why do you think I use it?' He then bounds up the stairs so fast I barely even get a head start. To be fair, there's no point trying to run in this dress. I'll just end up in a heap on the floor, which Brandt will find hysterical, and laughter is not what I'm after. Nuh-uh. I want full-throttle, bent over the bathtub, hardcore sex, with a moderate amount of pain involved. We've argued about my addiction to pain, but at the end of the day I like receiving it and Brandt likes giving it, so we managed to compromise. Brandt refuses to leave any lingering marks or bruises anywhere except my backside. That works for me. We can both get what we want this way, and besides, you don't have to leave marks to create pain. Brandt is rather devious like that.

'Don't even think about it,' I threaten as he moves towards me. 'It took me an hour to do my make-up, and this dress will wrinkle if you toss it on the floor.' The dress is amazing, made from this gorgeous velvety material that clings to every curve. It's stunningly draped to reveal nearly the entire length of my left leg and features a plunging 'V' neckline. I love it, and by the look in Brandt's eye, I'm not the only one.

'I won't touch your face and you can keep the dress on. We talked about this, princess. If you insist on wearing ridiculously sexy clothes that will torment me all through dinner, you'd better be prepared to suffer a little yourself. So, get in the bedroom, bend over the dresser, and lift up your skirt. You'd better not be wearing panties, either. You remember our arrangement I hope?' Brandt has the devil in his eyes.

'Our arrangement' as he calls it, means that if he catches me wearing panties he can dole out any punishment he likes on the spot.

'We're going to be late,' I say, backing away from him. 'You hate being late.' I'm just playing with him, of course. I need sex so badly right now I could cry. He's been away for the last two days studying some business module that his father recommended. Brandt wants to go into app development. He loves computers and nearly everything related to them, so he's testing the waters to see if it's for him. I've missed him like crazy though. Two days seems likes forever without Brandt.

'I hate being late when it's my parents or family. Dad's a pain about shit like that. But we're visiting friends tonight. We can be as late as you like.' The look he gives me is predatory as he moves forward and reaches out to grab me. I step back just in time.

'I think we need to talk about the no panties rule. This is a very short dress in places. Do you really want your girlfriend exposing herself in public?' I point towards the teal dress now riding up my leg in case he's forgotten the argument while running his eyes all over my body.

'No. I'd rather you wore a burka in public, if I'm completely honest. I don't want any other man setting eyes on what's mine. If you choose to wear dresses that are far too short and feel the need to wear panties, you'll just have to accept the consequences.' Brandt points his finger at me. 'Memo to you, dress more conservatively in future.'

My mouth opens wide at his high-handedness. 'Oh, you...' I don't get a chance to finish the sentence because his second grab at me is right on target.

'Was that a 'oh you devilishly handsome man, I've missed you so much and I need you so badly'?' Brandt's hand goes straight between my legs and finds out I am indeed wearing panties, and they're rather wet. 'Oh God, Harper,' he groans, 'you're going to kill me.'

'Makes a change from you wanting to kill me, huh?' I back away quickly, making a run for it down the hallway. Brandt is hot on my heels, which is exactly where I want him.

'Jesus, woman. Stay still.'

Huh? Where would be the fun in that? I run faster just to spite him. The trouble is, one of his strides equals two of mine and he's on me in two seconds flat.

Grabbing my arm he spins me round to face him, before pulling me to his chest and lifting me up in the air. Uh oh. Now I'm in trouble. Hallelujah!

Brandt flings me over his shoulder, and he doesn't let me down until we're in front of the dresser he mentioned throwing me over. He then does exactly that, placing my palms face down and my head directly in front of the mirror.

'You can safe word anytime you like, but if I have blue balls during dinner I'm making you wear the egg all night long.' The egg is a vibrating monster that fits snuggly inside my pussy and drives me crazy. He has a remote control for it, which means we can have the 'tolerable' level or the 'evil' level. Obviously it's much more fun to go evil, and that's usually where it stays. Anyway, this is a moot point. Why would I want to safe word? I've been gagging for this for days.

When I sit quietly for a few moments and there's no response I wiggle my ass. 'Please, Brandt. Please?' I whimper.

'God. The things you do to me, Harper. I haven't been able to concentrate all week because thoughts of you have been driving me crazy.'

I snort. 'Glad to know I'm not the only one. Now stick it in me, Brando, and wiggle it around. Oh, and hurry, because we're on a schedule here and you don't like to be late.' This is code for 'I need my orgasm yesterday'. He'll figure it out.

Brandt's mouth comes close to my ear and he bites my lobe, which drives me nuts. He always knows just how much pain to dish out without actually causing me bodily harm. It's a skill none of my other boyfriends has ever managed to accomplish. Oh, and he worships me as if I'm a goddess. Every woman in the world should be treated this way. It feels incredible.

'Hard?' he asks. It's a stupid question, and he knows it. Of course I want it hard.

'Yes,' I hiss, 'and don't rip the panties. I've only got two pairs left.' Brandt has a thing about tearing lingerie apart. The lady at Victoria's Secret now knows me by name and I swear she thinks I'm a prostitute as I'm in there nearly every week.

Brandt lifts up my skirt and then with one swift yank, tears the flimsy black lace panties in two. Men. Why can't they follow simple instructions?

'I like tearing them off. It's one of my favourite pastimes. And maybe one day you'll realise that buying new ones is pointless.' He undoes his fly and pulls his cock out of his boxers, rubbing it up and down my slit. Oh God, I'm about to explode. The merest touch on my clit is going to send me over the edge. Whoever told me the honeymoon period in a new relationship lasted six months was way off. I'm constantly like a lit firework around this man. It's got to be really bad for my blood pressure.

I let out a little growl of annoyance. 'You're buying my panties in future, Brando. The girls in the lingerie store probably think I have some sort of fetish by now.'

'No way. You're not allowed any. Ever. Either get used to going naked or learn to wear longer skirts.' His fingers lightly brush over my clit and my hips buck back into him, while the rest of my body crests on lightning waves of pleasure.

'Brandt,' my voice is ragged. 'Please.' My hands are shaking on the side of the dresser as his fingers dip inside me.

'Promise me you will never buy another pair of panties ever again.' There is no way I am making that promise. His fingers brush over my clit again, ever so lightly, but they make my whole body light up.

'I promise I am never buying panties ever again,' I mewl. 'Fuck me now, damnit.'

Brandt laughs and proceeds to do exactly that with hard, fast, deep and long strokes that have me coming in seconds. The feeling is amazing, and it never goes away. I am so lucky. All my fantasies have come true.

Anyway, the monster hasn't won. Either I'll use his credit card to buy all my panties in the future (so technically he's buying them), or I'll buy teddies, bodysuits or babydolls instead. Problem solved.

Chapter Twenty-Seven - Gabriel

When Harper walks into the restaurant and sees me she nearly does a double take. For a moment her eyes bug wide, and then she claps a hand over her mouth and squeals like a kid.

'Gabriel!' As she rushes over I just manage to get out of my chair before I am greeted with a bear hug. As far as bear's go she's a small one, but she looks a damn site better than she did the last time I saw her. 'What happened?' she breathes. 'Did you finally manage to get out?'

'If by that you mean did I finally manage to fake my own death, then yes, I am officially dead.' My eyes are eating her up, and her eyes on me are no less carnivorous. The dress she is wearing is almost indecent, so you can't blame me. I am a mere mortal, after all.

'You look really good for a dead person,' she says, grinning all over me. I have to admit, I do scrub up rather well. I've had two years to amass a small fortune, and in that time I've had a bit of a style update. It turns out that Armani suits are a good look for me, so I now have quite the collection. Tonight, I'm in a pale beige number with a white shirt, which does wonders for my tan.

'So do you. That dress should be illegal.' Smiling back at her, I then turn to Brandt and say, 'Thank your father for getting me out of there. I couldn't have done it without his help. It was a bit touch and go for a while, but we got there in the end.' Mayor Browning helped me pull off a massive sting operation where I basically gave him everything. The whereabouts of all the labs, the names of all my contacts, and where the drugs were coming in from. The only thing he didn't get was the money. There had to be some perks to the job. Anyway, there were pictures of my dead body plastered all over the tabloids, to make sure no one came looking for me. I have no idea where he got the makeup artist from, but oh boy did she know her stuff. I looked hideous.

'He says to thank you, funnily enough. He's almost certain to get re-elected after he's taken one of London's most notorious criminals off the grid, and crime is already down in the capital by ten percent. He's also grateful to you for saving my hide, as am I, funnily enough.' Brant gives me another hug and a slap on the back. I return it.

'I wasn't sure you'd come tonight,' I say. Now that Brandt's got the girl, I'm surprised he wants me anywhere near them. I wondered, up until now, whether Harper would be undecided between Brandt and me, but by the look in her eyes I can tell she isn't. She wears the look of a woman madly in love, and while I want what they have, I'm not prepared to destroy their happiness. For the first time in forever, I care too much for both of them to let my feelings interfere.

'Why ever not?' Brandt looks at me, puzzled. 'We owe our lives to you. Harper because of the stunt you pulled in Mal's warehouse with your men, and me due to all the strings you pulled in order to make some old 'evidence' disappear. We're not the kind of people who forget things like that, Gabriel.'

'No, not because of that, and you don't owe me anything. I didn't need any encouragement to tear Adley to pieces. That monster deserved everything he got.'

'Then what do you mean?' Brandt is grinning at me. The bastard is tormenting me in front of the woman I've been infatuated with for the past two years. Still, if he wants to fight dirty, I can sling a little mud of my own.

'I mean because of the way I feel about your woman.'

'Ahh. The woman. She's a feisty little thing.' Brandt raises his eyebrows and looks over at Harper. She winks and then picks up her wineglass and waggles it in the air.

'Gentlemen, we need wine. This is a celebration.' Beckoning a waiter over, she whispers in his ear and both me and Brandt stiffen.

'You're not bored with her then?' I bite my lip and look decidedly pissed off, because I already know the answer to that question.

Brandt nearly chokes but recovers himself quickly. 'I don't get bored, Gabriel. That's your thing and you know it. Harper is amazing. There is nothing I wouldn't do for her, and I mean that - nothing.' Brandt is smitten. He'll be building a white picket fence, planting roses and feeding a baby or two before the year is out. It's written all over his face. I am insanely jealous and I'm sure it shows. It's unlike me, but I can't help it. It doesn't help that the jealousy is twofold. I want both Brandt and Harper. I want their perfect life. I want what I can't have.

Pulling out my chair, I try my best to smile as the waiter brings over a chilled bottle of white wine. With napkin in hand, he pours a generous serving into each of our glasses, and I watch as the condensation dribbles down the bottle. I can't look at Harper. It feels like someone has wedged an axe in the middle of my chest, and it's a fucking great big one.

'Gabriel? Are you okay?' Harper sounds worried, and she reaches for my hand across the table. Oh shit. It's time to put on my brave face and pretend to be a big boy. I'm going to lose the two people I love tonight. They'll live their lives happily ever after while I'll be one of those bystanders that might get a glimpse of their euphoria every few months on Facebook, if I'm lucky.

'I'm fine.' My head snaps up, and I compose myself quickly. 'So, what have you guys been up to since I saw you last?' I smile, but it doesn't reach my eyes. They are focused on a large rattan vase at the back of the restaurant that is lit up in amber tones. It should be vaguely calming, but it isn't.

'Well,' says Harper, 'we've been studying, reading, exploring, travelling, playing house, and waiting.' There's a little note of excitement after her last comment. If she's about to tell me she's pregnant with Brandt's baby, I am going to lose it. Yes, I am going to lose it spectacularly, and I will start throwing all the glassware on this beautiful wooden table across the restaurant, as far and as hard as I can. The trouble is, I can't help myself; I have to know.

To prepare myself, I take a gulp of a rather acidic New Zealand Sauvignon Blanc which would be much better sipped delicately. Ideally, I could do with something much stronger. Vodka would probably do the trick.

'Waiting for what?' It takes me an age to raise my eyes to Harper's, and I swear I do it to torment myself. Perhaps I need to see the glow in her eyes, the look of ravishing happiness as she gushes out her wonderful news, or perhaps I'm just a masochist.

'For you, Gabriel,' she whispers when her eyes finally meet mine. 'We've been waiting for you, you silly sod.' They're both looking at me, and I feel even worse now that I am under intense scrutiny. Waiting for what? To make their enchanting announcement and ask me whether I want to be a godfather? Fuck. I can't do this.

'Oh?' I say, taking another enormous gulp of wine. I don't bother to tell myself not to ask this time, because I know damn well I'm going to. 'Well, I am honoured. What are you waiting to tell me?' My eyes flit between Brandt and Harper, and the pain in my chest expands. Someone could have injected a litre of Ricin in there and it couldn't have hurt any more.

'He's not going to make this easy, is he?' Brandt says, and his lips twitch. Harper frowns at him. They seem so comfortable around each other, and I feel horribly jealous of that fact. It's been too long. I shouldn't have come. The trouble was, I couldn't stop myself.

Harper takes hold of my hand again and pats it as I drain my glass dry. By now they probably think I'm either insane or an alcoholic. To confirm the latter, I'm itching to grab the bottle of wine from its fetching silver bucket and pour the rest of it into my throat.

Harper smiles, and I brace myself for the worst. 'Gabriel, we want to know if you'll come live with us for a while. Brandt and I are still both in love with you, and if you feel the same way about us, we want to see if a threesome will work. It's a big ask. You might already have someone back in England, or you might not feel the same way about us as you once did, so don't worry about being straight with us. We have no idea if this will work, but if you're up for it, we'd like to give it a try.'

My eyes explode out of my head and land on a table at the far end of the restaurant. There's no way I heard that correctly.

'I told you he'd already have someone,' Harper murmurs to Brandt. 'For God's sake pour him some more wine. He looks green.' I can't say a word for the life of me. I just sit there, watching, as Brandt pours me another glass, and all I can do is blink. This cannot be happening, can it? This is too much to hope for. There's no way I can get this lucky.

'I did warn you,' Brandt replies to Harper, patting her shoulder gently. 'Gabe usually has them on tap, running at him from all angles. Can you see him swapping his glitzy lifestyle for suburbia and Chinese takeout? Oh God, Harper, don't cry on me. I can't take it.'

Harper's eyes are filling up as she looks at me, almost pleading with me to say 'yes'. She looks as desperate as I feel. There is no baby. They want me. They both want me. Finally, someone removes the axe from my chest and I feel I can breathe again. Taking another gulp of wine, I then shove my trembling hands beneath the table. This is all I've been dreaming about for the past two years. They want what I want. This is a scenario that I never dreamed would be possible.

'I can cope with suburbia, and Chinese takeout sounds good. I'm not sure you two can handle me, but I'm willing to give it a go if you are. You are, right? Please tell me you're not fucking with me?' That would be too cruel.

Brandt shakes his head and punches me on the shoulder. 'No, we've talked about this at length. Harper and I are both still in love with you. We think this could work, but only if you're onboard with it. We don't want to pressure you. Take your time. Think about it. There's no rush.'

Fuck that. 'I've already thought about it. Tell me, is anyone on this table actually hungry?'

Harper and Brandt look at each other and two slow smiles spread across their features.

'We had a late lunch,' says Harper, shrugging her shoulders, 'and there's lasagne in the fridge.'

'Taxi!' I yell, making nearly everyone in the restaurant turn around to stare at me. I don't care. Throwing a wad of bills down on the table, I escort a laughing Harper and Brandt outside to the taxi rank and pay the guy double to get us back to their house in record time.

Two years later

It's ironic really. I've waited so long to finally fall in love, that when it happened I fell for two people at the same time. Life is funny like that. I've gone from being a nasty, East End criminal, to becoming a devoted househusband. Actually, we all share the chores, but now that Brandt and Harper are out to work I take on most of them - except ironing. I'm shit at ironing. Harper hates it too, so poor old Brandt has been left with it. Thankfully he doesn't mind.

And I don't mind being left home alone. My latest passion is surfing and now that we have a house right on the beachfront, I can go whenever I want. It was an impulse buy, but thankfully both Brandt and Harper love it. It's a five-bedroom palace with its own infinity pool that rests on the beach, with soaringly high ceilings, a gourmet chef's kitchen, an open plan lounge and dining room, and three incredible bathrooms - one that features a jacuzzi. If that wasn't enough, we even have our own wet bar and boat house. We've had a lot of fun times in that jacuzzi together.

At the moment I'm working on getting out to work myself, but I'm not sure what

I want to do. I can't just sit still. It drives me crazy. I always need to be moving, that's why prison very nearly killed me.

Hoisting my surfboard up under my arm, I make my way out of the warm sea and head back across the bright white sand, which is so hot it almost burns my feet. The day is picture perfect. The water is an incredible azure blue and the sky almost matches it. I am so fucking lucky. Untying the leash from my ankle, I get a better grip on the board as I begin to walk back to the house. I'm crap at surfing, but I love it. Every day I get a little better, though, and the locals have stopped taking the piss out of me. I even go out for a beer with one or two of the boys now. It's a nice life, and there isn't a thing I would change about it. Maybe I'll just practise with my board until I'm good enough to become an instructor. I'll probably be sixty before I have a chance at that job, but hey, it's something to aim for. Personal training is probably a better bet, or I could always set up my own martial arts studio. Now there's something I'm good at. It's a thought. I'm not in a hurry though. I certainly don't need the money.

Looking down at my watch, I realise Brandt and Harper will be due back in half an hour. I need to get moving. I have big plans for this evening. It's Brandt's birthday, and Harper and I thought we'd do something special. Seeing as he's into the kinky stuff, we've bought him a couple of presents we think he'll love. I've gone with a black steel spreader bar, with both wrist and ankle restraints. I grin evilly to myself. That will keep Harper out of trouble for the foreseeable future. Speaking of Harper, she's bought him a short suede flogger, which is also sure to be a big hit, although I'm going to get the most use out of that baby after tonight. We have an agreement on birthdays, though. You get to choose whether you want to be a top or a bottom for the night. Generally I top and that doesn't change on my birthday. Brandt swings somewhere in the middle, but on his birthday he always tops and for one night a year, he gets to top me. The fucker will put me through the wringer tonight, but it's a small price to pay for the other three-hundred-and-sixty-four days of the year, where I show him who's really boss. Harper always bottoms, except on her birthday. Brandt and I are always really careful to be especially nice to her on the week proceeding that celebration. She can be incredibly creative. Last year she made Brandt and I wear chastity belts for a week. She paid for that stunt for the rest of year, but I'm not sure she's learned her lesson yet.

Bounding up the stairs two at a time, I make sure the restraints are all attached to the bed, the candles are in place, and there's some decent music playing in the background. I changed the bedsheets this morning. Look at me, how domesticated am I? I have prison to thank for that. Anyway, I have paella in the oven (store bought; I'm not a kitchen god unfortunately) and a bottle of Sancerre chilling nicely in the fridge. I picked up the enormous chocolate birthday cake this morning - the one which we'll be smearing all over Harper later so we can then lick it off her again - and it looks incredible. Baking is also not my forte. The only one in this house who can bake is Harper, and even she has a hit and miss reputation, not that we'd ever tell her (remember the bit about the chastity belts?). Anyway, we're all set. All I have to do is jump in the shower and drag a pair of jeans and a shirt on, and I'm good to go. Sending up a quick prayer to anyone that will listen, I ask them if they can try to make sure Brandt goes easy on me this evening. Maybe he'll be in a good mood. He's just had a promotion, so there's that. Yeah, and who am I trying to kid?

When the door bangs open wide twenty minutes later and Brandt and Harper burst in full of giggles, I know they've been talking about me. I swear she enjoys this evening as much as he does. The two of them look like angels, but let me tell you, there is a devil lurking in everyone.

'Had a good day, Brando?' I ask, somewhat cautiously.

He is quick to reply as he saunters over to give me a hug.

'Brilliant, as it happens,' he says, his grin huge.

'That because of the promotion? Did they give you a raise?' No one in the household needs money, so I fail to see how this can be exciting, but each to their own. Maybe he sees it as a sense of achievement or something.

'Nah. I couldn't care less about that.' He waves a hand high in the air, telling me exactly what I thought. The promotion means nothing.

'Ah, it's because you won the lottery then?' I say hopefully, winking at him.

'Nope. You know damn well why I'm so happy and you'd better brace yourself, Rodriguez. You are in for a spell of hell-on-wheels this evening.' I breathe in deeply. Oh well. It's only for one night. How bad can it be?

'Oh, and Harper hasn't bought me a flogger. She's been lying to you.'

I turn and give her a dark look. I spot treachery on the horizon. What has she been up to?

'What did you buy him?' I hiss.

The two of them look at each other and burst into fits of giggles again. Jesus Christ. I'm living with children.

'Spit it out,' I say. We might as well get this over and done with.

Finally she manages to get herself under control, although she's now got a serious case of the hiccups. Serves her right.

'It's called the 'Ace of Spades',' she says, when she can finally talk again, 'and your ass is never going to be the same again.'

I close my eyes and pinch the bridge of my nose. Breathe, just breathe, I tell myself. Revenge will be mine tomorrow night, which is when these two will be screaming into the sunset.

'Don't you want to know what it is?' she asks me, with the cheekiest grin on her face. God, she is adorable. I don't know who I love more, her or Brandt. I couldn't decide even if I wanted to.

'I'd rather not know,' I say dryly. I have a feeling that a couple of painkillers before the session might be a good idea though.

'Good call,' Brandt yells, pulling me to him. We look at each other for a long moment, before melding our mouths together in a rough but intense kiss. This never gets old. I am living the dream. I don't kid myself that this will last forever because few things do, but if I can have a few years of it, then I will consider myself one of the luckiest men alive. When we finally pull apart we are both breathing hard, and Harper is looking on jealously.

'Hey, what about me?' she teases, with a wicked glint in her eye. She then squeezes her tight little body in between us, and my cock doubles in size instantly.

Raising my eyebrows I say, 'Oh, don't worry. You're going to get yours. I haven't bought Brandt a spreader bar either, as it happens.' I have, but that can go in storage for a bit. Now that we're waging war against each other I'm going to let Brandt have a little something I was saving for my birthday.

'What have you bought?' Harper demands, almost hopping in agitation now the shoe is on the other foot. Too bad. Two can play at this game.

'You'll just have to wait and see,' I purr. 'Brandt isn't allowed to open it until later, though.' The cooker timer then goes off as if on cue, and we all make our way into the dining room.

I'm going to need to do a quick wrapping job on a female chastity belt in an hour's time, but it's nothing I can't handle. The day Harper gets one over on me is the day I roll over in my grave.

Grabbing the wine from the fridge, I fill everyone's glass and raise mine in the air.

'To us,' I toast. 'May we always be this fucking good together.'

'To us,' they chant, and the celebration begins in earnest.

Chapter Twenty-Eight - Gabriel

No one has much of an appetite for the paella. It's not a bad offering if I'm honest, but nothing like they make at home. I miss tapas, Jamon Iberico, and churros. Maybe I'll have to take Harper and Brandt to Spain one day. Although I don't have any relatives to introduce them to, I'm sure we'd have fun.

'Everyone finished?' I ask, when no one has touched their plate for at least a couple of minutes. We've all been fairly quiet over dinner. The air is charged with sexual tension, and no one has their mind on food.

'Yes, let's get this show on the road,' says Brandt, as he rubs his hands together and winks at me. The grin he is wearing almost splits his face in two. I already know I am going to suffer this evening, but for some reason I get the feeling it will be more than usual. It's one day a year, I tell myself. It's a small price to pay for happiness. Suck it up and do as you're told. The trouble is, I really don't like doing as I'm told. This is probably why Brandt and Harper enjoy this evening so much.

'So, what's on the agenda tonight?' I ask casually, as I begin to stack the dishes. Harper stands up to help me, and we both begin loading the dishwasher. She is also smiling, but it's all right for her; she likes pain. She also enjoys submitting. I, on the other hand, do not.

Brandt clucks his tongue. 'No way am I going to tell you that, Gabe. You'll just have to be patient. It'll be your turn to have fun with me soon enough.' I glower silently. He is not wrong. I am already planning my retribution for tomorrow night and it is going to be epic. That sentiment is then ruined as I very nearly drop the plate I've been holding. Fortunately Harper grabs it before it has a chance to smash.

'Go easy on the big guy, Brandt. You know this is hard for him. Stop tormenting him and get on with it.'

Brandt looks at her and screws his face up comically. 'You're spoiling all my fun, you know that, right?'

Harper shakes her head at him. 'I'm pretty sure you're going to have more fun than you can handle this evening, so don't rub it in. Give the guy a break, Captain Evil.' She looks back at me and puts her hand on my arm, giving me an affectionate tap. 'He's just fucking with you, Gabe. It's his one night a year. He's going to go to town, but it is only one night.' She inserts her cute little butt against my crotch and grinds herself against me. If she was looking to divert my attention, she's succeeded.

'Come here,' I growl, spinning her around so that she's facing me. I desperately need a distraction, and getting my hands all over that incredible body will certainly provide one. Feathering my fingers in the hair at the nape of her neck, I pull her head towards mine until our lips are almost touching. 'Your job this evening is to keep him occupied, you hear me? If you can be a good girl, I might crack out the whip tomorrow evening.'

Her eyes widen in heated anticipation, but I barely see it because my lips are already descending upon hers. I have been waiting to cop a feel of this beautiful body all day and now that it's pressed up against me, it is too much temptation to resist. Slowly sliding my hand up the hem of her skirt, I groan out loud when I find she's naked under there. When I say naked, I mean really naked. There's not a hair upon that beautiful cunt of hers, and I should know because I suckle at it on a daily basis.

'You like that?' she breathes into my mouth. She knows I like it. I was the one who paid for her to have it lasered off. Now it's so silky smooth you could eat your dinner off it, and Brandt and I do, quite regularly.

'You know I do,' I growl. Gripping her bottom lip in my mouth, I bite down gently, pulling my head back so I can watch the flare of pain in her eyes before the rush of arousal floods in. That look undoes me. Thrusting three fingers sharply inside her, I smile when they are covered in soft, slippery heat. 'You're drenched,' I purr.

Harper smiles cheekily. 'How could I not be? I'm surrounded by two incorrigible reprobates. You keep me fully juiced from morning until dusk.'

I lick my lips as my fingers delve deeper. 'Just morning until dusk?' I frown darkly as my thumb dances hungrily upon her clit. I then pull my fingers out and pinch her clit in my knuckles.

Harper throws her head back and gasps. 'You are a monster. You know that, right?'

I love it when she gets that throaty little rasp to her voice. I love knowing that we make her so hot she walks around permanently wet, and I love that she does the same thing to me. Our unusual trio is working far better than any of us dared to hope.

'Just morning until dusk?' I repeat silkily, increasing the pressure on her clit. If she's not careful I'll bruise it, and then she'll really suffer this evening.

'A girl's gotta sleep,' she replies cheekily, grinding those lithe little hips into me once again.

Now I need help. 'Brandt, your woman is behaving badly again. She reckons we only keep her dripping from dawn until dusk,' I yell.

'Why is she always my woman when she misbehaves?' Brandt says, standing up from the table as he rolls his eyes heavenward.

'That's because I don't tolerate naughty behaviour, and if it was a normal night she'd be over my knee already, but seeing as how it's your birthday, you'll have to do all the hard work because I am officially on strike. You two have no idea how hard it is being the disciplinarian around these parts. You work me to the bone.' I tried to sound aggrieved.

Both burst out laughing, so my acting skills obviously aren't up to much.

'You love every second of doling out your punishments, and don't think we don't know it,' Brandt says. I'd call him a liar, but I'd be lying. The sadist in me loves everything Harper stands for, and with Brandt, well, I can't resist seeing the big guy brought low.

'Speaking of punishments, isn't it about time I tied you both up and showed you who's boss?' There isn't a chance he'll go for it, but you can't blame me for trying.

Brandt shakes his head as I knew he would. 'Get that woman upstairs on our bed, naked and smothered in my birthday cake,' he rumbles. 'Then get yourself naked and brace those beautiful biceps against my wall. Think you can do that?' He comes around the back of me, his breath fanning across my neck and I shudder. His hands press my head forward, so he can kiss my neck. 'If you don't do as you're told, you'll be wearing that chastity set Harper got you for the next week at least.' He slaps my ass hard, making me jump.

Grabbing Harper's hand, I give him a dark look and nearly drag her up two flights of stairs to the bedroom. She's giggling her head off the whole way.

'Honest to God, woman,' I grit out, 'this time tomorrow you won't be laughing. You are in so much trouble.' Yanking her roughly inside the master suite, I practically throw her onto the bed. She's now laughing so hard she's almost snorting.

'Is that supposed to be a threat?' she eventually manages to get out. Seriously. This is the type of attitude I have to deal with.

'Get naked now, or I'll come over there and tear everything off,' I threaten. 'You have three seconds.'

She takes me at my word, mainly because I've done what I've just threatened hundreds of times before. Hey, it's a fun game. I like ripping clothes. Anyway, the point is, she whisks off her skirt and blouse, and her bra follows seconds later. Brandt and I need to work on the bra thing. We've got her to go without panties; it's about time we upped it to the next level.

'How does it feel to be a sub, Gabe? I bet you secretly enjoy it. Come on, spill.' If Harper wants to get me riled she'll have to try harder. I wink at her.

'If you don't behave you'll get corner time with your brand-new chastity belt. You'll stick your nose in that corner,' I point to the far end of the room, 'and you'll be ignored all day while Brandt and I have fun together.'

That wipes the smile off her face. 'You wouldn't,' she breathes.

'Try me,' I say. I've been thinking of doing this for a while now. As far as punishments go for a masochist, this is about the only thing that might work. As if to confirm my thoughts, she goes quiet.

'I'll be good,' she says in a little voice. Ah, the sweet sound of surrender. How pleasant it is.

'You'd better be,' I say. She's already stretching her arms and legs out on the bed in order to help me get them fastened into the silk scarfs. I like silk. It's durable, strong, and it doesn't leave marks. I don't see the need to announce to the locals that we're all complete perverts, and thankfully both Harper and Brandt are in agreement. In less than two minutes I have the lady fully restrained, and let me assure you she is going nowhere, but just to make sure of the fact I attach my mouth to her clit and give it a good tonguing.

'Get off me,' she squeals, 'this is going to be bad enough as it is already.' She tries to kick her legs up but they don't move. Am I good, or what?

'Exactly. Why do you think I'm doing this? If you fall at the first hurdle it'll make me look good.' Our little trio is very competitive. No one likes coming in last, least of all me.

'You are a bastard. I hope he whips strips off that back of yours,' Harper shoots daggers at me, which is a pointless endeavour because it turns me the fuck on.

Suckling at her mound, I give her clit one last flick and then bring my head up so I can look at her. 'And are you going to enjoy that little spectacle, Querido? Will you enjoy watching me suffer?' My fingertips are worming their way inside her, spreading that delightful cunt open wide.

'Hell, yes,' she breathes. The little minx is not going to be able to walk for the rest of the week when I get my hands on her. Take my word for it.

'Then you can lie back and enjoy the show, darling, but don't think I'm not going to get my own back.' My fingers are now stretching her so wide she gasps out loud.

'I'm counting on it,' she purrs. Honestly. Personally, I think Brandt and I are far too soft on her. She's a cheeky little thing, and the little hellcat cannot be tamed. Well, she hasn't been tamed - yet.

Ignoring that comment I say, 'Now, where did I put that chocolate cake?' I know exactly where I put it, but it's fun watching her squirm at the knowledge of what's going to come next.

'Do we have to do this again?' she whines. We do. Brandt's birthday wouldn't be Brandt's birthday unless we stuffed Harper full of cake... and... other things.

'You already know the answer to that question,' I say, grabbing the cake box from beside the bed. 'Stop whining, woman. At least you aren't going to be whipped to within an inch of your life.'

'Can we swap places? I'd much rather be whipped,' she moans, groaning as I take out the massive sponge that is covered in soft, chocolate buttercream.

'Exactly. Why do you think you get to be covered in goo?' Sticking my finger in the middle of the cake, I pull away a large dollop of cream and smear it over her nipple. She grimaces. She hates being dirty. Hell, she can't even eat with her fingers without having a heart attack. She's the only person I've ever seen that needs to eat pizza with a knife and fork. It explains a few things.

'That is so unfair,' she mewls.

'Yeah, but you kinda like it that way. Now shut up,' I order, and before she can close her mouth I cram it full of chocolate sponge.

'Feel free to eat that mouthful, darling,' I say, winking at her. She won't. When Brandt found out she'd eaten a mouthful of his cake last year without him, he edged her on and off for five hours. You could hear the screams all the way over the other side of Australia by the time he'd finished with her. Sure enough, she glares at me. That's my girl.

It doesn't take me long to cover her from head to toe in cake, and I make sure the stuff goes everywhere. It's smeared all over her face, chest, tits, stomach and legs, and when we get bored with that I've filled every hole in her body with the damn stuff, and I mean every hole. Some are easier to fill than others.

When I've finished, I stand back to survey my handiwork. I've done a bloody good job if I do say so myself.

'Ah, the sound of silence,' I murmur, looking directly at her, while daring her to eat that mouthful of cake. She does no such thing. I get a string of garbled nonsense for my trouble instead. The woman's probably telling me how much she adores me.

'Right, my turn to get naked.' Standing at the foot of the bed, I take a big breath and begin unfastening the buttons of my shirt. Harper's eyes are on me the whole time, and I can feel my cock stir in response. There's a good chance I'm not going to be allowed to come all evening, so my balls are going to feel like clock weights tomorrow, but I will have my revenge. Oh yes, they will get theirs. When my jeans and boxers follow Harper's eyes land on my cock, which is standing proudly to attention wondering why no one's lips are around it. I'm wondering that too. I think we should cancel birthdays from now on in. Letting her get an eyeful, I finally hear the big guy's footsteps on the stairs and figure I'd better do as I've been told.

Sighing, I line myself up against the wall, leaning forward on my forearms. There are certain times in your life where you've just gotta grit your teeth, bend over and take it, and this is one of those times.

When Brandt opens the door he surveys the room with interest. Even though I can't see him, I can feel his eyes all over me. The connection I have with Harper and Brandt is remarkable. We are so in tune with each other it is almost uncanny.

'Like what you see, Brando?' I know the bastard is enjoying every second of this, but I guess he deserves his fun. It is only one day a year, and it does me good. Humility is good for the soul, or so they tell me.

'I'll like it better when you have stripes all over you,' he replies. There's then the sound of a drawer opening, and I know he's choosing a whip. It will be something nasty. On his one night a year, Brandt doesn't mess about. He goes straight for the jugular. Sure enough, when the drawer closes and he steps alongside me, I can see the rubber demon-tailed whip in his hands. It's one of my favourites, when I happen to be wielding it. I feel less inclined to sing its praises this evening, though.

Brandt wastes no time getting started. As the first lash lands on my backside I jump in shock, but now I've got a feel for it, I figure I should be able to hold myself still. Damn that thing smarts. How in hell can Harper like this shit? Don't get me wrong I'm glad she does, but wow, is her brain wired all wrong.

Brandt gives it to me full throttle. The thing flies in his hand, and while he isn't quite as practised as I am, he's not an amateur. He wields it with precision and grace, and it isn't long before I want to howl in pain. There is no way I'm ever doing that though. I'd never live it down, and I have certain standards to uphold around these parts as the alpha dog. To be clear, I'd rather swallow my own tongue than give Brandt anything more than a grunt. The trouble is the asshole knows it, and does his best to push me to my fucking limit. The only way I get through it is by imagining how I'm going to get my own back for the rest of the week.

'You've never forgiven me for that whipping back at Mal's warehouse all those years ago, have you?' I say, when he's been at it for a good half hour and I'm nearly on my knees. 'Every fucking year we have to do this so you can get your own back. Is this really necessary?'

He is quick to answer. 'Hell yes. If I don't do this, tomorrow you'll tear me limb from limb getting your own back. It takes at least a day or two for your anger to simmer down. I'm just protecting my own ass, Gabe.' He sounds smug, as well he should. But he won't sound so smug tomorrow. By the time I've loaded myself up with some heavy-duty painkillers, he'll be getting his.

'Your ass is getting fried tomorrow, whatever you do to me, and you know it. Move it along, Brando, else Harper will choke on that chocolate cake I've stuffed in her mouth.'

He frowns and looks back over his shoulder. 'You good, Harper?' The woman makes all kinds of squawking noises indicating she is anything but. There's nothing actually wrong with her though; she just wants in on the action.

Brandt winds his arm back for one final strike, and I snap my teeth together in preparation for the blast. Sure enough, it slices right through me and I want to scream my head off. Instead, I turn around and smile at him. He retaliates, of course.

'Don't think I've finished with you,' he says, giving me a dark look. 'Your ass is mine and let me tell you, it's never going to be the same again.'

'Yeah, whatever. Can we eat the girl out first?' My look suggests I am not at all bothered by that threat. I have to confess I am a little worried by it, if I'm honest. Still, how bad can it be?

'Go on then. You get the top half and I'm having the bottom.' Thank God. I'll have at least a few minutes to compose myself before the second round. That's something, at least.

'Can I join in with the bottom half later?' I ask cheekily.

Brandt rolls his eyes in response and I'm going to take that to mean 'yes'. Thankfully he seems to have turned his attention to Harper for the moment, as he's now looking directly at her.

'Darling,' he purrs, 'Gabe has given me the most wonderful present. Do you want to see it?'

She knows exactly what it is because her eyes bug wide. Ha-ha. It's about time she got hers.

Brandt takes his time opening my present. He's sitting on the bed beside Harper with this enormous box wrapped in shiny black paper and red ribbon, and her eyes are glued to it. She can't say a word, of course, but she'll want to in a minute. Have I mentioned that I get my own back in style?

'Hmm. I wonder what we have here?' Brandt says, as he tears off the paper. His eyes are shining, so I know he's excited. He should be. This baby is going to keep our little minx in line for years to come.

'Ooh, it's a female chastity belt, Harps. It says the RXC 2000. Sounds intriguing,' he says. My back is stinging like fire, and turning my head around is going to hurt like hell, but I can't resist watching Harper's face as he slowly unveils the beast. I chose this little beauty very carefully, and she's about to see why.

'It says it features generous stainless-steel plugs for both ass and pussy and a lockable waist belt and bra with an automatic timer release. Does that mean you can set it for however many days you feel like, and it will only pop open when the timer has run out?'

Brandt looks at me enquiringly, and I nod. It hurts to nod. The asshole has now stuffed up my surfing for the next few days because saltwater is going to sting like a bastard. Harper's ass had better be black and blue by the time we're finished with her, or I'm going to have words on the grounds of gender inequality.

'It has a few new little twists and tweaks. There are separate locks for ass and pussy. If she needs one released, you send her a code via text message which will work for however long you like. Anything from thirty seconds to three hours. It's a nifty piece of kit. She could wear the thing all year, if you were so inclined.'

Harper decides to voice her opinion on the matter, but as she is completely stuffed up with cake still, no one is listening to anything she has to say.

'That is incredible,' Brandt breathes.

'Yup,' I say. 'It is also very hygienic. With the stainless steel and silicone design, she can bathe in it and wear it comfortably for days on end. It should solve the short skirt problem, too.' Brandt and I have tried hard to get her to stop wearing short skirts to work. Yes, she has an awesome pair of legs, but we don't want the whole world to know about them. If she's wearing this beast, I'm pretty sure she'll want to keep it covered up. She won't be wearing those nearly see-through tops with that steel bra, either. Am I brilliant, or am I brilliant?

Brandt's face breaks into a wide smile and he looks at me adoringly. 'This is the best birthday present ever.' Harper's squawking over his shoulder suggests it is anything but, however. That's her problem, not mine. She started this war.

'Yes, she'll be wearing baggy tops and trousers from here on in, I should think,' I say, with a mocking little frown in her direction. Her eyes light up like lit fuses, and I'm really glad her mouth is still stuffed with cake. She's going to come at me with everything she's got as soon as Brandt releases her from those restraints, but I'll be ready for her.

'Won't she just?' Brandt enthuses. With one last longing look in the box, he finally closes the lid and pushes it away. 'We'll come back to that later,' he says, 'but for now Gabe and I are going to have some fun, aren't we Gabe?'

I narrow my eyes. This had better not be the fun at my expense kind of fun, that

I know I've got coming. Thankfully, he then indicates Harper, so we're good.

Standing up, he says, 'Harper, listen up sweetheart. Me and Gabe are going to lick that entire body of yours clean from top to bottom. Does that sound like fun?'

She nods enthusiastically, while I frown. Why should she get so lucky? I get whipped, and she gets smothered in cream with a gigantic tongue bathing to boot. How unfair is that?

He hasn't finished though. 'Just bear in mind that every time you orgasm, I will add twenty-four hours to your chastity belt total. Yes, you will have to wear it to work, to the supermarket, out to restaurants and cafes. Anywhere we go, you go. You won't be allowed to hide away indoors when it's on, so be mindful of that when Gabe and I are having our fun. Are we clear on the rules?'

Harper's eyes are currently peeled back in horror, but that's not my problem. The karma in the world has just been balanced and I am once again reasonably happy. There's no way my lot this evening can be worse than what she's got coming. Oh, I am going to enjoy myself so much next week. This is fantastic.

While she is lying there, wondering what just happened without her say so, Brandt and I decide to get to work. I have to confess this is my favourite part of the evening. I love licking cream off a hot, naked body. I love it even more when it's my cream and Brandt is doing the licking, but that will have to wait until tomorrow. Right now, my mission in life is to make Harper come at least seven times. I reckon if we have her locked up for the week, she'll never pull a stunt like she did today again. Now I wish I'd been given the bottom half, but never mind, I can still wreak some havoc from up here.

While Brandt's face dips between Harper's legs, mine begins to lick her cheekbone with carefully calculated strokes. No way will this girlie need a shower after we've finished with her. I will purposefully see to it that not a speck of chocolate remains anywhere on her body, and I mean anywhere.

I take my time with my cleaning duties. Starting with her face, I then lick her shoulders, her collarbone, and meander my way down the valley of her breasts. By this time her chest is heaving with the exertion of trying to hold her first orgasm back, and it's most amusing. There isn't anything she can do to stop it. Brandt's tongue is wickedly talented, and I should know. In order to hurry her along a little I decide to clamp my mouth around her left nipple and tug a little.

Sure enough, the woman comes like someone's just shot a hole in the Hoover Dam, with her legs and arms flailing about in the soft silk scarves that hold them. Brandt doesn't let up for a second, though. He just continues what he's doing with his fingers and tongue, and let me tell you, the man is blowing a veritable storm down there if Harper's eye sockets are anything to go by.

'Twenty-four hours in the suit, Harps,' I say, with a cheeky grin. 'Seems like a long time to me, but I have a feeling you'll be in it for a lot longer than just one day.' I waggle my eyebrows at her, and she tries her best to come at me, but that's not happening with those ties. I made sure to tie them tight, too. I've also made sure not to touch any of that cake in her mouth. I'm saving that until last. When she regains the use of her mouth, she'll no doubt whine incessantly for at least the next couple of hours.

162

'We're going for multiples, Gabe; get with the plan,' Brandt admonishes me, when he notices I'm not doing anything at the moment.

'Yes, Sir.' What is wrong with me? Harper needs at least a week in that thing. We have work to do. My tongue gets busy again, even where there is no cake. The delicate curve of her underarm, her nose, her ears. I bite them too, as I go along, watching the level of torment ratchet up in her eyes. She can't control her reaction to that. A little bit of pain and she's in raptures. A whole lot of pain all at once and she nearly sprouts wings. I use my lips, teeth and fingernails to impart as much as I can. Flicks, nips, bites, scratches and scrapes. I want every inch of her skin hypersensitised to my touch, so that when I start hitting her with a few impact play toys later, it'll send her headfirst into the clouds. I cannot wait.

Chapter Twenty-Nine - Gabriel

Orgasm number two is slightly harder to wring out of her. I can see she's trying her hardest to fight us, but you can't fight the dream team. We're too damn good at what we do. It takes us another two minutes, but then a tell-tale scream of frustration informs us we're right on track. Two down, and at least five to go before I'm anywhere near happy.

'Go get some toys, Gabe, and for God's sake eat that cake in her mouth. I know you're trying to keep her quiet, but it's my birthday and I wanna hear her scream.' Brandt is throwing around orders again.

'Suit yourself,' I say, shrugging my shoulders. It's his funeral. She's going to give him hell. Straddling her body, I let my hands explore her curves for a minute. In the years since she's left Mal's warehouse, she's rounded out a little and isn't so angular and pointy. I know it took a long while to nurse her back to health because Brandt told me, and even now we have to keep a close eye on her because she regularly forgets to eat. How can you do that? I have absolutely no idea, but she does, although not on our watch. There are lots of devilish punishments for not eating - which is perhaps why she does it so often.

Slowly lowering myself to my forearms I take her lips in mine. As expected she thrusts a mouthful of cake at me, as if to say I want to tell you exactly what I think of you, and I have to swallow the stuff back quickly. It tastes good, though, so I don't complain. When she's free of half a pound of chocolate cake she tries to come up for air, but I'm having none of it. Biting her bottom lip sharply to focus her attention, I let my tongue coax that vicious mouth back into submission. At first her lips are hard and hostile. Her body is tense because she's trying to fight her orgasm, and we need to get her to relax.

'Why don't you let yourself go for a change, Harps?' I ask her cheekily, when I've given up trying to steal her oxygen supply. Her mouth is so damn soft and velvety, I could drown in her forever.

'Just you wait,' she bites back. 'You're going to get yours next. Don't think you've won this round.'

Ah, but I have, and in a colossal amount of style, if I do say so myself.

'We're not stopping until you're trapped in that beast for a week,' I say smugly, both hands tugging sharply on her nipples. Her pupils are so dark, like black holes, and I find myself getting lost in their depths.

'There's no way I'm going to orgasm...' Harper doesn't get to finish her sentence because I sink my teeth into her neck and Brandt goes for broke beneath her. Once her hips start bucking it's all over, and she knows it.

'Nooo,' she wails desperately, her head thrashing from side to side, but it's too late. That's two days in her suit and the game isn't over yet. Drinking in the sight of her tormented face I can't help another grin.

'This isn't looking good, is it?' If she had the use of her hands I'd get a slap for my troubles, but thankfully, she doesn't.

'Come on, Gabe. Get the toys.' Brandt is looking at me, his lips wet and glistening, and damned if I don't want to suck that pussy juice right off them.

'Fine, fine,' I say. 'Hold your horses.' I don't move directly to the toy chest, though. My eyes have been hovering on those hot abs for far too long now, and he's well aware of my gaze.

'Permission to kiss the birthday boy first?' It kills me to have to ask, but it'll kill me even more if I don't get to do it.

He looks at me, his eyes twinkling. 'Hmm. Say please, pumpkin, and I'll think about it.'

Why the little fucker. Still, never let it be said that I can't play the game. Looking directly at him, I lick my lips salaciously.

'Oh, please will you let me suck those devilishly naughty lips of yours? I want to find out exactly where they've been.' I can beg when the need arises. I'll even get on my knees if necessary, though he'll pay for it tomorrow, mark my words.

'Permission granted,' he says, his smug smirk still in place. Yeah, laugh it up, asshole. We all know who'll be laughing tomorrow.

I take my own sweet time moving towards him. I can barely feel my back at the moment because my adrenaline is high, but I know that in a few hours it will sting like mad. I have a feeling I am going to be a little bit grumpy tomorrow, but by that time I'll be able to take out my bad humour on both Brandt and Harper. Hopefully, both at once.

He pulls me towards him, not that I need any encouragement. My hands go straight to the back of his neck and then I attack. Whereas Harper is all sweetness and light, Brandt is hard, rough edges and strength. When I push he pulls, just to torment me. With his hands on my chest I get the merest taste of him before he's breaking our kiss, and I feel like I'm gasping for air.

'This is my day. I get to kiss you, remember? Calm down, Rambo.'

This is why I hate Brandt's birthday. I don't do waiting and I hate being told what to do. It's probably good for me once in a while, but it doesn't mean I have to like it.

'Please, Brandt?' My voice is scratchy. I need this and he knows it.

'I love seeing you like this,' he whispers.

'I know,' I answer dryly. I'm well aware of how much he enjoys this day.

Thankfully, he doesn't make me wait any longer. Attaching his lips to mine with the suction power of a hoover, he tries his best to rob me of all my brain cells, and to be fair to the man, he does a fairly decent job of it. I swear the scent of Harper on his lips is like catnip to me. I go crazy and he knows it. When his hand descends to my dick and begins stroking it up and down I want to scream in frustration. I am not going to ask him for permission to come, though. Fuck that. I'd rather go without. My pride won't allow it.

'You are a stubborn one,' he says eventually, watching as my dick pulses in his fingers. I nod my head. He isn't telling me anything I don't already know, but he doesn't let it rest.

'Anything you want to ask me?'

'Nope, nothing,' I say, gruffly.

'Fine. If that's the case you'd better get the paddle out. We're two days down, with five to go.' Now we're talking.

Brandt and I spend the next two hours wringing climax after climax out of Harper. This is the most fun I've had in ages. Her face is an absolute picture, and she's screaming all sorts of obscenities at us as we work, but she can't fight us. We are the dream team, and she is a mere mortal. It's not her fault. We're just too good.

Flipping her over, amidst much struggling, we successfully manage to secure her the other way around, so she's now lying on her stomach. Then I let loose with the toys. As soon as I employ a bit of pain she is all too easy to manipulate and Brandt barely has to do anything to make her cream all over his fingers, lips and tongue. As the paddle, flogger and whip do their work she can't do anything to prevent the onslaught of desire that crashes over her, and all we have to do is watch the show. It's a fucking gorgeous one too, let me tell you. By the time I've reddened her ass to a nice deep ketchup colour, she is crying into the pillow. Not because of the pain; because we've just delivered her seventh orgasm. She knows she's got to wear the evil contraption I've just bought her for a whole week, and she also knows neither of us will back down on the matter.

'What say we go for day eight?' I ask Brandt as he reels back on his heels, wiping his mouth with his fist.

He shakes his head. Such a spoilsport, that one.

'Nah. A week is a good starting point. We need to break her in gently.' I shrug my shoulders. It's his party.

'So what's next?' I ask. I'm hoping he wants to fit Harper inside her sexy new suit. I am going to enjoy that show so much.

Brandt inserts his thumb into my mouth, and I suck it like a good little subbie. 'Next it's your turn.'

It's my what? I blink stupidly for a minute and he pulls out another present, this time wrapped in brown paper with a pretty green rosette placed in the centre. The box is about four inches square and looks benign enough, although I know it won't be.

He turns towards the orgasm queen. 'It's time to open your gift, Harper. Are you looking forward to this?'

'You have no idea,' she purrs. My face wrinkles up. She'll get hers soon enough.

My eyes watch Brandt's fingers carefully as he unwraps his package. He's going slowly on purpose. He needn't bother. I know exactly what is in that box, and I know that my life is about to be hell for the next thirty minutes or so. I can take it. If Harper can endure a week in the suit, I can deal with a little bit of pain and not cry like a baby.

Please don't let me cry like a baby.

'Oh look. It's a plug, and it's got your name on it, Gabe.' Brandt holds the shiny package in the air and sure enough, Harper has gone all out. The thing is a massive, teardrop shaped, black silicone butt plug. There's no way it's going inside me. No way in hell.

'I'm really going to enjoy locking you into that suit, Harper,' I fire at her. Inside, my legs are shaking. He's not really going to do this, is he? Of course he is.

Pulling the plug out of the box, Brandt admires it from all angles. I'm trying my best not to look at it.

'This is going to hurt, Gabe,' he says. Yeah. Tell me something I don't already know. I am going to make his life hell for the rest of this year if that thing comes near me.

'You aren't seriously going to do this, are you?' I ask. I confess, I am getting a little worried here. I'd barely be able to get that thing in my mouth, and that is most definitely not where it's going.

'Well, tell you what,' he says, 'if you decide to cancel Harper's week long punishment, then she can cancel yours. What say you?'

Oh, that is so fucking unfair. Now I'm going to look like the biggest pussy in the universe, and it's going to ruin my reputation around these parts. Where I'm from reputation is everything, and you do what you can to protect it.

'Nothing doing,' I say tightly. I hope I don't live to regret this.

'Are you sure?' he asks me again. He probably thinks I'm mad. Hell, even I think I'm mad, but I'm not backing down.

'Where do you want me?' I ask resignedly. I'd better not squeal. If I squeal my life will be made miserable for the next six months, at the very least.

'Bend over the dresser, palms down,' Brandt purrs. 'I'll just go put some lube on this beast.' These are the last words I want to hear. As he strides off I turn to Harper.

'You have no idea how much fun I'm going to have with you next week. Your ass is going to be red raw the whole damn time.'

She snorts. 'You'll be lucky if you can get to it through that contraption.' Her eyes linger on the chastity belt.

'Oh, I'll get to it all right. I made sure there is plenty of space for those naked ass cheeks to fit through it. You'd better brace yourself, princess.'

'Speaking of bracing yourself...' she goads, and sure enough, there is Brandt with his precious cargo. Dammit. I need to make sure all his future birthdays are cancelled. Either that, or I need to scare the bastard so much he won't dream of pulling a stunt like this ever again.

'Okay, Gabe. Harper had rules, so you get rules.' I don't like that sound of that, but I stay silent and wait for him to continue. 'If you take the whole of this beast, Harper wears the suit for a week. If you chicken out, she just gets forty-eight hours in the thing.' What? That is so not happening. Nuh-uh.

'Are you still talking? Let's get on with it,' I say testily. She is wearing the suit for a week and that's that.

'Suit yourself. I have a feeling you might change your mind, though.' Brandt sounds thoroughly entertained. I really hope he's enjoying himself because he's going to be on his knees tomorrow.

To be fair to him, he at least gives me a warm-up. Cold, wet lube is drizzled generously all over my sphincter and he then works the slippery fluid in with his fingers. For good measure he also runs a fist up and down my cock, and I can't help a moan. He has no idea how much I want him right now. My fingers are literally shaking with the need to throw him on the floor as I take what is rightfully mine, but somehow I stop them from moving.

Brandt, evil bastard that he is, slowly lubes up the massive plug in front of me. To put things into perspective, it's at least three times the size of the ones Harper will be expected to wear. How unfair is that? I have a mind to make a complaint, but just as I'm about to the plug disappears behind me, and before I have a chance to open my mouth he's pushing the beast forward.

'This is going to make your eyes water,' he warns unnecessarily. It's going to make a whole lot more than my eyes water, if I'm not much mistaken.

'Just get on with it. But if I were you I'd remember that whatever you do to me this evening, you're likely to be on the receiving end of next week. Just a heads up.' I don't get to say any more because he has already started pushing, chuckling to himself. Clearly I have a lot of work to do if I want to be reinstated as the alpha male around these parts.

The first six or seven seconds of torment are tolerable. Brandt starts gently and pulses the beast to and fro. Every second thereafter is not so much fun, but I try my best to keep quiet and think of how I'm going to reap my revenge.

All too soon I am starting to lose the will to live. My pain tolerance threshold is at its upper limit, and beads of sweat are dripping down my brow. If he doesn't shove the thing home soon I am going to admit defeat - and I never admit defeat.

'How far are we along?' I ask rather raggedly when my resolution to see this through starts wearing thin.

'We're just under halfway. You're doing really well, considering. I never thought you'd make it this far. Want to stop now?'

'Ideally yes,' I grit, 'but it would be a shame to waste all this hard work of yours. Can I get a little help for the next couple of inches?' I'm not going to do this without help, but if he gives me a nudge I might just make it.

But Harper has some things to say on the matter. 'Gabe, admit defeat for fuck's sake. There is no way you're taking that thing.' No way am I admitting defeat. She should know me better by now.

Brandt moves closer to me. 'This kind of help?' he purrs. His hand is once again around my dick and squeezing tightly, with a nice, reassuring, suffocating grip. When he starts moving I nearly come on the spot.

'That kind of help is perfect. Push the damn thing home. I don't care what it takes, shove the thing in and be quick.' From the corner of my eye I watch as

Harper's face goes slack. Seems she's a little shocked by this turn of events. Score one for me.

'Suit yourself,' Brandt says, 'but remember, you asked for it.' With no further warning he slams the thing home and Jesus Christ does it smart.

I scream. There is no avoiding it. Brandt will take the piss out of me over this for the foreseeable, but it will be worth it. To soften the blow he then pulls me into his arms and twists his face, so our lips meet with an almost crushing force. His hand is still on my cock and pumping me furiously. I come almost instantly, crying out as he drains me, and when he finally releases my lips he cups my cheek affectionately.

'Are you okay?' He gives me a lopsided grin.

I grimace in response. 'I'm not eating curry for the whole of next week, but yes, I think I'll live. It will be worth it to see that sneaky little woman locked up tight.' Now it's my time to smile wide.

Brandt looks over his shoulder and says, 'You lose the bet, Harps. I told you he'd pull out all the stops and take it. I did warn you.'

She doesn't say a word. Her face is devoid of all colour and she's looking a little peaky. Serves her right. She'll think twice before she pulls a stunt like that again. And our little minx has good reason to be scared; it's her turn now.

'Is it time to get Harper fitted in her suit yet?' I'm not asking because I'm eager to see all her holes squeezed onto those nice, fat, juicy plugs. Oh no. Not me. I'm not asking to make sure she doesn't frig her little clitty to furious pleasure while watching Brandt and me go at it all week, either. Nah, I'm not that kind of guy. I'm only asking because I think it might be a sensible idea to do it while she's still tied up. We might have some broken bones to contend with otherwise. Believe that, you'll believe anything.

Harper decides it's about time she piped up. 'If you two come anywhere near me I will kill you both...'

Brandt grins at me. 'Let's do it.'

That is all the encouragement I need. Grabbing the lube again we grease both plugs on the belt generously, namely so we can torment her with them. Pumping them in and out of her, we get her used to the feel of what her life will be like for the next week or so. She's screaming obscenities at us the whole time, but we pay her no attention.

We give our darling girl the works. I lock lips with her, mostly to stop her swearing, while Brandt teases her clitty to at least double its original size. I pull on her nipples, making them stand proudly to attention while Brandt eats out that pussy. He nearly lets her come... nearly, but not quite. Stopping just short he pushes into her dripping wet entrance and fucks her so hard she should be seeing stars.

'Please,' she whimpers when he's finished. 'Please let me come.' When Brandt shakes his head she looks at me. Ha! She must be desperate. There is no way I'm taking pity on her after the stunt she just pulled.

'No way,' I growl. 'You absolutely deserve this, and you know it.' That damn plug she bought is still in my ass and taking it out will require copious amounts of alcohol.

We stare each other out, before Brandt clears his throat to interrupt us.

'Would you like a turn with her before I stopper all those holes up, Gabe? I think she owes you at least that much.' Ahh, now that does sound like a good idea. Why didn't I think of it?

'No way in hell is he coming near me,' Harper spits, well aware that she's lost this fight. She is never one to give up though.

Giving Brandt a look, I take my place between her legs while he takes the top end for a change.

'No, you can't let him do this,' she wails. She's not bothered about me fucking her, she's bothered about losing and not being allowed to come for a week. She is so competitive. She's worse than we are, which is pretty incredible when you consider all that's happened to her.

'Are you going to give in gracefully or are you going to go down kicking and screaming?' Brandt doesn't give her a chance to respond; we already know the answer. He just stares into those pretty sable eyes of hers and works his magic. As soon as he wraps his hands around her neck the battle is lost, as I knew it would be. She melts like an ice cream whenever either of us go near her. Meanwhile I knead her thighs with my fingertips, while letting my mouth and tongue torment that deliciously naughty ass of hers. Hopefully she's still nice and greased up, as that's where my cock is going in a few seconds' time. It doesn't take me long to discover that she is. I am going to enjoy this so much.

When I slide into her she doesn't make a murmur. All she does is groan and buck her hips. How does that work? Oh, yeah; Harper likes pain. Anyway, I ease forward gently, guiding my cock inside her inch by slow inch. Brandt is now sucking down her moans, but I can just about make them out. She is going to be doing a lot of moaning this week, but she'll figure that out soon enough.

Increasing my pace I grab her hips and begin to slam into her. I know the woman is desperate to come, but I am hitting her in just the wrong spot on purpose. Besides, she's already come half a dozen times. How greedy is that?

Roaring as I spill into her I let out a deep, satisfied breath. God, that was good. Pulling out slowly, I watch as Brandt reluctantly releases her.

'Let's lock her up,' I say, giving her thigh a little nip with my teeth for good measure.

'Noooo,' she wails, her chest heaving up and down. 'I need... I need...' She can't get the rest of the words out because she is too exhausted. Thank goodness. Maybe we'll have some peace and quiet now. It's unlikely, but one can hope.

Brandt throws me over the belt, while he tackles the bra.

'She's going to be awful all week,' he tells me. 'There will be tears and tantrums, and she will refuse to cook. Are you sure you want to do this?'

Damn right I am. 'Absolutely. We can deal with a little bit of hysteria, and as to the cooking, we can get takeout. It's only a week. We'll survive. Harper needs to learn her lesson.'

Brandt nods, but he isn't looking at me. He's unfastening one of Harper's wrists so he can lock the metal belt of the bra into place. There's plenty of struggling going on, as you can imagine. Trying to keep the woman still is quite a challenge. Untying one of her legs, I also manage to get the lower belt circled around her waist and I take my time reinserting her plugs. I wonder how it's going to feel walking around in this beast all week. I'm pretty sure I'm going to hear all about it, so I won't have to wonder for long. When I get the plugs just where I want them, I tighten the belt and fasten it with the teeny tiny padlock I've been given. The plugs are held in place magnetically, which is how they can be released by app. It's a clever design. I fell in love with it the moment I saw it.

'Right, I'm going to get a drink for everyone. I'll leave you to untie the rest of her,' Brandt says, winking at me. Coward. He's worried she's going to scratch his eyes out. To be fair, that is a distinct possibility, but I don't think she'll try that with me.

'See you in a mo,' I say, waving him off.

Turning to Harper as I unfasten her other leg, I say, 'Are we even because I sure as hell think we're even after that. If we're not, I'm going at you all guns blazing and I am not going to be gentle. Just so you know.'

Harper turns her face towards me, and her pained expression mirrors mine, albeit for an entirely different reason.

'I think we're even,' she grudgingly admits.

'Good,' I say. 'We're not even with him though, right?' My attention is on the door Brandt exited just moments ago.

'Oh no,' Harper breathes, shaking her head. 'We haven't even got started on that.'

'Excellent,' I say. 'We'll reconvene this party tomorrow then?'

A sly grin slowly overtakes her face. 'Absolutely,' she whispers. 'Abso-fucking-lutely.'

So, Brandt may have won this round, but he most certainly hasn't won the war. This time tomorrow, my big tough guy is going to be shaking in his boots and I, for one, can't wait.

The End

Please help a starving author by leaving a review

Ok, so I lied about the starving part, but books need reviews on Amazon in order to sell. Without them they wither and die, and so do we authors. Honest, we do...

You don't have to say much, and you can stay anonymous - just set your Amazon reviewer name to something like *Amazon Reviewer 3982*. Anyway, here are a few examples of what you could write if you're a truly wonderful person who doesn't mind doing a good deed every now and again:

This book was so awesome I forgot to feed my kids. Thankfully they reminded me, over and over again, so they haven't died of starvation yet. Phew.

This book sucked. It was even worse than a certain president's infamous hairdo, and that is saying something.

Gabriel and Brandt are so hot I want a threesome with both of them. As long as I'm allowed a safe word, because Gabriel is a little bit on the seriously freaky crazy side.

I would rather read War and Peace than this ridiculous smutty drivel and nonsense. Seriously - all Mandara talks about is orgasms, sex, and hot blokes. Who wants to read about that?

Ms Mandara does not write quickly enough. I need her to release a book every month at the very least, yet she keeps me waiting for months, and worse - ends everything on a horrendous cliff-hanger. I have a love/hate relationship with this author. She should probably be spanked.

This is not a good book to read on the train. Especially when the hot guy sitting next to me kept trying to read it over my shoulder.

Don't ever read this book to your wife. She will demand sex for days on end and will suddenly become insatiable in bed. Seriously, I have been considering divorce...

Any of these will do (I'm more partial to the nice ones...) and it will give you extra karma points that will be returned to you in due course in the form of cookies, money, hugs and wine. Honest.

Thank You!

I just need to say a big thank you to all my wonderful beta readers who always step up to the rather tricky task of reading my books before they've had a good edit. Without you, my books would probably be unreadable as you manage to figure out that my heroine can't see things when she's wearing a blindfold, and that it's tough for her to talk if she's gagged. You also help me to correct my numerous errors and give me your honest opinions, which are more valuable than pixie dust (the stuff that makes you fly without wings). (That is what pixie dust does, right?) A special thank you to Nikki and Cassie! You know who you are :)

Another big thank you to all of my readers and fans - you always manage to brighten my day and make me remember why I started this journey. Please drop by anytime via my Facebook, Twitter page, or email me at christinamandara@yahoo.co.uk if you want to contact me. I don't bite!

So, for everyone who's helped me along the way, thank you, thank you, thank you!

Love 'n hugs to all xxx

Bio

Christina Mandara is a USA TODAY bestselling author and tends to write dark romance with lashings of kinky naughtiness. Her favourite pastime is travelling, and if it involves sun, sea and... sand then it's all good.

In her spare time she's usually cuddled up with a good book, exploring the countryside or baking in the kitchen. In fact, she loves her kitchen so much she's one of few women who wouldn't mind being tied to it! Her first and foremost love is writing, however, and more often than not you'll find her on a laptop spinning tales of romance, erotica or dark, paranormal fantasies.

Be the first to know about Christina's new and upcoming releases and get notifications on freebies and discounts by following her social media channels below:

facebook.com/cpmandara
twitter.com/cpmandara
christinamandara.com

www.ingramcontent.com/pod-product-compliance
Lightning Source LLC
Chambersburg PA
CBHW021046130626
46552CB00005B/2043